Beneath a Pale Moon

Victoria Morrow

Cover model: Jaci Janae Stanczyk

Photographer: Brian Baer of Baer Studios

Wardrobe courtesy of The Bridal Collection, Grand Island, NE
– Owners Liz Werner and Josie Ernstmeyer

Graphic Art by Rob Sturtz and Island of Selfpubbooks.com.

ISBN: 978-1-7329516-7-9 (ebook)
ISBN-13: 978-1-7329516-2-4 (paperback)

An *Original* Publication of Victoria Morrow.

For my sister, Cheryl Rae Bates-Lawson
and the proud, courageous people
of Wales and the British Isles.
May God bless you and may you remain
forever free.

SHE SAW THE SEETHING INTEREST
IN GARRET'S DARK BLUE EYES...

"Please you!" Charlotte stammered angrily, feeling hot, ragged and confused as she flipped her hair behind her shoulders. "I don't want to please you! I hate you!"

She pulled her robe around her in a whirlwind of white eyelet lace and ribbons, feeling better now that she had said it. She wanted desperately to believe it was true.

"I'm not your wife or your property!" she added vehemently as she tied her sash. "When I marry, it will be to a man who treats me as an equal, not as a servant, and someone I love!"

"I don't wish to be the bearer of bad news, Lady Charlotte," Garret said quietly, "but you are married—to me."

"Not legally!" she cried. She was well versed in feudal law and knew that an unconsummated marriage was invalid.

"That can be rectified this very moment!" he said. In one swift movement, he drew her to him and kissed her.

The sheer weight and power of the knight holding her made her dizzy. Last night he had been a shadow, nothing more than a dream. But this morning he was a man who claimed she belonged to him...

Beneath a Pale Moon

ACKNOWLEDGMENTS

With gratitude to Jaci Janae Stanczyk, a wonderful young lady and a friend who accepted the invitation to be the model for *Beneath a Pale Moon*. And to photographer Brian Baer of Baer Studios, whose talent made stepping backwards into the magical Middle Ages of the British Isles and the Welsh countryside visually possible and stunningly beautiful. The imagery would not have been complete without the wardrobe, which was made possible by Liz Werner and Josie Ernstmeyer of the Bridal Collection, located in Grand Island, Nebraska, and their lovely, timeless gowns. For advice, education, editing, and print layout and design, I'd like to thank Kimberly Hitchens and Barb Elliott of Booknook. Last but never least, Rob Sturtz of Selfpubbooks.com and Shoshanna Gabriel for amazing graphic art and classic book cover design. I am truly grateful.

Friends and Co-workers

I've enjoyed spending time with you. You are a blessing.
Vicki

Amy Abbott, Shirley Abbott, Wendy Albrecht, Deborah Alvarado, Jessica Bartek, Kerrie Bernstrach, Gunner Betz, Ankit Bohara, Ruth Boteo, Ashley Bower, Brittany Briggs, Stephanie Budden, Kendra Bult, Julie Burbach, Michaela Carpenter, Ashlee Carrillo, June Collison, Steve Coram, Erica Covey, Angie Crosby-Jepsen, Nicole Daffer, Brooke Darby, Shellane Dawson, Kristi Eichelberger, Stephanie Emmons, Stephanie Emerson, Rodney Gericke, Jordan Grooms, Travis Hahn, Angela Holke, Krystin Huges, Deb Zeleski, Judy Dietz, Ashana Ferguson, Grant Freeman, Shanda Fruhling, Jessica Gall, Maricela Garcia, Jordan Grooms, Amy Hasnat, Jessica Heaton, Kyrstin Hughes, Karese Hutchings, Marlene Johnson, Robin Johnson, Patricia Kistler, Ron Lauber, Shawn Leach, Julieta Lugo, Michele Marienau, Izabella Martinez, Kathleen Emry-Mefferd, Rhoda Mejia, Cassandra Milks, Terri Miller, Alexis Mishou, Kati Moore, Mcclain Narber, Starla Ortega, Elizabeth Pearson, Casey Peters, Teri Pinion, Nyoka Powell, Dustin Ritterbush, Teshawna Isenbart-Sawyer, Debbie Schaaf, Nathan Schema, Laura Schemper, Cynthia Schneider, Karen Shapley, Jamie Siegel, Carlie Skiles, Carla Smallcomb, Brandy Smith, William Speer, Sydney Spellman, Jennifer Stauss, Alicia Stewart, Erin Stone, Bonnie Streit, Curtis A. Sikyta, Beverlyann Trevino, Stephanie Trucano, Melissa Velazquez, Donna Westerbuhr, Corrina Whitney, Connie Witt, Nancy Zimmerman, Fr. Joe Hanappel, Fr. Richard Piontkowski, Fr. Jorge Canela, Fr. Art Faesser.

erworldly and fragile, she lay on a rough pallet of skins while the threads that wove her life were mercilessly sheared away.

The Baroness ignored the suffering of her daughter. With an impatient flourish of her cape, she adjusted a stray lock of rich ebony hair, tucking it back into a perfect ringlet. Her beauty was pure night magic: dark olive skin and striking eyes of piercing black velvet, as exotically Mediterranean as her Iberian ancestors. In the wavering light, she appeared more of a statue in her perfection than actual flesh and blood. Just as hard. Just as cold. The night was wearing thin, and her patience had long since come to an end.

"Must I do it myself, priest?" she admonished. "Or would a flogging from Gerald give you enough incentive to do your *saintly* duty?" She smiled wickedly, so comfortable with the control her power and wealth gave her.

The monk, a good and pious man who had devoted most of his life to the scholarly pursuits of theology and writing, had been routed from his bed in the middle of the night by the man who now stood so silently beside the Baroness. All these years, he had foolishly believed that he was safe behind the massive stone walls of the cloister house. But the shock of waking up with a knife at his throat had nearly caused his heart to fail. Frightened of the intruder's size and the cruel scar that ran the entire length of his face, the monk had believed him to be one of the fabled Vikings who struck such terror into the hearts of all Christendom, spilling the blood of the saints like water around the defiled temples of God.

"*Deliver us, Lord, from the fury of the Vikings!*" he prayed, crossing himself dutifully, and he watched in terror as a ghost of a smile played across the giant's face.

"No *Viking*... priest," he assured the monk. "But I'm just as capable of sending you to your paradise if you don't keep still!" He emphasized his words by pressing the tip of his blade just a little nearer, drawing a single, thin scarlet line above the monk's habit. "Come with me!" he ordered threateningly.

Choking with fear, completely petrified by the muscular man who towered above him, the little monk prayed fervently that his earthly mission had not yet been completed. Too afraid to cry out and doubting his ability to escape, he scrambled quickly from his pallet of skins and silently followed the towering figure into the night.

Two horses awaited the pair, and a wild ride followed.

Through shadowy woods with narrow, curving paths and along the darkened cliffs they rode, while the ocean rolled and crashed furiously against the breakers beneath them. One misstep would have been the end. And yet they didn't stop until the Vale stood before them, obscured, wrapped in silent mists. The only light that glowed in the manor issued weakly from the uppermost tower.

"Up there!" The guard pointed, and the priest nodded dutifully, following his "host."

But the scene that met his eyes shocked him to the core. A gentle man, who had not witnessed even one violent death in all his forty years, he fell to his knees and prayed, nearly fainting at the sight of birth. Such pain! Such purpose! His eyes misted in tears as he watched the frail young girl, so childlike in form, pushing with all her might, trading her life unselfishly for her child's.

"Help her!" he whispered, not sure whether it was God he pleaded with or the beautiful woman who stood half cast in shadow, staring morosely out the window. A young maid, not much older than the girl she tried to help, was on her knees, her arms awash in crimson blood. One final push, one heart-wrenching scream, and the baby was born.

"Merciful God!" breathed the priest, and only then did the woman by the window turn.

"What is it?" she asked quietly.

"A girl, my lady!" said the maid happily. "A real beauty, too!"

A faint look of disgust replaced the woman's curious gaze as she motioned for the maid to leave, while a look of infinite peace flooded her daughter's face as the baby let out her first healthy, wailing cry, comforted by the faint thundering beat of her mother's fragile heart.

"You, priest," ordered Isabel, "baptize her."

"Her father," he stammered. "Where is her father? Is he registered? Is *she?*" he asked. All questions needed to be answered before the child could receive the holiest of blessings.

"*She will be registered!*" Isabel spoke flatly and gave the priest the necessary genealogy of her granddaughter. But now what was he to do? It was a mortal sin to baptize a bastard child! Not simply a venial transgression that half a dozen prayers could negate, but one that could cost him his immortal soul, regardless of the penance he might make! Lost in thought, he contemplated the gravity of what he was being forced to do. Then a sharp command from Isabel caused him to look up.

"Gerald!" she snapped in exasperation.

The Captain of the Guard took a menacing step forward, drawing his sword with a loud hiss as metal slid swiftly across metal. With one hand, he took the child from the priest and laid her on the cold stone floor, the tip of his sword poised above her heart.

"Monster!" screamed the priest, throwing himself at the towering figure, his outrage giving him a courage he hadn't known he possessed. He grabbed for the arm that held the sword and was knocked halfway across the room, striking his head sharply on the wall. Before he could come to his senses, a massive hand closed around his throat and lifted him straight up into the air. With barely enough air to breathe, he looked into the unfathomable dark eyes glinting before him.

"May God have mercy on your soul…" he croaked painfully.

For a brief second the guard's eyes shifted, focusing on the man in front of him for the first time.

"I have no soul," he whispered lifelessly, dropping the priest to the ground. "Nor conscience," he added, placing his hand meaningfully on the hilt of his sword.

Swallowing, the priest backed away, rubbing his throat as he made his way to the infant and gently picked her up. He looked sadly from the quiet child in his arms to the leviathan figure, ready to kill for the woman he stood next to.

"Devils!" he hissed, drawing the child protectively toward him. After all, none of this was her fault.

"Devils?!" Isabel inquired politely, delicately arching her eyebrows over her almost hypnotic brown eyes. "I know of no such things, priest. *I* only know that *she*, my granddaughter, must receive the proper Christian ceremony to validate our claim with the Norman dogs who would occupy our lands. And *you will do it, priest!*" she warned softly, so close to fulfilling her dream she could nearly taste it. "Or *else*..."

Later, battered and weary, the little cleric agreed to what Isabel wanted, on one condition: that the child never be harmed.

"Baptize her, priest, and she will be worth a *kingdom* to me. I guarantee you that no one will harm her." Cruel though she was, Isabel's word was law, and she did not give her promises lightly. "But," she added, "remain a stubborn fool, and, well, who knows?" She shrugged, daring him to see just how far she would go.

Beaten, the priest gave in and the child was baptized. She became "Charlotte" after her tragic and timid mother, "Isabel" after her dark, Plutonian grandmother, and "de Clare" as was fitting for a child without the right to a father's name. The baptismal waters flowed over her face and tiny form, filling her nose and eyes, trickling coldly down her throat, choking her and ridding her of a sin she knew nothing about. On that mysterious December night, she became a cleansed soul, precious in the eyes of God, and an orphan, all within the space of a few minutes.

Sputtering from the acrid taste of salt lingering on her tongue, then sobbing in her childish need, and finally trembling violently from the bitter cold, she was taken from the arms of the battered and terrorized priest and given to her only remaining kin, a grandmother who detested even the sight of her.

"Find a nurse. Quickly!" ordered Isabel, handing her charge to Gerald without even a glance at the tiny, wrinkled face while the priest was ushered to the door with a bag full of gold for the poor and a warning to keep silent.

And so her life began, seventeen years ago, one remarkably bright night in early December's white world of snow and glittering ice. A silver crescent moon holding a jeweled star between its horns shone regally above the tower where she lay wrapped in soft skins. A Celtic crown, the ancients whispered, pointing knowingly heavenward. A fitting crown, they had all agreed, for a true Celtic princess. But this they dared not say too loud. The child born at the Vale of Clwyd at Camolodunn had entered the world in secrecy instead of splendor: hale and hearty, full of life and protesting her rude treatment loudly, orphaned and unloved.

Chapter 1

Night descended on the lush Welsh countryside with all the ferocity of a panther devouring its prey while pale starlight gleamed like beads of sweat on its endless back. The moon, wide-eyed and unblinking, stared down indifferently on the emerald-green forest below, where creatures of every size and shape roamed: fuzzy rabbits with pale pink noses and white cotton tails; graceful deer with their timid steps and liquid brown eyes; sleek black wolves lurking hungrily in the shadows. Predators and prey locked forever in combat, but none as savage and free as the wild Welsh who made this valley their home.

"By the saint's blood!" she muttered as her fingers slipped clumsily off the cold metal and her short sword clattered loudly to the stone floor. A loud "woof" and two shorter barks added merrily to the din.

"Bishop!" Charlotte hissed, looking worriedly from the tightly-closed door to the shaggy gray hound dancing with excitement by the faintly glowing hearth. "You'd better be quiet," she warned, "or you'll wake Grandmother!"

She reached tentatively for her sword as though it had turned into something alive. It was an ancient Druid *athamé*, pounded silver, beaten impossibly thin into a delicate angular tip, as deadly as it was beautiful, with runes of protection etched into the elegant handle. Picking it up, she carefully strapped it to her narrow waist, making sure that the razor-sharp tip was buried securely in its protective sheath.

"I've been moved two floors higher already this year!" She pouted furiously, tying her long silver hair with a single blue-satin ribbon. "Now I sleep in this dismal old tower, at the very top of this cursed pile of stones! There is no place left to go, Bishop! Nowhere," she added angrily, stamping her foot. A pale silver flame glowed dangerously in her clear blue eyes. "Except *down!*"

With more courage than common sense, she made her way to the narrow slit that passed for her window.

"Coming?" she asked softly with a grin, knowing nothing short of death could prevent her friend and protector from following her. Bishop wagged his tail furiously in reply.

Clad only in a paper-thin white chemise, with a pale blue gown and matching slippers draped carelessly over her shoulder, she padded barefoot toward her escape. Charlotte Isabel de Clare, the heiress of the Vale of Clwyd, more readily known as "Little Miss-Chievous" by the doting servants, or "Lady Charlotte" when formality was required, but *never* as "Mistress Charlotte," never anything so *proper*, poked her lovely face boldly outside and drew in a deep breath of the cool night air.

Nearly one hundred feet straight down, the wild Atlantic Ocean crashed furiously against the polished stone breakers. Spindrift, torn from the crests of foam-tipped waves, washed peacefully into a deep, purple-hued tidal pool that collected and swirled dangerously below her window.

The Vale had been built on a rugged precipice with the ocean, both protector and relentless foe, on the west side and a newly-formed Norman moat on the east. Though once a Saxon stronghold of wood and mortar, the manor had undergone a slow evolution. Stone slowly replaced wooden walls, polished green glass supplanted the thick, oiled skins of lamb, and a newly-formed bailey rose like an accusing stone finger on the west side, jutting out, obstinate and all alone on a thin lip, overlooking the lonesome sea. All those who opposed Isabel became familiar and long-staying guests in its inescapable rooms, including her own wayward granddaughter, the notorious "Lady" Charlotte.

Chewing thoughtfully on her lower lip, Charlotte calculated with experienced precision the path she would take. It was nearly a forty-foot drop to the narrow ledge that traversed the main floor, with nothing to stop her fall except the jagged rocks below. The ledge itself was barely more than a glorified pigeon roost. Its once-straight edges were now rounded and crumbling, cracked by the persistent lashing of salt and wind and the relentless, insidious tangle of suffocating ivy.

Sighing, Charlotte began her escape.

"You had better stay, Bishop!" she cautioned, regretting that she had said the familiar word "come" the moment she gazed outside. "This isn't like our other room." Afraid that his love for her would cause him to follow as it always had, she tied a sash about his neck and lashed the other end to the window's rotten timber. "You cannot climb, Bishop, she whispered softly. "And I doubt that you can fly, though you've always been an angel and my best friend."

Before, she thought angrily, it had been so much *easier*.

Their room had faced northeast on only the second level. It was hardly a challenge to scale the wall, and as for Bishop, it was only one joyous, bounding leap to freedom. But now, she would need all her strength to hold onto the gnarled ivy that clung so tenaciously to the keep. Such old ivy! Nearly six inches thick, and oh, so brittle! Ancient ivy really, she mused, trailing her slender fingers through its thick velvet leaves, knowing its vines had covered the Vale from nearly the very beginning, through dark Welsh warlords and fair-haired Celtic conquerors, from stern Roman magistrates to frightening Saxon hordes. The stubborn, enduring root seemed so much like the people of Wales themselves—they just refused to let go of land which belonged to them since the beginning of time.

Peering farther over the side, she calculated the depth of the ledge. It looked to be barely six inches deep and none too sturdy, and worse than even this, it ran directly beneath Isabel's drawing room window!

"Oh, Bishop," she admitted ruefully. "I'm not so sure about this! If I hadn't sent a message to Lon, I think I would just as soon lie down and wait for dawn!"

Bishop made a funny little sound, somewhere in between a growl and a whine. He rolled over on his back as far as the sash would allow, playing dead. He looked so comical, with his shaggy legs poking heavenward and his tongue lolling theatrically to one side, that Charlotte grinned.

"You're right, boy!" she agreed enthusiastically, interpreting his body language as only a long-time confidante could. "I am a horrible liar!" Her laughter filled the emptiness around her, joyful and reckless, and for a moment, she had escaped the manor without even leaving her room, free.

Hearing the merriment in his mistress's voice, Bishop whined again and turned clumsily over. Playing the clown, he crawled commando-style toward her, dragging his belly and the sash on the ground till his huge head was within scratching distance.

"You're absolutely right," she whispered affectionately, rubbing the big, floppy gray ears with both of her hands. "I probably would have tried it sooner or later, just to see if it could be done! And," she added wickedly, "because Grandmother wouldn't like it!"

Smiling, knowing she was once again tempting fate, she reached down between her legs and caught the back edge of her chemise. Pulling it up scandalously high, she tucked the end into her belt, forming a curious pair of trousers. Her long slender legs were bare, and the tight fit of her garment outlined the seductively ripe curves of her athletic young body, from her lusciously full, firm breasts to her supple, rounded bottom. With a sudden shift of weight and a tensing of deceptively strong arms, she grasped the worn timber outside her window and pulled herself easily through. Knowing better than to look down, she grabbed the thickest branch she could, searching blindly for a secure toehold with her agile foot. With a rush of nerve-tingling adrenaline and her heart pumping like mad, she tested her weight against the ivy's ability to hold her and swung outward, ready to spring back into her room in a heartbeat if necessary. Spread-eagle, with her well-muscled legs stretched as far apart as she was able, she distributed all one hundred and five pounds of herself as evenly as she could, balancing precariously on the ivy's straining limbs. Every muscle was tensed and shaking as she strained her ears, listening for the tell-tale squealing creak of breaking branches or the dizzying feel of too much pull.

"One thousand… two thousand… three thousand," she counted slowly, calming herself as Gerald had taught her, feeling the fear build in her like a smothering serpent, coiling upward as she accepted it, knowing she could do nothing about it, and then letting it go with a smooth exhalation of breath, until nothing remained except the faint, acrid taste of copper in her mouth. Seconds ticked by, and her palms were wet with sweat despite a cool, gusty breeze—and yet nothing happened. Licking her dry lips, she tugged a little—then held her breath and waited. A little sucker not more than half an inch in diameter, pulled away from the wall; it had given up so easily! But the parent vine, long since used to abuse, held tight. Reasonably sure that she had a marginally good chance of living through this night, she allowed herself the sweet luxury of breath as she cautiously began her descent.

Like an acrobat, hand over hand and ever so slowly, each movement precise and calculated, she made her way down. The climb was more difficult than she had anticipated. The branches broke and tore her skin, poking her in none-too-pleasant places, and the ivy's leaves stained her clothes, legs, and hands a deep, frightening green.

Somewhere in the forest a nightingale began to sing, its song so sweet it pierced her thoughts like a lance, causing her attention to wander, until all the sounds surrounding her became a deafening roar.

"Concentrate!" she demanded of herself, clenching her teeth as beads of sweat stung her eyes, and wave after frightening wave of vertigo washed over her, threatening to send her spiraling to her death. "Drat!" she cursed as a sliver of wood jammed itself painfully into her thumb. She couldn't afford the luxury of shaking her hand until the pain went away. With a herculean effort of will, she forced herself to ignore the splinter, thinking only of each separate movement she must make, focusing so strongly that all the sounds around her began to fade, until the crash of the surf thundering in her ears became only the rhythmic beat of her heart, slow and steady, and the wind's mocking voice and ghostly caress became no more than the whisper of her own breath. And then there was only the wall and the ivy, and her ever-increasing awareness of each straining muscle and tendon, as every inch gained became a victory.

Occasionally she would slip, cursing loudly and grabbing frantically for something—*anything*—to steady herself, sometimes finding only a handful of tattered leaves. In that moment she became frightfully aware of her own mortality. The fear, subdued but always there, came surging forward in overwhelming waves and threatened to paralyze her. *Fear* was her foe, she knew, her greatest enemy, and it always had been, not the rush of swirling waters or jagged rocks below. But her instinct to survive was strong, ultimately coming to her defense—making her reach *just one more time* for a branch or stretch *just a little farther* for a crumbling niche to dig her fingers into. *Try again*, her heart demanded, not willing to let fear rob her of her future as it had her past.

Scratched and scraped, leaves clinging to her silver hair, exhaustion threatening to engulf her, she continued until, much to her relief, she felt the ledge beneath one delicately shaped, slightly long, slightly calloused toe. Breathing deeply, her arms and shoulders aching, she tried to steady her racing heart as she rested first one toe, then another, and then another after that until both feet balanced perilously on the fragile outcropping of wasted limestone. Licking her lips, scarcely daring to draw a breath, she began to inch her way along, now above dry land instead of surging tide and worn rocks. But she was still nearly thirty feet in the air.

Nearing the darkened casement of Isabel's study, where she hoped to gain a few moments of rest, a light bounced off the wall and settled in the room, sending a golden glow out into the night and nearly stopping her heart.

"Drat again!" Charlotte cursed, so tired she was shaking. Holding her breath for the hundredth time that night, she flattened herself out against the wall as much as she could, searching desperately for a tenuous finger-hold of ivy, or cracks deep enough to shift some of her weight into. Then she waited, listening.

* * *

"Charlotte will be of no use to me if *that* happens, Gerald!" stormed Isabel, sending a glass crashing into the hearth as she paced furiously around her elegantly decorated drawing room.

"What can I do about it, m'lady?" asked an exasperated Gerald in his thick, gravelly voice. The years had not been kind to the old soldier, who was battle-worn both physically and emotionally. His deep brown eyes lacked the luster of life. His face, once ruggedly handsome and firm, sagged as if gravity had such a severe hold on him that he had begun to melt, and his mustache, once so pert and virile, so richly black, had faded to a cold, lifeless iron gray.

"You can *keep* her in the manor, for one thing, Gerald!" snapped Isabel.

"We try, my lady," he offered wearily. "But she refuses to obey!"

"I do not understand how a tiny slip of a thing like *her* can outsmart every guard in the Vale, and *you* as well!"

Unconsciously, she adjusted her thick, plaited hair, patting it expertly into place.

Gerald watched her every movement and couldn't help but wonder at her meticulous perfection. The years had not diminished *her* beauty one bit, he thought ruefully, nor her vile temper. A few lines guarded her fiercely mesmerizing brown eyes, and her hair, which had once glowed as blue-black as a raven's wing, shimmered with lightning streaks of white at her temples. Regal, he thought. Even her form, which had driven him to distraction countless times and homicide at least once, had refused to age. Beautiful, he mused sadly. So beautiful, my Isabel…

"If you had not treated my granddaughter like a common soldier," she raged, "schooling her in war and riding and *combat*, for God's sake, *this would not be happening!*"

Gerald's head sank a little lower, his mustache sagged a little deeper, and his spirit, long since banked and dark, died a tiny bit more. He said nothing, knowing her hysterical accusations were undeniably true. Lady Charlotte could not be dominated nor cajoled, would not bend to Isabel's will. In short, she would not submit to her grandmother's control. But even without his diligent tutorage, he had suspected long ago that Lady Charlotte would have been just as stubborn and willful—just as *defiant*—and he was so *proud* of her! Though she was not nearly as physically strong as even the smallest of his hand-picked guards, she had the wits and courage to best nearly all of them.

"She fights with no scruples!" his men would complain when they were gouged or bit or kicked a little low.

"Yes," he would admit with a hint of pride coloring his words, "no scruples, nor principles, nor ethics, and no hindering, misplaced honor that could get a man killed in battle!" Her only intent, he knew, was to *win* in any way she could, and she did! Ah! How she did! With fire and fury and bloodcurdling cries! There was passion in that girl's veins, he thought with secret satisfaction, and such heart and courage.

"Gerald!" Isabel snapped, his silence further irritating her. "Are you *listening* to me?"

Her temper had been on a short leash ever since she'd received the King's order that *her* manor was to fall under *his* fiefdom! Worse than this royal dictate was the unanswered question as to *whom* the King would appoint to be the Vale's keeper and lord. Isabel had done her best to assure King Henry of her loyalty, carefully omitting expressions like "noxious Norman progeny" and "conquering filth" from her letters, all written in elegant French script, so patronizing, so flattering, such lies! Letters sent with the intent to mollify and placate the Conqueror's heirs and keep *her* in the manor.

Yet nothing she'd written had generated the type of response she wanted. Ready to shift the burden onto the already oppressed shoulders of her people, she had promised him increased taxes. Tribute to a great king! But a relatively curt reply had been sent, assuring her that he could collect all the "tribute" he wanted without her help. His only intent for drawing the Vale into the fiefdom was to create a unified front to discourage any would-be invasions, including the still-frequent raids of the Vikings—and *he* would do this with or without her help.

Gloomily she realized that the days of the Celts and Anglo-Saxon lords were gone. Now the Normans, who were the French-speaking cousins of the marauding Vikings themselves, ruled *her* land, controlled *her* very future. As she chewed absently on the tip of the King's letter she'd just received, a plan began to form in her mind. There was one way out of this dilemma, he had "suggested." One way that she might keep her castle and her lands—perhaps even *enlarge* her estates—and she held the very means locked safely away in the tower.

"Come with me, Gerald," she said quietly. Her sudden shift in temperament alerted Gerald to the probability that even more of her scheming treachery was afoot, just as surely as black clouds foretold a summer storm.

"I've a letter to send and a ransom to pay," she informed him; her decision was made. "And I'm sure, Gerald," she added dryly, without even the faintest trace of humor, "that I'll need your help with the 'payment'!"

Outside, her energy nearly gone and her limbs shaking violently from the exertion, Charlotte exhaled gratefully as the light left the room and the door shut with a resounding echo. Thankful, she inched forward, wanting only to rest a moment, needing to catch her breath, and she reached with trembling fingers for the ledge. But the stone was old, a crumbling ruin eroded by countless winter freezes and repeated summer thaws. Carefully she wound her fingers possessively around the rough edges and shifted her weight—and the ledge crumbled to powder beneath her hands!

"Oh, NO!" she cried in alarm, not caring who heard as she windmilled her arms and scrambled frantically for a hold as she felt her center of gravity move dangerously away from the wall. She grasped at leaves, air, and slippery stone, finally catching onto a branch, but too late to try again, she heard a sickening, splintering crack, and she began to fall.

"Oomph!" A huge, spine-cracking moan escaped her lips as she landed full on her back, severely bruising her tailbone and knocking the wind clean out of her. Dizzy and suffocating, she lay motionless on the coal-dark sand, feeling as odd as a gasping fish out of water and, for a second, just as terrified. Her gown of pale blue silk hung limply, like a defeated flag, from the greedy ivy nearly thirty feet above her head while her slippers, not to be outdone, performed several curious flips before landing in the deep, swirling pool and vanishing forever beneath the lacy spume.

With her head pounding and her ears ringing as merrily as church bells announcing vespers, she ravenously gulped her first life-giving mouthful of air—no wine had ever tasted so sweet—as she waited for the glare of probing lights or the warning sound of the sharp, staccato beat of tramping feet.

Quiet. All still. No glaring light, no feared guard, and, most important, no Grandmother!

Very carefully, with the numbness from her fall wearing off, she gingerly tested her fingers and toes, sure that something had to have broken. Her hands, though aching, horribly scratched, and beet-red, moved easily, and her limbs, though stiff and sore as well, soon got the idea and joined them. Standing was incredibly painful, but then, so was life, she mused as she pointedly ignored her discomfort and rubbed her sore behind with both hands, longing for a warm bath to soothe her muscles—and a gulp or two of brandy to numb her head. But that would come later.

Now she must find Lon!

Hearing a familiar "Woof!" of approval, she looked up just in time to see Bishop standing on the casement, with half the window's rotten timber hanging like a pendulum from his sash.

"Bishop! No!" she whispered frantically. Her heart had flung itself into her stomach as she gazed up at her furry, good-natured friend, motioning for him to *stay.* "Go back, boy!" she begged, keeping her voice as low as possible. "I'll be back for you in the morning! I promise!"

Leaving him to her grandmother's keeping for any length of time was unthinkable, but taking him now was simply impossible!

He had been a gift from Gerald on her seventh birthday, and he had been beside her nearly ten immeasurably long, lonely years. She wanted a sword that birthday, boastfully claiming that she was now old enough to fight with "her" men. A big sword, she had insisted, just like the *other* soldiers carried, only prettier—one with a gold hilt instead of brass and a sleek two-foot blade of beaten silver. But instead of a blazing sword of steel or a somber lance she could carry proudly into all her imaginary battles, she had gotten a lively bundle of rollicking fun, with ears and paws so large they seemed completely out of proportion to its fat little body.

"But I wanted a sword, Gerald!" she pouted, purposely ignoring the pup sniffing curiously about until he did the most undignified, *comical* thing she had ever seen. He waddled clumsily toward the towering, fierce-looking Captain of the Guard, squatted bravely on the tip of his thick leather boot and wet! There and then, she had loved him with all her heart, sensing some kindred spirit in his outrageous behavior. Giggling, she had protectively gathered him up in her arms while Gerald just scowled and shook his boot, issuing a powerful string of Gaelic curses she eagerly memorized as he made his way out the door.

"I think I'll call you 'Bishop'!" she had told the squirming pup as she touched his cold black nose against hers, hoping God would look kindly on a creature named in honor of one of His holiest servants. "I think you are going to need all the help you can get, boy!" she explained earnestly.

From that day on she became his fiercely devoted friend, tending carefully to all his needs, and he had rewarded her by helping to fill her lonely days with a small measure of love. From a playful, frolicking puppy, chewing up all her favorite toys, to a full-grown hound who sat quietly by her side—he was always there with his slightly moronic, tender brown eyes gazing up at her as if she were his god. And now he meant to follow her again as he had so many times before, even if it was to his death.

"Stop, Bishop… please…" she cried again, only much louder, leaping desperately for the wall, her pain long since forgotten as she tried to climb.

She had barely gone four feet up when all one hundred and forty pounds of persistent canine landed directly behind her in the pool with a heart-breaking thud, sending twenty-foot geysers of water shooting into the air and inundating Isabel's study.

"You stupid dog!" she screamed in terror, jumping from the wall, certain that he had fallen to his death on the hungry rocks surrounding the pool, all because of her. Down she ran toward the water, running as hard and fast as she could along the shadowy black beach, leaping far into the center of the still-rippling water searching for her friend.

Bishop had fallen fast, his weight and the relentless pull of gravity accelerating his speed to a dangerous level. When he hit the water, its smooth, liquid surface felt as solid as a brick wall—stunning him, knocking him nearly senseless but not stopping him. Down through the deep purple pool he fell until the suffocating fluid lost all light, becoming blacker than a moonless flight, a bottomless, airless void his simple mind could not comprehend. The worm-eaten timber, still attached to his neck by the strangling blue sash, first acted like weight, dragging him down—then like a buoy, slowing his descent, then mercifully stopping it before dragging the plunging, nearly unconscious animal back from the gates of perdition.

Charlotte watched in amazement and indescribable relief as her old friend bobbed to the surface, looking with frank astonishment at the world he thought he would never see again before he paddled unfailingly toward her.

Standing waist-deep in freezing water, she hugged his great soggy gray head. "Silly, silly dog!" she crooned as he gazed with unabashed adoration at his mistress, acting like nothing at all out of the ordinary had happened. "You're really more trouble than you're worth, you know!" she chastised Bishop sternly, mock irritation lacing her voice. But he knew her and took her insult for what it really was, proof that his beloved mistress cared, and he dutifully raised one huge paw, laying it with grave dignity over her hand, letting her know everything was all right and thanking her for her concern while above them in the empty tower room, a huge, seldom-used iron key grated noisily in the slot before the massive oak door was pushed forward, squealing furiously in protest.

Isabel strode forward, grim determination etched in every line of her finely sculptured face, followed closely by the ever-obedient Gerald.

"Charlotte!" she demanded. "Wake up! We've something important to discuss."

She walked confidently to the bed where a lump rested securely in its center. "Charlotte!" she said impatiently, jerking the rumpled covers away, exposing only a plumped pile of clothing and a thick blanket rolled into a ball.

"What in blazes!" she said. "I've been tricked!"

Turning sharply toward the silent guard, her surprise hardened into fury at being duped once again. "*Now* do you understand what I've been trying to tell you! Our very futures depend on you finding her before it's too late!" Angrily she shoved past him, shouting loud enough to wake the entire household and alert her granddaughter.

"Guards! Guards! The Lady Charlotte is missing… *again!*"

Chapter 2

Charlotte and Bishop were making their way from the pool to the beach, she thinking of what she could possibly find to cover herself with and he following, as usual. It wouldn't be proper for Lon to see her nearly naked, she mused happily—at least not yet. With Bishop beside her, there was now no reason in the world to return to the Vale, except at the proper time, to claim her title, birthright and the mythical Sword and Crown of Wales. And when she did return, she vowed, it would be on her own terms, with a husband beside her and perhaps even an army behind.

Her thoughts wandered, giddy with the promise of freedom, until her grandmother's voice ripped through the fabric of her dreams like the cruel blade of an intruding knife. She looked up in surprise, just in time to catch the shaft of glimmering yellow light fading from her hated room.

"Bishop! We've got to get away!" she cried feverishly, fully expecting Isabel to chain her to the wall this time. She could not go back to that dark room and the horrid, maddening seclusion. She would rather die! "The forest, Bishop! We must make it to the forest!"

The deep woods surrounding the estate were nearly half a mile away across open meadow. But it was their only chance. The forest hid things, magical things and dangerous things, and things that could not be explained by the ancients. Would it not hide her as well?

"Hurry!" she urged her friend, and she started to run as though her life depended on it. Oblivious to her drenched appearance, she instinctively hiked up what was left of the nearly transparent chemise with her hands, exposing the long, smooth, muscular curves of her furiously pumping thighs, and ran for all she was worth, rounding the manor in a heartbeat and heading for the sheltering seclusion of the trees.

Inside the manor, chaos reigned. Gerald's booming baritone rolled like thunder, crashing painfully into sleep-filled minds. "You drunken louts!" he roared, kicking his men, who sprawled at odd angles beside a newly-opened cask of ale on the manor's narrow marches. "She's gone again! Get up, you lazy dogs, and earn your keep! Find her, or I'll have your heads for breakfast!"

Bleary-eyed soldiers rolled drunkenly from walkways, gathering neglected swords and clumsily trying to mount horses that just refused to stand still.

Twelve good men, thought Gerald. Brave men, who could hold an army at bay indefinitely, gave quarter to no one and would face death without hesitation for the Vale, grumbled quietly. They didn't really want to follow his orders this time because this situation was different. Charlotte was not a common enemy, she was their *lady*, and they respected her, hating to see her a captive in her own home. Still, they must bring her back.

"I don't want a single hair on her head touched, do you understand?" bellowed Gerald.

"Aye," they muttered softly among themselves, exchanging meaningful glances, sure they were in for a fight. Mounting up, they rode noisily across the open courtyard and out into the night.

They saw her, nearly a quarter of a mile in the lead, heading for the safety of the woods, as a blur of white: flawless, ivory skin; flashes of silver hair; piercing glances from eyes that glowed like sapphires. They spurred their horses on, closing the gap, and then they were around her, careful not to get too near.

Surrounded and cut off from her escape, she stood silent and furious in the center of *her* men, panting for breath, while Bishop, sensing her mood, growled menacingly.

"We've come to take you home, mistress," offered one young soldier, whose gaze traveled helplessly over her heaving breasts and flushed skin.

A slow hiss of breath slid through her parted lips as she drew her dagger from its sheath, automatically shifting her weight to first position—a fighting stance that Gerald had taught her many years before and one she now adopted as easily as walking. Bathed in the incandescent glow of the moonlight, she was as hauntingly beautiful as a wood sprite and as deadly as the gray-eyed Athena.

The men looked at each other with obvious worry on their faces. It was not that they wouldn't like to accept her challenge and the possible rewards it would offer if a man remained alive, but they had their orders.

"No, mistress," argued the young soldier uncomfortably. "We're to take you unharmed."

She laughed quietly, a dangerous gleam shining brightly from her half-lidded eyes. Never again would she be locked up; never again would she be a prisoner in the Vale. Shrugging nonchalantly, she walked deliberately toward his mount, sheathing her dagger and looking for all intents and purposes as though she had given up.

Smiling prettily, she reached for him, keeping his attention focused directly on her face, while the other hand grabbed his horse's reins and twisted them violently, wrenching the poor animal's head painfully to the side and throwing the young soldier savagely to the ground.

Laughing, Charlotte sprang lightly up toward the empty saddle, sure of her escape, when a firm hand, with skin as hard and rough as stone, pressed itself meaningfully against her shoulder. Furious, she turned and lashed out with her knife, drawing it back quickly, missing by a bare fraction of an inch the man who stood quietly behind her. He was her teacher, father figure, friend, and, lately, her most hated jailor.

"Gerald," she whispered, "why do you betray me?"

They stood facing each other silently under the curious gaze of the full moon. She, with eyes at first confused, full of pain, hurt and reluctant love, hardening into unforgiving anger, and he simply accepting the accusations thrown by her heated stare as he held the horse, knowing she would mount for him and follow him like a child back to the Vale.

"Call me Judas," he said. "Yet I love you, Charlotte. With each betrayal I crucify myself, yet I know it is for a greater good. Your good, Lady Charlotte."

"My good? Your god, Gerald, is my grandmother, and she will never love you, anymore than she has ever loved me."

With a dignified toss of her head, she turned away, hurting him more than she knew. Surrendering without a fight, she began to walk arrogantly back to the manor with her dog at her heels while the guards followed at a respectable distance.

Between her sweat-dampened skin and the soggy garment she barely wore, she was chilled to the bone, and the cooling night breezes blowing in off the black, wind-swept waters of the wild Atlantic added miserably to her discomfort. She shivered.

Gerald, eager to make amends, to do something to give her comfort, strode forward, draping his cape gallantly over her shoulders. But she wanted no patronizing comfort from him. She wanted nothing he could offer except her freedom, and it was obvious he wasn't willing to give her that. So, from a careless shrug of her stiff little shoulders, the black velvet mantle fell, rustling softly to the ground. Swallowing, Gerald ignored it, walking over the cape as if it didn't exist while his soldiers followed silently, exchanging knowing glances.

Charlotte's stride was purposeful, defiant and proud, with her high-stepping, swinging hips and her flowing cape of silver hair, innocently uncaring of the reaction her nearly-naked body had on the soldiers.

"You!" Gerald growled, pointing to a man whose eyes lingered too long on the shadowed curves of her thighs. "Look away!" he ordered sternly.

She was so naive, he thought bitterly, so totally unaware of the powers and perils a woman's seductive charms had on a man. As always, he felt protective toward her.

"All you louts," he added, "keep your eyes averted, or I'll tear them from your face with my bare hands!"

They did as they were ordered, not just out of fear of the captain but out of pity for their little mistress, feeling a stab of shame for their thoughts.

Into the shadowed courtyard they marched silently. Charlotte Isabel de Clare, the heiress to the Vale, surrounded by guards like a common prisoner. They escorted her back into the castle and led her into the dimly-lit drawing room where her grandmother waited.

"Leave!" was the imperious command. "Gerald, you stay."

Without a moment's hesitation the guards all obeyed the dark figure staring morosely into the flames.

Charlotte stood quietly in the center of the room, readying herself for one of her grandmother's scathing remarks or acid stares. Slowly the old woman turned, and Charlotte marveled at her beauty and vitality, even now when she was nearing sixty.

"*You*," Isabel said quietly, aiming her remark directly at the young girl, "have given me nothing but trouble!"

Charlotte drew herself up, thrusting out her chin boldly, even though inside she had begun to quake. There was something elemental in this woman, something savage and severe. She had never given her granddaughter one kind word, instilling in her a fear so deep that not even the years had been able to soften its chilling effect.

"Well," she added with a sigh, "it seems I must ask you this, Charlotte, since I well know where you were going this night!" Her words were fairly hissed at the girl. "Have you bedded young Lon yet?"

Charlotte was stunned by the bluntness of her question. "That," she replied icily, "is none of your affair!"

"Oh, but it is!" Isabel answered, her voice purringly sweet, while a cruel light shone from her dark, probing eyes. "No *honorable* man will take a wife who has lain with another!"

"*Honorable* man?" she retorted sarcastically. "I know of no one as honorable or as good as Lon ap Llewelyn, and *he* is the man I intend to marry!"

The color highlighting her grandmother's cheeks began to drain away, and her eyes seemed to burn with something other than anger. *Fear?* Charlotte wondered for one brief moment. But before her mind had time to dwell on this new and marvelous possibility, Isabel came toward her with dizzying speed, grasping her arm until her flesh burned.

"You are my *ward*, Charlotte, and as my ward, you will do *exactly* as I command. Do you understand?"

Gerald had moved closer, wondering if his slowed reflexes would be enough to contain Charlotte, should she lose what little control she had left.

Yet Isabel seemed blissfully ignorant of any danger she might be in as she doggedly persisted in trying to bend Charlotte to her will. She needed her. Just how much, she was not willing to say.

"I," continued Isabel, glaring at her granddaughter with barely concealed hate, "have given my word to Lord Charles Montgomery, promising him that you will marry his son three days from now, and I never break my word!"

"No!" Charlotte cried, unable to believe that even the possibility could exist that she was to marry someone other than sweet, gentle Lon—and a Montgomery! She had heard stories of Charles's sons from soldiers and lords alike. Garret, unforgiving in battle, ruthless in war, a terror and a menace to all who opposed him, while Cole and Ransom, his ambitious and eager younger twin brothers, were no better. No, she could never marry a Norman, especially a *Montgomery* Norman, *ever!*

"Let go!" she cried. Wrenching her arm free, she began to turn, wanting only to escape.

"Guards!" Isabel called, determined to have her way.

Reaching out, she caught the back of Charlotte's hair and meant to hold on.

In that instant, whatever control Charlotte had managed to maintain all these years vanished. Turning, she slapped her grandmother hard, regretting it the instant it was done.

With that slap burning her cheek, something cold and cruel shone in Isabel's eyes, something totally unforgiving. Enraged, she placed one hand on her cheek, where a faint pink print was blossoming into scarlet, growing brighter by the second.

"Put her in the *West* Tower," she commanded softly, while her gaze seemed to bore holes right through her granddaughter's soul.

"My lady!" Gerald begged softly. "Not there!"

But the widow of the late Baron Arnulf de Clare would not listen, feeling nothing but her own desire to strike back.

"To the *Tower!*" she shouted, losing all composure.

The guards half-carried and half-shoved the frightened girl up the winding stairs, tossing her reluctantly into the dark little room at the top of the manor that hadn't been used for nearly seventeen years.

The room where her mother had died giving her life.

There, alone with no light but the borrowed glow from the moon shining through the arrow slits, Charlotte sank to the dusty floor. Shivering, she drew her legs against her, refusing to cry. It all seemed like just too much; too much pain, sadness, too many lonely, hateful hours. Sighing, she choked back her tears, not willing to waste them on herself. She felt that her whole life, no matter how hard she had tried to make it better or please her grandmother, to be "good," the *whole* of it had been nothing more than a horrible mistake, a mistake her grandmother seemed to take great pleasure in reminding her of.

Crying softly in the tower, Charlotte wondered what it would have been like to have been loved. She looked upward and sensed something good near her, but only the moonlight drifted through the arrow slits in this small, cold room. Drawing her legs upward, she wrapped her arms around them and bent her head, resting it on her knees. She was filled with an indescribable sadness. Shivering, she imagined that if her mother had lived, she would have loved her and cared that she was sad and hurting so much that her heart ached! Trusting in her imagination, she took comfort in the thought and said softly, "Mother in Heaven, I love you." The dust fell. The spiders continued to spin their webs, and all was silent in the tower.

Down below in the study, with the silent, accusing eyes of Gerald watching her, the Baroness finalized her plans. A letter giving permission for Charlotte to marry Charles's eldest son, Garret Montgomery, was receiving its final seal. With the betrothal of her granddaughter to Garret, the senior Montgomery had promised her a handsome share in the fortunes of his territory as well as exclusive rule of her own, all with the blessings of the King!

The merging of the two families would create an alliance that would stretch from the northernmost part of Wales to the far southern province of Pembroke. *And*, thought Isabel, smiling smugly to herself, *it would put an end to the annoying problem of the Llewelyns once and for all.* It was inconceivable that her granddaughter could even toy with the idea of marrying Lon. After all, she sniffed distastefully, he was her half-brother! Of course, she admitted (to only herself), Charlotte didn't know that, and now, with this marriage to Montgomery, well, she would never have to!

Feeling that she had satisfactorily taken care of everything, she gave the letter to a messenger, and with Charlotte safely locked away, she went to bed, intent on a refreshing night's sleep, not even noticing the absence of Gerald or Charlotte's hound.

As quietly as he could, he slid the key into the lock while Bishop snuffled and whined behind him. Opening the door just a fraction, he stood back, and the dog padded happily into the room with his tail wagging, his claws clicking loudly on the stone floor, and a heavy, warm blanket in his mouth, which he dropped at his mistress' feet.

"Bishop!" she cried happily, looking up in time to see her grim-faced tutor silhouetted against the light for just a second before the door banged shut. But not before a tray of steaming food and several mugs of juice, water, milk and mulled wine were passed over the threshold.

"Gerald!" she called, desperately wanting his help.

"Gerald… please!" she begged, beating her tiny fists against the door. "Please let me out!"

In the corridor, all alone, the old soldier rested his head wearily against the door.

"Long ago I would have, little one," he whispered. A lifetime ago, when he was young and strong—and still harbored dreams. Now, with his head pressed against the old oak door, he felt as shriveled as a prune, useless, *old*.

After a while her pounding ceased, and she stopped calling for him to help her. Her silence was worse than her cries, for now it seemed that *she* harbored no dreams, no illusions about *him*, knowing that he didn't have the power or courage to open the door and set her free. That was the ugly face of reality, and reality was her grandmother's will.

With an effort, Gerald reached into his tunic and pulled out a packet of parchment wrapped in ribbon. He knew that giving this to Charlotte and being caught in the act would seem an act of treason to Isabel, but he could not banish the sounds of crying.

"May this give you comfort, Charlotte," he said beneath his breath. He opened the door a fraction, slid the packet inside, and quickly shut and locked the tower's door.

"Gerald?" Charlotte said quietly, knocking on the door again. "Please, set me free!"

"I can't, mistress," he whispered. "Your grandmother would have my head."

Quietly he turned away as the first pale, shell-pink rays of searching morning light fanned outward from the horizon and he made his way quickly down the winding turret stair.

Knowing she was alone, Charlotte picked up the packet and pulled the ribbons away. Inside was a paper, written on with ink and sealed with wax. Sinking down, she read her mother's name and the name of their priest. Her mother was baptized a Christian, witnessed and registered. Beneath it was a second parchment. In fine script was her name and that of a witness that she was baptized, too. She touched the wax seal gently.

"I'm a Christian," she said softly.

In the packet was a silver chain, beautiful and finely crafted. Hanging like a pendant from the chain was an artfully-made silver Celtic cross emblazoned with sparkling blue topaz.

Instinctively Charlotte placed the beautiful cross around her neck. Somehow, perhaps because it was her mother's, she felt better. Eating a bit of food and comforted by Bishop's incessant attention, she wound herself into the warm blanket, held the baptismal record tightly in her hand, and fell into a deep, peaceful sleep.

Outside, night had fled, morning had won, but Gerald didn't see the victory in the rosy light of dawn with his heart wrapped in the cold, deceitful shadows of his past. The sinister tower loomed menacingly behind him. He turned away from it and made his way quickly to the stables.

Chapter 3

The sky was on fire.

The rising sun licked the bloated bellies of last night's clouds until their coal-colored rims exploded in golden flames, burning the mist from the ground and driving the darkness away.

Garret Montgomery sat confidently in his saddle, walking his horse slowly up the coast, flanked by twenty of his best men. He was a dark, intensely passionate man who radiated an unmistakable aura of power even at the tender age of twenty-three. A thick, unruly mane of silky black hair flowed down his neck, curling seductively along the collar of his leather jerkin, reflecting turquoise lights in the early morning glow.

He was not "pretty" in any sense of the word, yet he was undeniably handsome. His features, each one taken separately, did not seem to fit. His deep-blue eyes were too large and fierce beneath his slashing black brows. His nose was too slender and hawkish, his mouth too wide and sensual, his jaw far too square and stubborn. Yet, seen all together, along with his natural confidence, his mannerisms and pride, his virile strength and self-assured speech, his slightly dangerous, predatory looks gave him an indisputable masculinity that made women weak in the knees and caused hearts, young and old, to skip several beats.

He was Norman-French. A distant progeny of Hardrada and a cousin of William the Bastard, Conqueror of England. Like the rest of his line, he stood well over six and a half feet tall, towering above both stocky Anglo-Saxons and lithe Celts alike. He had been born in the summer when the constellation Leo shone overhead, with fierce Scorpio on the rise, and the fabled star Antares glowed brightly like a jeweled eye in the morning sky. He was born to rule, the old magician told his father, poring over his charts and calculations with a practiced eye, and Garret never doubted it for one minute.

Moodily he gazed out over the gray-green sea that seemed to blend imperceptibly into the horizon, keenly feeling the effects of too much ale as he watched a gull dart through the sky and scoop up a fish for breakfast with its hooked beak.

They were now twelve miles past Cardiff and heading north. Viking raiders had struck several settlements along the coast recently, and it was up to him and his band of well-trained soldiers to stop them—and he would, with a vengeance.

Cole, one of his younger brothers, his junior by ten years and one of a set of twins, rode beside him. They were so alike in looks it was uncanny, yet they were completely different in temperament. The only common trait existing between them, outside of their physical resemblance, was their innate love of a good challenge, whether it was a simple fight to gauge each other's strength, a reckless, potentially neck-breaking horse race in the middle of the night, or even a chess match that might go on for days. The red god of war ruled their lives, filling their minds with fire, and the love of pure, cold steel resting in their hands.

Cole, with his reckless temper and caustic speech, could be angered by a glance, throwing his glove down in a second and demanding "satisfaction," while his older brother seemed to take forever to explode, never letting his expression belie his true feelings until it was too late for the other man.

"How much farther?" Cole asked sullenly, already wishing it was time to return to Pembroke. He had wanted to fight, and all this trip had been was one drunken revel after another. If he had just wanted to drink, he could have done that easily at home.

Sensing his younger brother's disappointment, Garret smiled.

"Soldiering not to your liking?" he asked politely. He grinned wickedly, deepening the cleft in his chin.

"Well, no, not exactly," Cole admitted, scratching a tuft of black hair that poked outside of his helmet, while he stretched his long, graceful frame, looking like a young willow beside his brother, whose massive biceps and stout, sinewy thighs appeared as strong and as thick as the branches of a hundred-year-old oak.

"There will be many fights in your life, Cole, I promise," Garret added, knowing his hot-tempered younger brother was feeling all the insecurities of growing up, wanting his body to muscle out and watching for the first faint hint of a manly beard and body hair—lots of body hair—afraid it would never come.

Sensing his big brother's amused gaze, Cole looked up sheepishly, knowing that, without saying another word, Garret understood. Then his older brother, whom he adored like a father, frowned and peered closely at his face, stopping his horse dead in its tracks.

"What is it?" he asked curiously, beginning to worry under Garret's intense gaze. Lifting a hand, he touched the area his brother seemed to be staring at, wondering if he had suddenly sprouted a horn. "What?" he asked, mystified as Garret reached out with his massive hand and touched him gently beneath the nose.

"There!" Garret cried excitedly in his deep, melodic voice.

"There?" repeated Cole, stammering and squeaking uncontrollably.

"Yes, right *there!* Say, Torin," Garret called. "Did you see this?"

Torin, Garret's best friend since childhood, rode up, looking from his friend's serious face to the younger man's worried one with interest. Instantly he understood. A broad smile swept his handsome Gaelic features.

"You're right!" he shouted for all the men to hear. "The boy's got *a hair!*" Both men roared as Cole struck out blindly, hitting only air.

Garret ducked the blow easily and kicked his horse, laughing loudly as he thundered across the open sand with a wild shout.

"I'll get you for that!" Cole yelled, beet-red from embarrassment but feeling a stab of pleasure at the thought of his singular manly hair—hoping it was just as black as his brother's.

Up ahead the two friends rode, still laughing, when the sound died suddenly in their throats.

On a narrow lip of shore, partially hidden by sand, a sleek dragon ship over fifty-four feet long had been dragged onto the bank. Its massive fifteen-foot serpentine prow arrogantly poked heavenward while sixteen pairs of elegantly crafted oars lay at rest along its sides.

Like a magnet, all eyes were drawn to the abbey in the distance.

"Vikings!" Garret shouted, savagely kicking his mount while he automatically unsheathed his double-handled sword, his body hardening in expectation of what lay ahead, especially with the added burden of worrying about Cole. Yet he knew he mustn't let on that he doubted his brother's ability.

Cole wasn't very big compared to the other men, but he was as fast as a banty rooster and just as eager to fight, and it was crucial that Cole feel Garret had total confidence in him. Yet Garret couldn't help but wish Cole had gone to London with his twin Ransom who was more concerned with learning about laws and women than war.

With practiced precision, his men fell in line, instinctively donning helmets and reaching for their swords while below them on a narrow isthmus of sand, a score of fair-haired, ruddy-complexioned giants crouched low, waiting for a signal from their leader.

"Now!" shouted the burly red-haired man. His men, as of a single mind, leapt the low retaining wall, howling madly and waving razor-edged swords and blood-drinking axes wildly, striking and felling anything that moved.

The watch fires, which burned day and night, were dark. The guards slept in a drunken fog as the monks prayed. No warning bell rang.

"A wicked wind is blowing the sea into fits," said one brash young soldier confidently to his mates. "We've nothing to fear. Only a fool would try that boiling mess!" He was one of the first to fall beneath a Viking's sword.

St. David's was burning, burning, and the monks were running, running, and the guards were bravely dying, dying—all on a lovely spring morning.

"Don't beg, boy," admonished Harold Halfdanson, the chosen leader of this band of freemen. "The Valkyries will hear you, and your death will be for naught."

At the mention of death, the young monk he'd captured began to struggle.

"That's better," said the old pirate kindly, a trace of satisfaction seasoning his words as he slammed the boy face down on the stone walkway. "At least you're *trying* to be a warrior now—so I'll honor you as such!"

With his men watching, he calmly split the boy down the middle of his back in one lightning-quick sweep of his ax.

Stooping over, Harold picked up a golden chalice, shrewdly estimating its worth. "Let's move along," he told his men, their arms full of booty and their axes dripping, already tired of this game. "We can make Hedeby in a week with a full hold and time to spare."

Suddenly movement from the east caught his eye and he turned, peering into the distance through callous green eyes. "Soldiers," he grunted with little enthusiasm, rolling his eyes as he grinned at his men. Then his gaze caught a flash of gold and a hint of red. He stared a little harder, just making out the double-headed eagle emblazoned on the leading man's shield. His gaze narrowed.

In the pack of approaching men, one stood out. He proudly carried the shield of the House of Montgomery, but he was dressed more like a barbarian than a knight. While those around him were shrouded in suits of chain mail and helmets of beaten silver, he wore almost nothing. Covering his chest was a light, open-throated leather tunic. His head was bare, letting his black hair take flight in the wind, while his legs were devoid of both trousers and tights. His massive thighs gleamed nakedly like cut marble in the glowing morning light, with only a pair of low-heeled boots covering his calves—all outlined starkly against the muscular black stallion he rode. And to Harold's disbelief, the devil was laughing!

"Garret Montgomery!" he said out loud, recognizing the man from all the stories he had heard. Warrior—some said devil—but he appeared only flesh and blood to the tall Viking.

"By Thor," he whispered happily. If he could beat this man in a fight, *this Montgomery*, who had defeated Sven Forkbeard with his bare hands, crushing the life from the mightiest of Viking warriors—then the news would follow him up and down the coast. And the Skalds, who now sang of him as only the last of those to go "a Viking still," would compose a new song—one to immortalize his bravery until the very twilight of the gods silenced their lips forever.

"No man can live till evening whom the fates have doomed at dawn," he whispered, feeling the expectant thrill of adrenaline coursing through his veins, wondering which of them would die.

"We fight!" he shouted hoarsely, and his men formed a barrier of flesh along the wall, swinging axes, flexing rock-hard muscles, hearing the warrior's drum in the beat of their hearts.

Garret watched as the Vikings formed their line—and he grinned, loving almost nothing better than a good fight.

"Engage!" he shouted as horses and men leapt the wall, the sound of steel striking steel reverberating for miles.

Garret worked his horse to flank Cole, keeping an eye on the young man who stared in horror at the bloody carnage. "Cole!" he shouted angrily, ramming his horse into a Viking who had his brother's neck in his sights.

Startled, the boy looked around just in time to see his brother's horse, used to battle, snorting furiously, viciously stomping the man beneath his sharp hooves.

"Watch what you're doing!" he growled, as Torin fought to gain the other side of Cole.

A loud roar and the keen-edged tip of Harold's ax ripped through the soft leather of Garret's jerkin, drawing a line of blood along his back.

"Garret!" Cole screamed, unsheathing his sword. He swung wildly, his inexperience obvious as he tried desperately to get to his brother.

But the blow had been a glancing one, meant to smart and only draw Garret's attention. Garret spun, turning enough to see a man who was as tall as him and appeared to be just as well muscled, motioning with his hand to "come and get me!"

Grinning, he obligingly swung one leg over his horse's head and slid to the ground, touching the back of his shoulder, which was dark with his blood, as he faced his challenger.

A moment of silence passed between the two while they sized each other up. And then with a bellowing roar of rage, Harold ran toward him, bringing his razor-sharp, two-headed ax high over his head in one powerful arc.

Garret's sword was four feet long, weighing well over forty pounds, with a hilt of inlaid silver. Holding it easily in his two hands, he deftly brought it up in a wide half-circle which caught the ax and drove it to the right. The pressure from the blow was immense. When the two weapons connected, blue sparks shot out like falling stars while the vibrations the blow set off flowed along both men's arms and shoulders and necks, shocking even the delicate nerves of the spinal cord. Yet there was no hesitation—no moment needed to recover—as Garret countered his block with a savage, curving blow to the right that caught the Viking squarely on his massive chest. The big man staggered from the blow, his tunic rent, his skin torn, saved only by the thin, chain-linked metal shirt he had learned to wear.

Grunting, he lifted his ax again, using it this time as a shield to fend off Garret's next blow. Again and again the two men struck, reeling from the force of each other's power, glorying in the intensely alive feeling of battle while the skirmish around them turned lukewarm, then waned as all eyes focused on the pair of sweating, powerful men.

"Give up, Norman!" shouted Harold, feeling a kinship with the dark-haired warrior that went beyond the boundaries of land, as his ax whistled through the air, causing Garret to step back and trip, falling roughly to the ground.

"I'll see you in Hell first, Viking!" he countered as he rolled to one side, followed by the laughter of the red-haired giant.

Coiling his body, Garret sprang lightly to his feet. Within the space of an eye-blink, he jumped straight up into the air, concentrating all two hundred pounds of his muscular build into one ferocious kick leveled directly at the laughing man—catching him squarely at the throat.

Harold fell with a groan, watching in horror as Garret's sword followed his kick by mere seconds, flashing overhead, preparing for the final blow, then it arced savagely downward.

Harold couldn't breathe, but he could move, and he did, rolling to the right—but not far enough, as the sword bit through his tunic again, this time neatly slicing his hand away at the wrist before burying itself nearly six inches into the ground.

Silence fell on all the men as Harold watched in horror as his blood poured from his severed stump.

"Finish me!" he demanded hoarsely, not wanting to be left a cripple. "Finish me!"

Garret, breathing deeply, stood quietly over him, a curtain drawn across his eyes, masking any emotion he felt.

"Take him," he ordered his tired men. "He'll stand trial in London for his crimes."

Obediently, Torin and the rest rounded up the few remaining Vikings, tying them securely with stout ropes.

Harold was furious. At least if he had died, he would have entered the warriors' hall in Valhalla as a hero! Not a cursed cripple! But now he was nothing more than a maimed thief, a common criminal, who would swing from the tower at Gateshead Prison.

"I swear to you, Montgomery!" he cursed loudly as a man tied a rag around his upper arm to stop the bleeding while another approached him with a sword fired white and hot in the flames. "You'll pay by Thor's hammer!" Hot metal seared his skin, melting his flesh, cauterizing broken blood vessels and tiny veins, saving him from bleeding to death so he could die on the gallows for the Englishmen's sport.

"You'll pay!" he whispered, fighting the cloud of oblivion ready to welcome him into its black embrace.

The Viking's threats were like the chatter of gulls or the rush of surf, white noise which was heard often enough but meant nothing. His words were yesterday's news to Garret, whose mind was on other things.

The Vale...

The scraping of the door and the squeal of its rusted hinges brought Charlotte out of her troubled sleep with a start. She jumped to her feet, her first impulse to try to overpower the guard and run.

She stood to one side as the door opened hesitantly a few scant inches and a tray of food was shoved inside.

She started to move around the casement, tensing her foot to kick or her hand to pull—and ran straight into Gerald, who stood behind a cowering serving girl, with two more guards behind them.

His face held no expression, looking only like the dutiful castle guard.

Glaring hatefully at him, she backed away while the door was shut again, and she heard the key turn in the lock once more.

Alone again, she sighed, always alone, especially inside of *herself*, even when surrounded by dozens of people.

Frowning, she looked down at the tray at her feet. Her first thought was to send it and its steaming contents flying against the wall, but Bishop had already deduced that the shank of raw meat was for him, and he had helped himself, greedily tearing into it with obvious relish.

The only things left were a bowl of lukewarm porridge and a steaming tankard of sweet-smelling honeyed tea.

"Ah-choo!" she sneezed, with a chill inside of her threatening to bring on a cold. She sat down cross-legged on the cold floor by her dog and decided to drink the tea to warm herself. It was very hot green-leafed tea laced strongly with cinnamon and overly sweetened with honey. But it warmed her going down, and for that she was grateful.

For the first time, she really noticed the room she was in.

It was, perhaps, the smallest room in the manor, without even a hearth or a heating vent to give some measure of comfort in win-

Prologue

Wales, A.D. 1100

"On with it!" the Baroness impatiently ordered, wrapping her cape tighter in a futile attempt to keep the swirling north wind from chilling her already frigid form. Several candles had been lit for the christening; their weak, sputtering flames, prisoners of wick and wax, jerked convulsively against the icy air in protest, throwing darting black shadows against the tower's stone walls. Salt and blessed water waited in golden bowls while a very frightened priest, trembling more from fear than cold, took the screaming infant from the arms of her mother.

"Please..." begged the pale, delicate beauty with the silver mist-colored hair falling like a shower of moonlight around her tiny face. "Mother..." she pleaded vainly, her eyes as shimmering blue as a summer sky, as ethereal as a dream, while her life slipped further away with every breath taken. But her words had no more effect than the wind on the dark and coldly beautiful Isabel, who surveyed her daughter with little more than remote indifference.

"My child, Mother," the girl whispered in despair. "Please give her to me!" With not even the strength left to sob, she reached beseechingly toward her baby with one slender, delicately shaped hand. "Cold. I'm so cold," she breathed, drawing her legs as close as possible to her tiny form, searching for some measure of warmth to thaw the ice that grew so oppressively around her heart. Othter. The walls were still crude stone, never having been replaced or paneled in the warmer woods, and not one stick of furniture graced the area she was in. The only thing in it, outside of several inches of dust and tattered cobwebs lacing the walls, was an old pallet of skins shoved into a corner.

Curious, she took her tea and walked toward it, wondering who had made their bed in such a dismal place. Frowning thoughtfully, she bent forward, her lips suddenly dry, while her tongue began to feel thick and clumsy in her mouth as she touched the faded skins. Simple furs, peasant furs, sewn crudely together; deep black and spotted brown pelts of hare. It was then that her blurring vision caught a silver glitter, and she reached unsteadily for it, suddenly grown dizzy.

"What?" she wondered, plucking a long strand of silver hair from the rough bed. There were others. More silver hairs fanning out like a faded star on the crude wooden block that served as a pillow.

"Who?" she whispered out loud, trying unsuccessfully to focus.

The hairs were the same color as her own, the same silver ash. Then, wavering ever more unsteadily on legs suddenly grown weak, she noticed that the center of the bed was darker than the rest of it. A crusty brown stain flowered out from the middle—like old petals of dried blood. Her lips tried to form the question that shot through her mind but was instantly lost as she wondered vaguely what on earth was the matter with her.

A new thought occurred, one that stuck like a knife in her mind and dug itself in.

"Poison," she whispered, staring in disbelief at the half-empty mug in her hand. "She's poisoned me…"

A loud crash caused her to turn. Bishop, with breakfast finished to the bone, had fallen to the floor with his eyes shut, looking as though he were barely breathing.

"Gran… mother…" she tried to say, knowing that Isabel hated her but still unwilling to believe that she hated her enough to *kill* her.

Stunned, she tried to walk.

"Ger… ald…" she called, still believing he would help as she wavered unsteadily toward the door while the fingers holding the mug in her hand lost all feeling. The cup of poisoned brew crashed to the floor, followed seconds later by the unconscious girl.

Chapter 4

Planter's Inn sat squarely in the middle of the eternally overcast city of Cardiff, flanked on the north by the wheelwrights' stalls with their belching, smoking forges and raucous, ceaselessly clanging hammers, and on the south side by the cordwainers' lane where shoemakers and candlemakers and other bourgeois merchants plied their trades.

The inn itself was nondescript, built with crude, rectangular brown lar stones heaped carelessly one on top of the other while a shock of fresh golden thatch crowned its low-peaked roof. It had seen many a weary traveler in its service: clerics who lusted for more than the cross; kings who desired nights of anonymity beneath its old timbered roof; and bands of young men who rioted merrily with the sweet abandon of youth in its massive common room almost every night.

Garret opened the door and stooped low, his head missing the lintel by a fraction of an inch. "Alice!" he called, twisting his body a bit so he could enter. His wide shoulders were nearly the same width as the door and scraped both sides of the jamb as he pushed himself through the narrow opening and into the large common room where the gray-hued light from outside grew even dimmer. He and his mob of well-bred men were no strangers to the inn.

"Well, bless my soul! 'Ere he is again!" The carrot-haired proprietress of the inn chuckled good-naturedly. "It's been a while, hasn't it, lad?" she joked while she finished scouring the worn wooden table with a rough stone before she let drops of tallow fall from her lighted candle to wax its porous surface to a gleaming rich amber. "Wasn't it you and that band of brigands what drained my casks and exhausted my girls *just last night?*" she asked sweetly, smoothing her rumpled brown cotton work dress and tidying her mop of outrageously hennaed, unruly red hair, still artfully playing the coquette at the ripe old age of fifty.

"I'll never tell." He grinned roguishly and gave her an affectionate hug. "We need a room to freshen up a bit, Alice, before we can play," he told her with a devilish wink.

"Surely, my lord," she replied with mock gravity as she curtsied, dropping nearly all one hundred and eighty pounds of her fleshy form into a charming bow. "Right over there, my lord," she warbled, trying hard to curb the harsh sound of her vowels as she extended her arm elegantly toward the stairs. "I think you know your way by now, you scamp! 'Play' indeed! More like a circus in here with you boys!"

He laughed, giving her a teasing slap on her overly-developed posterior, then he rounded the worn wooden brace and headed for the room, delighted as always by her sauciness.

"Bring us up some ale, luv, and some hot water, too," he ordered loudly.

"And food," added a dusty, road-weary Cole, always hungry.

"Forget the refreshments," said a lusty-eyed Torin, scanning the darkened hall with his twinkling, restless gray eyes. "Where's the girls?"

Everyone laughed as some of the men found their way into the common room, sprawling onto benches while Garret and Torin took the stairs two at a time.

Up above, in the low-ceilinged room overlooking the sea, the two men busied themselves, peeling off their clothes.

"Do you think the magistrates will show those brigands mercy?"

asked Torin, a speculative frown creasing his narrow features, giving him a slightly feral look. Magistrates were, after all, human and just as subject to bribes as the next man.

"Would you?" Garret replied icily, a piercing stare causing his friend to look away, slightly shame-faced, as if he had read his corrupt thoughts.

Knighthood demanded the highest ethics from any male valiant enough to obtain its coveted belt. Sadly, ethics and honor were mere words to most high-born males, but not Montgomery. He *lived* the code of honor, believing in it with the passion of a man who has little else to hold onto, defending those weaker than himself with a heart filled with righteous wrath and a steady hand that wielded an unforgiving sword.

If Torin could have chosen only one word to describe his powerful friend, that word would be *noble*, dangerously so, a characteristic much talked about in these changing times but seldom practiced.

"You know," Torin offered philosophically as he pulled his shirt over his head, "I think there is a new order coming in with King Henry. A time of peace and forgiveness, a time of law."

"Go tell it to your priest," Garret said tiredly, jerking the tunic away from his shoulder with a grimace. Fresh blood began to pour from the reopened wound. "Men are what they are, greedy dogs of war, and have been since the beginning. Look in those history books you're always reading, Torin. If a man cannot sniff out a good fight or stumble into one, he will start his own with his neighbors or his brother or even out of boredom with his own wife," he added with a wry smile.

Torin appeared to think about this for a moment before a timid knock at the door drew his attention.

"Enter!" Garret shouted, standing in the middle of the room, nearly naked except for the thin white piece of loincloth wrapped around his middle that accentuated his ample endowments remarkably well and hid nothing.

The thick door to their room swung slowly inward, and a short young man, gasping and out of breath, with cherry-red cheeks and a matching pug nose, poked his head through the door.

"Lord Montgomery?" he asked in a shy, faltering voice.

"Yes?" answered Garret, turning toward the young man with interest as he recognized one of his father's messengers by his clothes: six horizontal red stripes decorated his tunic of bleached muslin.

"These are for you, sir," the boy offered politely, handing him a packet of papers with grave formality, an aura of pride surrounding the young serf with the completion of his orders.

Garret frowned slightly, taking the papers from the boy. He immediately recognized the familiar wax seal that held the edges together and was used only in times of grave secrecy and war.

"What is it?" Torin asked curiously, combing his brown hair into neat waves. "Is something wrong?"

Garret threw him a look that silenced him, then broke the seal, and read quickly…

> *To my first-born son, Garret,*
>
> *I send you greetings and hope all is well with you and your brother.*
>
> *This document is being sent to inform you that since you seem to have no interest in uniting our great family with another, I have taken that responsibility from you.*
>
> *By the time you return from your mission to Pembroke, you will be legally married to Lady Charlotte Isabel de Clare, heiress to the Vale at Camolodunn.*
>
> *Lady Charlotte comes with considerable dowry, although her pedigree is somewhat in doubt.*

However, this minor blemish is amply compensated for by the fact that the Baroness Isabel has assured me that her granddaughter has a legitimate claim to the rulership of Wales because of some pagan artifacts in her possession.

It is a fortunate match, my son, and has the blessing of the King. It is also one that we cannot help but profit from for generations to come. However, I must forewarn you that any attempt on your part to defy my wishes will result in the immediate loss of your birthright and of any future claim you might have to a share of the manor.

How do you say, my son?

Your father,
Lord Charles Montgomery

"How do I say?" said Garret softly, sitting down on the long bench that ran the length of the wall beneath the window while Torin finished reading the letter over his shoulder.

The room had grown impossibly still and close; even the sounds of the boisterous men downstairs seemed to fade while a nearly tangible tension filled the air with a feeling of crackling electricity. No emotions of any kind played across Garret's handsome face. Not anger, nor indignation, nor indifference; nothing showed. He sat perfectly still for the space of several moments, looking like a Greek god in repose with his rounded, powerful muscles and tight, gleaming thighs shadowed artfully by the slanting rays of the setting sun poking curiously through the small window.

"Do you have a quill?" he asked quietly, finally looking at the young messenger, whose face had grown uneasy under the steady, unrelenting gaze of his master.

"Certainly, my lord," he stammered, and he brought out a

small quill and silver powder, mixing the dye with a drop of his saliva before handing it to Garret with unsteady hands.

Garret immediately wrote on the bottom of the page in a tight, controlled script:

As you will.
Your first-born son, Garret

He folded the paper, sealing it with a bit of wax but leaving no crest mark. That was the sole right of the ruling Lord Montgomery, and it would not fall to him for perhaps another twenty years.

Quietly he handed the paper back to the young man.

"Your lordship." The messenger acknowledged him respectfully, then exited as quickly as he could with the fatal document.

"Why did you do it?" Torin asked in horror. "I've heard of those Welsh women, like bloody cows with dour faces and fleshy thighs! For God's sake, Garret! You've never even *seen* her!"

Part of Torin's ranting had to do with the fact that he was in the same boat as Garret. Someday, if he could not present his family with a suitable match, one would be made for him, and seeing how easily it had been done, especially to someone as strong-willed as Garret, was the most frightening spectacle he had ever beheld.

"Why?" he asked again but with less force, hoping Garret would shout out of the window, stop the messenger, show him that there was hope at the end of this bleak tunnel for all in the nobility who must marry according to pedigree instead of love.

"Because," Garret stated sarcastically, "it is my *duty*," while secretly wishing he could wring the neck of the innocent messenger, knowing it wasn't his fault but not really caring.

Torin watched him silently, seeing him for the first time in years as others must see him: so controlled, so responsible, yet so potentially *dangerous*. But the years had tuned him in to all the subtle changes in Garret's rigid demeanor, not just the illusive facade he had learned to wear. Torin's quick, restless eyes watched in growing apprehension as he saw the huge calloused hands clench into powerful, relentless fists of steel, and he noted the rapid breath and the silver flames in Garret's dark eyes growing brighter by the minute, ready to explode.

Suddenly Garret rose from the bench and walked toward the door.

He was too quiet. Torin had come to fear the calm before the storm, and just like the eerie end of the tranquil eye of the hurricane, his expectations of fury were realized when Garret's fist crashed into the thick timber of the door, thoroughly destroying the vertical slats of wood with one thundering blow before he half-turned to face his friend.

"It's war or women, Torin," he said evenly, feeling the frustrated anger building in him by the second, needing physical release. "But I need one or the other!"

Torin nodded solemnly, understanding completely. Marriage was a lifetime sentence, worse maybe than even a noose around your neck because *it* went on forever and ever and ever…

"Let's go!"

He agreed wholeheartedly, intent on getting very drunk out of sympathy for his friend and fear for himself. "I buy the first cask," he offered, suddenly very thirsty as he followed his doomed friend down the stairs.

She was dreaming.

She was an infant, swaddled from head to foot in tight muslin, and someone kept bouncing her painfully up and down, up and down, like an abused toy. Fortunately, she could breathe, but she couldn't move at all. It seemed as if someone had put a candle right in front of her eyes, which glowed brighter and painfully brighter by the minute. Her head ached and felt as though it were swollen to twice its normal size while something heavy pressed against her eyes. It took her a full minute before she realized it was only her lids, yet they felt as heavy as lead and refused to open. Other senses came gradually into play, with the sensuous feeling of silk, the cold kiss of steel. A bird was singing somewhere above, and a wind blew, so real she felt it stir against her cheek.

Like a piece of cork floating up from the bottom of a deep, black well, she came awake, cringing at the jangling sound of traces and the booming clip-clop of horses' hooves.

"Palfreys," she whispered, recognizing their peculiar, high-stepping gait. Beloved pleasure horses of the aristocracy.

Finally she opened her eyes just a crack, making out the edge of a thankfully overcast gray sky and the emerald-green forest of slowly receding mountains.

So I'm not dead, she thought. *Grandmother has failed at least once.* And then she heard a voice she didn't recognize.

"I think the lady's wakin' up!" it said.

She struggled to focus, seeing a pair of burly Norman soldiers riding close behind her. Riding? Her fuzzy mind, still full of the poisonous nightshade, could not comprehend what was going on.

It was then that she realized she was in the back of a wagon, her hands tied above her head and shackles of iron binding her feet. Startled, her dulled senses flooded back, overwhelming her mind with a torrent of fragmented information. She saw that instead of a tattered chemise, she wore a gown of the finest blue silk and a cloak of purple satin lined with silver fox. Her dress was royal in appearance, even to the jewels adorning her tied wrists and the weight she could feel bouncing on her chest. Satin pillows had been strewn in the wagon's bed, and warm rugs of fur tucked into the sides.

Apparently, nothing had been left out in an attempt to give her at least the appearance of comfort.

Behind the wagon, tied to the wooden rack, her old friend trotted a little unsteadily.

"Bishop!" she whispered in horror, seeing the strip of leather that closed his jaws and the noose that hung around his neck.

Instinctively she reached forward, forgetting about her bindings, only to be rudely reminded by a stinging pain in her hands as the blood made a feeble attempt to circulate.

"Looks a little tight," said the younger soldier to his friend. "Why don't you let me loosen them a bit? Besides, she don't look all that dangerous to me!" he asserted, gloating over his royal prisoner, greedily admiring the view he had been afforded all day of the sleeping beauty.

They had left the Vale in mid-morning with their unconscious charge, taking the inland route through the narrow pass splitting the southern Cambrian Mountains. Now the sun was setting, falling rapidly behind the mountains, staining the cold gray sky a violent black. With luck, they would reach Pembroke by early afternoon with Montgomery's bride.

"Let's stop here for the night," said the soldier. "I'm weary, and she's probably hungry and needs to take a rest."

"We're not to let her loose," said the older man, reining in his horse. "That was our orders."

"Humph!" the young man snorted, busily twirling the ends of his overly long yellow moustache while his eyes greedily followed every bounce of her full breasts. "Even *thieves* get to take a break!" he said with some feeling. "She's a royal and worthy of respect and privacy!"

He wondered sympathetically how such a wonderful, tempting-looking girl as herself could be called anything but adorable. That good-looking older woman at the Vale had filled them full of stories: claimed she was dangerous, would slit a man's throat in the twinkling of an eye if he weren't careful… Yet to him, she didn't look to be anything more than a frightened, captive bride.

"That Garret's a lucky man," he said enviously. "I sure wouldn't mind finding that girl in my bed or calling her wife."

"Watch your mouth!" the older man growled. "Our job is to get her to Pembroke safely and *untouched*, so you can keep your thoughts, and anything else, to yourself!"

The older man knew the de Clares, knew of their prowess in battle and their courage. If the Baroness Isabel said Lady Charlotte was dangerous, the odds were that it was true. He would take no chances.

"Ah, mind your own business!" The younger man scowled.

"Mind my own business?" The old soldier scratched his beard and laughed, remembering the foolishness of his own youth. "Let me just give you a piece of advice. As a matter of fact, I'd say it's something that you can stake your life on: I sure wouldn't want to be the man caught looking at a Montgomery woman. They'd rip your eyes out, and that would just be for starters! Do you know anything about the Montgomery men? Lord Charles, the twins or Lord Garret? Only a fool would toy with the idea of touching anything that belonged to them!"

"Cor!" snorted the other. "Garret's never even seen her! Why, he's got himself half a dozen women at the manor and a village for the taking whenever he wants 'urn!" Sourly he remembered how even the girl he had been seeing on a regular basis had succumbed to the flashy Montgomery smile. The thought of her with him had rankled him more than he cared to admit.

The Montgomerys were gentleman, however; there was never a tale told of a woman who was with them who didn't want to be. This transport of the captive bride they were delivering to Pembroke conflicted with all past deeds involving women and the Montgomery men. No woman proposed to by one of the Montgomery men had ever had to be forced. Most considered themselves fortunate.

"What makes you think Garret would care a farthing for this one? She's thin and tiny, wiry as a kitten and not at all happy about being betrothed to the lord. Her eyes shoot daggers at me every time I look at her!"

The older man looked at him in disapproval.

"The truth is, if you ever told it, the lady is beautiful beyond compare. Even in this cruel situation, her charms are apparent. A pocket Venus—a goddess we've bound lest she spirits herself away before her wedding day. I confess I've never seen a more beautiful woman."

The older guard allowed himself to *really* look at Charlotte for the first time. Twilight only enhanced her charms, making her look a bit more mysterious, with her eyes downcast and her veil of mist-colored hair cascading like liquid moonlight around her face. The approaching night shadows swarmed jealously around her glowing form like dark-winged moths attracted to a silver flame.

"Look at her," he said quietly. "No, Gregor," he said impatiently when the boy ran his eyes over Charlotte. "Not just the obvious! She's different—special."

"Ahh! You're a daft old bird what's got the hots, that's all!" Gregor snorted. "*Different!* She's not the Virgin Mary—she's just a woman! Like all the rest. Sure, she's prettier than most, probably never worked a day in her bloody life... But *what* is she? Nothin' more than a hank of hair, a nice form. They're all the same. Put a sack over her head, she'd be no different than the wenches in the pub!" Gregor yawned and scratched himself tiredly. "Come on, Henry, I got to get some sleep!"

Reining in his horse with a painful tug, he prepared to dismount. "Light's nearly gone, and I ain't stumbling around in the dark ruining my horse just because you're scared to death of the Montgomery family!"

"You'd better learn to watch your mouth, boy!" growled Henry, thoroughly sick of his companion. "You've given your oath of fealty to the Montgomery family, and they've done well by you!"

"Aye, my oath—not my soul!" he spat.

They had stopped beneath a clump of birch and aspen trees, where night birds had begun to call and new leaves rustled happily under the caress of a warm southern breeze. "'Ere, Lady Charlotte," said the smooth-talking Gregor, his one-track mind on hold as he walked toward the wagon with what he considered a sexy smile on his sour face. "Let me help make you a little more comfortable for the night," he offered with a self-serving smile and wink.

During their conversation, Charlotte's face had remained downcast, but at the sound of his voice and hastily approaching step, she looked up, spearing him with her eyes. No fear registered on her face, no demure reticence, just a frank appraisal of the situation that made the young man frown slightly until his artificial smile fixed itself back into place, his ignorance causing him to misread her expression.

"That's a good girl," he chirped patronizingly, talking down to her as he did to all women. "Let Gregor loosen those nasty ropes a bit!" he crooned, treating her as if she had the intellect of a three-year-old imbecile.

"I wouldn't, Gregor," advised Henry, watching the girl watch Gregor with all the predatory interest of a mountain lion with a helpless bunny in its sights.

"Keep it quiet, old man. You think Montgomery's the first nobleman to be cuckolded by his intended?"

He crawled into the back of the wagon, purposely lying halfway across her shackled legs as he reached upward to loosen the ropes, letting the side of his hand brush against her lips. "Why, it's practically an obligation amongst us."

To his delight, she smiled, and his blood stirred as his hand lingered, feeling the satiny smooth texture of her lips. His smile broadened to show his pleasure—sheer seconds before she bit down so hard on his hand that she drew blood.

"Ow! Oh!" he howled, sitting up so quickly that he nearly fell out of the wagon as he shook his hand rapidly in the cooling air, drawing it back and preparing to teach her a lesson. But another hand caught his hand and refused to let go.

"I wouldn't," the old knight warned quietly, his free hand resting on the hilt of his sword. Both drivers stood ready to back him up.

"She is to be left *unharmed!*" he repeated, intending to enforce his words with muscle instead of logic if necessary.

"Fine with me!" Gregor shouted like an injured child who didn't get his way. "Charles Montgomery's got to be loony to want a woman like *her* for a daughter-in-law!" He pointed a finger at Charlotte. "And you just wait! Wait till Garret gets a hold of you! I guarantee *he'll* teach you what a woman's place ought to be, you little witch!"

"Gregor!" barked Henry. "Go lie down!" he commanded, treating his younger comrade like the misbehaving pup he was.

"No problem!" he shouted, with a head full of wounded pride and a smarting hand. "Who'd want her anyway!" He grabbed his bedroll and skulked off into the trees without looking back, wanting to sleep as far away from her as he could.

"Lady Charlotte," said the old guard quietly. "I beg your pardon for Gregor, my lady. He's young." She nodded quietly, not expecting even this much civility from a Norman.

He offered her water, bringing a flask to her lips. She drank her fill, and the old man bowed.

"Can I…" the aging soldier started to say, groping for the right words. "Can I escort you *somewhere* to freshen a bit?" He spoke timidly, his cheeks blooming crimson.

"No, thank you," she replied quietly, thinking it would be pointless to ask him to loosen the ropes.

But it appeared he read her thoughts and, quite unexpectedly, he unlocked one side of the shackle attached to her ankle, careful to keep his gaze respectful. He then attached the circle of iron to the strut on the back of the wagon. With that done, he untied her hands from the seat, still leaving them bound together. At least she could feel the blood as it began to circulate once again.

"Thank you," she said quietly as he bowed his head. Then he too retired, stretching out his bedroll at the foot of the wagon, right next to Bishop.

It was strange how this one simple gesture made her feel secure. She was glad for the old battle-scarred knight at her feet. For a moment, the wisdom in his eyes reminded her of Gerald, and she felt a stab of loneliness for her old friend, forgetting how he had betrayed her when she needed him most.

Laying her head against a pillow, she tugged the fur rugs up around her, trying to sleep. Her head still throbbed from the drug she'd been given, and she hoped she would feel better tomorrow.

Gazing upward, she searched the clouds for an occasional glimpse of the elusive velvet-black sky, trying to see an end to the stars and the night, which seemed to go on forever. The crazy moon was but a fingernail's width, a sheer, tipsy crescent holding the treasured black pearl between its points, rocking with its cargo and hiding behind clouds as the ghostly white galleon sailed across the night-black sky, grinning as if it knew something she did not.

Tomorrow she was to be married to a man she knew nothing about—except that he was a *Norman* and she hated him already!

All her life she had longed to be loved and cherished, yearned for the tender touch of someone who truly cared, someone she could confide her deepest thoughts to, someone who wouldn't turn away. But now there was nothing except this painful reality that cut through her heart like a hot knife. Unless she could do something about it, tomorrow night she would find herself in a stranger's bed—a stranger who would have the legal right to use her body as he saw fit! She shuddered violently as all the illusions she had ever harbored about love and her wedding night were shattered. What would it be like when he touched her, if he touched her? She wondered fearfully. Could she find a way to escape? Perhaps Lon would come…

"Yes," she whispered out loud. "Find me, Lon," she begged desperately. "Before it's too late!" Her prayer was lifted gently on the breath of the rising mist and carried slowly away by a lazy breeze. "Find me," she pleaded, knowing sleep would elude her tonight as she thought about lying captive in a stranger's arms.

Night had settled comfortably around Planter's Inn like a well-worn blanket. A white phosphorescent cloak of mist crept in from the sea like a ghostly thief, slowly enveloping it.

The common room was filled to overflowing. Ale was poured and spilled and drunk with unrestrained glee while full-breasted women served and laughed and tamed the ferocious men into growling kittens.

Cole looked as green as the brocade lining in his cape. He hovered above the table, barely holding his head up.

"Here you go, Cole!" Torin laughed drunkenly, pouring ale from a full pitcher into the boy's already full cup. "Drink up!" he urged gleefully. "You're getting behind!"

"Oh!" he groaned. He could hardly see his hand in front of his face, let alone drink another swallow of that foul-smelling beer!

"C'mon, Cole," Torin chided. "Let's drink a toast to your brother, then we'll have us a bit of eggs and kidney pie. How does that sound?"

The young man looked at him, blinking rapidly, seeing two of the devilish Torins before his drunken gaze. He then wobbled, teetered, and started to fall.

"Look out!" hollered Torin, grabbing his beloved pitchers of ale. "A good man's goin' down!"

Feet moved, and a bench or two were drawn back as the boy hit the floor with a loud *whoomph*, passing out face down on the reeds.

Torin squinted one eye, looking at the boy curiously out of the other. "Must've been tired," he concluded, draping his own cape over Cole's head. "Let the lad sleep," he commanded the others, who nodded in agreement, never suspecting it was the gallon and a half of ale that had caused the boy's abrupt departure.

"Let's see, what was I doin'? Oh, yes!" he remembered gaily. "A toast!" Torin could drink continuously through the night, apparently without any ill effects. "To Garret," he offered somberly. "May he find true happiness, if not with his new lady wife, then with one of you!" He winked as he toasted two busty beauties perched near his friend, one with hair as dark as Garret's and a slightly feline appearance to her face, while the other was a collection of circles, blonde curls and dimples, rosy cheeks, and plump arms and thighs—both thoroughly besotted with wine.

Garret raised his glass in salute, then drained it in a single gulp, quiet as a man sentenced to the gallows in the morning, totally lost in his own thoughts tonight.

"Your lordship," said the dark-haired girl, her cat-shaped eyes drinking in his wonderful form as she lifted his hand to compare it to hers. "What big hands you've got!" She raked her long fingernails across his calloused palms. "They say that a man that has big hands and feet is big *elsewhere*..." Her eyes traveled the length of him meaningfully. "Do you think that is true, your lordship?" she asked sweetly, fluttering her eyelashes ambitiously.

For a moment, all was quiet as Garret looked at her.

Then, quite to her surprise, he tipped his refilled tankard of ale over, sending the entire contents splashing coldly over her exposed cleavage.

"OH!" she exclaimed in surprise, starting to stand up, sure that her plans at seduction had backfired and that she had offended him. "I'm sorry," she started to say, her words tumbling over her tongue. But before she could get any farther, his hand shot out and hooked her around the waist, pulling her close to him. The look in his eyes frightened her as he bent his dark head and kissed her ale-soaked cleavage.

"Shall we find out?" he asked, his voice a husky, deep-throated whisper.

"Find out, my lord?" she stammered a little shakily, her composure shattered by the intensity of his gaze.

"How the rest of me measures up?" he answered, grinning like Old Nick himself.

She started to laugh with pleasure, and then the giant of a man stood up, towering over her, lifting her with one hand. He tossed her carelessly over his shoulder amid the hooting approval of his men, pausing for just a moment by the inebriated blonde, looking down at her as though considering.

"Well?" shouted Torin, knowing his lusty friend so well. "'Tis your last free night!" He slammed his mug angrily against the table for emphasis. And then Garret grinned, his foggy mind made up. He reached down with his other arm and grabbed the blonde, carrying her like a sack of flour under his arm as the three of them made their way upstairs, two of them giggling in delight.

Later, when the moon had traveled nearly the length of the sky and the mist had settled in for good around the town, he had sent the girls away, physically satisfied but emotionally empty.

The bed was a tangle of sweat-dampened sheets. He lay naked and alone with his arm under his head, gazing up through the window at the partially overcast sky, dreaming of *her.* He had never told anyone, not even Torin, of his dream.

After all, in his father's ambitious schemes, there wasn't any time for something as foolish as a dream which had haunted and bewitched him from the onset of his youth.

How could he explain to anyone that he knew with unshakable conviction that out there, somewhere, *she* was waiting for *him?*

His father had told him time and time again that love was fantasy. Power was the only real thing that existed. With it, he lectured, all things were possible, even maintaining the *illusion* of love.

"But, sir," he had argued at fourteen, after a fitful night spent dreaming about her—she had called to him, and he had blindly fought through the shadows of his subconscious, searching desperately for her, knowing she needed him. "True love must be real." He was sure he could will love into existence even if it didn't exist, as his father insisted.

"You say that with such conviction, boy," his father replied scornfully. "Tell me, how is it that you're such an authority on the subject?"

"I just know!" he stated stubbornly, holding his father's gaze like no other could, until the older Montgomery turned away, as if to hide something that shone in his eyes and he was afraid his son would see.

"There is no such thing as *love*," his father whispered, a hint of tragedy lingering in his words. "Love is only the mask of lust, which is nothing more than a clever demon in disguise. It uses you, Garret! Plays with your mind! 'Love' will drive you half-mad with want on moonlit nights and leave you standing alone like a fool in the cold reality of empty mornings with your heart shattered!" He grabbed Garret and shook him hard as if trying to force his words into his maturing brain. "Don't give in to that doomed apparition, Garret! Don't do it! *Take* all the women your manhood desires!" he urged passionately, his hands still firmly holding the boy, even though they had begun to tremble. "Take them, do you hear? Take them, one and all—*use them* till the burning flame they've started in you is nothing more than a cold, decaying ember! But *don't* give in to the wicked illusions of 'sweet romance' and 'eternal love,'" he warned softly, his eyes glowing fiercely, moist with the first hint of tears Garret had ever seen him shed. "It will destroy you!"

His voice trailed off to a choking whisper as he reluctantly released his son. Turning, he walked quickly away.

Garret watched his tall, powerful form climb stiffly up the stairs, meeting his silent mother coming down. His father paused for the briefest moment, and Garret's heart skipped a beat as he held his breath and watched his father tilt his mother's beautiful face upward as if searching for something in her eyes. For a second, his father didn't appear to be the all-powerful man he had come to know. He watched spellbound as, for the briefest time, the stone-cold mask dropped from his father's face, and his eyes appeared to be pleading, begging for something from his chaste wife that she refused to give. The lids of her eyes remained downcast, drawn against him like an ivory curtain, while she nervously fingered the rosary dangling from her dress. Slowly, a sad, ironic smile lit Charles's features, making him seem tragic as he turned to face his staring son.

"It will destroy you," he whispered quietly, and Garret swore he saw a tear trail down his father's cheek before he turned and made his way up the few remaining stairs, going toward his bedroom, with his broad shoulders visibly sagging.

His mother had acted as though nothing had happened,

continuing quietly down the stairs, going, as always, toward the chapel, where she prayed night and day. If she saw her son, she didn't acknowledge him. It was as if he and all her other children didn't exist except as crosses she was forced to bear, like the heavy burden of being married to a man she claimed to never love.

But that wouldn't happen to him! His wife would love him and their children. She would want his touch and be there when he needed her, not hide behind the Church!

He had seen her so often in his dreams, and sometimes she had called to him. He tried oh so hard to find her. Yet she always seemed just a little out of his reach. He would run and run, glimpsing her behind a tree, swimming in the ocean, gliding motionless on currents of air. And he would reach for her, aching in every part of his body, needing her almost past the point of endurance. Her face, though always before him, was never clear upon awakening, yet he knew she existed *somewhere* out there, waiting.

Now his dreams seemed pointless. He was to marry another, who was probably just like most of the other well-bred noblewomen he had known—quiet, contrite, docile creatures, schooled in obedience and religion.

Dutiful, so dutiful and obliging that they made him ill. No doubt she would lie stiff as a board on their wedding night, *allowing* him to perform the necessary consummation. Then what? Why, children, of course! He snorted. That kind of women were like broodmares, kept only for the purpose of continuing the line.

Sighing, he stretched and yawned, remembering how his father had reminded him that he could keep a mistress. Although in all the years he'd been able to recall, he had never heard of his father keeping other women. It seemed that Charles Montgomery was faithful, even if he didn't believe in love.

"How many nights have I lingered in your shadows?" he whispered softly, quoting a much-loved Arab verse. "With girls... both blonde and dusky, who pierced my soul like blazing swords, like somber lances…" He laughed softly then, knowing that all the women he had known in his life were sorry imitations of the *one* woman he longed for—the woman of his dreams. He smiled sleepily, stretching out on the little bed until his legs dangled over the end. He began to drift into sleep, wondering if she really was out there somewhere, beneath this grinning April moon, needing him as much as he needed her.

Chapter 5

The noose around her neck was pulled tighter. Glaring hatefully at the tall man with the deep-set hawk-blue eyes standing beside her, she could feel the bristly bits of hemp sticking painfully into the tender skin of her throat as she gasped for air. The last hopeful thought of being rescued fled from her mind like a cowardly shadow, and still the frightened priest droned on, dabbing the sweat from his waxy brow as he asked for the third time this morning, his timid voice shaking with urgency and fear: "Wilt thou have this man to be thy husband and wilt thou pledge thy troth to him?"

"Never!" she spat again, the word cutting into her throat like a shard of broken glass, scratching painfully against her battered windpipe as the rope that held her was instantly tightened once again.

Her grim-faced captor sighed in apparent disgust, indicating his growing displeasure over her answer.

Only this morning she had arrived at Pembroke. Its massive gray-stone edifice rose out of the mists to greet her like a gigantic primordial beast. High stone walls encircled the low hills and lush, freshly-tilled valleys for miles. Villagers had materialized out of nowhere, swarming curiously around the wagon to see "Montgomery's woman," talking constantly, laughing at her shackles, leering lecherously at the "fine tidbit fit for Garret's table," all thinking

Montgomery was a very lucky man until the fair-haired beauty with the sky-blue eyes was untied from the wagon's forward strut and all hell broke loose.

"What a shrew!" shouted a merchant's wife. "I've never seen the like!"

Charlotte ignored her.

Still shackled, hand to hand, foot to foot, with barely enough room given to walk, she had struck out blindly, using her tiny hands as clubs, elbows gouging, teeth biting, cursing wildly at all the strangers who had surrounded her the moment the wagon pulled across the drawbridge and into the central open courtyard.

"Look out!" shouted one man, wisely ducking when Charlotte grabbed a shepherd's crooked oak staff with both of her hands, thanking the surprised man with several swift, wheeling hits to the side of his unfortunate head. Then she turned, glowering savagely, jabbing the staff threateningly toward her captors while she backed toward her dog, protected by the very fact that the guards were under strict orders to bring her in *unharmed.*

Gregor, still nursing his wounded pride, began to draw his sword, eager to show the "lady" who was the boss, when Henry laid a firm hold on his arm and pointed toward the manor. Following his direction, Gregor visibly paled. In a cloud of dust, with the accompaniment of the clattering hooves of several mounted guards, Lord Charles came riding toward them, head down and elbows up, apparently in a great hurry, with fire spitting from his dark eyes.

"Lady Charlotte," Henry pleaded quietly as she tried unsuccessfully to work the tiresome knot free from the back of the wagon while also trying to protect her open flank with the staff. "His lordship is coming, Lady Charlotte! Please, put down your weapon!" the old soldier begged, knowing the lord of the manor was capable of anything so long as he got his way. He would not stand for anyone, especially a *woman*, thwarting his authority.

Charlotte's eyes flashed, boiling mad, their clear blue turning to the palest shade of ice-blue Henry had ever seen. "The devil take all of you! I'll never be your lady and I'm no shrew! I'm Princess Charlotte de Clare of Wales! How dare you treat me like a piece of baggage!" she snapped. Furious, she stubbornly worked the obstinate knot, even as the horse of the manor's lord clattered loudly to her side and stopped.

Silence descended on the crowd in a nearly tangible thickness, and still she worked the knot. She knew he was there—everyone knew he was there. She could smell the strong leathery scent from his horse, hear his mount's outraged snorts at being pulled up too short. Yet she chose to ignore him. Though she didn't claim to be psychic, she swore she could feel his eyes boring holes into her skull. Still she refused to turn, stubbornly showing him her back and her total disregard for his authority, ignoring him as if he were nothing more than an irksome peasant or a stranger standing too close. In short, she was determined to be as rude as possible for as long as she could—until she felt the noose drop over her head and it was too late to wrench it free. Charles Montgomery, Lord of Pembroke, pulled it painfully tight.

"The priest is waiting, daughter," the lord said evenly, each word seasoned with scorn and dripping with acid as he jerked her around, appraising her as indifferently as one might appraise a stock animal or a newly-purchased horse. His cold eyes probed everywhere, noting her hair color, size, the well-rounded shape of her hips, the tilt of her nose…

"You'll do," he said casually, meeting the glaring hatred pouring from her eyes with total indifference. He clucked softly to his horse, who began a leisurely walk back to the stables.

The elder Montgomery pulled his future daughter-in-law

through the jeering, laughing crowds and into the double-doored private courtyard of the manor with as much dignity as an animal being led to slaughter.

Once inside the castle, she was struck by its sheer enormity and its obvious wealth. Rich wool tapestries adorned every wall, depicting scenes from daily life—pastoral peace and bloody wars, martyrdom and magic. Gold and silver plates and goblets gleamed softly from above the huge fireplace which could easily have held twelve leisurely diners and a long table but now retained only a softly burning fire in its massive hearth, glowing a cheerful orange and casting darting shadows of light against the blue-and-white marble floor.

With remarkable agility, her captor slid from his horse, still holding firmly to her "leash" as servants poured from every niche and darkened corner in the room. But the lord didn't stop to talk to the waiting servants; he simply dropped his reins and continued walking, dragging her behind.

She could see him clearly now. His skin, dark and swarthy, was wrinkled into a permanent frown while his frame was both tall and wide. He was a formidable blend of Gaul and Viking, regal and proud in his wine-colored clothes and massive gold chains. White hair flowed from his high, intelligent forehead like a frosted lion's mane, and a thin, hatchet-shaped nose split his face into two distinct halves. He would have been handsome in a rugged, masculine way if the years and the choices he had made hadn't stamped his face with such cruel and callous disregard of others.

He pulled her along impatiently, leading her through a narrow hall and into a partly sun-drenched courtyard. If she stalled or dragged her feet at being led, he would give the rope a vicious yank, sometimes nearly jerking her off her feet. But she wouldn't cry out, even though the rope burned her neck like fire, choosing to suffer in rebellious silence rather than give this cruel old man the satisfaction of knowing he had the power to cause her pain.

Into a separate small building they went. The light from outside drifted through windows of finely-colored stained glass, patterning the smooth white limestone floor into a multihued, moving work of art. Incense burned; myrrh and jasmine drifted lazily up into the shadowed alcove by the altar where an impossibly white, cruelly thin Christ looked down upon her with sorrowful, pain-filled painted brown eyes. A coven of stained-glass saints had their overly large, staring orbs fixed heavenward as if trying to reassure her that "all this, too, will pass away." Somehow, she had her doubts.

Beneath the hovering effigy of Christ, a woman knelt. She was dressed all in white, with her head covered and bowed, concealing her face from sight. A priest wearing robes of scarlet stood silent and nodding in front of her, listening to her confession with pious concern.

"What, my dear?" Montgomery sarcastically chided, his voice echoing darkly through the hallowed hall. "Asking for forgiveness for yet another grave sin?" he mocked. "Or is it my soul you're seeking salvation for? I assure you it is far too late."

At the sound of the familiar voice, the white-cloaked figure lifted her head slightly and turned. Charlotte was shocked into silence. She was beautiful, gazing impassively at Montgomery with the darkest, most luminous eyes Charlotte had ever seen. The woman looked as frail as porcelain and as long-suffering as the Christ she knelt before.

"I do pray for you, my lord," she replied, so softly that her voice seemed to come from a long way off, drifting toward them like the rustling whisper of a breeze through dry fall leaves.

Standing up gracefully, she moved away from the priest to hover like a ghostly white illusion by the wall of smoking votive candles, lighting all those that had gone out with patient obsession, praying quietly all the while, and ignoring Charlotte and her husband as if neither one existed.

"This," Montgomery indicated to the priest, suddenly full of anger as he held up his end of the rope, "is the woman I told you about. You will marry her to my son *now*, and I will stand in as his proxy until his return."

The priest, wide-eyed and obedient, nodded and began. "Dearly beloved, we are assembled here in the presence of God to join this man and this woman in holy wedlock, which is instituted by God—"

"Just get to the vows," Charles growled impatiently, stopping the priest in mid-sentence, his eyes never leaving the hovering white-robed figure near the wall. "It is nearly sundown, and I'm expecting my son tonight."

"Yes, my lord," replied the priest quietly, blinking slightly as he tried to readjust his thinking, fishing for the phrases that would close the ceremony and seal the vows. "Garret de Montgomery, wilt thou have this woman to be thy wife?"

Tonight! No! thought Charlotte. Not tonight! There would be no time to think or plan. No time for escape!

"In all love and hon…"

Not tonight, she pleaded silently and began to struggle against the rope, not knowing where she would go even if she could get away.

"To live with her and cherish her, according to the ordinance of God, in the holy bond of marriage…"

Charles pulled his end a little tighter, cutting off her air for just a second and giving her a taste of what he could do—would do—if she didn't remain still.

The priest had finished the husband's vows and looked nervously at Charles, who controlled Charlotte as easily as a disobedient puppy.

"I, Lord Charles de Montgomery, acting as surrogate for my absent son, Garret de Montgomery," he started, pulling the rope so tight that Charlotte sank helplessly to her knees, "take thee, Charlotte Isabel de Clare, to be my wedded wife, and I do promise and covenant before God and these witnesses to be thy loving and faithful husband."

The rest was a noisy blur, a mass of recited phrases that held no meaning.

"Charlotte Isabel de Clare," spoke the priest softly, bending as near to the kneeling figure as he dared, "wilt thou have this man to be thy husband?"

"No!" she cried vehemently, choking out the phrase. "I will not!"

The rope was pulled so hard that she could not even draw a whisper of a breath into her starving lungs.

"Repeat the question!" Charles roughly ordered, giving the rope a painful yank that Charlotte swore broke her windpipe in two. But still she would not relent.

"Say 'yes'" came a soft, feminine voice in Charlotte's ear.

She was on her knees, tears springing from her eyes as she struggled to put even a finger-breadth distance between her aching throat and the cruel rope.

"Do you hear me, child?" came the sweet, lilting voice, and an angel-lady knelt beside her, a luminous blur of white and midnight-black hair.

"Listen to me," she repeated, the urgency in her preternatural voice sounding like the hiss of the sea in Charlotte's ringing ears. "It is your cross to bear, your tribulation as set down by the Lord to test the faithful. It is our punishment as the living descendants of a deceitful Eve," she whispered. Charlotte felt her hand gently graze her cheek, collecting her salty tears as if they were diamonds. "Say 'yes,' my dear."

The pain was nearly gone, everything in the room turning into the shimmering, wavering shadows of a dream instead of the clear, dark lines of blunt reality. She couldn't speak, but her will, which had kept her alive and going for so many years, refused to bend. No—and she nodded her head weakly—she would not marry Garret Montgomery. She would not marry anyone, except for sweet Lon.

"There is always tomorrow, child," whispered the angel-lady, now so close she could smell the cloud of lavender and rose that enveloped her. "There is hope in a new day…" she offered wisely, careful not to touch the rope and earn her husband's displeasure.

"Hope?" croaked Charlotte. She wanted to laugh, except that it would hurt too much. By tomorrow morning Lon would probably not want her after she'd spent the night in another man's bed. And yet, she would be alive… and, maybe, that was enough for now.

"Charlotte Isabel de Clare… wilt thou have this man to be thy husband?" the priest urgently repeated for the third time, not wishing to give the last rites to one so young and detesting the thought of having to absolve Charles of yet another crime.

"Yes," she rasped, the word hurting so much, both physically and emotionally, that for a moment death seemed a kindness. The moment the word was said, the pressure on her neck vanished.

"Take her to my son's room," ordered Charles. "Have the maids bathe her, give her something to eat, and make her ready to receive her husband."

With his tedious chore out of the way, Charles dropped the rope into a waiting guard's outstretched hand and left the chapel, mentally dictating the letter he planned to send to the King.

Charlotte held her hands to her burning throat and heard the fateful words: "By the authority committed unto me as a minister of the Church of Christ, I declare that Garret de Montgomery and Charlotte Isabel de Clare are now husband and wife."

The shock sent her spinning mercifully into darkness.

The sun had dipped tiredly below the courtyard's walls, going from lemon yellow to faded orange in a matter of minutes while long shadows stole from hiding places to show themselves in the deepening twilight, growing larger by the second as they gorged themselves on the remaining light of day until nothing but darkness and clinging mists swirled around Pembroke's stone walls.

A band of weary riders rode into the deserted courtyard.

In the lead, seated on the broad back of his fiery black *destrier*, in a velvet swirl of a midnight-colored cape, his raven-hued hair hidden beneath a sooty wing-edged hat, Garret rode. His hard face was streaked with dirt and his eyes sparkled with impotent rage as he rushed angrily toward the manor and his waiting destiny.

He pulled up hard on his horse's reins, and the animal wheeled back, screaming furiously and pawing the air in a display of temper at being treated so rudely. But Garret gave the seasoned warhorse little thought as he slid from his saddle and slapped him on his backside, sending the indignant animal trotting off to the stables as its master strode toward the huge double doors of the manor.

Cole and Torin followed close at his heels, exchanging uneasy glances as they watched Garret push both massive oak doors open with a single mighty shove, opening them easily with the broad palms of his hands and sending them banging loudly against the foyer's polished stone walls.

"Father!" he shouted, striding toward the library where a merry fire was burning.

When he entered the room his mother looked up from her sewing, giving him a quiet nod before returning her attention to the intricate cross-stitch pattern that filled all the hours that praying did not, while his father, forcing himself to smile, stood up to face him.

"Well, my son!" offered Charles cheerfully, sensing the storm building in his first-born with the keen perception of someone who knows all the signs in another by studying himself. "It seems the weather is turning," he offered somewhat dryly, the double meaning in his words clear as he watched the man who was so much like he had been in his younger days ball his hands into powerful fists, careful to keep them at his sides.

A timid servant brought Garret a tankard of strong ale as he had been instructed to do hours before, then backed fearfully away from the powerful, glowering man as quickly as he could.

"I have heard that you and your men caught the rogue who's been terrorizing the coast and he is to be hung this May Day. That is good, Garret. The King will look favorably on you and our family for such a brave deed!"

The conversation, which had been entirely one-sided, lapsed into an uneasy silence when Garret failed to respond to his father's flattery.

Cole and Torin stood silently in the doorway, watching the two men eye each other the way bulls do before they butt horns. Garret's mother had the good sense to slip discreetly from the room.

"Why, Father?" Garret asked quietly, his voice sounding like the rumble of distant thunder, threatening to bring a storm near. "You could've at least consulted with me first, before you made such a choice!"

"Consulted you?" his father roared, dropping the pretense of civility at once. "When have you ever given any thought to finding a suitable match?" He brushed back the waves of white from his forehead in frustration. "The only thing you ever appeared to be interested in is hefting that damned sword!"

Laughter, low and dangerous, issued softly from his son. "And whose fault is that?" Garret retorted icily, gazing at the aging patriarch from beneath lowered lids. "*You* were the one who wanted a soldier instead of a son!" He drew himself up to his full height, his fists clenched so tightly his knuckles went white. "Let me see," he mused, sarcasm lacing his words, "how does the story go, Father? What is it that you tell others as often as you can—and have told *me* since before I could walk?"

His father blanched slightly, shaking his head, but Garret would not let it go.

"Doesn't it go something like this, Father?"

"Let's see," he started, tapping his lip softly. "'When that one was born,' you said, 'I laid him down none too gently on the ground and held the sword above his head. With *this*, I told him, and only with this will you ever have anything, for I will give you nothing!'" Garret recited easily, his eyes glowing from the memory. "And now that I've learned the soldiering trade quite well, still you find fault with me. I think the fault is with *yourself*, Father!" he asserted with chillingly accurate perception. "I would have found my lady—when the time was right! I didn't get your help before, and I'll be damned if I need it now!"

"Fine!" roared Charles, hurling his mug into the fireplace, its contents spattering the walls and floors. "But what is done is *done!* And since you say," he continued, "that you're such a good soldier, my son, remember, a *good* soldier always does his duty!"

"Since when is bedding wenches *duty?*" snapped Garret.

"Since this *wench* is your *wife!*" replied his father, his face livid with rage. "Picking your own wife is not the romantic dream you think it is. It is far better that those who have more understanding choose your wife for you."

"Such as *you* and your court of sorcerers and star-gazers?"

"Exactly!" his father replied, not even trying to conceal the fact that his own astrologer, an aging cabalist, had given his endorsement to this union after comparing Garret's chart to the de Clare woman's.

"You're mad," Garret stated tiredly, not wishing to engage his father in a debate on the lunacy of the "divine arts."

"She is the only woman for you, my son," his father stated, more gently this time.

Charles refused to believe in love as the binding of a happy marriage, seeing it more as the result of compatible trines and sextiles of beneficent planets and the absence of malefic. But even without the use of charts and calculations, the de Clare woman had certainly shown him that she was a fit wife for a warrior.

"You must do your duty," he stated earnestly.

"Of course, Father," Garret replied wearily, instantly quiet and once again under control. To see him struggle with his monumental temper was like watching a man tame a team of wild horses with a single line—it was done by sheer willpower and nothing more. "But tell me," he asked, his stinger once again to the fore, "this Welsh woman you've wed me to, shall I put a bell around her neck and send her out to pasture? Or is this woman merely another comrade-in-arms who will want to borrow my shaving knife?"

"Just do your duty, Garret!" Charles rasped irritably. "I'll speak to you again in the morning, provided the bridal sheet is flying scarlet from the balustrade!"

With a weary shake of his head, Charles left the study, intending to seek his wife.

After his father left, Garret stared moodily into his second mug of dark ale until a commotion at the study door caused him to turn.

A group of harried-looking house servants entered the room. They appeared to have been caught in a whirlwind. Their clothes were shredded, and deep scratches laced their chests and flushed faces into a crimson web. Some sported brightly-colored bruises and bleeding lips.

"What is this?" Garret asked, an amused grin on his face. He was not used to seeing the docile servants of the manor in such a warlike condition.

"Your bride, m'lord," replied the oldest steward, hat in hand, his left eye swelling shut.

"My *bride?*" Garret asked, instantly forgetting about his ale.

"Yes, m'lord," he answered softly, sucking on his swelling lip. "She is ready."

"Ready?" Garret repeated, arching his eyebrow, wondering how these men came to look like they'd just returned from battle and just what *that* had to do with his new bride.

"Yes, my lord… ready!" responded the old man, proudly now, squinting through his purple pansy-colored eye at his master's son. "We had to tie her to the bed," he explained, making a slipknot in the air. "But she is vanquished and under control!" He spoke enthusiastically, feeling as though he had conquered a fierce enemy instead of welcoming a new bride into the castle.

"Tied her to the bed!" Garret roared incredulously, rounding on the men with an outraged gleam shining from his dark blue eyes.

"Yes, m'lord," gushed one particularly plump boy, hosting so many bruises on his fleshy form that he appeared to be more blue than white. "Otherwise, I think that devil would have killed us all!"

"Devil!" Garret shouted, unable to believe his servants had just called the future lady of the manor a devil to his face, nor shown such uncivilized behavior to any woman under a Montgomery's protection.

"Yes, m'lord," replied the boy, feeling as though he had accomplished a great deed. "The lady's maids have stripped her down—"

"Stripped! Tied!" snapped Garret, his blue eyes fierce. He was shocked.

The servants moved as with a single mind, seeking a corner, wondering just which one would be worse to deal with: an irate Montgomery or that wild heathen Welsh woman upstairs.

"Sir," said the plump steward, showing him a painful bite on his forearm in his defense, "I think the lady's hydrophobic—and quite possibly possessed!" Most of the others shook their heads in agreement, and several remained silently terrified. "She surely would have killed us if we hadn't subdued her! And then," he stammered, his eyes growing wide as if the memory were just too horrible to deal with, "and then… that *woman's* devil-dog came bounding out of nowhere, with its rope bit clean in two, lather pouring from its mouth and snarling like a wolf. Arghhh! Arghh-rrr!" He demonstrated, shaking his round face from side to side like a savage dog. "We were in fear of our very lives, I tell you!" he added, spittle flying, his eyes wide with amazement and shock while his pudgy arms windmilled, and he nearly hyperventilated from reliving the traumatic ordeal.

"Well, Steward," Garret drawled softly, "if you were afraid *then*, you should be terrified *now!*" He advanced menacingly toward the cowering servants. "What you have done is grounds for flogging! The 'lady' you've so proudly bound and trussed like a goose is my *bride!*" he shouted, surprised by how easily that word came to him. "From this day forth," he commanded, his face livid and within inches of the cowering men, "you are to treat my *wife* with every kindness and every consideration. Kindness! Do you understand?" Garret was furious.

The servants nodded in unison.

"If my *wife* wishes to bite your arm off, then offer her your leg as well! Do I make myself clear?" he asked, his deadly gaze impaling each man.

"Yes, your lordship," they whispered.

"And if my *wife* is 'possessed,' and you fear for your immortal souls, then sprinkle yourselves with holy water, make the sign of the cross, and *do as she commands!* She, God help me, is my *wife*—and I will not stand for anyone mistreating her ever again!"

The servants nodded timidly as their master turned with a flourish. His swirling black cape twisted around his tall, broad figure like a dark whirlwind as he made his way upstairs to his new bride, secretly wondering what sort of monster his father had brought into the house.

Cole and Torin looked at the silent servants and then at each other in wonder. A *woman* did this!

Frowning, Torin asked the oldest steward, "Is she a giantess?"

"No," said the wizened old man in frank amazement. "She is a beautiful young woman! Small-boned, perfect—quite petite!"

"Does she wield some sort of magical weapon?"

"Only relentless fists and cruel little feet," he answered honestly. "And a set of devilishly sharp teeth!" He gazed ruefully at his swelling hand, where she had bitten down hard and refused to let go until the blood flowed and three other stewards had pulled her off.

"No one helped her?" Torin asked incredulously.

"No, your lordship," he answered quietly, feeling as though he had been thoroughly castrated by those soft words and the fragile-looking woman upstairs. "She didn't even need her dog!"

If Torin was surprised by the steward's story, he gave no sign. He simply looked at Cole and shrugged his shoulders in amazement.

"Do you think we should stand guard?" Cole offered with a concerned frown.

"No," Torin answered slowly, placing his arm reassuringly around the younger man's shoulder. "Your brother can handle himself."

"Imagine!" Cole exclaimed. "A woman with such fire!"

Torin saw the light in the boy's eyes and understood its meaning all too well.

"Frankly," he answered dryly, "I prefer my women to be pudgy, docile, giggling fools, as the Lord meant them to be, completely subservient to a man the way nature intended. War, on the other hand, is meant to be fought on the battlefield, not in *bed*."

But the shining, youthfully lustful look in Cole's eyes confirmed Torin's belief that this was a lad who took after his older brother. Nothing to Garret was worthwhile unless it was to be had through a fight or conquest, not even a woman.

"Let's get us a bite," offered Torin, and the two walked out of the library lost in their own thoughts.

In a fever to get this bothersome mess out of the way, Garret had taken the stairs two at a time. He didn't ask for water so that he could bathe—or even trouble himself to dispose of his hat or cloak. All he wanted to do was get this "formality" out of the way as quickly as possible. He only hoped she wouldn't be so ugly that he wouldn't be able to perform his "duty" properly.

Outside his room he unbuckled his sword, electing to keep his dagger close at hand. A tingling excitement was growing by the second in him—a thrilling through his entire body, an electricity he didn't fully understand. It was not the battle fire coursing through his veins making him giddy or aroused or the heat of lust that drove reality from his mind; it was something *in* him that went beyond his conscious thought, welling up from the darkest, most irrational corners of his soul. It was desire and anticipation, wondering and somehow *knowing* what waited for him just beyond that door. Or was it simply hope that led him on like a blind fool? Whatever it was—illusion or reality—the feeling had started a pleasant humming in his groin which grew stronger by the moment, as though a massive switch had been fired in his psyche, waiting, then building toward some climactic event. All these feelings he ignored as simple nonsense and fatigue, as if they were nothing more than a broad, sweeping undercurrent of idiotic thoughts flowing just beneath the surface of his mind; a separate dialogue, whispering simple nonsense in his brain, generated by too much ale and a hard day's ride, mere fragments of a long-forgotten dream.

Taking a deep breath, he entered his room, relieved to see that no lights were lit, secretly confirming his rational belief that any woman who could deal out such misery to a group of men *had* to be cursed with a degree of ugliness he had yet to witness. But even with these logical conclusions whirling through his brain, the *excitement* of the moment refused to leave him, making him wonder for the hundredth time that night just what it was that he expected to find.

A small fire burned in the hearth. Quietly he moved in front of it and stood before his massive four-poster bed. Its drapes of purple velvet had been pulled back and secured against the posts, revealing startlingly white linen sheets. In the center of this island of white, a girl of amazing beauty was tied. Her arms and legs were spread across the sheets and secured to the posts with stout hemp ropes. She resembled an open flower in the heat of summer, her skin glowing like the ripe, fragrant petals of an alabaster rose, while her hair shimmered and flowed like a silver waterfall spilling across the pillows, framing the most beautiful face he had ever seen with rivulets of liquid moonlight.

Lightning struck him full in the stomach, knocking the wind from him completely, pulverizing his groin, cramping him and making him ache with the tingling messages crackling all up and down his spine.

It was *she!* He knew it in that second, and he could neither speak nor move. So completely mesmerized was he by her charms that he ignored the hatred pouring from her beautiful sky-blue eyes, preferring only to dive deep into their cooling depths, longing, with every quickened beat of his heart, to pull her close.

"Cut me loose!" she cried, fed up with his quiet scrutiny. She strained her already-aching wrists and feet against the ropes.

A growl from a darkened corner jerked him back to reality. He half-turned to see the huge "devil-dog" snarling at him from the other side of the room, a heavy two-inch chain holding him in place.

"I said, let me go!" she demanded again, gazing at the dark figure who stood between her and the hearth. She was afforded no view of the person who stood towering above the bed, gazing down so quietly at her. He was covered by an ankle-length cape and wide-brimmed hat, and he appeared to have been born from the shadows of the room, a column of darkness in the massive shape of a man. Yet, for all his silence and obscurity, she felt his gaze as keenly real as if a gentle hand explored every inch of her body, traveling wantonly over her exposed skin, and she shuddered.

The few seconds that had ticked by had stretched into a memory of a lifetime for Garret. The firelight touched every shadowy recess, revealing eyes as ripe and blue as a late summer sky, night-kissed black lashes and brows, and a tiny upturned nose, poised arrogantly over a mouth as freshly pink and delicate as a new rose.

He was so affected by the sight of her that he failed to note how she glared at him, how her pouting, perfectly-shaped lips were pressed so firmly together that the color was slowly fading, while her eyes snapped and sparkled their displeasure at him like a late-summer shower of meteorites in a twilight sky.

He noticed that, although she was stripped of clothes, someone had tied a wide ice-blue ribbon of silk around her graceful neck. Frowning, he began to feel a sense of guilt and anger at how she had been treated, and an overwhelming protective urge soared through him as he noticed how she still struggled against the ropes.

"Not like this..." he murmured, so softly that she thought his words were no more than the sigh of the wind.

Suddenly she heard the familiar hiss of metal sliding against metal, and her eyes grew impossibly wider, warier, as she saw the flashing gleam of a blade.

"Monster!" she cried, pulling hard against her restraints as he walked closer to the bed. Another second passed, and she saw the blade arc. Then she felt confused as he used it against himself, sliding the razor-sharp edge across the broad, flat part of his calloused palm, leaving a thick line of crimson in its wake.

"Not this way," he murmured again, with a flash of startlingly white teeth, and he held his hand above her naked thighs, letting his blood flow between them, staining the sheet scarlet between her legs. He calmly sheathed his dagger.

"Someday, you will come to me of your own free will."

It was a prediction and a prophecy. She was part of him now: his wife, and no one would dare harm her unless they were prepared to battle the lord of the manor.

"You're under my protection, Princess Charlotte." Lord Garret bowed low, appearing calm, but a storm raged in his eyes when he looked at her, confused and filled with emotions he could not identify.

She felt the warmth between her legs and stared incredulously at the tall, cloaked figure with the raven-black hair and sparkling blue eyes standing beside the bed.

"Never!" she said. "I'll never come to you of my own free will! Never!"

Smiling to himself, he opened the door, intending to sleep in the hall tonight, but not too far away. He would woo her and win her; of this he had no doubt. Some women were worth the wait, and he wagered his young bride would be his soon.

He turned to look at her and his eyes lingered on her beauty, glittering dangerously.

"My lady," he said with courtly grace, bowing, "sleep well and peacefully. Refresh yourself. You are safe under my care. No harm will come to you."

A young maid servant was waiting outside his wife's room.

"Cut the bindings from your mistress," he ordered calmly. "Then fly the bridal sheet high from the balustrade this very night so that all may see that she is *officially* mine."

"Yes, m'lord," she said enthusiastically, wanting to get a good view of the woman she would be serving for the remainder of her life.

"But first," Garret warned her, "before you cut her loose, tell the lady that a squadron of guards waits outside her door and beneath her window. Make sure you tell her this *before* you cut her free. Otherwise, you might not make it out of that room!" He grinned and then, as he watched the girl turn ashen, he patted her reassuringly on the shoulder. "I'll order the guard," he told her kindly. "Just wait till they arrive before you set her free. Do you understand?"

"Yes, m'lord," she stammered, eyes wide as saucers as she thought about her new mistress with something akin to awe at the thought of a real warrior maiden.

Whistling softly to himself, Garret went in search of Henry, fully intending to post the guards as he told the girl he would.

Lady Charlotte was just too valuable an asset to let slip away. And now that he had found her, he knew he could never let her go.

Chapter 6

Charlotte awoke in a tangle of rich furs, her throat and hands throbbing—painful reminders of the last few days. Groaning, she stretched, only to be greeted by a sloppy wet tongue and the panting grin of her old friend.

"Bishop!" she cried, smiling and hugging him, taking comfort in the familiar shaggy neck and childish brown eyes.

"Morning, mistress," came a soft greeting, drawing Charlotte's attention to the windowed recess at the far side of the massive room.

The girl who had freed her the night before was busy laying out an assortment of rich dressing gowns in front of a steaming tub of perfumed water. Food had been brought, and strong, sweet tea. The sight and smell of such comfort caused Charlotte's stomach to growl in anticipation. It seemed like more than a week since she'd eaten, and the bath smelled so good, promising to soothe her aching muscles and wash the dust from her skin.

The girl, mistaking her mistress's intense scrutiny for displeasure, lowered her eyes nervously, toying with the fabric of a soft white gown.

"What time is it?" Charlotte asked politely, and the maid instantly brightened.

"Half past ten, my lady," she replied, and, as if Charlotte's cordial query were an invitation to chat, the girl's tongue flew immediately into action. "Isn't this wonderful?" she asked, her bright little eyes glowing as she stroked the white dressing gown lovingly, and then she hurried on: "It's spun several times, me mum says, combed at least half a dozen, too, very soft. Do you like it? I like it. It's such a lovely color, like a cloud. You would look wonderful in it, my lady, simply wonderful! Does he bite?" she asked quickly, talking so rapidly and changing subjects so quickly that she made Charlotte grin in spite of her discomfort.

"Bishop?" she asked politely, rubbing her sore wrists with an amused smile on her face. The princess sat in the middle of her bed, naked and unconcerned like a woodland sprite, with only the blue silk ribbon tied snugly around her throat and a cape of shimmering platinum hair flowing around her shoulders.

"Oh, Bishop, is that what you call him? Nearly scared me to death, he did! He is so big, got the biggest ears I've ever seen and such a tail—why, it's twice as long as most. Do you like him?"

"Bishop?" Charlotte said again, confused now, nearly laughing.

"Well, no, my lady," the girl replied quickly. There was a note of apology in her voice as she poured even more of the expensive oils into the steaming water. "Lord Garret, of course!" she answered enthusiastically. "He's a big one, isn't he? And so beautiful! Don't you think he's beautiful? I do! So do all the girls! Even my mum!" she admitted with an embarrassed grin. "I think he's got it all! Such a smile, and those hands of his? Why, one of them is bigger than most other men's feet! But of course," she said with a sigh, capping the empty bottle of oil with a worn cork, "you must think he's grand—he's your husband after all. But then," she frowned again, sorting absently through a pile of hairpins and her disjointed thoughts. "He wasn't exactly your choice, was he? Pulled you in here like a lamb, didn't he? But you must understand, mistress," she stated matter-of-factly, with a fatalistic shrug of her rounded shoulders, "that's just his way. Really quite kind, he is."

"Lord Garret?" Charlotte asked, mystified, failing to keep up with the rapid changes in the young girl's gushing dialogue.

"No, Lady Charlotte," she answered impatiently, coming toward the bed to offer her mistress her hand and a winning smile. "Lord Charles, of course!"

Charlotte nodded in bewilderment, wondering how anyone could think that ogre of a man was "kind."

"But I bet you weren't disappointed after last night, right my lady?" she asked slyly, having heard so many stories of Garret's prowess in bed that she was sure he could charm anyone and make the earth shake. There was such dark magic in his mysterious eyes, and oh, such forbidden excitement in the flash of his smile! "Such a gentleman, too!" She sighed dreamily, conjuring up the image of Garret in her mind with studious attention to every detail. "Such a man!"

She was not more than sixteen, with light brown hair and matching eyes, and she harbored one wish all of her life: that just once the great warrior lord of the manor with the flashing blue eyes would look at her with something other than indifferent politeness. "He's a real hero, my lady," she crooned rapturously. "Not like some of them others what comes and brags by the well. And rich, he is! Rich as old King Midas!" The maid sighed deeply, her pubescent adoration coming out full blown in the reverence of that single sound. "You must feel just like a queen!"

"What's your name?" Charlotte said. She was laughing in spite of her confusion as the girl's incessant chatter finally began to cheer her up.

"Sparrow," she said quickly as she led her mistress to the soothing water. "My father is a shepherd," she stated proudly as Charlotte stepped into the warm water. "A freeman, he is, and my mother was allowed to join the Seamstress Guild. Lord Charles arranged it. You've such lovely hair. Looks just like spun silver! Mine is brown, rather plain—like me. Why do you suppose they named me 'Sparrow'? Because of my hair?" she asked, pausing to catch her breath, a frown wrinkling her round, cherubic face into an overripe, moon-faced melon. Then, with lighting speed, her thoughts changed direction again.

"Did you really wield a sword and fight against men?" she asked incredulously and somewhat breathlessly while her square, capable hands piled Charlotte's hair atop her head, securing it into place with elaborately decorated pins of extraordinary length.

"Yes," Charlotte replied, relieved that there was at least one question she could answer. She sank back into the soothing water with a contented sigh, the young maid's constant chatter adding to her comfort.

"Saints alive!" gasped Sparrow, her fingers stopping in mid-flight through the tangled mass of her mistress's silky hair. "Why would you want to do that? It is so much nicer when a man hugs you. I wouldn't want to fight with one," she stated emphatically, pretending to be very grown-up and sophisticated as she busied herself with Charlotte's hair. Her youthful face showed all the signs of dreamy, adolescent lust until she admitted thoughtfully with a frown, "If I had one, that is," her worldly façade evaporating like early morning mist in the stiff wind of reality.

Sighing helplessly, Charlotte relaxed against the copper-colored, polished metal back of the tub, classifying Sparrow's words with the inevitable flux and flow of the tide or the constant hiss of the surf—relentless, insidious background noise that meant very little but was always there.

With her eyes half closed, she let Sparrow soap her aching legs, never ceasing her chatter, until Charlotte nearly dozed in the warm water, listening with half an ear and an occasional nod as the "baker's son did this," and the "wheelwright's daughter Chloe was caught right in the middle of doing that," pleasantly submerged in the water and the one-sided conversation until the sweeping bang of the door drove her, curling like a soldier, to her senses, and the tall, powerful figure of Garret Montgomery strode confidently into the room, whistling gaily.

No cape hid his form, nor hat covered his thick mass of shining ebony hair. He had bathed and carefully shaved his blue-black beard, spending more time on his appearance this morning than he had done in years. The result of his careful attention was a devastatingly handsome man who walked with an arrogant, self-assured stride toward his glowering, wet bride. He was intensely interested in her, not just because of her physical beauty, but because he felt an almost supernatural, spellbinding magnetism that pulled him in her direction with an elemental, uncanny force that was difficult to describe.

"Good morning," he said brightly. He sat down on the window seat with easy grace, acting as someone would if they had been invited into her bath. Smiling, he settled back against the wall, propping his leather-clad feet on the edge of her bath. "Lovely day, isn't it?"

Charlotte's reaction to his intrusion was instinctive and almost feral. She retreated beneath the cover of water, oils and aromatics, scrunching down as low as possible in the opaque water with her knees drawn up and her hands folded protectively over her breasts. Her heart quickened and she glowered at him, hatred pouring from her eyes as she stared at the intruder before her.

Garret sighed and pulled absently on a loose thread. It wasn't going exactly as he had planned. Admittedly, he was enjoying the view. He loved every naked inch of her.

Sparrow giggled and left the room in a flurry of brown muslin and damp hands, eager to tell the others in the kitchen just what she had seen, while, to Charlotte's outraged amazement, Bishop walked over to Garret, begging to have his head scratched while wagging his tail in fond appreciation of the attention he was receiving.

Garret, seeing her astonishment at the obvious friendship between himself and her hairy protector, smiled apologetically.

"Last night while you were sleeping," he explained, "I brought your shaggy friend here a meal and took off his chain. As you can see, he was very grateful. He's quite a beast. I'm very fond of him already. Incidentally," he teased, his eyes twinkling merrily as he remembered how, last night, when he was too restless and excited to sleep and needed to prove that she really existed, he had walked to her room, standing in the doorway like a man bewitched by her presence. She was sleeping; the innocence of that moment lingered in his mind long after he left. "Do you always sleep without covers?"

He was a man conflicted by desires, laws and reality. He was her husband, yet not planned and definitely not wanted by her. Still, he found himself compellingly drawn to her.

"No worries," he said. "I covered you. You never know what sort of rogue may be wandering around at night."

"The only rogue I see is you!" she said angrily. "Now, get out of here!" The water had cooled to the point of being uncomfortable, and she shivered, aware of his eyes on her.

Garret sighed. "Beloved enemy," he said softly. "I covered you and ensured your room was secure. Yet I cherish the memory of your sweet slumber, your innocent escape into dreams and places where I could not follow. If I have taken your hand, would you have led me to a place where your eyes welcomed me?"

Her silence felt sharp and the chasm separating them eternal.

"Burnt bread?" he offered softly. He offered her a thick slice of toasted bread oozing with honey and butter which had been prepared for her and placed on a silver serving plate. His hair fell forward across his brow, shadowing his intense eyes with a veil of humility. He was falling for her, falling in love in a way he could not quite explain.

"What?" she snapped. "Oh, I see! Offer me food and I'll grovel at your feet as my dog did? Is that your misbegotten logic? Let me tell you something, Lord Garret Montgomery! I am not an animal to be bribed or petted into submission! Now for the second time, I'm demanding that you leave my bath!"

Charlotte was furious. She wanted to throw something at him. Her dressing gown was just out of reach, and in desperation, she wished the butter knife were just a little closer. Adding to her ire, Lord Montgomery ignored her order to leave. Staring at her, he simply settled back against the window as though it was perfectly natural that he be in her bathroom. Unwilling to let a good breakfast go to waste, he took a healthy bite of toast.

"No, wife, I don't think I'll leave. After all, we are married."

"Don't insult me by referring to that farce as a marriage!" she shouted. "Now get out of here!"

"Make me, Charlotte," he said softly. He smiled and took another bite of bread, this time licking the honey from the tip of each finger very slowly and smiling so wickedly that she blushed.

"You've no right to be here!"

"I've every right."

He stood up and stretched languidly.

"I don't know how to bridge the distance," he confessed. "Here I am, your husband, lusting after you and loving you in my mind, and there you are, pushing against me. Is there no truce between us, Charlotte? Will you make our marriage bed a battlefield and I only the victor? We are legally wed. I am your husband."

"You'll never be my husband!" she said.

"Oh, I beg to differ!" He smiled innocently, a dangerous light in his eyes. "I am your husband, and as your husband, I have a great many rights, and we've only just begun to explore the possibilities.

"Shall I scrub your back, darling?" he offered sweetly. She saw the searing desire in his eyes.

He made no pretense at hiding his intentions as he walked to her bath with a sinful glitter in his eyes.

"You're not my husband!" she said. She assailed her enemy with the only weapon she had available—her now-tepid bathwater, dousing him with several handfuls in rapid succession and thoroughly drenching the front of him, from the top of his dark head to the bottom of his leather-shod feet—making it frightfully clear to her that he wanted her and was not about to step down.

"Quit acting the shrew and welcome your husband," he said. It was almost a growl.

"You're a brute! And you are definitely not my husband!"

"It's normal that you should feel a little anxious—virgins usually are—but don't you think you are taking this a little too far? Perhaps you are overreacting?"

"Overreacting? You called me a shrew! You tell me I'm your wife. Your father roped me and dragged me here, treating me worse than a servant or a hostage. I've been tied to a bed. And now you are telling me, over breakfast, as I am in my bath, that I'm overreacting?! Clearly you and your people are insane!"

Garret calmly picked up a cloth and soaped it, preparing to hand it to her.

"Lay a hand on me," she hissed threateningly, backing up against the metal as far as she could, her blue eyes crackling and spitting fire, "and I'll scratch your eyes out!" She meant it, too, every word, secretly wishing she hadn't chewed her nails to the quick. "You're not my husband!" she repeated, glaring at him as if her belief that they were not *truly* married would negate any claim he had on her—any right to possess or touch or hold her body.

Hearing her, he turned his face away so that only his profile could be seen, as though he were trying to conceal something from her, and she wondered crazily if he were *laughing* at her. Yes, that was it! He was laughing at her! Thinking what a helpless, silly fool she was! But then, after a few moments of tense silence while she strained to hear his snickering, surprisingly, she couldn't hear a thing except the wild beating of her own heart. Then he looked at her—truly looked at her—with such longing shining from the deep blue depths of his eyes that she gasped and nearly forgot her nakedness. *He was handsome!* Sinfully so, dangerously so, a fallen angel cast in clay, too achingly good-looking to be a mere man.

"You called me a devil last night," he said. He couldn't stop staring at her. "A fallen angel."

Water dripped from his raven-hued hair in crystal rivulets and beaded like liquid diamonds on the thick spray of his spiky, jet-black lashes before each droplet fell, trailing down the strong line of his high-boned cheeks, lingering on the firm set of his square jaw, moistening the sensuous curve of his luscious mouth.

"Stars and angels have fallen," he said. "And so have I. Tell me, Princess Charlotte, will I find salvation in your touch, redemption in your eyes, or will you simply turn away?"

Then he smiled again, but this time so sweetly and earnestly, so wistful and wanting, that the cleft in his chin deepened in response, and his eyes shone with the soft dreaminess of a calm summer sea, elusively pure and chivalrously honest.

"Save me from myself and endless nights alone."

"You're not my husband," she whispered, as though trying desperately to convince herself, feeling an odd, unfamiliar tug deep inside of her that made her catch her breath in wonder: a peculiar sense of déjà vu. As if she had gazed into those searing blue eyes at least a million times before. She was a captive bride: her marriage made under terrible circumstances, vows spoken by a surrogate to solidify an alliance of families, joining her to a man she did not know who now claimed her as his wife.

"I could be," Garret offered solemnly. The ferocity was gone, the arrogance banished, as he plunged his hand, shirt sleeve and all, into the water and lifted her foot reverently, with all the humility of a servant instead of a proud and pompous lord.

Gasping at his touch, she tried to pull back, but the firm pressure of his hand held her there as he slowly began to rub the bottom of her tiny foot with the cloth, tickling and teasing, mesmerizing her with his touch, holding her gently in his big hand, tracing delicious little circles along her instep, moving upward with a slow, hypnotic grace. "I could be your husband, I *would* be..." he pledged softly, his heart in his words, "if you'd only just let me." His gaze never left her face.

Charlotte's body betrayed her spirit. The woman responded to his noble looks. She could not deny that she felt a powerful attraction to this man.

"Adversary," she said. "That is what you are."

"Beloved adversary?" he encouraged.

Every nerve in her body seemed to be centered in the area where he touched, every electric shock a miniature bolt of lightning that traveled the length of her spine before plunging sharply into her groin, exploding in bursts of liquid heat, making her heart pound and her head light.

"No," she whispered, her eyes locked on his, unable to believe she was letting this happen. Her body was betraying her! Her flesh, hot and wet, refused to move, responding to this stranger's touch with shameless abandon, yearning for him as if it didn't sense the awesome danger in this man.

"Let me love you," he said. His voice was deep, filled with the rumbling timbre of barely restrained passion. One hand traced the smooth path of her calf, lingering beneath her knee. "Let me be your husband and let yourself be my wife. Our families will be united, and I will protect you and these lands and your people and cherish you all of my life."

"No!" she said. "I'm not a pawn to be brokered by my grandmother to satisfy her security and keep that *pretender*, which she is, on my throne!"

She pulled free from him as though waking from a dream and stood up proudly, defying him as she reached for her dressing gown.

Garret was quicker. Anticipating her every move, he grabbed the robe and held it out in front of her. The hunter's light now gleamed from his eyes.

"We are both pawns, Charlotte," he said. "We've been led to this place by politics, not our hearts. Consolidating the shires is for the greater good of all our people."

"Our people? I'm Welsh and you're a Norman invader. I suspect there is a slight difference. We are Welsh, and we are not nor will we ever be a captive people!"

"Never?" he replied, a teasing light glowing from his eyes, giving them a nearly predatory glint as he held the robe above her head, dangling it like a carrot in front of a pony's nose, smiling at the full-length view of his beautiful new bride that her frenzied movement afforded him. *God! So lovely*, he thought, and the man in him, never too far beneath the surface, was passionately aroused, surging forward, wanting to take her as she stood—against the wall, on the floor, in the tub—the *place* didn't matter, but the *need* to claim her, to make her belong to him now and for all time was greater than any force he had ever known.

"No!" she replied hotly, seeing the desire burning in his eyes like the all-consuming fires of Hell as she grabbed once more for her robe, feeling the flames licking at her heart. So close, sweet Jesus, she prayed desperately, so close to the flame…

"NEVER!" she screamed, backing up half a step, afraid for the first time in her life—afraid of *herself*—as she hovered on the brink of desire, the imp in her wanting nothing more than to give in and leap into the scorching flames.

The force of her words drove him back to reality with a painful start, her anger giving her the power to ignore his insolent, hungry gaze.

"Never! Never! Never!" she raged, glaring at him. "*Your* idea of a wife would be someone—someone like your *mother!*" she told him scornfully. "And I could *never* be like that!"

"My *mother?*" he replied icily, the teasing light leaving his eyes in a flash, replaced by a wary, barely concealed anger as, quite by accident, Charlotte had found and pierced his Achilles heel. "What has my *mother* got to do with you or me?"

"I know you," she replied furiously, forgetting her nakedness in her anger, her hands poised on her hips while her hair fell out of its pins, swinging around her like a silvery cape. "I know what *kind* of a man you are!" she hissed. Although he towered above her, she gave him no ground, gaining the half-step she'd lost and advancing half a step closer still, locking eyes with him until a nearly visible electricity seemed to crackle through the air—a challenge—as she pitted her will against his. "The only way a woman could ever please a man like you is by staying on her knees several hours a day in prayer!"

One black eyebrow shot up in surprise, followed by a brief nod, trailed by low, menacing laughter, coldly dangerous and without a trace of humor in its brittle sounds.

"There are *other* things a woman can do on her *knees* that are infinitely more pleasing to a man than praying," he replied dryly, picking up the gauntlet she had thrown down and retaliating with his stinging tongue and equally quick wit as he dropped the robe over her head.

"Blast you, Montgomery!" she muttered, pulling the gown from her face, then becoming silent as she saw the seething intent in his dark eyes as he let his gaze roam wherever it wanted, as though he had the *right*, across her heaving breasts, along the shadowed cleft of her thighs, traveling, traveling, and finally settling hungrily on her mouth… And his gaze *did* things to her, things she could not admit, even to herself.

"*Please you!*" she stammered angrily, feeling hot and ragged and so confused as she flipped her hair behind her shoulders. "I don't *want* to please you… I *hate* you!"

"Indeed," he replied nonchalantly, as if she had just mentioned the weather or an uninteresting bit of trivia.

"Yes!" she raged, pulling the robe around her in a whirlwind of white eyelet lace and ribbons. "I hate you!" She was feeling better now that she had said it, wanting desperately to believe it was true. "And I'm not your wife, and I'm not your property," she added vehemently, tying her sash. "And I'm not a woman to roll over whenever you would want me to and whisper sweet words to pacify your lofty ego! Someday, when I marry, it will be to a man who treats me as an equal, not a servant, and someone I love!"

"I don't wish to be the bearer of bad news, Lady Charlotte," he said quietly, a tightness growing in his chest that threatened to choke him, "but you *are* married, and to *me*."

"Not legally!" she cried, versed well enough in feudal law to know that an *unconsummated* marriage was invalid. "That sheet flying out on the balustrade this very minute is a *fake!*"

"That," he said fiercely, drawing her to him in a single swift movement, "can be rectified this very moment!" And he kissed her, winding his free hand roughly into her hair, feeling every curve as he urged her, with the firm, demanding pressure of his mouth, to want him as much as he wanted her.

The sheer weight and the power of the man holding her made her dizzy. She had never been kissed. The unyielding pressure of his mouth on hers, the warm, silky touch of his breath, and the strange magic of his touch caused her heart to pound.

Charlotte was confused. According to law, she was married. Yet he was a stranger. According to law, she had no choice—yet last night he had given her a choice. Last night he had been a shadow, nothing more than a bad dream. This morning he was hot flesh and blood, real and demanding, a man who claimed she *belonged* to him.

Oh! If only she had kept her head instead of losing it to her vile temper, she might have gotten out of this! Now there was nothing in the universe that existed except the touch of this man, the *way* he tasted, the scent that enveloped her as much as the liquid warmth of the water had, and the distant memory of Lon, sweet Lon, whom she had promised to wed, plaguing her like a remnant of a guilty dream…

Lon! she thought with a sudden stab of shame, not able to remember a time when she had *wanted* him as she did this stranger. Lon… sweet, gentle Lon… whose only intent had been to make her happy, to soothe her loneliness and give her hope—to be her friend. The memory filled her with remorse, acting like a wedge, driving her arms back, causing her to remember the humiliation that had led to this moment. The anger fired her temper, driving her knee upward, intending to hurt the man who held her as much as possible.

He felt her pull back, felt the knee move upward, and caught it easily, still intent on finishing his kiss.

Holding her firmly by the waist and hair, he moved her to the wall, knocking jars of powder and bottles of perfume to the floor, pinning her against the tapestried wall as the hand that stopped her knee slid upward, cupping a full, silky breast in one fluid movement.

"Better men than you have tried, little one," he murmured, his voice husky with passion, as he nuzzled her ear, tracing the winding path with his persistent tongue, probing and nuzzling her, drunk with the want of her, till her body went limp with the torrent of new emotions that flowed through her.

"You're lying!" she whispered, her voice nearly a moan as she twisted her face away from the delicious torment of his mouth, conscious of his hand and the swelling warmth of her breasts.

"How is it..." he murmured softly, his hand finding the opening of her robe, letting his fingers slide sensuously over her satiny flesh, "that I am a liar?" He paused then, a deep groan escaping from his lips as her twisting body pressed innocently against his groin and a spasm of white-hot pleasure shot up his spine. With a voice ragged and nearly beyond conscious control, he finished his question, barely able to remember how to form even the simplest words. Beads of sweat glistened on his brow as he searched her face, his body trembling so violently from his restrained emotions that he hurt. His eyes, filled with the mystery of a midnight sky and the promise of glittering stars, seemed to demand and plead with her for release at the same time. Physically and mentally, this little woman had the power to torture him as no one ever had.

"Well," he whispered, "how is it?"

"Last night," she stammered, held more forcefully to the wall by his unyielding gaze than his arms could ever hold her, "you said it should be of my *free will!*" Powerless to prevent him from taking her, she hoped to appeal to his honor—if he had any—because she knew that a few minutes more of this torture and *she* would be begging *him* for release.

Garret looked at her. Sorrow and pain clouded his eyes.

He tried to speak to her without words, stroking her cheek, tracing the curve of her lips, trying to make her understand that, as unbelievable as it might be to her, he had fallen in love with her the minute he had seen her. Indeed, he had been in love with her all his life, waiting, always waiting for *her.*

Shivering uncontrollably, her mouth dry, she jerked away from him.

"You're not a gentleman!" she breathed, exhaling slowly, trying to clear her mind and slow her heart.

He drew several cooling breaths to still the wild hammering in his chest as he gazed at her, regaining control second by second, struggling to tame his body with his mind.

"Only soldiers and those of bad breeding swear," he replied dryly.

"Only brigands and *cowards* bully women!" she retorted, seeking her salvation from this man in anger.

"I don't recall bullying you, Lady Charlotte!" he replied in exasperation, sure that there had been moments when she *enjoyed* his touch, clinging to that hope like a drowning man.

"No?" she asked sarcastically, pulling the ribbon from her throat. "Then," she taunted him spitefully, her eyes studying his face carefully for any reaction to her words, "you're saying that you are not like your *father?*"

He was very quiet, surveying her neck with eyes that missed nothing. His gaze narrowed as he saw the nearly inch-wide burn that circled her white throat like a ring of fire.

"Are you implying that my *father* did that to you?" he asked quietly. His eyes, once filled with desperate fire, had turned into blocks of solid blue ice.

"Oh! Of course!" She laughed in disbelief. "How *stupid* of me! *You* didn't know anything about this, did you?"

Swallowing, she turned, wrapping her robe around her, gazing with an agonized expression out the window, wondering *why* she had told him. What did she expect him to say—or do, for that matter? Why *should* he care? It was only arrogant pride that kept him from forcing himself on her anyway… not some chivalrous, gallant honor.

"Why did he do it?" he asked softly.

Not turning around, she told him. "Your father put a rope

around my neck and pulled me into the chapel. There he married me to *you*, forcing me to say I would by choking me nearly half to death."

Utter silence filled the room.

"You didn't marry me willingly?" he asked, a tightness in his words that was nearly painful as he remembered last night… the ropes and how she fought. Suddenly he felt like a fool.

"No!" she stormed, whirling around. "I didn't *willingly* marry you, nor would I ever!" She spoke harshly, her words intended to punish.

"And I suppose," he replied, suddenly feeling very old, "that you tried to fight *him* as you did me?"

"Yes! Yes! Yes!" she hissed. "And I would do it again!"

"No doubt," he murmured. "Perhaps you should've tried tears instead." He gave a shrug of his shoulders as he picked up a soft cloth and began to dry his hair.

"I don't cry!" she replied forcefully, surprising herself by the feeling of stinging tears that welled up in her eyes, threatening to make her look like a liar by spilling down her cheeks.

"Never?" he asked softly, gazing at her sparkling eyes. "Not even for *yourself?*"

"Especially for myself!" she retorted, showing him her back once again.

A silent nod was his reply as he bent over and picked up the fallen ribbon.

"It was only a suggestion. Women use tears as men do swords, often with greater results," he told her, yawning and seeming apathetic about the whole thing. "Enjoy your breakfast," he finished lightly, leaving the room with a polite bow and a soft click of the door.

She had observed his behavior out of the corner of her eye with a feeling of intense humiliation. Why had she expected him to care? Why should he? Suddenly a horrible feeling came over her as she realized that she had *wanted* him to feel sorry for her.

"See?" she whispered to the empty room, choking back a sob as she saw herself many years ago as a small child, holding up her injured hand in front of an aging apple tree.

Her Grandfather Tree, she called him. "I hurt," she told the gnarled old tree, who seemed to sigh in sympathy at her outstretched hand. Then she had climbed into her special place, way up high, where boughs had met and twisted, forming a curious lap that held her even when she slept, while the wind rocked and sang to her. "One, two, three, Grandfather Tree, hold me, save me… I love thee!" she had crooned softly, laying her head against the rough old bark, her silhouette outlined against a luminous summer moon.

She had believed that the old tree had a soul and was alive and, most important of all, that it loved her and cared that she was hurt. But that was imagination, a place in her mind where she had run when the pain of living grew too great. Reality was a place where pity and those who offered it were scorned.

"Hate me!" she whispered to the empty room, slamming her fist against the wall, easily able to combat enmity with her own anger. It was that inner boiling rage that had driven her to succeed against all odds—not pity, which crippled and defeated and had shone from so many eyes.

And yet, she had *wanted* it from Garret Montgomery. For a moment, when she had pulled the ribbon from her neck, she was again the child. "See?" she had wanted to say. "See how he *hurt* me?" She had *wanted* to rest her head against his wide shoulder, hear his heartbeat, and feel his arms surround her like the strong branches of a tree, to know for the first time in her life that someone truly cared.

All this, she mused sadly, she had wanted, not from Lon, whom she had promised to wed, nor her grandmother, her only remaining kin, nor even Gerald, the closest thing to a father she had ever known, but from a man who was a virtual stranger, a man who claimed he had the right to share her bed.

Sniffing softly, thoroughly miserable and as full of self-pity as any human could possibly be, she curled up into the farthest corner of the window seat and *almost* cried.

Chapter 7

Garret's bedroom window was not on the seaward side of Pembroke. His view was of his people. Below, in the teeming center of the courtyard, freemen plied their trades, shops were opened, casks of wine flowed, wedges of cheese rose on makeshift stands, guards patrolled regularly, the beginnings of a busy town.

Charlotte observed all this orderly chaos with something akin to detachment, seeing everything but so overwhelmed by her own feelings of misery that it took her a full minute before her eyes caught the drama being played out right below her window.

A large, fat, bald man in flowing saffron robes and black pantaloons, with a bright red sash tied around his bulging middle and a thick gold hoop dangling from his ear, was plastered against the far wall, trying to conceal his outrageously costumed form against the dreary gray limestone without much luck.

"There he is!" shouted one heavily armed guard brandishing a two-foot sword as he rounded the gate opening.

The chase was on!

Leaping straight up into the air with a curious, nervous "Whoop!" the brightly-colored clown ran as fast as his girth would allow. He shook, his belly bounced, his arms pumped as fast as his pudgy legs pedaled—up and down, side to side, while his overly-stuffed rump kept up with a curious shaking rhythm all its own.

"Whoop-ooh-ahh!" he cried, lumbering up onto the wagon

full of new cheese, crushing wheels of dark cheddar beneath his curious shoes with their pointy toes and tingling bells.

"Hey!" shouted the guard. "Stop that thief!"

Over the wagon he tumbled, rolling to his feet, pulling his shirt front out from his pants as though it had suddenly caught fire. Copper coins, gold and silver, glittered in the morning light, tinkling to the ground as he ran.

"Blimey!" shouted the cheese woman. "It's raining coppers!"

Chaos soon ensued. Shoving the guard, she began to scoop up as many of the shiny objects as she could, stuffing them down the front of her dress, while others in the square dove straight for the stolen loot, pushing and kicking, cursing and punching their neighbors as viciously as they could. Tomorrow they would be friends and sip ale and swap lies, but today, yes, today, with money on the ground, it was every man for himself.

"Look out 'ere!" shouted the guard indignantly. "That's the King's money!" He was promptly rewarded with a shattering blow from a smoked leg of lamb as he put his hand down the cheese woman's dress.

"Fresh bloke!" she raged, and she hit him again for good measure, intent on keeping her coins.

Meanwhile, the thief had hidden himself behind several wine casks. Charlotte watched in amusement as he crept on hands and knees toward the cloister house, where the friars had left their washing out to dry.

With a surreptitious look at the brawling mass of townsfolk and guards, he grabbed the nearest robe, a dark brown, coarse woolen garment with a bit of twine strung through the arm to use as a belt, and he put it on, pulling it over his bulk until he looked like a gigantic overstuffed pillow with pointed toes and a bald head.

Then a curious metamorphosis took place. He stood up, and Charlotte watched in amazement as his expression seemed to melt, the crafty look evaporating from his face as he miraculously took on the guise of a somber friar. He loosened the gold hoop from his ear and tossed it behind him, then bent his knees so that his odd shoes wouldn't show because his robe was too short. The transformation was complete within the space of several heartbeats, and with all the dignity of a man of the cloth, he clasped his hands before him with saintly grace and began walking with "holy" light shining from his eyes.

Charlotte was nearly doubled over with laughter as she watched him walk right past the crowd of scuffling soldiers toward the gate and his freedom. Then suddenly, scarcely missing a beat, he pivoted a neat hundred and eighty degrees and walked back toward the men as a group of the King's soldiers clattered across the bridge.

Suddenly Charlotte had an idea.

"Sparrow!" she shouted, tying her robe securely around her. "Sparrow! Come quickly!" she called, and the curious little maid with the mousy brown hair appeared from behind the door like smoke.

"Yes, Lady Charlotte?" she asked a little fearfully, seeing the intense light burning from her mistress's fair eyes.

"Call me 'Charlotte,'" she told the girl impatiently, "if you must call me something."

"Yes, m'lady, ahh… Charlotte," she replied hurriedly, knowing that was not the reason she'd been summoned. "What can I do for you, Lady Charlotte?"

"I've need of a priest!" she told the girl with enthusiasm, her eyes sparkling.

"Priest, m'lady?" Sparrow asked doubtfully. Somehow the idea of her lady being religious just didn't fit.

"Yes," she replied softly, chewing thoughtfully on her lower lip. "There is a monk walking toward the manor right now, a big, fat monk with a bald head. Bring him to me! Tell him," she added after a moment's careful thought, "that your mistress bids him come and he will be safe!"

"Hurry, Sparrow!" Charlotte cried, urgently pushing her toward the stairs. "Or he'll get away!"

"Yes, mistress!" she replied quickly.

Charlotte watched with satisfaction as the seed of her plan began to take root and grow when Sparrow yelled at the top of her lungs: "Get the priest! Hurry! Get the priest! My mistress has need of a holy man!"

Garret held the blue ribbon tightly in his hand.

Anger was a bright blue flame and rage was its pure white center. That spark, that ivory light, glowed intensely from his powerful blue eyes as he stalked down the stairs, ignoring Cole, ignoring Torin, ignoring his mother—as she had ignored him all her life.

"Father!" he shouted, his voice reverberating eerily through the high-ceilinged manor. Like a wolf, he wound his way through the corridors, knowing where to find his father with an instinct that bordered on the uncanny.

Below the main floor was a small room used to plan raids and wars and hold secret ceremonies that only Charles and his sorcerers were privy to. Garret found his father there, hunched over stacks of bleached parchments, his eyes swollen and red from lack of sleep and the poor ventilation in the cellar.

"What is it?" he asked in irritation, his expression changing instantly as he recognized the murderous gleam shining from his son's eyes.

All Garret felt was the thin slip of satin in his clenched hand, and all he saw was the horrible burn encircling his beautiful wife's throat. It was beyond logic: a woman he just met—a virtual stranger lying in his bed—his wife, they said; a princess, treated worse than a servant, brought into his home under protest. Where were the roses and champagne? The wedding dance and the celebration?

Garret was outraged by what had been done and who had orchestrated the events that led to a princess being bound like prisoner and led in shackles to her new home.

Without a word, he caught his father around the neck and drove him back against the wall with one mighty shove.

Guards, who followed Charles everywhere, immediately unsheathed their swords and came forward, only to be motioned away by the lord of the manor, who stared warily at his son, waiting for an explanation.

"If you—or *anyone*—ever touches my *wife* again," Garret vowed, his words spoken so softly that Charles strained to hear him, "I will kill you!" With his warning issued, he dropped his hand from his father's throat and stood silently, waiting for yet another "punishment" to be exacted.

"It seems," his father replied quietly, rubbing his sore throat, "that you have taken quite a fancy to your new *wife*— is that correct?"

Garret didn't reply. He just continued to look at the man who had controlled his life so thoroughly, so completely, since the day he was born, with an emotion bordering on contempt.

"Ah! I see," remarked Charles dryly. "Well, I don't imagine you will *thank* me for bringing her to you, eh, my son? Or my court of 'sorcerers'?" He waved his arm at the scholarly-looking men clustered together in the corner.

"The *way* you brought her to me has ensured that she hates *me* as much as my mother hates *you!*"

Charles flinched at Garret's words as though he had been slapped, but he continued to stand his ground, nodding his head in dispassionate agreement.

"She would have come no other way," Charles countered

smoothly, adding, "Lust is a vexation, my son. It will have you believe in all manner of happy endings... only to realize one day what an idealistic *fool* you've been!"

Without asking for permission to leave, Garret turned.

"Since you are here," Charles continued, and Garret stopped with his hand resting on the door, "I am told that Halfdanson has escaped the Gate. There are reports that he has joined with yet another band of Vikings. See that you take care of it." He then settled himself once again at his desk, brushing the blue silk ribbon onto the floor with a complete lack of interest.

Watching his father shut him out once again, Garret stooped to pick up the ribbon, tucking it into his shirt.

"Well?" his father asked impatiently, not bothering to look up.

"Nothing, Father," Garret replied quietly, a trace of sadness in his voice as he looked at the bent form that he resembled with mocking accuracy. "Nothing at all..." And he walked stiffly from the room, calling for his men to make ready to ride.

In the back of a cart filled with stray and squealing pigs, Harold Halfdanson crouched beneath filthy hay and stinking feces.

His face was bathed in sweat. His body burned with fever.

His arm was little more than a crusted-over stump filled with noxious poison. Cursing softly, he pulled the ragged stub close to his chest when the cart hit a rut in the middle of the road.

This stinking ride had cost him half a crown. Yet, he grinned wickedly to himself, the coppers jingling in his pocket had not been acquired with too much difficulty. Even with only one arm, he was still more man than most of these peasants could deal with.

And then, he mused, looking at the faintly glowing ridge of mountains to the east, Gloucester wasn't much farther. There he would find shelter under Alaric of York's roof and he could rest until his wounds healed. After that? Well, he had a score to settle. He didn't give a damn if it was done with honor, just so long as when it was over, Garret Montgomery's body was fit only for dogs to eat.

"Aye," he growled. "Pig slop, when I'm through with you, Montgomery! By Thor's hammer, I swear you'll die by my hand!" A momentary pause in his thoughts occurred when a curious pig poked her snout near his leg. "Get your stinking self away from me, you dirty thing!" he roared, then kicked her viciously in the face, sending her squealing. "Pig slop," the old Viking repeated to himself. "When I'm through with you, Montgomery!"

He settled back with a grin against the rattling cart to finish his ride, contemplating the sweetness of his revenge.

"Riders approaching!" shouted a guard.

Gerald looked out the drawing room window as a group of young nobles rode toward the Vale. In the lead, with his dragon banner of red flying above his head, was Lon ap Llewelyn of Aberystwyth, his light hair flying in the breeze and his smoky blue eyes locked tenaciously on the castle's central keep.

"Who is it?" asked Isabel irritably, studying the letter she had just received from King Henry with growing alarm.

"It's Llewelyn," Gerald replied quietly, and Isabel stared in shocked silence.

"What do you want me to do?" Gerald asked gently, watching as his mistress nervously toyed with her hair, her slim foot tapping in rhythm to the accelerated beating of her heart.

Sighing, a hopelessly trapped look clouding her penetrating eyes, she shrugged her elegantly sloped shoulders in resignation and replied dully, "Ask him in."

She walked with stately grace to her divan, sitting down as carefully as someone who was posing for a picture, settling her gown of emerald-green brocade around her like a fan. But her attempt at indifference was wasted on Gerald, who knew her all too well. He noticed everything about her—the crimson stains blooming on her cheeks and how her hands trembled while her breath came so rapidly that he thought she might faint.

"Well?" she asked sarcastically, tired of his scrutiny, motioning to the door with an impatient wave of her hand. "*Ask him in!*"

Nodding silently, Gerald walked into the foyer, where the servants were already ushering in the company of youthful knights.

"The Baroness will see *you* in the study," Gerald told Lon quietly, pointedly ignoring the others.

Lon nodded and started forward. His men followed until the crusty old soldier positioned himself between them and the door.

"The Baroness will speak only to *him*." He spoke roughly, and though their expressions told Gerald they didn't like what he had said, they stayed where they were with a nod from young Lon.

"This way," Gerald offered courteously, and the heir of Aberystwyth followed the lumbering giant into the shadowed room.

"Good afternoon, Baroness de Clare," Lon murmured softly, bowing low, exposing the aristocratic elegance of his slender hands and long neck in that one simple gesture. Though he was not nearly as tall as Gerald, his build was the slender desire of most women: athletic, supple, and lean. Yet it was his *face* that caused heads to turn and stare, not so much from the sum of his physical features, but for the hidden strength one read in its chiseled lines. Still, for all his capable actions and words, there was a poet in young Lon, a Celtic bard and a Druid mystic—also a stubborn set to his jaw that made it plain he did not give up easily, and that was why he was here.

"Llewelyn," she replied with a haughty tilt of her head. "Lon, I believe… is that correct?"

"Yes," he answered calmly, knowing full well she knew who he was but allowing her to play whatever games she deemed necessary in order to maintain the comfortable illusion of civility. If he took any offense at her childish attempt at snobbery, he gave no outward sign.

"How is your *grandmother?*" Isabel asked with acid sweetness, lightning flashing ominously in her dark eyes as a mental image of the aging Llewelyn matriarch presented itself full-blown and painfully clear in her mind.

"Well, Baroness. She sends her regards," he lied, rationalizing that it was just a little *white* lie, one that he hoped wouldn't count. All that mattered to him was the outcome of this meeting, not the verbal battle this hard-faced woman seemed intent on trying to wage. Lon knew that his grandmother hated Isabel with a singularly intense passion, although she would never tell him why. Seeing the malice seething in Baroness de Clare's eyes, he suspected that *her* feelings for his grandmother were even less charitable.

"Indeed," Isabel replied dryly, with a contemptuous, *knowing* smile, making Lon flush with the knowledge that she knew he lied. Unknown to him, once, long before, Isabel and his grandmother had been quite close, co-conspirators in a plan to satisfy their mutual lust for power. That was seventeen *long* years ago, years in which they had not spoken a single word to each other, detesting even the mention of the other's *name.*

Unable to cover up his blunder, Lon stumbled on, still intent on his goal. "I've come about your granddaughter, Baroness de Clare," he began honestly, wisely leaving out the part that he and his precocious friend were to have met by the sacred oak two nights ago, and he had been sick with worry about her ever since.

"My granddaughter?" Isabel asked sweetly, pretending ignorance.

Yet Gerald could detect the note of jealousy in her voice, and he watched with deepening sorrow as Isabel wound a lock of her midnight-colored hair around her finger, bending forward, the low cut of her dress giving Lon an unhindered view of her full breasts.

"Yes," he replied evenly, gentleman enough to ignore her obvious efforts at seduction, yet man enough to wonder why this aging beauty appeared to be flirting with him.

"Well…" She sighed, sitting back on the divan and draping her arm along the top. "Come," she told him, patting the seat beside her and flashing a smile at him that sent an involuntary chill up his spine. "Come sit beside me and tell me just what it is you *want.*"

"I prefer to stand, thank you," he told her calmly, and he watched as, like a cat deprived of its cornered prey, her eyes narrowed to mere midnight slits. He swore he could hear a growl escape her clenched lips.

"As you like," she retorted, unable to keep the anger out of her voice. "Now, young man, I really don't have all day… so please get to the point!"

"I have come to ask for Charlotte's hand in marriage," he stated boldly. "Before you protest," he hurried on, holding up one hand to silence her, "you know my family is one of the oldest in Wales, and our wealth is second to none. I wish no dowry for her—I simply would like your permission to make her my bride."

A low, wretched laugh issued from Isabel's lips. Her eyes were blazing infernos, filled with more hate and pain than he had ever seen, and he marveled at how it seemed to be directed at him.

"You wish to marry my granddaughter?" she asked incredulously and laughed again, until Lon thought she might be mad. "Well, my young…" She stopped for a moment, appearing to lose herself in thought as she drank in his features, one by one, stopping to gaze wistfully at his long, slender hands. "…*handsome* friend…" she began again, tears forming unexpectedly at the corners of her eyes. "I'm afraid you're too late."

"Too late?" he asked, confused, fearing something horrible had happened to Charlotte.

"Yes, too late!" she triumphantly crowed. "It seems," she stated, apparently in more control of herself as she got up and walked to the opened window, "it seems our *dear* Charlotte has gone off and married someone else!"

"What!" he cried in surprise, unable to believe that this could possibly have happened in the space of a few days.

"Oh, yes," snapped Isabel, enjoying the confusion and pain in Lon's eyes. "*She is married.* The Montgomery family must deal with her now. Do you know them?" she asked, her stomach clenching convulsively at the mention of their name. "Excellent family." She smiled bitterly. "It seems," she continued in a low, biting voice as she glared maliciously at the letter lying on her sideboard, "that they have very close ties with our Norman king. *Charlotte* was really quite pleased with the match."

"You're lying!" he stormed, advancing half a step closer to Isabel. Gerald seemed to materialize out of nowhere to stand protectively beside his mistress once again.

"Oh, no," she assured him harshly. "I am most certainly not! Here," she told him, snatching up the letter she had just received from the King. "You see," she handed it to him, "even *dear* Henry sends his congratulations, along with, of course, his orders!"

Lon reluctantly took the letter and read it. The seal was official. It *was* from Henry, sending his best wishes to the new couple and the proud grandmother, along with the order to transport all of Charlotte's worldly possessions, titles, inheritances, etc., to the castle at Pembroke, including the fabled Sword and Crown of Wales. And to do so without delay.

"It's not possible," Lon whispered, remembering their plans: May Day, the wedding. He cherished her, wanting nothing more than to give her a good home, a happy place where she could live and know peace and security—perhaps, in time, even love. Charlotte, he mused sadly, *his* Charlotte. The images whirled like a collage in his mind: sweet, kind Charlotte, always willing to listen; high-spirited vixen, loving nothing better than a good prank; courageous warrior maiden, willing to die for those she loved; and, most important of all to him, *friend.* She was his best friend. It was inconceivable that she would have married another—not without telling him. Not of her own free will…

Carefully, he placed the letter on the table, fixing Isabel with a look that made her flinch.

"I think you can find your way out," she told him coldly. With a wave of her hand, she dismissed him as she poured herself a tall goblet of deep purple wine, turning her back on him and ending the interview.

"Would Lady Charlotte consent to marry a Norman?" Cedric Dai asked Lon on their long ride back to Aberystwyth.

"No," Lon answered slowly, "I don't think she would." He fell back into silence, staring moodily at the passing coast without really seeing it.

Only a few weeks before, their plans had been made. At the May Day festival in Cardiff, two days from now, they were to be married. Frowning, Lon could not ever remember a time when Charlotte's word had been given and not kept.

Now her promise seemed less than the dust that whirled in the distance. Useless. She was married to another. Lon suspected that it was a forced arrangement, and if that was so, he intended to find out. If Charlotte did not want to be there—a Montgomery husband or not—he would find a way to free her. Even if it meant securing an army.

"Let's go!" he shouted, clenching his teeth in determined anger as he kicked his horse with renewed energy. "There is a letter that needs to be sent!" A letter, yes, he thought savagely, backed up by a sword and a thousand men if necessary!

Chapter 8

"Hello, Father!" Charlotte cried brightly, smiling sweetly at the dubious-looking monk cowering by her door. "You may *leave* now, Sparrow," she told the staring young maid, who promptly did as she was ordered, reluctantly shutting the door behind her with one last curious look.

With a smile on her face, Charlotte walked toward the big man who was stuffed so uncomfortably into the monk's stolen habit. He tried to look humble. She tried not to laugh.

"Tell me, *Father*," she asked softly, rocking back and forth on her heels patiently, like a slowly circling shark—waiting for her prey to wiggle the wrong way, "how much penance is required of a man who defiles his neighbor's wife?"

The impostor started in surprise but recovered almost instantly, then replied in a grave voice mimicking the priest in the great cathedral with uncanny accuracy: "For three years he must fast three days out of seven on bread and water." He droned on soberly, keeping his eyes glued to the floor, secretly relieved that his mother had beat the Archbishop of Canterbury's penitential system into his wayward bones.

"And," she went on, undaunted, in a deceptively soft voice, "what punishment is exacted of a man if he commits fornication with a virgin?" She continued to rock back and forth on her heels as if she had all the time in the world, watching in satisfaction as beads of sweat broke out on his rounded forehead.

"He shall do penance one year," he recited easily, having committed that sin at least half a dozen times. "*If thy right eye offends thee*," his first shrewish wife had scolded, bringing the broom down across his head when she caught him staring at all the young girls bathing in the stream, "*pluck it out!*" Whap! She had hit him again, but the sight of those rounded, youthful curves didn't offend him at all. No, he thought with a groan of pure pleasure, *not one little bit.* Both eyes had remained, and he had gotten rid of his wife instead, running from her nagging voice as fast as he could, and he'd kept running, taking whatever pleasures he could along the way.

Sighing unhappily, he thought about rubbing his bent legs, which had begun to cramp. And damn it all anyway! Now his toes were beginning to curl inward, and it hurt! What did this woman *want* with him anyway? he wondered sadly. The King was said to be a man of conscience. Perhaps if he threw himself on his mercy…

"And a thief," she continued slyly, drawing him out of his reverie as she dropped down so that she could gaze up into his face, "how much penance shall a *thief* do?"

"Well," he replied soberly, licking his lips and doing his absolute best to avoid her probing eyes. "I suppose…" he began, "I suppose that would depend on the circumstances behind…"

Low, sweet laughter filled the room, cutting him off in mid-sentence. He watched with growing concern as she picked up the butter knife from the tray and pricked her middle finger.

"Oh! Sharp!" she murmured, shaking her head before she turned and pressed the tip against his throat. "And for slaying a monk?" she quizzed again, watching in amused silence as his eyes grew as wide as saucers.

He didn't dare cry out. There were enough guards outside her door to do him immeasurable harm, and he didn't care to try his hand at grappling with her, lest she make a horrible mistake and stab him. And damn his greedy eyes anyway, but his knees and thighs were beginning to give way with all the pressure he was putting on them, squatting beneath this cursed robe!

"Well?" she prompted, pressing the edge a little closer. "How long would I have to do penance for slaying a monk?"

"A 'lady,' let me see here," he stammered. "Seven *long*, incredibly long years!" he added quickly. "Or serve God." He fervently hoped he wouldn't be seeing His face any too soon.

The knife disappeared, and he felt her walking behind him, though he didn't dare turn around to see just what it was she was up to.

"Well, well, well…" she began softly, and then she grinned. Reaching down, she grabbed a handful of his swollen rump and pinched him, *hard!*

"Ow!" he shouted, coming to attention rapidly as he rubbed his sore behind with both of his hands.

"My, my, my," she said. "What strange shoes for a priest!"

"I'm not a priest!" he admitted guiltily, finally able to stand at ease and enjoying the feeling of his muscles slowly uncramping.

"You can say that again," she agreed with a smile.

"I'm ARMANDO BUSTAMANTE!" he said loudly. He lifted his hands theatrically in the air as though he was expecting applause. "Actor, magician and, occasionally," he said beneath his breath, "Master of the Art of Acquisition." He bowed.

"In other words," she replied with a grin, "a *thief?*"

"Yes," he admitted with a sigh as he sat down on the window seat. "I *have* been called that."

"Good!" she exclaimed enthusiastically, rubbing her palms together.

"Good?" he asked with a confused smile, making the slim outline of his mustache disappear into the folds of his cheeks as he helped himself to the last piece of her toast, lifting it unconsciously to his lips.

"Yes, *very good!*" she reassured him with a hearty slap on the back that nearly made him choke. "You see, Armando, I have a problem that I hope you can help me solve."

Cocking his moon-shaped head to one side, he swung his legs back and forth, listening with interest and wondering *why* a beautiful, *rich* lady like herself would need help from *him.*

"How much do you know about Garret Montgomery?" she asked slowly, cringing at the mention of his name and the involuntary, tingling wave of heat that washed over her.

"Well, of course, I don't know *everything* about him, but I have heard quite a few stories in my wanderings."

"Who," she began, wanting to phrase this question as carefully as possible, "who is the single *male* person that he *hates* above all others?"

"Oh, that's easy!" he replied lightly, tearing into a piece of hard cheese left on the tray. "That would be Robert, the Earl of Gloucester. He's a cowardly young man who fights only with his mouth and behind other people's backs," he confided, sniffing distastefully at the thought of the simpering rogue who would probably sell his mother for the right price. Even thieves had more honor than Robert did. "Why do you ask?"

Turning her back, she asked Armando in a biting voice, "Is this *Robert* of Gloucester man enough to want to make Garret Montgomery look like a fool?"

"Well, no," he admitted with an ironic laugh, and her heart sank. "But his uncle, Alaric of York, would love nothing better! Those two have locked horns on several occasions. But York is too smart to ever let their feud fall into the realm of a personal vendetta. Something like that usually ends up on the jousting field, and I don't think York likes those kinds of odds!"

"And yet Garret hates Robert more than Alaric?" she asked, a frown crinkling her forehead as she tried to understand the man she was tied to a little better.

"Oh, immeasurably!" he told her with authority. "You see, Garret Montgomery is quite a devil, but he does respect a man who will fight for himself, even if it's only with words, and is at least honest in his hate. And Saxons—*true* Saxons—hate Normans. It's a fact of life. But Robert would never admit to that, not in a million years, because that would mean he is taking a stand, and he is too much of a coward to do that."

"Then this Alaric of York, if he knew something—something that would make the *Norman* Montgomery family the laughingstock of the land—he wouldn't be afraid to let this *scandal* be known?"

"Oh, I would say not! Alaric would probably consider a scandal involving the Montgomery family, Garret in particular, better than a Christmas present!"

"I see," she said thoughtfully, tearing off a bit of cheese for herself. "The pieces are falling into place," she whispered happily.

"Pardon, my lady?" Armando asked politely, cupping his hand to his ear. "I didn't hear what you said."

Waving her hand impatiently for him to be quiet, she stared for a few seconds at the door, lost in her own thoughts, and then she said, "Armando, this is what I want you to do. Take this..." She began furiously scratching a note on a piece of paper left on Garret's secretary.

"Take this note to Robert of Gloucester. Tell him," she added, a speculative gleam shining from her blue eyes like a warning light as she tried to shove the note into his hand, "tell him the *virgin* bride of Garret Montgomery wishes to cuckold her new husband!"

"What?" Armando gasped, recoiling from her outstretched hand and the piece of parchment as though it had become a serpent.

"Take it!" she ordered impatiently. "Tell him this *woman* wishes to cheat Montgomery out of his *rights*. But the act, when it is complete, must be acknowledged in *public!*"

"Why… why would this *woman* wish to do this to her *husband?*" asked Armando in horror, having kept several women from time to time, each blissfully ignorant of the others' existence. The thought of them being unfaithful to him was simply beyond his comprehension.

"Because she didn't want to be married to him in the first place!" she snapped. "And second, by participating in this irrevocable act, the marriage that she didn't want in the first place becomes *invalid!*"

"A woman can be killed for such an offense against her husband," Armando said.

"I won't live as a captive or a slave," she said furiously. "I'm Princess Charlotte de Clare, and I will fight to the end for the freedom that has been denied me and my crown! And you will help, Armando, because I might live, and if I do, you will be wealthy beyond your wildest dreams."

"Yes," he said slowly, swallowing the cheese with a thoughtful frown wrinkling his skin, "I see why she *might* want to do this. But once it happens, if her husband lets her live, that is," he muttered, suddenly feeling sorry for a fellow man who was about to be put through the wringer, "her *bargaining* power is greatly diminished. Very few men enjoy used property."

Turning on him, her face contorted with rage, she stormed, "I am a *person*—not someone's property—and this is *my* body, not an object to be bartered to the highest bidder!"

"I only meant…" he stammered, sinking as far back into the alcove as he could, "that, that, a woman's *place* in society demands purity, vigilance, chastity. What else does she have?"

Her eyes were simmering, shimmering summer-blue lights, dancing with outraged fire. *What else does she have?* echoed hollowly through her brain, making her hate a society that put so little value on a woman.

"Respect," she offered quietly, with the dignity of a queen, controlling her words as she was forcing herself to control her hands to keep from clouting him on his shiny head. "*Self-respect*, even if it means she must always be alone!"

"Uh-hmmm," he murmured, sliding the butter knife across the table. "And just what would this, uh—" he almost said "crazy" but thought better of it as he pushed the knife off the table and kicked it back underneath the seat with a sigh of relief—"woman offer in the way of compensation to the man foolish enough to attempt this deadly mission?"

"Enough to make a friar forget about Heaven," she replied softly. "Or grant refuge to a fugitive, or perhaps even enough to content a bedraggled thief such as yourself."

"A home, too?" he added hopefully. After all, he wasn't getting any younger.

"For as long as he likes."

"I hate to bring this up, m'lady, but if you go through with this *scheme*, I doubt if even you will have a home. Except in Paradise," he added, making an elaborate sign of the cross across his chest and peering upward piously.

"I'm going back to the Vale," she stated matter-of-factly, "and if I'm not welcome there," she murmured, more to herself than him, "then I will go to Aberystwyth to my friend Lon and ask for his protection, and a permanent place for you."

That decided it. There was only so much traveling a person could do.

"Where shall he meet you, uh, this *woman?*" he asked eagerly, coming to attention as if she were his captain instead of a frail-looking, silver-haired beauty with an unfortunate lack of sense.

"The bathhouse," she replied quickly. "The first available moment I have. My *priest*," she added, pointing meaningfully at him, "will escort me there so that I may take a mineral bath for my rheumatism!"

"Yes, m'lady…" he replied, feeling deeply apprehensive, knowing that this beautiful bonnie nymph held the power of life and death over him and the promise of wealth and contentment, should he succeed and she stay *alive* long enough to fulfill her end of the bargain.

"Well, go!" she ordered impatiently, giving him a shove. "I haven't much time!"

Garret's face flashed unexpectedly in her mind, and his twinkling, mischievous eyes danced before her while his hands began…

"Oh," she breathed softly, suddenly flushed and very warm, "I haven't much time at all!"

Chapter 9

With the hastily-scribbled note tucked beneath his robe, Armando Bustamante walked smugly down the stairs in the manor house, right past the guards, blessing them along the way.

What a pack of fools! he thought gleefully, walking confidently through the empty room, past the gallery, in front of the fireplace, alongside the tapestried wall. *What a bunch of morons!* he gloated arrogantly. "Stupid, metal-headed soldiers," he muttered in delight as he steered himself toward the huge double doors, wondering why he had never thought to dress up as a cleric before as he walked right in front of the study.

"Whoah!" he cried in alarm as a huge hand clamped down on the back of his neck and lifted him off his feet, pulling him through the door and slamming him against the wall with the unrestrained force of a hurricane.

"My son!" he squeaked, nearly biting his tongue from the impact of the jarring blow, and then he lowered his voice an octave as he stared into a pair of magnetic blue eyes, glittering dangerously. "My son… is this any way to treat a man of the cloth?"

"Which 'cloth' might that be?" asked Garret icily, his gaze traveling from the tight-fitting robe to the bright, lemon-yellow shoes poking out beneath it. "Papal brown or circus yellow?"

Armando's confidence left him in a sigh. Being caught was beginning to become a most unpleasant habit today.

"*Who* are you?" Garret demanded coldly, twisting the material enough to make Armando squirm. "And just what the hell were you doing in my *wife's* room?"

"Nothing, your lordship," he reassured him, praying the note Lady Charlotte had given him would stay tucked safely in his drawers. "Your lady wife wished to make confession."

"Really?" he asked sarcastically. "Are clowns in the habit of hearing confession?"

"Only this clown, your lordship," Armando sorrowfully replied. "This foolish, foolish, *greedy* clown. Could you…" he hesitated, motioning at the floor as he tried to swallow and found it impossible, "could you please put me down, your grace? My nose is beginning to bleed."

Snorting, Garret dropped him to the ground.

"Unless you want to end up as target practice for my archers," he warned quietly, "you'd better tell me what is going on."

"If I do," asked Armando hopefully, angling out of habit, even though he knew he was out of bait, "what will you give me?"

"A chance to draw another breath," Garret answered lightly with a smile that froze Armando's blood and caused his spit to turn to sawdust.

"Yes," murmured Armando. "I can live with that." Sighing in resignation, he made his way over to the divan and dropped down upon it with a satisfied groan.

"I'm waiting," Garret prodded with a chilly smile as he made himself comfortable on the library's table, drawing one leg up so that he could rest his chin on his knee.

"Well," Armando began, licking his lips, "I don't really know how to say this, sir." He suddenly felt a stab of loyalty to the fair-haired lady upstairs and wondered in amazement *who* or *what* had placed such a foreign thought into his mind. "But I must beg you to go kindly on the lady, sir," he said, feeling almost guilty. "She is really quite attractive." He felt that anyone as lovely as she could be forgiven anything.

A searing glance from Garret silenced him.

"It seems," started Armando evenly, as he tried to adjust the ends of his rope belt, "that she, uhm, how would one put it?" He frowned as he fidgeted with his girdle. "It seems that she is not *happy* with her present circumstances."

"How so?" Garret asked politely, tapping his finger on his lower lip, his eyes glowing with interest.

"Oh," stated Armando with a wave of his hand, dismissing the whole situation as simply typical female hysteria. "You know *women!*" he snorted, rolling his eyes and grinning.

Getting up, he began to pace the room, acting as though he were on a stage. "Oh what, oh what, do women want?" he began very theatrically, holding up his hands in mock confusion. "The stars?" he asked, pointing elaborately to the ceiling. "No," he answered, wagging his finger at Garret and shaking his head. "The sun?" he offered, making a large circle out of his pudgy hands and then fluttering his fingers down to the floor as if they were rays of golden light. "No," he stated loudly, straightening up. "Wealth?" he questioned, raising his eyebrows as high as they would go while he turned imaginary pockets inside out. "Definitely not!" he answered with a snort. "Some say," he offered sagely, suddenly looking very wise, "beauty," and he held his hands cupped beneath his chin and fluttered his eyelids like a misshapen Venus come to life. "*You* might say love," he added, changing expressions once again, looking syrupy sweet as he pointed to Garret and received a nod of approval. "Yes," answered the aging thief, "I knew *you* would, and others might agree." He sighed sadly, as if he suspected that at least half of the human race clung to that particular deception in desperation—the *male half.* "But *I*, ARMANDO BUSTAMANTE!" he said with a smug, knowing grin, "know what it is they *really* crave!"

"Kindly enlighten me," said Garret, thoroughly amused as he watched the man prance back and forth with a growing smile of pleasure.

"They want," he said quietly, cupping his hand to his mouth and bending as close to the handsome knight as he dared. "They want," he whispered, looking suspiciously around the room as though he suspected spies. "They want *their way!*"

"No!" exclaimed Garret, pretending to be shocked.

"Oh, yes!" he replied adamantly, shaking his head vigorously up and down as though this were an offense to man and God. "They want to do what they want, when they want, whenever they want, *just like a man!*"

"What a revolting thought!" Garret murmured with a wicked grin, suddenly seeing Charlotte in front of him with her hands soldered to her hips and her hair swirling around her, looking as though she would like to hit him squarely in the nose.

"Oh, I agree!" Armando enthusiastically replied, rocking back and forth on his heels, deep in thought. "You see," he told Garret eagerly, knowing this thoroughly *masculine* man would understand him completely, "I have *three*, no, *four* women," he added up, holding up one hand and counting.

"*Wives?*" asked Garret with a merry grin, relaxing against the table. He was beginning to like this impostor very much!

"Well, they all call themselves such," he said, shrugging, "and I see no reason to deprive such simple creatures of their illusions."

"Ah!" Garret sighed, immediately understanding. "Do these 'simple creatures' know about each other?" he asked curiously, folding his arms across his solid chest.

"Oh, Heaven forbid!" Armando said quickly, his eyes widening in shock. "Why, if that gaggle of geese ever got together, this would be one cooked goose, I can tell you!" he muttered fearfully, shuddering at the vivid mental image parading across his mind of four women with cleavers flashing, chasing a fat, bald-headed goose dressed in a monk's habit. Gulping, he closed his eyes as they caught him, torturing himself with one last vision of feathers—his feathers—flying in the air…

"Armando," Garret prodded gently, drawing the suddenly-ashen thief out of his reverie, "this is all very interesting, but I really don't see what it has to do with *my* wife."

"Oh," Armando said, recovering from his day-mare. "Yes. *Your* wife." He nodded in understanding as he hiked up his robe, revealing his brightly-colored clothing beneath. "We *men* have to stick together," he told Garret with a grin, and he pulled his trews out as far as they would go, looking inside until he found the note, now a little smudged and moist with sweat. "We men have to stick together." He treated the sentence like the Universal Anthem of Men, feeling a kinship to this dark-haired giant simply because they happened to share the same gender—and enemy. "We stand," saluted Armando, waving the note in the air, "while they sit!"

"Absolutely," agreed Garret, laughing at Armando's wonderfully concise logic. He had said with a few words what philosophers had taken volumes to relate. "And," Garret added, shaking a finger in the air in mock anger, "we men must stand together!"

"Otherwise," Armando warned, shuddering involuntarily, finishing his newfound friend's train of thought, "those *women* would have each of us sporting a leash like a dog, and sitting by the hearth at their beck and call *every day!*"

"So true," agreed Garret, snapping the note open with a flourish of his wrist. He began to read the urgent scrawl with intense interest.

Armando watched nervously, knowing that women had driven men to homicidal rages for far less heinous schemes than this one. But, to Armando's surprise, Garret threw back his head, his dark waves of hair spilling down his back, shimmering in the muted light. *And he laughed*, a rich, deep chuckle that seemed to begin at his toes and curl up through his body like smoke, becoming a full-blown roar.

"So," he murmured to himself a few minutes later, wiping merry tears away from his eyes, "she *wishes* to lose her virginity," remembering his chivalrous promise to take her only if she were *willing*, something he had thoroughly regretted at least a hundred times today. "Well…"

Suddenly hard and ready and very *hot*, he flexed his brawny muscles eagerly, continuing to laugh while fire glowed impishly from his midnight-blue eyes. "I think I know just the man for the job!" he said with a roguish grin, his eyes glittering wickedly. "Armando, go to Robert as Lady Charlotte instructed you to. But tell him," he paused as he collected his thoughts, "tell him to meet the lady by the garden gate, where the old stone bench is. But first," he added with a sly wink, "creep back upstairs and tell the good *lady* that you overheard the guards say that her husband will be gone for two days next week. Set the rendezvous at the bathhouse for then. Do you understand?"

"But if Robert is to meet her at the gate," Armando murmured, playing out the game on his fingers, "then why must she go… Oh! Oh!" he said suddenly, as though he'd been pinched. Once again, understanding dawned slowly in his mind as he looked at Garret's twinkling eyes. "Oh, I see!" he added slowly, his smile growing broader by the second. "To you, sir!" Suddenly sober, he kneeled before the dark-haired knight reverently, deep respect shining from his worshipful eyes. "And to the future honor of all *men!*"

"Indeed," replied Garret with a devilish grin, pretending to knight the kneeling thief with the opened letter, tapping him on each shoulder and then on his shining pate. "And to the future *deflowering* of all women!"

"It's war, then. isn't it, sir?" asked Armando, scrambling to his feet, breathless with excitement.

"It always has been," Garret replied lightly, feeling the blood pound in his veins as he gazed at the intricate, beautifully sculptured chess pieces he loved so much on the table beside him. With a sly smile, he placed the bishop and the black knight against the white queen. "Check," he said evenly, cornering the only *female* piece on the board with a smile of sheer delight as he winked confidently at his friend.

Chapter 10

"And I say!" shouted an enraged Halfdanson as he rose from the table, striking it with his withered stump, "that we take the manor *NOW*—not play some child game of cat and mouse!"

"Really," Robert murmured, straightening the lace adorning his cuffs. "You are a most quarrelsome beast!"

"Beast am I!" roared the red-haired giant, flinging himself across the polished table at the effeminate-looking young man perched on the other side.

Robert, pale brown hair, pale brown eyes wide with shock, instinctively moved away from the lunging figure, toppling over backward in his chair as the Viking landed squarely on his chest, pinning him to the floor, while his one good hand tried to choke the life out of the impertinent younger man.

"Enough," Alaric of York ordered quietly, and Halfdanson felt the tip of a sword pressed against the back of his neck. Pausing, he was slyly calculating his chances against both these men when a *Whoosh!* of bowstrings being pulled back caught his attention and he remembered the guards.

"I meant no harm!" he offered, grinning, though still sitting astraddle Robert with his hand poised in the air. "I was just having a little fun with your nephew!" He rose from the cowering youth, but not before he slammed his knee against the younger man's chin, causing him to bite his tongue and make it bleed as he cried out in pain. "See, what a clumsy fool I am!" he said, sizing up Alaric with a practiced eye as he turned around, wanting nothing better than to wipe the perpetually superior look off his arrogant features with the edge of a blade. But not yet. Now he needed him.

"Clumsy," Alaric agreed, studying the lumbering giant with contempt. "And stupid."

A scowl replaced Halfdanson's sly grin as he stared at the pale man before him. Black and white; night and day. Alaric was a study in sharp lines and extremes. Black eyes. Black eyebrows. Black hair, white bloodless skin, and sharp-edged, high cheekbones. Though not tall, he radiated a dangerous power. Pure Saxon, he refused to speak French, hating the conquering Normans above everything else in his life. They had taken his birthright. Reduced him to a mere retainer on *his* land instead of its rightful ruler. They did not recognize his crest nor his nobility, but had taken everything away from him except his life, and what was that worth now?

Sighing, Alaric took his place at the head of the large rectangular table, motioning for Halfdanson to sit down.

Assembled in the huge dining hall at Gloucester, seated around the old oak table, was a curious band of infamous strangers, brought together for one purpose: to reduce the House of Montgomery to ruins.

"This," Alaric began, pointing to a large map spread out across the table, "is an exact replica of the bay at Pembroke, and this," he pointed to a drawing of a castle on the upper right-hand corner, complete with windows, doors, cellars, and various measurements, "is the original design of the manor."

"How is a *picture* going to get us into Pembroke?" Nell Gwynn asked, pouting.

"This picture isn't, Nell," Alaric quickly informed her, letting his gaze wander over the beautiful creature with the flaming hair sitting next to him. "*You* are."

Narrowing her heavy-lidded hazel eyes, she surveyed the dark-haired man before her critically.

"How is someone," she asked, moistening her full, curving lips with her tongue as she tipped her head back, exposing the long, slender curve of her throat and the full, rounded mounds of her breasts, "as *helpless* as myself going to do that?"

A deep, brittle laugh erupted from Alaric's throat. "*Helpless.* Nell? Don't make me laugh! Once mistress of our *beloved* king? Helpless? You are about as helpless as I am, my dear."

"It is said," Alaric told the group of assembled mercenaries, brigands, and Vikings, "that a Norman never refuses to show hospitality to *anyone* who comes to his door. Surely he will not turn away two *guests* as pleasant as Nell and myself?" With a mirthless grin, he rose, drawing Nell to her feet beside him. "You see, manors were built to keep people *out.* But doors are easily opened from the *inside.*"

With a victorious flash of dark eyes at the grinning Halfdanson, he turned his attention back to the woman. "Shall we take a walk, Nell?" he asked with an inviting grin.

"Whatever gives you *pleasure,* my lord," she purred, playing the docile female so well.

"Ahh." He sighed, a dark, sadistic fire gleaming in his eyes. "I like that, Nell. Whatever gives me pleasure!" His hand dropped below her waist as they walked out of the room and into the darkened corridor. Nell's laughter filled the air.

Chapter 11

The plan was half complete. Armando had told her that Garret would be gone for two days and that, if Robert was agreeable to her plan, she would be free by the third—one way or the other.

Grimly determined, she finished dressing, lacing the bodice of light blue silk that Sparrow had laid out for her. It was time to take a walk and assess her situation in more detail.

"Bishop," she murmured, and her ever-attentive friend rose from his pallet by the fire and followed her as she made her way out of the door. As soon as she entered the hall, two guards fell into step behind her. Down the stairs she walked with her head held high. Two more guards appeared and flanked her on both sides. She waited irritably as the main door was opened for her.

Sunlight streamed into the shadowed hall as she entered Pembroke's main courtyard—the common ground that she could observe out of Garret's bedroom window.

Noise and light greeted her as she began her walk. Being out of the room for the first time would have been exhilarating if the guards hadn't surrounded her. Along the stalls she strolled, looking at the wares. Everywhere she went, people stopped their chatter and stared, gaping with open curiosity at their future mistress, until the courtyard became as silent as the bowels of an empty church.

Trying not to pay any attention to this, Charlotte observed the main drawbridge and the side door, noting how many guards were posted on either side. The wall was high, over fifteen feet, and she saw with dismay that the stone was well kept; there were no cracks large enough to hold her feet and no ivy to help her climb.

Stopping near the cheese woman's heavily-laden wagon, she happened to glance up. The woman, with heavy, doughy features and stringy brown hair, was leering at her, her gaze bouncing back and forth between the beautiful, delicate beauty and the gaudily-stained red sheet flying high above the courtyard.

Noticing her lewd grin with a feeling of disgust, Charlotte wanted to scream, "It isn't what you think!" But she knew better than to betray this secret, so she bit her tongue, reaching for a piece of cheese and popping it into her mouth, chewing as hard as she could as she felt her cheeks glowing a brighter pink by the second.

"Do you enjoy staring?" she asked the woman quietly, pinning her with her eyes as she tried to work up enough saliva to swallow the suddenly dry cheese.

The old woman grinned, purposely letting her eyes slide to the sheet and back to Charlotte with an "I know what *you've* been doing!" look all over her face.

"You like a little show, is that it, then?" Charlotte asked slowly, biting back the urge to slap the silly grin off the woman's leering face. "How's this?" She looked at her nose, causing both of her azure-hued eyes to cross. "Or this?" Her voice rose in intensity as she turned and wiggled her petite rump rudely in the woman's startled face.

"Cor!" shouted the cheese woman in surprise. "Such manners!"

Charlotte only laughed. Turning around once again, she hooked her thumbs in her ears. "You want manners? I'll show you manners!" she said loudly, crossing her eyes and sticking her tongue out as far as it would go as she did a little dance, jiggling back and forth and chanting, "Nyah-nyah-nyah!" in a perfectly childish voice, not caring who saw her ridiculous display.

"Well!" the cheese woman indignantly exclaimed, reaching for her ragged leg of lamb as the villagers yelled their approval. "Lady or not, I'll teach you to poke fun at an old woman!" She snorted, swinging the bedraggled club which had taken so much abuse from the indignant soldier that it had split in half, and the upper shank dangled by only a thin piece of sinew.

"Ya-ya-ya! You can't catch me!" Charlotte chanted, easily dodging the woman's crippled blows.

"Fresh little Welsh witch!" the red-faced woman shouted, her cheeks puffing up angrily and her ill-gotten coppers falling unnoticed to the ground as she kept on swinging and the crowd kept on cheering while Charlotte kept on ducking, laughing gaily the entire time.

"Nosy old crone!" she snapped. "Nosy, nosy, stinky, *smelly* cheese lady!" she chanted merrily, jiggling around even more wildly, alternating between bouts of sticking out her tongue and crossing her eyes, thoroughly enjoying herself.

"Perhaps," said a familiar voice that nearly stopped her heart, "you're sticking that thing out at the wrong person."

"Oh, Lord," she murmured, swallowing hard, hoping that she would simply die, cease to exist, fall into some crack or crevice, or blow away like a leaf in the wind—do *anything* to escape that insidiously masculine voice.

Closing her eyes, she pulled her fingers from her ears, where they seemed to have taken root, and wished with all her heart that she could swallow her offending tongue.

"The only thing I would like to stick at you," she forced herself to say in a tight little voice, "is the sharp edge of a knife."

"Indeed," he said with interest, coming around to stand in front of her and blocking most of the sunlight with his huge form. "There are a great many things I would like to stick at you, my little wife, one thing I can think of in particular!" he said slowly, giving her a lecherous wink and flexing his rounded pectorals at her, which were exactly at eye level, causing her to take a stumbling step backward.

"You're impossible!" she stammered, whirling around.

Again he was there, blocking her exit as he placed both of his brawny arms on either side of her, fencing her in against the cheese woman's cart.

He loved to tease her. He saw what she could not possibly see.

"I think you like me, Charlotte," he said confidently. "Even if you won't admit it to yourself. And you know," he murmured, his eyes glowing dangerously bright, "I really am very good—very good indeed!" he assured her in a lazily husky voice as his gaze traveled boldly over her form, settling possessively on her lips.

"Umm!" he murmured, licking his lips as if anticipating some sweet, honeyed delight.

"That may be true," she replied scornfully, pretending to ignore his sexy, pouting, *moist* mouth. "But the question is, at *what?*"

"Perhaps we should find out," he murmured encouragingly, moving a step nearer, flexing his muscles, his smile deepening while she watched his masculine display with hypnotic interest, utterly fascinated by the play of light on his pearly teeth and the shiny wet tip of his pale pink tongue.

"Oh!" she said when she looked at him. Her body reacted to his presence as naturally as the earth turning toward the sun. It was physical and beyond her control. He was right. She did like him. There was something about his presence that she understood; a kindred spirit perhaps, something which attracted her despite the circumstances. She struggled against it, but it was rather like the oceans resisting the pull of the moon; the tide reacted to the elemental magnetic force as naturally as her body reacted to him.

"You're a beast!" she shouted, shoving past him. "And you're not *good*, either! Not at anything!" One more step away from him, and her foot caught in the hem of her dress, sending her crashing clumsily to the ground. "What?!" she spat, tasting dirt and hearing *laughter* all around her, his laughter rising loudly above the others.

"I'll show you!" she muttered angrily as she pushed herself up off the ground. Keeping her head down more out of anger than humiliation and her fists clenched tightly at her sides, she stalked across the open courtyard. Her dress was covered in dust, and her pale, beautiful blonde hair fell loose from its pins around her shoulders. Charlotte admitted to herself that she felt positively homicidal. "You just wait! I'll show you!"

And suddenly *he* was walking beside her at a leisurely pace as she hurried for the door and her salvation.

"Don't you have something better to do than harass me?" she hissed. She refused to look at him.

"Actually, I do." he admitted, brushing back an ebony wave from his forehead as he thought about the red-haired giant who had escaped the Gate. "But teasing you is so much fun!"

"You're a dog!" she spat.

"You *like* dogs," he replied easily.

"You're a *swine!*" she countered savagely, kicking a clod of dirt and wishing it were him.

"Interesting," he noted casually, never breaking his stride. "You say that you're my… *equal.* So, I suppose, if you are my equal and I'm a swine, that would make *you* a little *piggy!*"

He chuckled evilly.

"You're a perfect—"

"Yes, I know," he admitted arrogantly. "I've often been told how incredibly *perfect* I am. Say, shouldn't you be walking a few steps *behind* me?"

"What!" she snapped incredulously, stopping dead in her tracks to look up at the man who was looking down at her so seriously.

"A *few steps behind,*" he repeated slowly. "The *proper* place for a woman," he added innocently, pointing to a spot directly behind him on the ground while he rocked back and forth on his heels, whistling a silly, meaningless tune and waiting for her to *heel.*

"I'll show you proper!" She swung all hundred and five pounds of herself against him, hitting him right in the middle of his stomach, nearly breaking her hand. "Ow!" she shouted.

She stared at him. No human being was that hard. He must be made of stone. She cringed when she heard him laugh, feeling the hairs on the back of her neck rise in response.

"Don't you know, little girl, when you've been beaten?" he said quietly. He gazed at her and his beautiful blue eyes were warm and incredibly soft. Secretly, he felt very protective of her; somehow wishing he could tuck her next to him and protect her from the world and herself.

She was lethal. Garret knew that. He had watched from the tower as she wielded her sword. The old guard had trained her well. Her archery skills exceeded every knight in his service. His admiration grew as he watched her on horseback, riding at breakneck speed over the marshes, hurdling fences as if they didn't exist. She had absolutely no fear, and he found her courage and uncompromising attitude, especially in her situation, admirable.

Garret respected her.

"I haven't been beaten yet, and certainly not by *you!*" she retorted angrily, still shaking her reddened knuckles up and down.

"You can't beat me," he told her simply, in a gentle, fatherly tone, baiting her for the pure hell of it. "Women were made for men, out of a man's *rib.*" He pointed to a spot just below his barely concealed nipple, and suddenly Charlotte thought of a brace of ribs roasting on a fire and wondered what *he'd* look like, spitted above the flames.

Smiling wickedly at the vivid mental image she was entertaining, she looked him squarely in the eye and replied, "I can do *anything* you can do!"

"*You!*" He snorted, laughing. "You, my dear little *wife*, could never do everything I can do. Therefore," he deduced, with typical male logic and a shrug of his broad shoulders, "*you* cannot possibly be equal with me, because *we* men are superior to *you* women," he stated chauvinistically with fatalistic pride. "It is only natural that we are superior—a biological fact that can't be overlooked. So, *little girl*, why don't you accept your place in life and behave like a good wife should?

"I've been patient—very patient—kind, understanding, tolerant."

Unknown to Charlotte, Garret had stood between her and his father, and between her and the condemnation of his society, and he would continue to be her protector and her friend—the man the law recognized as her husband—a man who couldn't help but fall in love with her and her indomitable spirit, holding onto a thread of hope as he recognized that his princess *liked* him and for now, that was enough.

"What?" she snapped. "Standing *behind* a man instead of *beside* him?"

Sighing, as if her mind were just too simple to understand certain indisputable facts, he murmured softly, mockingly sweet, "*Darling*, it is *behind* men that pedestals are erected, upon which objects of beauty and devotion are placed."

"I don't want to be on a pedestal," she cried, pouting obstinately, staring into his gorgeous face, "like some perfect piece of stone to be admired as a possession of some foolish, egotistical man!" She advanced like a miniature whirlwind toward the dark-haired giant, who stepped back in surprise at the fury burning in her eyes. "I want to stand beside my *chosen* mate—and if I can't have that, then I choose to stand alone!"

Her words stung Garret. He wanted to murmur, "*Choose me, and I will spend the rest of my life making you happy*," but he didn't. Instead, she kindled his anger and he retorted: "How can you possibly think you are equal to a man?" His eyes narrowed perceptibly as he studied her face, readying himself for the next attack. "A woman's place is behind a man, *serving him.* Or on her back with her legs poking heavenward, *serving him.* For pity's sake, woman," he purred, letting his hand slide innocently against her waist as though to pull her close, "that's all women know how to do!"

"I can do anything you can do!" she challenged, swatting his overly friendly hand and swallowing hard as she remembered the rock she had just recently hit that was supposed to be his stomach.

Shaking his head in wonder, he smiled and looked around. The entire population of Pembroke had been watching the confrontation with keen interest.

Seeing what he was looking for, Garret walked to the wheelwright's stall and picked up a three-foot rod of iron nearly an inch thick in diameter. Holding it out to her to show what he had, he placed the bar over his shoulders like a yoke and grasped both ends in his huge hands, with an indrawn breath and a sound like the growl of a lion.

Charlotte watched in amazement as the thick shaft began to curl inward, more and more, while Garret strained like a dark-haired Hercules until the two ends overlapped, and he had a circle of iron curling around his broad shoulders.

Smiling smugly, he lifted it off and cast it at her feet, sure of his victory. Much to his surprise, his petite little wife with the fiery blue eyes grabbed another rod from the wheelwright's stand, held it up with both hands for her husband to see, stalked over to the front gate, went through it—trailed by Garret and most of the townspeople—and shoved and twisted the rod into the ground. Pausing to make sure it was positioned just the way she wanted, she turned and walked with a determined stride back into the gatehouse. She pulled a huge wooden lever with all her might, releasing the drawbridge.

"Look out!" Garret shouted.

People of all sizes and shapes rolled or dove for cover as the huge gate came crashing down on the metal bar with a horrendous creak and a frightening, two-ton WHIRRR!

Peering out of the gatehouse and looking quite unperturbed as she watched her husband brush the dust from *his* clothes—glaring angrily at the woman who had just tried to smash him like a bug—she began to slowly crank the bridge up, grunting and sweating with the effort.

"Let's see," she murmured, surveying the wooden sprocket with its deeply grooved teeth as she slid the lever back into place, securing the gate once again. "There," she said with satisfaction, "all better!" Wiping her soiled hands on her new gown with a total lack of concern, she walked haughtily over to the group of glaring people.

Placing her hands once again on her hips and spreading her legs wide, she gazed pointedly from the bar, which was demolished, to her glaring husband, with a fiendish smirk lighting her features, making him wonder how he could ever have thought she looked like an angel with such devilish eyes.

"Brute force is a poor substitute for intelligence," she quipped mockingly, turning her back on him with a flourish and punctuating her remark with an insulting little wiggle as she stalked back to the manor house. The townsfolk moved back silently, respectfully keeping as far out of her way as they could.

Garret watched her leave in utter amazement, looking from her to the smashed iron rod, then back again. Suddenly, in his mind, he saw the white queen trapped on his chessboard by his zealous black bishop and eager knight. Her eyes opened and she came to life. With a proud "Humph!" she hiked up her skirts and jumped easily to one side, out of danger and into safety, sticking her tongue out as far as it would go—at *him!*

"My move," he whispered with a crooked smile, throwing back

his head and laughing uproariously at the antics of his beautiful wife. "My turn!" he vowed with a grin while the cheese woman looked at him suspiciously, clutching her battered leg of lamb to her breast, wondering just what sort of deviltry was blowing in the wind this fair day.

"You like me, Princess Charlotte de Clare-Montgomery, and I vow, one day, you'll love me."

Chapter 12

Robert of Gloucester was a brown man. Brown hair, brown eyes, brown, brown, brown. The only remarkable thing about this brown man was his image of himself. In his eyes he felt as if he was God's gift to women, a treasure meant to be spread as thinly as possible amongst the fairer sex.

Sniffing at his perfumed hanky, he shuddered as he remembered the vulgar Viking his uncle had given refuge to. Really. He couldn't understand all the fuss that Alaric made about things. Saxon, Norman, Celt, what was the difference?

The only things that really mattered were gentility, nobility, *love*. Ah, whatever language that word was spoken in, be it French or Anglo-Saxon, it made no difference to him. Neither did his loyalties. He had the amazing ability to get along with whoever was in power, fondly thinking of himself as a great diplomat. But the truth was that Robert of Gloucester was a cowardly fool.

"Your lordship," called one young steward, breaking into his reverie with a timid smile. "There is a priest outside who wishes to speak with you. He says it is most urgent."

"Blast!" shouted Robert, wondering just which one of his recent liaisons had come to the cleric's attention. "Well," he said irritably with a wave of his hand, "send the man in!" The boy was gone in a second.

Robert went to a chest, looking for a few coins to redeem his lecherous soul.

"Your lordship" greeted him soberly from his door, and he turned, plastering a smile on his sullen face as he counted out several silver zecchins.

"Yes, Father! So good to see you!" he gushed, placing his hand on the back of the huge monk and escorting him into the room. "What can I do for you?"

"I have a note for you, m'lord," he replied humbly, careful to keep his eyes downcast as he handed the folded parchment to the curious man.

"A note?" he asked, a worried frown wrinkling his average features and giving him at least the look of character for a moment.

"Yes, your lordship," murmured Armando, suddenly developing an itch in the worst possible place, hoping Robert would get to the business at hand so that he could step out back.

Frowning thoughtfully, the young man opened the letter as though he expected a snake to jump out at him and then he read it, his eyes bulging wildly as he read it again and again, making sure his eyes weren't playing tricks.

"What sort of nonsense is this?" he demanded.

"No nonsense, m'lord," answered Armando, beginning to fidget as he tried not to think about his itch.

"This… this young woman wishes to, uhm, *meet* me?"

"Oh, yes, most definitely, sir," answered Armando, chafing his thighs together to try and relieve the niggling sensation of prickly skin beneath his sweating jewels. "She has long heard of your beauty and virility, and she wishes to experience it for herself."

"Indeed," Robert answered with a grin, swallowing Armando's lie as readily as if it were the sweetest elixir. "And she is," he suddenly frowned, "a *comely* woman?"

"Oh, more than that!" Armando honestly offered, seeing the little flaxen-haired spitfire vividly in his mind and swallowing as he remembered how easily she had placed the knife against his throat.

"More than comely?" prodded Robert, his interest growing by the second. Virgins, *real* virgins—not some experienced girl pretending otherwise—were incredibly rare.

"Oh, yes!" gushed Armando. "She is exquisite!" He molded a petite little hourglass shape in the air. "Eyes like a summer sky after a rain, lips as pink as a newly-opened rose, breasts as ripe as autumn fruit—"

"Enough!" moaned Robert, sure that he was in love again. "Tell your mistress I will meet her at the garden gate as she requires, flying to her side on the wings of love… most profound!"

"No doubt," muttered Armando, rolling his eyes as he turned to take his leave, scratching himself as he walked out of the door, relieved on at least two accounts.

Pacing in Garret's room, Charlotte heard a shout in the courtyard outside.

"What now?" she whispered, running to the casement to peer outside.

Below, in the muted afternoon light, with the sun's bonnie golden glow hidden behind masses of gray clouds and the typical fog rolling in from the sea, Garret stood in the center of the courtyard, shouting orders.

"Torin!" he bellowed, drawing his sword for the hundredth time over the wheelwright's whirring whetstone. "Get a move on it! It'll be dark in less than an hour, and I doubt if we'll have much of a moon."

"I'm hurrying!" muttered a slender man surrounded by squires who were diligently encasing their young master in layer after layer of metal. First came thin links of chain covering his breast and groin. Then sleeves of the same, then interlinked metal pieces shaped into chest plates and leggings, and gloves of mail. Topping all of this steel was a conical helmet sporting a visor.

All the men in the courtyard were similarly attired except for Garret. Standing up, he tested the edge of the sword against his finger. With a satisfied grunt, as a thin line of blood appeared simply from the act of touching his flesh to the cold metal, he slid his sword into his scabbard. He wore no metal, no shining plates of tempered steel—nothing except leather trews held securely in place by four-inch straps crossed tightly over his burly chest. Reaching up, he smoothed back his midnight hair, tying it in place with a leather thong.

"By the saints' blood!" he cursed. "Where is my horse!"

As if in answer to his question, a shrill whinny pierced the air, and a huge, solid black stallion came clattering out of the stables with half a dozen stable lads running in terror. His saddle was half on and half off. Like his master, this horse wore no armor, no footcloth reaching to his high-stepping knees, no hindering heavy plate adorning his tossing, screaming head. His power was as evident as his master's.

Mesmerized, Charlotte watched as Garret walked boldly toward the outraged brute, talking softly, inaudibly, until the great beast stood still with his ears pricked forward, intently watching the man who held out his hand. As though in a last attempt to show that he belonged to no one, the stallion reared back, bringing his powerful, slashing hooves up into the air in a threatening display of power.

"Be careful there!" Charlotte called out to the man she thought she hated. He was going out to fight for his people, to push the Viking storm away from the coast.

Garret paused and turned to look at her. There was a moment of profound silence between them, an understanding.

You like me, he thought. The knowledge that she cared, even a little, helped.

He smiled at her, and Charlotte thought the sun had just appeared from behind the clouds above. She was confused in his presence, drawn as the tides to the shore by his smile.

He nodded and turned back to the horse. He held out his hand and the animal settled down, walking two steps toward Garret in an act of resigned submission.

"Arion," she heard him croon, stroking the glossy black head as he straightened the saddle and slid the bridle over his head. He cinched the strap tightly, then leapt easily onto his back. And as if he had been conscious of his wife watching him the entire time, he looked directly up at her window, speaking to her with his gaze and smiling roguishly.

"Aren't you going to wish your husband a safe journey, wife?" he asked, holding the straining beast easily with one hand firmly wrapped around the reins.

"The Lord is said to look after fools and little children," she said.

He paused as though considering her words. When he looked at her, she caught her breath. It was his masculine beauty, his arresting and unsettling blue eyes and wayward ebony hair. He smiled at her and she swore a thousand suns instantly flared to life.

"Into which category do I fall?" he said. Emotionally distant of necessity, he set aside his armor for a moment—long enough for her to witness her husband standing amid staring townsfolk, letting down his guard to publicly ask his wife her opinion of himself.

"Take your pick," she said. Her reply was saucy and meant to maintain distance; to get close to him, she feared, would bring disaster.

A scowl replaced his smile, and Charlotte pretended to study the bulging black clouds with interest until she heard him laugh.

"*Adieu*, my beloved enemy," Garret said softly beneath his breath.

His breath quickened. The gentle, rumbling timbre of his voice did little to conceal his anger.

In the distance a shard of lightning bit through the building clouds, followed by the growl of thunder.

"See if you can find some way to torment yourself, my love, while I'm gone," he said. Then he laughed and shouted to his men: "We ride!"

The group of suited knights with a bareheaded barbarian in the lead clattered across the courtyard and out through the gate.

Suddenly depressed and refusing to admit why, Charlotte watched them leave until they were completely out of sight. Straining her ears, she listened for the last beat of the horses' hooves, until there was nothing left but the sound of her beating heart and the echo of distant thunder.

Chapter 13

Mist and moonlight greeted Charlotte on May Day Eve. It marked the return of spring. The world, once withered and white as an old woman, had freed herself from the shackles of darkness and cold to become a maiden once again.

Bonfires lit the countryside. The music of lute and harp filled the air, accompanied by the merry sweet laughter of pursued women playing hard to get and the deeper groans and pleas of pursuing males bent on their prizes. It was the fabled Night of the Phoenix, a night of midnight magic, a night of desire and dreams fulfilled beneath a pale moon.

In the courtyard, like a huge phallic symbol thrust promisingly against a midnight sky, a maypole stood with colored streamers draped from the top, ready for the maidens' hands and gentle dance.

It was a time of fresh promises and new beginnings—a night of sweet awakening and a night meant for love.

"Now," Charlotte murmured gloomily to herself, "what does one wear to one's 'deflowering'?" She critically surveyed her choices, finally settling on a simple black dressing gown and matching cloak, in keeping with her mood. Picking up her camisoles of lace and elegant satin undergarments, she looked at them. "Waste of time," she said. "The more I wear," she reasoned, a dangerous gleam in her eyes, "the longer it will take to get them off!" So with a simple, vicious toss of her hand, her dainties were thrown to the floor and the black frock was pulled on over her bare skin with a savage tug.

"Calm," she whispered to herself as she smoothed her dress. "I must remain calm." But she had started to sweat, even though the breeze blowing through the opened window was misty and cool.

Swallowing, she tried to think of this evening as a necessary evil, something that had to be done. Just like the time when she was ten and a fever had overtaken her, and she had to be bled. Leeches, all over her arms! Shuddering, she recalled that incident all too well; the black loathsome slugs were feeding off her, growing larger as she watched. She had gotten so weak and so dizzy she was sure she would faint, but the fever left her in the infected blood they drank, and the leeches were removed, sated, bloated to ten times their normal size.

Nothing to it. Like tonight. Nothing to it.

In her mind she imagined a chess board and saw the great Sword of Wales, gleaming with silver light like the lesser glory of hidden moonlight, illuminating the board. The white queen moved, a brazen tactic, castling the white king. For the briefest moment, Lon ap Llewelyn's face impressed itself on her mind and she closed her eyes. The queen must sacrifice herself to draw the black knight into battle. In order to take his prize, the lines of fate would open, like dominoes falling from an irrevocable act—an act of infidelity that would nullify her marriage to Lord Garret Montgomery and deny the Norman knight access to the Crown and Sword of Wales forever.

She saw the bishops armed with their canon laws.

"Shall I die a thousand nights, if my lack of courage fail me and I surrender my birthright to an invader; or rather pass the scepter to one who is worthy by birth and blood though I martyr my good name and lay with another?

"It is only my body. What am I compared to a kingdom? Who am I if I do not love my people more than myself?

"I would be unworthy of the blood of kings which flows in my veins and the Crown, which I hold in my hands.

"Only God can make a king."

Charlotte was determined that the Sword and Crown of Wales be given to Lon ap Llewelyn and she was willing to risk her fortune, future and life on a scandalous act of infidelity to ensure that no other than a Welsh prince inherit the throne of Wales.

"Forever free," she whispered. "My people!"

Her eyes were fierce and her skin pale.

"He'll kill you, mistress, for what you are going to do tonight," said Sparrow beneath her breath.

"He'll try," said the princess with a deadly gleam in her eyes.

The maid would not venture down that path again. She shuddered. The conflict of nobles was a war of titans. Sparrow watched them from afar at games—jousting, fighting with sword, ax and rapier, hurtling cross country on palfreys outfitted for war; the sound of steel upon steel and blood-curdling oaths echoing for miles. They gave no ground and expected none. They fought to win, and no one bragged at being second best; their crests were adorned with lions, signifying courage, nobility, royalty, strength, stateliness and valor.

The Crown of Wales was at stake and Sparrow knew that the princess did not want a Norman knight to ascend the throne, even if it were to cost her life.

"Mistress?" said Sparrow sweetly. "Is your rheumatism hurting?"

She looked at her mistress and understood. Not waiting for a reply, she continued to turn the comforters down on the huge oak four-poster bed, her tongue immediately slipping into gear. "Me mum swears by onion poultices. I'll have one ready for you to put on when you get back from the baths, if your back is still hurting you, that is!"

Smiling wryly and managing a dark little chuckle while her eyes flashed dangerously, Charlotte didn't think it would be her back that would need a poultice when she returned to her rooms tonight. The thought made her close her eyes and groan aloud.

"Mistress!" cried Sparrow sharply, now truly concerned as she made her way to the foot of the bed. Her lady seemed to be in a great deal of pain and looked ill.

"I'm fine, Sparrow," Charlotte reassured the young girl, patting her on one rounded solid shoulder. "Really." And then a thought occurred to her as she listened to all the young people laughing and loving below. "Why are you here, Sparrow? Don't you *want* to be out there with the others, enjoying the festivities?"

"Oh, I don't know." She sighed, turning around to look at her lady with a guilty blush on her cheeks. "I've been talking with that new priest of yours lately. I confessed to him that I have been having some perfectly wicked, sinful thoughts as of late!"

"You told 'Father' Armando this?" Charlotte asked incredulously, thinking of the lecherous, unscrupulous man with a mental groan.

"Oh, yes!" she answered seriously. "I told him all about how lately I have to practically stand before a fire several times a day just to dry the wet between my legs and that my privates burn just like the fires in Hell."

"Good heavens, Sparrow," Charlotte said, She shut her eyes as she thought of what a man like Armando would do with such knowledge. It was like inviting a fox into a henhouse and handing him a fork. "And this confession, did Father Armando offer any suggestions?" she asked, holding her breath as she waited for Sparrow's reply, hoping for the best.

"Yes, he did!" she answered gaily, her bright brown eyes twinkling cheerfully. "He had some perfectly wonderful ideas, as a matter of fact!"

"I should've known!" Charlotte groaned, forgetting completely about her nefarious tryst out of concern for her young and naive maid. "Well, Sparrow," she asked gloomily, holding the girl by the shoulders so that she could look into her easily readable face, "what did the merry monk suggest?"

"Well," Sparrow answered slowly, wondering why her mistress seemed so concerned about her but feeling a deep sense of pleasure that this beautiful, powerful woman cared about *her*, "Father Armando said that most likely I was *possessed!*" The last word was whispered, nearly hissed, as though Sparrow expected the Devil himself to pop up from under the bed at the mention of one of his minions' wicked tricks and poke her in the butt with his red-tipped pitchfork for telling on one of his kind.

"Possessed?" Charlotte questioned with an ironic snort, her eyebrows shooting up cynically.

"Yes!" Sparrow replied, her eyes grown impossibly round and shiny as she remembered how the corpulent man with the wonderfully warm brown eyes had placed his hand upon her head and began to shake as though filled with some divine energy while chanting words in—what did he call it? Oh, yes, Sanskrit! Or was it Saint's Skirt? She mused in utter confusion, scratching her head.

"Sparrow?" Charlotte prompted impatiently. "What did Armando *say?*"

"Say?" she murmured, adjusting her thoughts with difficulty. It was like sweeping up dust during a whirlwind—a nearly impossible task. But she rallied, remembering the cleric's wise words. "He said," she whispered, her voice gaining momentum with every word, "that I was possessed with the spirit of lust!" She blurted out the last part all in one breath, feeling for a moment like someone special, different; like the wave breaking free from the ocean to rise above and be noticed for one brief, shining moment.

"No doubt a spirit he is quite familiar with?" Charlotte questioned sarcastically.

"Oh, of course!" Sparrow answered breathlessly, thinking about how wonderfully knowledgeable the friar had seemed when questioning her about all her burning thoughts, wanting to know all her secret sins in detail. "Why, the man's a saint!" she gushed, following this with a wondrous sigh. "He told me that tonight, after he returns from ministering to you at the baths, he will meet with *me* in my room and together we will hold a vigil—light candles, everything—and pray for my salvation all night if necessary! A saint!" she added worshipfully, her pert little breasts heaving up and down in adoration. "The man is a perfect saint!"

"I hardly think so," Charlotte replied dryly. "I'll discuss your salvation with Father Armando tonight on my way to the baths!" she promised her, smoothing the serving girl's crown of light brown hair gently, wishing now that she had clouted him over the head the other day.

"If you like," Sparrow answered with a polite shrug, not understanding what a woman—even one as grand as her mistress—could tell a learned man, especially a *holy* one like Father Armando, remembering with a sudden, quickened beating of her heart how wonderful his hand had made her feel. "It's a pity Lord Garret won't be here to share your bed tonight, mistress," she murmured dreamily as she smoothed the last of the wrinkles out of the coverlet.

"Oh!" She started in surprise, raising her hand to her mouth in horror as she realized with acute embarrassment what she had just said and blamed the lustful thought in her mind. "Satan be gone!" she intoned gravely, making a hurried lopsided cross in the air, and she sought to reassure her mistress that she wasn't thinking what she really was thinking. That, she rationalized, like a good Catholic girl, had been the lustful imp inhabiting her mind—and certainly wasn't her! "I only meant that the mists coming in off the seas this night are so cold," she stammered as her mistress's translucent blue eyes speared her and held her like a fish on a line. "He could've at least kept you warm!" she hurried on, trying desperately to cover her blunder.

"Yes," Charlotte murmured, savagely cinching her gown around her waist with a vicious tug on a golden cord. "Such a pity!" she replied, and she walked out the door, to be followed by the dubious Armando and several waiting guards. "Courage," she murmured beneath her breath, knowing it meant doing what one had to do even when one was afraid. Nothing to it.

"What was that, m'lady?" asked Armando politely, cupping his fleshy oversized hand to his ear and leaning toward her as they marched down the stairs.

"Letch!" she snorted in disgust, popping him in the stomach and eliciting a surprised grunt from him and a strangled cry from Sparrow, who stood watching their departure from the landing up above.

"Your ladyship!" she cried in horror, her voice echoing through the massive foyer as she made a quick sign of the cross, half expecting a bolt of lightning to shatter the roof and strike her mistress dead. "You don't clout a priest!"

"No," she muttered under her breath. "You're probably right, Sparrow. You don't clout a priest." The huge double doors were swung wide and she entered the swirling mists. "But I know one I'd love to castrate!"

This time the cry was from Armando, who followed his mistress a little less closely out into the night, protectively cupping his jewels in his hands.

"Oh, happy, happy girl," recited Robert of Gloucester from the shelter of the stone wall. "Why are you all too long a maid?" Advancing half a step closer, he stared curiously at the pastel-robed figure seated demurely on the stone bench in front of him. Frowning, he couldn't remember ever seeing a maiden with such large shoulders.

"Robert of Gloucester," Garret called in a high falsetto voice. "I have waited breathlessly for you!" Then he *tittered*, trying to giggle like a sweet young girl, but his laugh sounded more like the grinding of rocks than a flirtatious chuckle, and his back ached with the effort he made at holding himself hunched in.

More confident, the brown man advanced, surveying the area cautiously. Certain of his imagined legendary prowess, he extended one arm high in the air, touching his heart with the other, preparing to further advance his epic amorous adventures by quoting poetry. A troubadour to the bitter end.

"My desire has flown!" he said sweetly. He overextended his arm and fell forward, bumping clumsily into the cloaked figure. "I'm so sorry," he muttered apologetically. He had expected her to fall forward from the force of his fall or at least move an inch or two, but she hadn't budged, not even an inch. "Curious," he murmured, furrowing his brown brows. Steadying himself, the flats of his hands placed on the maiden's broad back, he frowned again. Such firm, hard flesh… then a muscle rippled beneath the silk. Robert jumped back with a gasp, his hand tingling as though he had just touched a huge, coiled snake.

"Say on," Garret encouraged sweetly. The second word in the sentence dropped down nearly two octaves and sounded like the resonant tones of a baritone instead of the bell-sweet notes of a soprano. "Continue," Garret persuaded softly. His face was downcast, and Robert could not see the murderous gleam shining from his eyes nor heed the warning of the clenched fists beneath the azure silk of his disguise.

Robert hesitated. He cleared his throat and smoothed his satin frock. He had spared no luxury on himself tonight. He wore silk stockings, a lace doublet, the sweetest perfume his servants could provide. He doused himself with it to cover the fact that he had an abhorrence to soap and water, bathing only twice and year and then fully clothed. His nightly toilet included basins of scented water, but the ritual bath was left to six months and no sooner, to prevent the possibility of contracting pneumonia or some other virulent disease.

He glanced down at himself and smiled smugly.

A narcissist to the bitter end.

"Onward and upward," he said beneath his breath. He braced himself and stood at an angle, tipping his head slightly to give the maiden a view of his better side; his profile, he knew, distinct and handsome.

"My desire has flown, kiss me, my sweet and we shall fly away together on the wings of love most profound."

He extended his hand and received no response. Insulted by her lack of interest, he cleared his throat. Then he knelt and attempted to gaze at her veiled face.

"Let me gaze at your beauty, my love," he implored sweetly. "Let me look at you, fair maiden, before I love you!"

Garret had enough. When Robert's hand grazed the veil and he attempted to move it away from his face, it took every ounce of restraint to keep from strangling him.

"Let me look at you, princess, before I love you…"

It was there that his words stuck in his throat as the maiden began to stand. Uncoiling from the bench, Garret towered above him. The veil of mauve-colored silk fell away to reveal waves of jet-black hair and blistering blue eyes.

"Oh my God," whimpered Robert as recognition began to dawn on him. "Oh, my dear sweet Jesus! This was a trap!"

Garret nodded, reached down with one hand and lifted him by his family's jewels until the two men were eye-level and Robert of Gloucester was staring into the coldly dispassionate face of the single man he feared above all men in the world—Garret Montgomery.

"So," said Garret. "What exactly was it that you wanted with my *wife?*"

"Your *wife?*" Robert was desperate.

He lied.

"I didn't know she was your wife! I didn't even know that you were married! Must you twist so hard?" he whined pitifully, squirming painfully against Garret's ironlike grip.

"I'll twist the little worm off if you don't tell me what you were doing in my garden and what it has to do with my wife!" Garret warned icily. The breeze whipped the mane of his thick black hair into a midnight halo that glowed with blue fire in the light of the torches.

"Your wife!" Robert shouted, eager to shift the blame. "*She* sent a note to *me!* Naturally, I wanted to catch her in the act so I could inform you!"

"Is that so?" Garret responded quietly. His eyes flashed dangerously in the moonlight as a thin smile played across his handsome face, making him look savage and absolutely mean. "I see, you only wanted to help me by trespassing into my private gardens, wooing who you thought was my wife with your pathetic acting…"

"Pathetic?" protested Robert. "I thought it was pretty good, actually."

"Pathetic," repeated Garret. "And here you are, and I am expected to believe that you were only trying to help me by attempting to sleep with my wife?"

"Yes! I mean, no! Absolutely not!" swore Robert. "She could

have flung herself down naked, in front of me and begged me and I would never have betrayed you, Lord Montgomery"

"Begged?"

"Begged. I wouldn't have touched her, even though I've heard she is absolutely beautiful!"

Garret tossed him to the ground.

"She is," Garret admitted, breathing hard. "Absolutely beautiful. And it wouldn't have mattered anyway."

"No?" Robert said. Hope. Perhaps Garret didn't care enough about his wife to let a little thing like infidelity bother him.

"No," Garret answered darkly. "From what I could tell, you would've done very little damage, if any. In fact, I doubt that she would have known you were there except by your stench!"

Robert's ego was thoroughly crushed and so, he knew, was his reputation. This story was destined to make the rounds of all the noble houses for years.

"I could travel," he mused beneath his breath. And then there were the monasteries; seclusion could do wonders for the soul.

"Henry!" shouted Garret. "Henry!" He tossed the rest of his robes aside and stood in front of Robert in leathers and steel. "Henry! Escort Robert of Gloucester to the cellar. Perhaps he can charm a few rats!"

"No, Garret! You can't do this! Forget all this! I'll give you money, gold, whatever you want!" His words died in his throat at the contemptuous look Garret threw his way.

"I don't want your money," he told him quietly. "Neither do I want your gold nor your worthless life! Take him!" he ordered.

"You can't do this!" Robert shouted as Henry hauled him to his feet. "I'll go to the King, Montgomery! Do you hear? I'll tell—"

But his pleas and threats were wasted on Garret, who watched impassively.

"Montgomery! You can't hold me as a prisoner for something that never happened."

"Actually, I could kill you," Garret said. "Or I could take you to the King, and he could kill you. The consequence of a crime of passion: no greater provocation can a man have then another try to steal his wife. Or borrow her, as in your case. Frankly, though, I'm somewhat disappointed. I thought my wife had better taste. Toss that fop in the cellar, Henry. I can't stand the sight of him.

"No one will ever touch my wife *except me!*" Garret warned. Hellfire was dancing in his eyes as he watched Robert led off by the manor guards, bent nearly double.

"I'll tell!" Robert screamed futilely.

Garret laughed. "No one will listen, you fool." He watched their departure until the tramping feet of the guards faded in the distance, leaving the garden in silence.

He drew in one deep, cooling breath. Iron and steel, a knife's bitter edge. That was his life, and he had accepted it with stoic pride. But now he wanted *more*, needed more, feeling as if he were about to explode with the intensity of feelings flowing through him.

His life was never his own.

He wondered how he came to this moment. Was love a comedy of errors, a foolish enterprise? Here he was, ready to take on the identity of fool in order to spend his wedding night with his wife, a woman who neither loved nor wanted him.

He wanted to teach her a lesson, to block her foolish machinations and game-playing. Neither had wanted this situation, this marriage of convenience and state.

"We're both prisoners, Charlotte, we've no choice but to surrender to our fate."

Her situation was precarious. Her willful, reckless behavior and defiance was not only contrary to society, but dangerous to her person.

Garret closed his eyes, seeing her bound and gagged, tied to his bed like a prisoner. He cringed when he remembered his servants relating how they fought her and subdued her with force—this young princess, his wife. He heard how the townsfolk jeered when she was brought into the city through the gate, all standing to watch the captive bride and witness her humiliation.

Garret was ashamed of how she had been treated. She should have been greeted with music and flowers, gifted with kindness, and welcomed to her new home. Her wedding should have been a celebration and an event to commemorate the unification of her country and the beginning of her new life as his wife.

He didn't wonder why she hated him. It was her crown and her people, her land and her ancestry which were sought after and required to consolidate the alliance and power, which he needed. But the cost was high.

If he let her go, the animosity which was growing daily between his people and those born of this land would escalate. If he took her by force, as his father reassured him was his right, she would never forgive him, and he knew from the fire in her eyes she would retaliate.

He must play the game tonight and pretend to be Robert of Gloucester, let her think she had outsmarted him and deprived him of his rights as her legally wed husband. What bothered him more than this whole sordid situation was that he knew Charlotte understood feudal law. If she had succeeded in sleeping with Robert, her actions would be considered adultery—a crime whose punishment was death. Even should he forgive her, the King would not, and neither would his people. She would be killed. Yet he knew she preferred death to being a captive bride and would never be tamed or cajoled into behaving as expected.

Once again, the image of her lying so helpless in his bed forced itself upon his mind. He had pitied her and yet been overwhelmed by her incredible beauty, which had struck him like a bolt of lightning that night. He had never seen a woman so incredibly beautiful. She took his breath away.

Though he did not believe in love at first sight and would argue that he did not believe in love at all, only duty, yet he did love her at first sight.

And he had been acting as her best friend for a fortnight, running interference and brooking no insult of his lady from any man, woman or child, instructing others on how she should be treated: with kindness and respect.

He loved her.

"Love," he whispered sardonically, instinctively understanding the duality of the word. At its best, it could make the commonest fool a king; at its worst, it could destroy the strongest man, like his father, and like him.

Above him in a tree, a nightingale took heart in the stillness and began to sing. The bright plumage identified the bird as a male. Garret looked upward, seeing the bird outlined in silver, hearing the melody of his call and knowing that he sang for his mate.

"Beautiful," he whispered, listening with rapt attention as he gazed wonderingly at the full, silvery moon and the countryside bathed in luminous mist.

"My desire has flown like a dream. Kiss me yet once again. The last, long kiss, until I draw your soul within my lips, and drink down all your love."

Like the nightingale, his song finished and he mounted his waiting horse. Fueled with a burning desire and a heart brimming full of love, he shouted "Yah!" and slapped the sorrel-colored rump of the frisky palfrey, who bounded across the moors. He left the reins slack, guiding the sensitive beast with the lightest touch of his hand over streams, around curing rocks, giving her the freedom to run. And she did. At times all four of her feet were off the ground as she stretched out, sensing her master's urgency. Garret lay against the back of her neck, compelling her forward, until it seemed that the horse and rider were one.

To save Charlotte's life, he must masquerade as her lover. The knowledge of who she slept with would be his and one other's, whose silence was guaranteed. He would play the game if it would keep the princess safe.

Garret knew he needed time because he was convinced that she liked him and, given time, perhaps the princess would fall in love with him.

"Hurry," he encouraged the mare as the wind whipped against his skin, feeling cold and moist. Her pert ears twitched, listening to her master, and her stride lengthened. The two became one thundering shadow flying across the moonlit moors, heading for the bathhouse to fulfill a lifetime of yearning. Tonight was Lord Garret Montgomery's wedding night—something his wife apparently knew nothing about.

* * *

With the Roman conquest of the British Isles came also the Romans' fondness for bathing. Huge domed buildings were erected beside flowing rivers and streams. Fires were lit. Heated water scented with fragrant oils trickled forth from ornately-carved fish heads or scantily-clad water nymphs. The public baths became a duty—indeed, a sacred pleasure—to be enjoyed by even the commonest folk. Then the Dark Ages emerged, and the houses of joyful splashing became things of the past, objects to be scorned by the pious. Only a few of the ancient structures still dotted the land, and one very old, very elaborate one on the banks of a raging river at the very heart of Pembroke still shot water into a central pool from the tiny flaccid penis of a very lovely Cupid.

"Leave her alone, Armando," Charlotte warned, as the two approached the courtyard's main door. Her voice had been kept low so the trailing guards wouldn't hear. "She is much too innocent and young for the likes of you!"

Pretending extreme contrition, Armando bowed his head before her stern gaze, wisely keeping to himself that *innocent* and *young* was exactly the combination he liked best in women.

"Did you hear me, Armando?" she asked irritably.

"Yes, m'lady," he answered. "It seems," he murmured somewhat gleefully, "that we are here!" There was at least *one* man he knew of who could put the woman back into this haughty little viper.

Looking up with a startled "Oh!" on her lips, she turned pink, then ashen, as she remembered just why they were here. "So it seems," she murmured with a careless shrug of her shoulders as the door was opened.

Armando held out his hand, bent on keeping the grin now blooming on his face hidden as he ushered her in.

"You!" Charlotte ordered her guards sternly before entering. "Stay here. My priest alone will accompany me."

Shrugging indifferently, the men were more than happy to stay out of doors. Townspeople were trailing by, laughing and talking gaily, and one sweet, slightly inebriated young lady was already offering them a taste from a well-squeezed flask of deep purple wine.

"Lead the way," she told Armando dully.

"Princess Charlotte?" Armando said, alarmed at her ashen appearance. The old thief suddenly felt fatherly compassion. "Are you sure about this, Princess Charlotte?" he asked gently.

"It is all arranged, isn't it, Armando?" she said. She turned to look at him, and the caped hood she wore fell away and a river of platinum blonde hair spilled down her shoulders.

Armando saw the girl then, a man's daughter and a knight's wife. He felt a sense of pride in what his lord was doing, understanding feudal law all too well. Garret was protecting the princess the only way that he could: by becoming her husband.

"I almost hoped something went awry," Charlotte said. "Perhaps the note had been lost or Robert of Gloucester had been stricken with some virulent disease."

She remembered her bath and Lord Montgomery entering her chamber in broad daylight. She was struck by his towering height and handsome good looks; yet his confidence made her feel confrontational. He called her *beloved adversary* under his breath and laughed as he left the room.

"I didn't want this life, Armando. I wanted to marry Lon and stay at Pembroke. You know that, don't you?"

Armando nodded kindly.

"Things may yet work out, Princess Charlotte. You might still have a good and happy life if you'd but give your new life a chance. Lord Montgomery is a good man."

Anger and resentment reasserted itself. In defiance she looked at the wily old thief and said, "Robert of Gloucester is meeting me at the baths, is that correct, Armando?"

"Yes," he answered kindly, conveniently ignoring the second part of her question. "It is all arranged. There is a door near the river seldom used. *He* will use it," forgetting to tell her who the *he* was! "No one will see him, including you, because the lights will be out."

"What does he look like, Armando?" she said softly, wondering why, after all that she had planned, that small detail should even matter.

"I have never seen a man that could be his equal," Armando answered honestly, with a feeling of immense pride.

Suddenly, in Charlotte's mind an image of Garret planted itself firmly there, with beads of water shining like diamonds from his lowered lashes, and a hint of blue-black beard shadowing the curve of his chin. Then the image smiled, so sweetly, so *beautifully*, that her thighs trembled and her knees went weak.

His presence provoked unbidden passion in her; a chemistry that she could not describe. She was powerfully attracted to the lord of the manor, dangerously so, and had no power to prevent what nature defined.

"Don't be so sure," she whispered gloomily as the image of Lord Garret Montgomery continued to taunt her. "Don't ever be so sure!"

Whipping up her resolve to follow through with her plans, reminding herself that it was the *only* way to be free, even if it cost her life.

"Lead the way, Armando," she said. "Nothing to this," she muttered firmly as she followed the smiling monk into the echoing silence of the deserted bathhouse. "Just something that has to be done so that I may be free—one way or the other!"

* * *

Outside, in the shadows of newly-budded yews and fragrant aspens, Garret watched silently as she entered the courtyard, the large double doors closing behind her.

"Tonight, my wayward bride," he vowed roguishly, seeing the white queen glare as she refused to accept defeat while he angled his black king's rook directly in her path, giving her a choice of moves. She could take the offered bait of the black rook and thus sacrifice herself to the king's bishop, which would be an unlawfully *stupid* move, exposing her king to automatic checkmate from the threatening black knight. End of game. Or she could use her other pieces against him, which would make the game last longer and a whole lot more fun! Smiling, he slid from his saddle, ready to do battle.

"All for love," Garret said and laughed.

* * *

"This way," motioned Armando, drawing back a heavy black drape, exposing one of the narrow cubicles lining the walls of the main room. The cell was barely five feet by eight, sparsely furnished, with only one weakly-burning oil light glowing from an alcove in the wall and a bed covered in white satin sheets and pillows that nearly took up all the space.

The floor was cold stone. But instead of warming rushes covering it, someone had cut enough boughs of freshly blooming lilac bushes to cover the entire room with their emerald green leaves and gloriously scented lavender blooms. Tiny bunches of the fragrant blossoms tied with white satin bows even adorned the waiting pillows.

"It seems," Charlotte murmured icily, "that Robert of Gloucester has gone to a lot of trouble for very little reward."

"Oh, good lady!" Armando reassured her enthusiastically. "I am sure you are worth a few flowers—perhaps even a bottle of wine!" The wily thief bowed low, thinking he had given his mistress the finest of compliments.

"Humph!" she snorted, jerking the ebony-hued drape out of his hand. "A *bottle of wine* and a bunch of raggedy old flowers for the only *worthy* thing a woman has to offer a man?"

"I only meant," he hastened to reply, standing upright, "that someone as lovely as you would be worth all that a man has."

Armando suddenly felt very foolish. "You see, Princess Charlotte, I don't have much, so for me, a bottle of wine *is* a great treasure."

Charlotte quietly surveyed the corpulent man in his newly-made habit. "Be careful, Armando," she warned softly, smiling reluctantly. "Or I may just begin to think there is hope for you yet."

"Oh, there *is*, my lady!" he assured her with a shy smile.

He bowed low once again as she shut the curtain behind her.

"There most certainly is!"

Chapter 14

Long legs carried a splendid black-haired knight unerringly toward his waiting bride. His hair was loose, flowing about his face like the mane of a great stallion.

"My lord." Armando greeted him grandly with a reverent bow, yet as quietly as he could.

"In here?" Garret murmured quietly, eyeing the black drape with undisguised interest.

"Yes," Armando assured him, feeling as though he were part of something truly monumental. Something incredibly beautiful was to happen tonight—he could sense that. Something wonderful.

"The light?" Garret asked softly. "Where is it?"

"As you walk into the room, barely a hand-span from the door. It rests in a little alcove," Armando replied, showing him on the outside of the room about where the oil light sat.

With a satisfied nod and a tingling sensation growing stronger in him by the minute, the kind of feeling one gets when walking in the rain and lightning is about to strike *very near*, Garret took a deep breath to steady his nerves.

"Wish me luck, Armando."

"Oh, sir," Armando gushed in admiration, "you won't need luck. Why, just *look* at you!"

"Let's just hope the *lady* in there won't get a chance to do that!" He smiled ruefully. "At least for a while!" he added with a wink.

So saying, Garret reached his hand into the room, the drape

hiding his form, found the alcove, and snuffed the light between two fingers, sending the cubicle plunging into total darkness. A startled "Oh!" from the interior told Garret that he had gotten just the reaction he wanted, and he and Armando exchanged a devilish grin. Now was the time for a little fun! He would teach his lady wife to invite another man to *his* bed.

Garret parted the drape, becoming nothing more than a shadow. He closed the curtain behind him and melted into the darkness in the room.

The scent of lilacs was overwhelming and the scent of the woman lying on the bed was subtle and distinct. Garret closed his eyes, breathing in the humid aroma, and smiled in the darkness, thinking of musk, roses, and ambergris.

He would know the scent of this woman should his eyes grow dim and his limbs weak with age.

The princess was quiet. Her heart was pounding. She did not expect the darkness. *Was he the darkness? The anima of her life? Was he the avenue to freedom or a cleverly disguised suicide?*

There was no hope for her after this night; no marriage to Lon and no return to Pembroke, except as the heir to the crown. Never having been loved or cherished, she did not expect that she should be. Having been tutored to war and power, equated with a crown and born to a life where her every whim or decision impacted the lives of many, her personal life and feelings did not matter.

She was Princess Charlotte, and much was expected of her. For a moment, her decision haunted her. The hope was to return to Pembroke and to claim her throne and care for her people; they were her family. If necessary, she would go to Lon and take Pembroke by force. Never again would she be subjected to her cruel grandmother's treatment or be played like a pawn on a chessboard for her grandmother's benefit!

Charlotte knew this night would irrevocably reverse the alliance between the two houses and provide her people with their much-prized independence, but at a cost.

"*I'll pay it,*" she said beneath her breath, for her people. Charlotte was willing to risk everything for Wales. Even a night of indiscretion, so that the Welsh would remain free and not be subjugated as a captive people of the Norman conquerors.

Not willing to be cowed by the darkness like a child, she pushed up on her elbows, still reclining.

"Robert?" she said. "Is that you?" She heard the rustle of fabric. "Let's get this unfortunate business out of the way!"

Pausing as he stripped off the last leg of his trews, Garret reached downward and pulled his tunic over his head and exhaled. Narrowing his eyes, he went to his bride and knelt beside the bed. Gently he reached out and touched her cheek with his hand. His heart was racing, and his mind was in torment. He had vowed to risk it all to keep the princess safe. His penance was silence; the price of a knowledge of what they would do to Charlotte if her plans had been successful.

He would not allow it.

With chivalrous grace, he lifted her trembling hand and kissed her fingers. He felt her wedding band. It matched his own. Overcome with infinite tenderness, he lifted the silk sheets and lay down next to his wife.

* * *

Nearly an hour later Charlotte awoke. She was covered by silk sheets and a warm comforter. Wine, hot, aromatic tea, sweet treats, meats, cheeses were left beside her. And a rose. She stared at the long stem rose of deep red. The oil light was lit. The sheet, folded discreetly beside her bed, was stained deep red. A path was left amongst the lilac boughs to the drapes covering the door.

Outside her door, Armando waited, diligently guarding his little mistress with a feeling of devotion he had seldom experienced.

"So it is done," she whispered. Sitting up, she drew the cover over her naked breasts. Tears formed unexpectedly in her eyes and she began to cry.

Chapter 15

Holding the stained sheet in one hand, Charlotte swallowed hard, trying to steady her heart. It was now nearly noon. Only twenty minutes before she had been curled up in bed, sleeping peacefully. No dreams. No fitful waking. Just the pleasant peace of nothingness, from which she had drifted up reluctantly. Her head ached, and she was so tired that when she lifted her head from the pillow, it sank back down as though it were made of lead. Sighing, she had risen nevertheless, sipping water and dressing hurriedly, looking at herself in the mirror.

No different. Somehow, she had expected there to be an *outward* sign of her scandalous tryst, but there was nothing at all.

Inwardly she felt a profound sadness. Growing up with her grandmother left her feeling unwanted and unloved. Secretly she hoped that someday soon she and her best friend Lon ap Llewelyn would marry. In their home there would be love and laughter, children and peace and heirs the Welsh would accept.

Personally, the thought of living her life with someone she knew who loved her was her secret joy and hope.

Perfect. So perfect! To be loved for who she was and not just a title.

Yet this was not meant to be. Powerful political currents and ancestral domination of lands and people had led her to this moment of uncertainty, using what little personal power she had to change the course of her life and the future of her people.

Princess Charlotte loved Wales and she loved her people—the

Welsh. Whatever personal desires she had meant little in comparison to their future. She would do whatever it would take to keep her people safe. Including defying Lord Garret Montgomery and any invader who would be pretender to the Crown!

The rightful heir to the throne was Lon ap Llewelyn, and Princess Charlotte was determined to do everything she could to see that he would rule Wales unchallenged, including sacrificing her life and happiness for the greater good of her people.

"*God bless Wales*," she whispered beneath her breath.

Knowing full well what she was doing, she lifted the stained sheet she now disdained. It was time to face Lord Montgomery and take responsibility for her actions.

Outside in the corridor, Princess Charlotte's maid was nowhere to be seen, yet she had the feeling that if she found Armando, Sparrow would be there as well. Sighing, knowing there was nothing she could do about it now, she made her way downstairs.

"Is Lord Garret home?" she asked the guard.

"Yes, Princess Charlotte," replied Henry respectfully. "He's been up for hours. In a wonderful mood, I might add. He told me to tell you that he is waiting to speak to you in the study."

With a resigned shrug and a sigh, she decided to let the gods decide her fate. She would play the martyr if her ill-advised scheme would prevent a Montgomery from ever usurping the Welsh throne and hoist the Norman flag above the balustrade.

"To war, then," she muttered without much enthusiasm, and she rounded the corner and entered the brightly-lit study.

Garret was seated at his table, dark head bowed, his hand flying over a page of a book, writing like a demon. He worked all the time and slept little. Princess Charlotte heard the servants speaking of him and how his stamina was unmatched. He administered his estates and did not delegate the task to another. And the shire's priests told of his quiet humility, finding him praying in the chapel alone, and his devotion to tithing and his compassion for the poor, widowed and orphaned. He kept a storehouse of grains and dried meats, and it was widely known that no one in the shire went hungry at night. Each harvest, he directed his people to put away their abundance for times of hardship, and storehouses had been erected near each field for fodder, grains and meats. And the wise women in the shire were encouraged in their healing arts and listened to regarding times to plant and times to reap. He valued their knowledge and skills. The lands and the people under his protection thrived, even during hardship.

Princess Charlotte did like him. She admitted this to herself, remembering his teasing, but she would not allow the feeling to go any further, vowing to never love the dark-haired knight. But she did like him, and it was the most traitorous feeling she had ever experienced. She did not know why, but she did. His frankness appealed to her as well as his honesty.

He ruled his people wisely and well. What he said was to be done was done; his arbitration during disputes was just and sincere. And his unrelenting ferocity in defending his people was known throughout the kingdom. "*Don't challenge the lion," the royals said jokingly at the games. "He bites!*"

"Lord Montgomery," she said formally, "I need to speak to you."

The quill stopped in mid-flight and he looked up, flashing a smile at her that would've driven an angel to its knees.

"Darling girl," he said softly. There was warm, soft light shining in his blue eyes as he gazed at his wife. "I'm delighted to see you this morning. I trust you slept well?"

He meant every word. He stood in her presence and stretched languidly with the gracefully beautiful movements of a large, predatory cat.

"Please, stay where you are," she said.

"Here?" he said. He understood intuitively what was wrong. He saw her as his wife. She saw him as her enemy. Time, he thought, could turn the tide. Time.

He pointed to a spot on the floor near his leather-shod boots.

"Is this where I should stay, Princess Charlotte? Close enough for conversation but far enough to prevent more intimate attention?"

"Yes," she said.

His smile faded and he nodded. He thought of his parents, living separate lives, separated by distance within the castle, polite and civil and eons apart emotionally. She delivered him three sons and her role was complete; she retired to her rosary, and out of love, his father respected her wishes. Garret knew he loved her, and it was with profound sadness that he gazed at his parents and the loneliness of their respective lives. He did not want to suffer the same fate.

"I think you like me, Charlotte," he said softly. "In spite of everything, I think you do. I want to start over, if that makes sense. To invite you to your new home. To ask you what I can do for you. I want you to be happy, Princess Charlotte. I want us to be friends."

He remembered last night and every curve of her body. The thought filled him with desire and longing. Yet he must remain silent, for her sake. She was unpredictable and he had never met a lady with such independence and unshakable courage. Arranged marriages were common, yet Princess Charlotte did not come to Pembroke willingly and had been treated horribly. Garret wanted time—time to be with her—time to make amends for his father's ill treatment of her and given time, perhaps she would want to stay and not feel as though she was a captive bride.

"I have something to tell you," she said. Her throat was suddenly dry and tight; she felt dizzy and lightheaded and began to sweat.

The ordeal of the last few weeks had settled harshly upon her shoulders this morning. The numbing shock of being locked in the tower, then forced into a prearranged marriage by her grandmother who hated her, being led to the altar under armed guard and in shackles, it all made her furious. Then meeting Garret, who seemed kind and good and treated her with respect and dignity. It was too much to expect that she should forgive such treatment of her person by anyone, including the man who called himself her husband.

She had acted boldly, and some would say unwisely last night. Her objective was clear in that Lon ap Llewelyn, with her out of the way, would inherit the throne and no other would usurp his right to rule.

"Oh?" he said, feigning an innocence he did not feel as he thought of his masquerade in this charade. He saw it coming and felt it as clearly as if a bitter northeastern wind were blowing against him. It was about the Crown and Sword of Wales. Garret knew this. Whatever their relationship could have been, the legend of the mythical Sword of Wales and the Crown with its jewels formed from the tears of their ancient queen, and the right to rule Wales would overshadow the events. He felt the weight of history piercing him when she looked at him with her sky-blue eyes.

His intention was to protect her, but she would never believe this after what had happened.

She approached him as an adversary, not as his wife, reminding him that their marriage had been arranged by her grandmother and his father. Their hope was that an heir would be produced who would consolidate an alliance between the two families and be accepted as the legitimate ruler of Wales and the rightful owner of this legendary Sword and Crown.

"What do you want to tell me, Charlotte?" Garret said. He recognized the sheet in her hand.

"I didn't want this life," she said.

"You mean you didn't want to be my wife," he said evenly.

It was a statement.

She searched his face, trying to find the words she needed to explain how she felt and why she acted as she did.

"I've never had a choice," she said. "All my life I've been trained and told what I must do. I have always done my duty and risen to the challenges which have come my way, for my people—for the Welsh."

"And I'm a challenge," he offered. "I'm not Welsh, and you were forced to marry me because your grandmother and my father saw the alliance as a practical consolidation of power. Something for *their* benefit."

"Yes."

"In addition to that, the man fortunate enough to be your husband, Princess Charlotte, becomes a contender for the throne and also the rightful owner of the legendary Sword and Crown of Wales?"

Charlotte closed her eyes.

"Yes," she said. "But that won't happen, now or ever. The crown belongs to Lon ap Llewelyn and every house in Wales will support him.

"I've a confession to make to you this morning, an irrevocable action that will ensure that I never rule and that you, as my legal husband, cannot possibly ascend to the throne."

"Does that sheet have anything to do with it?" he said quietly. His blue eyes were on fire.

"Yes," she said, flinging it down on the floor. She felt triumphant, even if her decision was about to cost her life. "I'm not a virgin any longer."

"No?" he said sweetly. Leaning back against the fireplace, he crossed both arms across his brawny chest. He looked at her with the oddest expression on his face and smiled. He was jealous of

Lon, not because of the crown but because he could see that his young wife cared about him.

"Where there is no jealousy, there is no love," he said beneath his breath.

He rose and crossed the room, knowing that he was in love with Princess Charlotte: her courage and love for her people, her kindness and compassion, and her beauty that literally hypnotized him. He was addicted to his wife and he wanted her to love him. He knew she was attracted to him; he sensed it when he neared her, and she stepped back—not out of fear—but something natural. Garret felt their chemistry and her animosity. He was determined to win his princess bride any way he could, and if that meant masquerading as that fop Robert and trysting with her in a bath house with a lecherous thief standing guard, then that is what he did.

"Did you hear me?" she said. "I'm not a virgin any longer."

"Oh. You're not a *virgin,*" he said. "And that should nullify any agreement between your grandmother and my father, correct?"

"Correct."

"No," he said sweetly with the utter guilelessness of a child, advancing one step closer still. He looked so deceptively innocent. Like a beautiful little boy with that wavy black curl falling across his forehead.

"No!" she said forcefully. He was the most infuriating man she had ever known! Coming out of her stupor and self-imposed martyrdom, she noticed the slow, lazy grin appearing on his face. "What do you mean 'No'?"

"We're still married," he said, "whether you like it or not. Would you like a cup of tea and some burnt bread?'

"Did you hear what I said? I slept with Alaric of York! I'm not a virgin. My grandmother and your father's agreement is null and void!"

"No," said Garret with a bored expression on his face. "We're still married." He was trying very hard not to laugh. Picking up a cup of tea, he sipped it and then looked at her over the rim. "You *slept* with *Alaric of York?*"

He gave an exaggerated shudder of his immense shoulders, making a little expression of distaste that made his full sensuous lips look as though he were preparing to kiss someone. Charlotte was convinced it was her and she gasped and stepped backwards *two* steps this time.

"Really, my dear, I thought you had better taste than that. Alaric of York? Biggest fop around and not very good-looking, if you ask me," he chided. With an exaggerated sigh, he raked back his hair and smiled at her. He'd tell her someday. Maybe.

"Not with Alaric," she hastened to explain, struggling up through her mental fog. "His nephew, Robert of Gloucester!"

Garret took a bite of toast and sipped his tea, appearing deep in thought.

"Was he any good?" he asked conversationally.

"What!?" she shouted. She was unable to believe he wanted the details of his humiliation, and *hers.*

Garret set his teacup down and advanced boldly toward her.

"*Good,*" he said. "In bed. Was he any good in bed?"

Standing very close to his wife, Garret touched her chin gently and traced a path toward her cleavage. Charlotte jumped backward a full three steps with a startled "Oh!" on her lips.

"How can you ask me something like that?" she countered in a strangled little voice as she bumped into the table.

"Curiosity," he said. "That's how I can ask something like that." He fenced in her against the table with both of his hands. His handsome face was within a scant few inches of hers. She had never seen a man in her life as handsome as Garret Montgomery. She would never admit this to him or anyone else, but he was.

Garret smiled slowly as if he read her mind.

"Men are rather preoccupied with certain things in life. Sex, as you know, is one of them," he said with a shrug, as though it were something they couldn't be blamed for.

"What are the other things men are preoccupied with?" she said, trying to redirect his attention.

He blinked slowly and looked at her.

"Their wives," he said. "Some men are positively addicted to their wives. And sex. Sex with their wives. It doesn't get much better than that," he admitted. "Would you like a demonstration of my preoccupation with you? An upper persuasion of a lower invasion? I admit I'm addicted to you."

"You're disgusting!" she said. She ducked quickly under his arms and rounded the table, looking for something to throw.

Garret bit his lower lip to keep from laughing aloud and telling her that she didn't seem to think he was disgusting last night. But then, she didn't know it was him.

"Thoroughly disgusting," he agreed. "And hot." Garret pulled his shirt over his head and tossed it on the floor.

"I can't believe that you don't *care* that I slept with another man!"

"Oh, I wish you had a little better taste in your choice of *potential* lovers," he admitted slyly. *Potential* is as far as you'll ever get, he thought darkly. "But no, I don't care that you're no longer a virgin."

"You're not going to have our marriage annulled?" she said, watching, totally mesmerized, as he walked across the room bare-chested and slammed the door shut.

"Of course not," he said as he made his way toward the table and her. "I'm just going to enjoy the rest of our honeymoon."

Her eyebrows shot up as her eyes caught sight of a slim, silver dagger lying on the table near a stack of parchment. She lifted it and stood ready to defend herself.

"You'll have to enjoy it alone," she said.

"You're my wife and I'm your husband. I have a right to be with you."

Charlotte threw the dagger.

And Garret stopped in mid-stride, surprised, as he looked down with his newly-acquired frown. The knife was embedded in the wall right between his legs.

"Another inch or two," he said, "and I think we would have *both* been unhappy."

"Don't flatter yourself!" she said. "I'll never be your wife and I'll never love you!"

"Never?" he asked.

"Never!" she said.

"You're trembling."

It was an observation born of the sympathy he felt for her that reasserted itself when he looked at her. He wondered what it would have been like to have met her under different circumstances; to meet her and to know her—to hear her laugh and make her smile; to earn her praise and friendship instead of her hatred and disdain.

"Let's start over, Charlotte. Let's take what has been given to us, though neither had a choice, nor did we own our lives until this moment, but have been merely pawns in all of this. Let's start over and make the best of this; otherwise, they win."

"They?" questioned Charlotte. She didn't trust him; she had no reason to and did not realize all that Lord Montgomery had tried to do for her these past weeks.

"Your grandmother and my father. They have overshadowed our lives since our birth, but no longer. I'm your husband and your ally. Together we can rule and create the kind of lives we choose for ourselves and our people, instead of being manipulated by others. You're my wife."

Garret's decision to support her was firm.

"And you're my enemy," Princess Charlotte said softly. "You cannot be my husband and my ally because I don't trust you!"

"You can trust me," he said.

"No. I can't! You're a Norman and I'm Welsh. Your people invaded our country and have taken over our lands. I won't be tricked by you, Lord Montgomery!"

Garret was silent. There was nothing more to be said.

"I will never stop fighting for my people or their independence," she said. Her voice was soft and the exhaustion she surely felt apparent in the dark circles beneath her eyes.

"There are Vikings attacking these shores," Garret reminded her. "The alliance we are forming between the Welsh and the Normans by our marriage is strong enough not only to defend against their attacks but to repel them from these shores.

"You may see this situation between us as inconvenient to your personal desires, but there are issues far above ourselves which demand that we unite.

"Also," he added angrily, "I did not mean for you to be treated so badly and knew nothing of the plans of your grandmother and my father. I would never have allowed him to treat you so badly, Charlotte. Ever.

"However, their intentions were politically correct and strategically valid in light of the Viking attacks, though their methods were deplorable."

Princess Charlotte nodded her head quietly.

"Somewhere between the message I'd received from my father at the inn and this morning, I became your husband. It was not my choice either, but I found myself drawn to you in an inexplicable way, caring about you and not merely as a convenient alliance between two families.

"Do you understand what I'm saying?"

"That you like me?" she said bitingly.

Garret shook his head slowly.

"No," he said. "That I love you. I didn't intend to. But somewhere, in all this madness and preparation for war, I fell in love with the bravest woman I have ever known. You. It is somewhat of a shock to me when I realize daily that my *like* has turned to an inconvenient love.

"You cloud my senses in a dangerous way and captivate my attention when my mind should be pursuing other things. I want you to be happy, Charlotte, with me. And even if you don't love me, give this marriage a chance. If not for yourself, then for our respective people.

"We are the only hope our people have against the Vikings."

In silence, Princess Charlotte turned and left the study, retiring to her room, shutting the door soundly to keep Garret Montgomery out and herself, deep in thought, secluded within.

Downstairs, Garret sat down on the divan. *Time.* Time to build the forces necessary to repel the Viking invasion. Time to form alliances.

Princess Charlotte was his wife and it was true. He loved her. They were married and he had time to make her his.

"Someday, Princess, you will love me."

Of this Lord Garret Montgomery was certain. Someday, she would love him.

Stretching out on the floor, he lifted the white queen from the chessboard and held it in his hand. Sunlight streamed through the windows, and he fell into a tranquil sleep, holding his little queen in his hand.

Chapter 16

Charles walked up the winding, narrow stairs with a heavy heart, feeling as though he were carrying the weight of the world on his broad shoulders. *How much could a man age in a day?* he wondered tiredly, feeling as though every time he drew a breath a year had gone by, and his mounting responsibilities were becoming more than he could bear.

"How many mistakes have I made?" he whispered out loud, and those words conjured up fragmented memories of his life, where picture after picture of days gone by slammed forcefully into his consciousness. Behind each scene he stood, directing the lives of his family, the villagers—playing God by bending and twisting the wills of others to conform to his own. But his intentions were good, he rationalized, even if the outcome of his actions *wasn't.*

Absorbed in his own thoughts, he entered the sunlit study, his eyes falling on his son sprawled on the floor. Fear. A heart-stopping, spinning fear that curled up through him like a cobra, threatening to explode from his throat in a scream, gripped him. Frozen to the spot, his hand went out.

"No," he moaned. "This cannot be!" Stumbling forward, he prayed this was just another one of his dreams, another nightmarish jaunt through his subconscious, as he knelt beside the still form.

"God!" he whispered in relief, wiping the sweat from his forehead, trembling so violently that he nearly fell. Garret was only sleeping. Closing his eyes tightly, he summoned what little strength he still had left and gazed at the form before him, watching greedily as Garret's chest rose and fell. "Yes, my son," he whispered, "breathe deeply. Live well and always, even when this relic you call father is no longer on this side of the veil."

Tears, long since held in check, flowed down his pale skin. Love, like a protective shield, flowed from Charles, wrapping itself like a golden cloud around the form of his beautiful son.

Like Endymion, beloved of the moon goddess Selene, Garret lay motionless before his father.

Charles could only gaze at him in wonder. Magnificent, so *perfect.* Garret was everything to Charles, everything. How many nights had he stood beside his son's bed, looking down at him as he slept? How many hours had he stood in the corridor, listening as he wept? How many times had he wanted desperately to run to his side and comfort him? How many times had he looked at *himself* in the polished copper mirror in absolute loathing, hating himself for trying to force Garret to live in a world without love? Wishing to make him hard, to shield him from the one emotion that could bring even the strongest man to his knees as it did him. If he had never fallen in love, he would have been the happiest man in the world or, perhaps, if he had never fallen in love with someone who didn't love him.

Murmuring in his sleep, Garret turned slightly, still clutching the white queen to his chest, and smiled in his dreams. Such a lovely face. In sleep the lines became soft, the mouth lost its cynicism. The brows didn't rise skeptically over his dark blue eyes. In sleep, Garret looked like an innocent little boy. His boy.

Sighing, Charles stood up. Whipping the cloak from his shoulders, he carefully laid it over Garret, stooping once more to brush a wisp of unruly hair away from his forehead. "Sleep well, my son," he whispered. Then, pausing for just a fraction of a second as he drew a quivering breath, he murmured, "I love you, Garret." Swallowing hard, he pushed back a lump that had suddenly grown to throbbing proportions in his throat. "I've *always* loved you," he whispered, barely able to control the waves of love pouring out from his soul toward his son. Sighing, Charles left the room, clearing his throat as quietly as he could.

In the hall his wife approached, glimpsing her son for a second before Charles closed the door.

"What is it?" he asked icily, still drawn to the dark fragility of her beauty as much now as he had been years before.

"We have guests, my lord," she answered quietly, humbly, refusing to meet his gaze.

"Who?" he asked, shutting the door firmly behind him, not much in the mood for company.

"Sir Alaric of York and a young lady," she replied hesitantly, fingering her rosary nervously. She had seen Alaric of York before, many times, but never the woman with him.

"What does he want?" Charles asked almost savagely. He had no use for York, and he knew the feeling was mutual.

"They wish to stay at your hospitality, my lord," she replied again, suddenly seeing the dark-haired, dark-eyed man in her mind and driving his image away with a hasty prayer.

"They know I cannot refuse," he told her flatly. "Make them welcome."

"Yes, my lord," she whispered, giving a polite curtsy. As she was about to leave, Charles grabbed her arm and pulled her close. His heart was hammering loudly against his chest and his eyes looked moist and so tired. What was wrong? Before she could speak, he kissed her, placing his mouth firmly on hers and wrapping his arms around her.

He needed her now as he had never needed her before. He needed her strength. He needed her acceptance. He desperately needed her *love.* But she gave nothing. No returning kiss, no circling warmth from her arms, which remained firmly fixed at her sides. She was utterly yielding, tolerating his touch as she had done so many times before. Tolerated, he thought darkly, never *wanted.* He released her from his grip without so much as a sigh. There was nothing left in him. Nothing.

Feeling her husband's dark, probing eyes on her, she hastened to fill the empty space between them with words.

"It is most unseemly for Garret to lie on a floor in the middle of the day."

"Yes," he admitted, watching as she counted her beads, her lips moving as she murmured her prayers in silence. "It is totally unseemly, yet somehow very sweet—very *human.* Something you would know nothing about," he added with a polite bow, walking away from her and into the courtyard of Pembroke while she walked the familiar path to the chapel, hiding her feelings behind the Church as she always did.

Back in the study, still lying on his stomach, Garret slowly opened his eyes, which were shining brightly with tears. *He loves me,* he thought in absolute wonder. His father had never spoken those words to him or given him the slightest indication of any affection. Garret clutched the little queen tighter, drawing his father's cloak over them both, as one wound in his heart began to mend, washed in his father's tears.

Chapter 17

Nell Gwynn hated men. Young or old, rich or poor, it made no difference—she hated men. Yet she *needed* them, their power, their connections, their protection. She *needed* them and hated them for it.

Holding a small joint of lamb in her right hand, she gently nibbled on the warm, smoky-flavored flesh, letting the juice roll over her lips, making them shine. Smiling prettily at Charles, she placed the shank of meat to one side, licking the juice from her lower lip with the slow, languid grace of a cat preening itself.

"More wine?" offered Charles, his gaze roaming helplessly over the beautiful woman seated on his left while his wife, covered from head to foot in a shielding veil, kept her eyes glued chastely to her plate.

"Why, yes," she purred, extending her cup to meet him halfway, boldly catching and holding his gaze as only a certain kind of woman could, while one hand trailed lightly down the emerald-green satin of her dress, her lips forming a delicate little pout as if she enjoyed caressing herself *just that way.*

Loveless sexuality. A vampire of flesh and blood, who could not see herself through her own eyes, but only in the reactions of others to her physical charms. Her sex was not even of the animalistic kind, done with instinct for a divine purpose. Her sex was manipulation, pure and simple. She used her body with the same cold calculation that an officer used his troops: for gain and nothing more. But her schemes hadn't worked with King Henry. How many days had it taken him? Three? A week? She couldn't remember. But he had cast her out, calling her a succubus, a demon, who would surely try and suck the very life out of him.

Anger at the memory caused her eyes to flash, and Charles frowned, wondering where the soft, yielding gaze had gone.

"Nell?" he asked solicitously, shocking his wife into looking up when he used this woman's first name. Grace had never seen Charles so animated, so charming. Seldom had she seen him smile this much in the course of an entire year. This Nell was *seducing* her husband, and the thought made her *uncomfortable.*

"Forgive me, my lord," she whispered sweetly, gently fanning herself with her hand. "I seem to be in need of air."

"I would be delighted to show you our gardens," offered Charles, his dark eyes gleaming lustfully.

"Oh," she replied breathlessly as she rose to meet his outstretched hand. "I would *love* to see them!"

Garret stared hard at his father, who didn't appear to notice him or his new bride seated at the long table, or his wife, as he took Nell by the arm and went strolling through the door into the shadowed gardens.

"It seems," offered Alaric of York dryly, speaking French for the first time in years as he drained the last of his wine, "that your father is quite taken with Lady Gwynn."

"I see no *lady,*" Garret replied coldly, his blue eyes locking with Alaric's until a tension so thick filled the room one could have cut it with a knife.

"Your Norman King Henry seemed to find her such," goaded Alaric, flashing a solicitous smile at Princess Charlotte. Lovely woman, he thought, wondering how loyal she was to her noble husband.

"She didn't fool him for long," Garret answered tersely, able to see through this woman, Nell, with remarkable ease and wondering why his father couldn't and just what she was up to.

"True. True," Alaric agreed with a wave of his hand and turned to look at Charlotte, who refused to look at him or Garret, concentrating on her dish of rabbit and currants as though it were the most interesting dish she had ever eaten. "But then, once the initial curiosity is satisfied, what is left?" he asked spitefully.

Garret hated Alaric, and he liked him even less the more he looked at his wife. One thing pleased him, though: Charlotte, unlike most women, didn't seem affected by his obvious charm. There was nothing about Alaric that was real—not his smile, not his friendship, not his compliments. Neither fish nor fowl—he was a snake with two legs.

Quietly, without letting his voice rise in anger, Garret caught Alaric's eyes. Charlotte was amazed at the hatred that burned in them. Perhaps, she thought with embarrassment, Alaric knows about his nephew Robert and I and the bathhouse tryst...

"I don't like playing games, York," Garret told him softly, laying aside his knife, placing his broad, firm hands flat on the table. "I don't know what you're doing here—but I know *you*, and I know that you're planning something, and I swear by my last breath, if you do anything—*anything*—to harm any member of my family, I will kill you."

"Point well taken," Alaric replied lightly, tearing off a huge chunk of meat and chewing thoughtfully. "But then, I think you are too suspicious for your own good, my *friend.* We've simply come to pay our respects and homage to the *noble* house of Montgomery. Incidentally," he added, keeping his remark very casual as he watched Charlotte to gauge her reaction, "when are your lovely wife's possessions to be brought to Pembroke?"

Charlotte gasped, looking up, her goblet of wine spilling across the table.

"My possessions?" she asked, her gaze going from Alaric to her husband, her expression changing from soft disinterest to one that appeared to be as hard as a nail.

"Why, yes," replied Alaric in undisguised delight, slipping back into his native Anglo-Saxon with relief. "All your inheritance is to be brought to Pembroke. Didn't you know that?" he asked, thankful for his host of spies. "In all haste, I might add, including, I believe, the legendary Sword and Crown of Wales!"

They were artifacts whose power and prestige were more than legend. Alaric had longed to possess them ever since he was a child, knowing that simply having them was an act of Divine Will, signifying the owner's right to rule. And he had wanted to rule this land for as long as he could remember.

"It's the transportation of the relics that is troubling. How to get the mythical relics transferred without some unscrupulous thief or brigand pinching them. Can't imagine anyone who would do that, can you? Pinching the relics, I mean?

"I've heard the sword is so magical that when it's lifted by someone other than the rightful heir, the blackguard is blasted by some invisible force or entity. Now, I'd like to see that personally, you know? Just never seen anyone blasted by an invisible force before. Sounds so interesting. But if the rightful heir lifts the sword, it is supposed to sing, a high-pitched tone that resonates for miles."

Princess Charlotte looked up. Her eyes darkened as she stared at Alaric of York. In her mind she heard her grandmother's voice, "*Magic will always be with you, Charlotte. It is who you are.*"

"Rumors travel fast. I've heard there are a few who can lift the Sword of Wales safely and survive, Lon ap Llewelyn being one, your grandmother, Princess Charlotte, being two and then, of course, the third, *which* is you! Or rather, should I say that you are the *witch* who can lift the sword and hear the angels sing? Now, isn't that just special?"

Alaric speared the rabbit and popped a tidbit into his mouth.

"Yummy," he said, smiling as he watched with glistening eyes the effect of his words on Princess Charlotte and Lord Garret Montgomery.

"How do you know this?" Princess Charlotte demanded, so angry she wanted to throttle Garret. The relics must never leave the Vale!

"Ask your husband," Alaric replied casually, stretching, happy as only a bitter man could be at stirring up trouble for Garret.

"Is it true?" she asked Garret quietly, watching as her husband finished chewing. His expression was completely unreadable.

"Yes," he said. "But it was by order of the King. I had nothing to do with it." He had only just found out about it today.

Why? he had asked his father earlier today. His father had stared at him in this ageless game of thrones and powers. Charles wanted Princess Charlotte's grandmother's ancestral power, if not for himself, then for his heirs.

The relics were everything legend described. Unknown to Garret, Charles had sent a messenger to pick them up and the situation had ended badly. A terrified guard said that when the soldier reached out to lift the Sword, he was lifted off the ground and appeared to be throttled before being flung across the room by an unseen force. A clear blue flame appeared above the Sword and the sound of banshee wailing could be heard above the winds. The guards fled the room in terror, followed by the laughter of the Baroness Isabel, recounting her words as they ran for their lives, "Men can elect officials, but only God can birth a king!"

The ancient symbols bestowed the ancestral right to rule.

"They are supernatural, then?" asked Garret skeptically.

Charles nodded.

Garret's father told him that the Baroness Isabel was still the right-

ful owner of the Vale and its contents, including the Sword and Crown of Wales. Princess Charlotte was her only heir, and Lon ap Llewelyn, via complicated ancestral blood ties, was linked to the Sword—and only Isabel knew why. He could, she knew, with the proper knowledge, legitimately claim them, but Isabel forbade it, bequeathing the relics to Princess Charlotte, and no one understood why.

"But by possessing the Sword and Crown of Wales, removing them from the Vale," said Charles, "if we must and bringing it to Pembroke, our family will have unlimited control of the coastline, second only to the King! And your marriage to Princess Charlotte has insured that you, my son, can take possession of the relics!"

"You're saying I won't be throttled if I lift the Sword?"

"No," said Charles, shaking his head. "Princess Charlotte must remove the Sword and bring it to us."

"She will never do that, Father," said Garret. "She would rather die first, than see a Norman in possession of the Sword and Crown of Wales."

"Even her husband?"

"Even her husband. Let them be where they are," warned Garret. "There are forces at work here and an ancient people whose affection, not animosity, I want."

"Make her," said Charles.

Garret became furious, remembering the way his wife was brought to the castle.

"I will never force my princess to do anything against her will."

Charles stared at him.

"You're in love with the girl," said his father.

"Yes," said Garret. "I love her, and she will never, as long as I draw breath, be mistreated again by anyone."

For a second Garret had almost forgotten about the moment in the study, seeing only a greedy, grasping man before him, bent on acquiring as much power as he could.

"If you'll excuse me," Charlotte told him quietly, suddenly very pale. Another betrayal. There was no one she could trust, not even her husband.

Garret stood up, granting permission for his wife to leave, feeling such a murderous rage build in him that he was afraid he would strangle Alaric of York right here in front of his mother.

"Lady Charlotte." Alaric stood and bowed, watching with glittering black eyes as the beautiful princess left the great hall.

"I want you out of my house," Garret ordered quietly. He couldn't stop himself from seeing his wife's face, the expression of betrayal, horrified over what they were planning to do. And he understood why. If she had a heritage *separate* from his, she had a sense, a *feeling*, of being independent, not totally at the mercy of others. Hearing that everything she was to inherit was to be absorbed into the Pembroke holdings, stripped away all her hope. He understood this, and he cared about her enough to feel her pain.

"Garret," chided Alaric softly, seating himself once again, "your *father,* the *lord of Pembroke,* has offered us *his* hospitality, and I don't think," he turned halfway around and stared at the empty garden door, "that he is quite ready for *us* to leave just yet!"

Seeing the gloating expression in York's eyes, seeing his mother seated at the table, so utterly passive—so uncaring of what could be taking place in the garden at this very minute—hatred poured through his veins, making his muscles stand out in sharp relief, causing his fists to clench, knowing without a doubt that he could break Alaric in two, but frustrated at being unable to do anything about it.

"Sleep lightly, Alaric," Garret warned. The knight of Pembroke grinned coldly, his expression freezing Alaric of York to the marrow of his bones.

"Threatening a guest, are we?" Alaric said, forcing himself to smile as though he weren't suddenly very afraid to lie down tonight.

"Take it however you want," Garret whispered, bending over the table, his eyes burning into York's, causing the man to draw away, while Garret wished with every fiber of his being that he would shove him, just once—or even just *act* like he would. He wanted a reason to shake the life out of the man, knowing his intentions were to somehow hurt his family. Family was everything to Garret. No one, not so long as he had a breath left inside of him, would ever harm a Montgomery.

Alaric stared into Garret's face, knowing what he wanted and wondering if he had pushed just a little too far this time. But no, he wouldn't give him what he wanted; the odds were simply not in his favor.

"Really, Garret," he said quietly, his gaze traveling to Grace, who was watching the confrontation between her son and their guest with a look of absolute horror on her face. "Your *mother...*"

A laugh, low and dangerous, rumbled from between Garret's lips. He marveled at how this man would use anything to gain his ends, even his mother.

"*Bon appétit,*" he murmured lightly, thrusting his knife into the oak table with a vicious stab as he straightened up. "Mother." He spoke softly, bowing low to her, noting the extreme flush in her cheeks. Instantly he felt guilty for having caused this saintly woman any pain. "Good night," he murmured when she gave no reply. He left the room, leaving Alaric of York and his father's wife at the long table, alone with only the servants to stand guard while he went to find Princess Charlotte.

Chapter 18

Knowing he had just escaped with his life, Alaric pretended to be quite busy with the rest of his supper. Minutes passed, and each time he glanced up, he noticed how Grace kept looking at the garden door—the *empty* garden door. With each furtive, wistful peep, Alaric's spirits soared. His plan was turning out just the way he wanted! Soon, he thought to himself… soon. He tossed down the last of his wine with a satisfied grunt of approval.

"Your gardens must be quite extensive," Alaric remarked nastily, trying without much success to keep from gloating.

Flushing slightly, Grace looked from him to her garden's empty doorway and back down to her plate of uneaten food.

"They *are* quite large," she offered lamely. Her voice had the injured quality of a small child expecting to be scolded. It was as soft as silk and as far away as a dream, the words starting out reasonably strong and trailing away to a whisper, while her hands folded and twisted the napkin lying in her lap into one gigantic knot.

"Perhaps you would show them to *me*, lovely lady," he replied with a charming smile. The idea of seducing a nun had always appealed to him, simply because it was so *wrong*, so *forbidden.* And she, swathed head to heel in thick white wool and wimple, with her rosary dangling from her girdle like an amulet, fit his fantasy perfectly.

He admitted to himself that she was beautiful. Her skin was alabaster and porcelain, a quality of ivory that shone like polished stone. Her cheeks were high and blushed with pink as were her lips. But it was her eyes that struck him. They were sapphire-blue with thick lashes and dark brows which matched her ebony hair.

Her son looked a great deal like his mother, just much more masculine.

"I hardly think..." she began timidly, searching through her plate of currants and lamb for divine inspiration. "That would not be appropriate."

"Appropriate?" Alaric goaded. "Are you saying it wasn't *appropriate* for your husband and his guest to be walking in a moonlit garden? Alone?" He baited her and humiliated her at the same time. So chaste. So pure and docile. Such a perfect example for womanhood everywhere, he thought in disgust.

"I only meant..." she stammered, blushing furiously now, her pale hands darting nervously in her lap like imprisoned doves.

"Yes?" he prompted, laying aside the shining, clean bone of his meat to give her his undivided attention. *Quite pretty, really.* he thought. *Quite fragile... so easily broken.*

"I..." she started to say, and he watched in amused silence as she fingered her beads, unable to meet his gaze.

"He is the lord of the manor," she began to recite.

He smiled darkly as he saw her tremble. A delicate porcelain doll. Hardly a match for a snorting bull like Charles.

"What's good for the goose," he challenged as he lifted the silver goblet to his thin ruddy lips, "is a veritable *feast* for the gods." He ended his suggestive remark with a lecherous wink. "Have you *feasted*, Lady Montgomery?" he asked with a cunning smile as he boldly caught her gaze, letting his eyes travel brazenly over her face, finally settling on her tiny heaving bosom. "Or are you starving?" She gasped, and he smiled. "There are some things, madam," he murmured evilly, lecturing her with a calculating grin on his lips as he continued to undress her in his mind, "that one does not *pray* for. One simply reaches out," he paused dramatically with his arm extended, grasping at an imaginary object in the air, his ruby rings glittering on his long, wan fingers like baleful scarlet eyes, "and takes, as your husband did, I might add. You don't really believe they've been out there all this time *smelling the roses, do you?*" He spoke with acid sweetness, and he watched with satisfaction as the pale woman turned the color of marble. He began to chuckle.

"Of course," he said with a thoughtful frown, swallowing a small piece of a crisp new turnip, "you're the type of good woman who would *ignore* such behavior. Turn the other cheek. Yes," he murmured evenly, as he picked up his goblet of silver and sipped the fragrant red wine, appearing to be deep in thought. "You'll *forgive* him, won't you? Forgive him… and perhaps not mention that you knew he was… he was making *love* to a virtual stranger in your garden, practically right in front of you—while you were having supper, I might add. Hardly appetizing, I should think," he muttered disdainfully as he turned another shank of cold lamb over, examining it carefully as he held it delicately between two long fingers. "Or perhaps," he added thoughtfully, letting the piece of meat fall to the gilt-edged serving tray with a rattle, "*you* might be the type of woman who is *grateful* that she came along and released you, however temporarily, from your *loathsome wifely duties.*

"Sleeping with a man you don't love, even if he is your husband, or so I've been told, is such a burden. Don't you agree, Lady Montgomery?"

Alaric smiled wickedly. He dabbed his lips with a flourish of his handkerchief and a dignified sniff.

With a strangled cry, Grace rose from the table. "I love my husband," she said. "You're vile, and so is that horrible woman you've brought here to seduce my husband. She won't win. Lord Charles won't betray me! He is a good man, like our son Garret!"

"We'll see. By the way, are you going to pray for me, Lady Montgomery? Isn't that what a saint would do?"

Grace began to cry and fled from the room, pursued by Alaric's wicked laughter and the staring eyes of the horrified servants.

"Nicely done, Alaric of York! Very nice work indeed!" Alaric complimented himself. His dialect changed back to his familiar Anglo-Saxon dialect. He was neither Welsh nor Norman nor Saxon. His heritage was as shadowy as his past, and his deeds were nefarious and legion.

Smiling at the empty table, he dabbed at the corners of his mouth with the snow-white linen napkin, laughing beneath his breath. He knew Grace would never confront her husband to ask what transpired in the garden; therefore, he deduced accurately, she would never tell Charles what *he, Alaric of York*, had said to *her*. And the servants—well, they would never open their mouths to the lord of the manor. Each other, perhaps, behind the stairwell or in the stables or kitchens, but never to the fierce lord of Pembroke.

"Now," he mused out loud, pouring himself a congratulatory cup of wine, "if my darling Nell is doing her job properly, Pembroke will be *mine* in three days' time!"

* * *

"Come to my room, Charles," purred Nell. Her attempts to seduce him in the garden had failed.

"You don't understand," Charles said softly, not entirely understanding why he had left the dining hall with her in the first place. Perhaps it was flattering that such a beautiful woman so boldly flirted with him in front of his other guests. Yet he was sick with himself at what he had done, but he had good reason.

"I'm a married man," he said firmly "Your note to me beneath the table said you needed to talk to me regarding the safety of my family. That is the only reason I am here."

Nell frowned. Thinking quickly, she said, "Lord Charles, you must come to my room. I've something to show you regarding Alaric of York. I can't translate it. It is written in French, but he kept it hidden and I know it has something to do with you, your son, and the Sword and Crown of Wales."

Lord Charles bowed. "All right. I'll go to your rooms to see what it is that you possess that threatens my family, Lady Gwynn."

"How *chivalrous* you are," she murmured sweetly, tearing a blade of grass down its middle, thinking he was the biggest *fool* she had ever met. "Charles, *look at me.* Since you won't let me be your fantasy, then let me be your sin. I've a need of a man like you."

"Show me the message you intercepted," he said. "That is all I want to see. Your reward will be great, Nell. My family is all that matters to me."

Nell laughed. "You'll regret rejecting me, Lord Charles," she predicted. "I know you are a man of honor; therefore, I'll show you the message I intercepted from Alaric. The price will be high, Lord Charles. Are you willing to pay it?"

"I'd give my life for my family," he said softly.

Nell smiled slyly. "Yes, I believe you would! Come to my room, Lord Charles, and I will give you the message Lord Alaric gave to me. You better hurry, however, before I change my mind!" Her green eyes were glittering.

Chapter 19

"What am I, Gerald?" Princess Charlotte had asked sweetly, with her characteristic directness, so many years ago. Gerald had nearly fallen from his horse. Now, sitting in Montgomery's secluded garden, with her hopes of escape thwarted time and time again and her heritage being transported over a road to Pembroke, leaving her with nothing, she clung to that memory with her last vestiges of hope.

"Nothing to concern yourself with," he had growled that soft summer day, pretending to search the rugged peaks with interest for something which might divert her.

"I'm *not* a lady," she argued stubbornly. "I'm a *brat*—Grandmother said so."

"You're not a brat!" he countered with feeling. The edges of his deep black mustache, which curved arrogantly over his firm lips, dropped even farther when he frowned, making his face, with its wide slashing scar, appear even more fierce, but not to her.

Never to her. To her, he was her friend.

"Then what *am* I? An orphan, when my mother died as I was born," she said softly, pulling absently on the mane of her little dark pony. "I would have liked to have known her, Gerald. My mother. Why does Grandmother hate her so and me as well?"

So sad, he thought, so confused, so *alone*...

"You're the heiress to the Vale, m'lady," he stated truthfully with satisfaction. "A true Celt, and the rightful ruler of *all* of Wales, not just the Vale!" he said with pride.

"Like Grandmother?" she ventured, looking cautiously at him from beneath long, spiky, jet-black lashes that matched her eyebrows perfectly. The thought of being like that dark and brooding woman was beyond her comprehension.

"No, not like her at all," he admitted ruefully, scratching his beard. "More like *your* mother, the first Lady Charlotte, for whom you're named. Only, little miss, *more* the rightful ruler than even she because—" He stopped, a pained expression on his face as his loyalty to Isabel fought with his damaged conscience. "You're like the *old* queen of Wales… Boudicca!" he said with satisfaction, smiling brilliantly.

"Who?" she asked curiously, a frown threatening to solder her midnight-hued eyebrows together permanently as she tried to remember a Boudicca, queen or otherwise, among her small circle of acquaintances.

Gerald laughed softly, gently brushing back a loose tendril of her hair from her cheek as he gazed down at his charge with utter devotion and genuine love. "Long ago, little one," he whispered, feeling the magic and beauty of the legend filling him at once, "there was a great and powerful queen of the Iceni with raven-black hair, who loved her country and king *even unto death*."

"Ah, a story!" Charlotte cried excitedly, sitting up in her saddle with renewed interest shining brightly from her wild blue eyes.

"Yes." Gerald smiled indulgently. His façade, hardened by years of pain and frustrated denial, began to melt, and his hard, obsidian-shadowed eyes took on a dreamy quality so uncharacteristic of the burly old soldier that Charlotte peered at him curiously. "A *true* story," he offered. "A story about the power of love and courage and birth—and destinies that are set *even before we breathe…*"

Charlotte looked confused again. Destinies and birth? What

did that have to do with her? And if he was going to tell a story, why couldn't it be about the faeries that haunted the glen or the nasty-tempered trolls that lurked beneath fallen trees, waiting to get you—or at *least*, she pouted sullenly, twirling the ends of her fine hair into one gigantic knot, dragons that breathed fire and flew high above everyone's heads with maidens gripped helplessly in their claws? Why did it have to be about some old queen?

Noting her displeasure, he shook her loose, swinging hair, carefully sorting out the knots, and laughed softly.

"You must know your people, mistress," he admonished sternly, patting her hair into place with both of his huge hands. "We Welsh do not bear the yoke well—not even from our own brothers!"

Nodding her head obediently, Charlotte pretended to understand until a bright blue butterfly hovering near a sunny head of clover caught her eye and her attention began to wander.

"That butterfly is quite beautiful," Gerald reprimanded her softly. "But do you think *he* can tell you the story of a *warrior* queen?"

A warrior queen! she thought with a gasp, her head snapping around so fast that she heard a loud pop.

"A warrior queen?" she asked dubiously, not believing there ever was such a thing. But the bright gleam in her eyes foretold her avid interest.

"Aye," answered Gerald, keeping a note of disinterest in his voice. "A real queen. One who fought against the Romans hundreds of years ago."

"Tell me!" she begged. "Did she use a sword and have her own pony? Did she wrestle?"

"Quiet, now," he scolded. "I'll tell you what she did, if you just give me half a chance!" he said, laughing at her enthusiasm and loving her for it.

"Well?" she prompted when the story didn't begin with his

next breath, her patience wearing thin as her old teacher collected his thoughts.

"Well, mistress… long ago," he began, slowing his horse to a gentle walk, "it seems the arrogant Romans wished to rule the world, invading our beautiful land. They had come over the water in lumbering ships sent by their Emperor Claudius, who was bent on proving to his subjects that he was a great general. You see, up until that time, the Romans saw Claudius as nothing more than a lame and stuttering scholar—hardly the image of a god."

"What's that got to do with a warrior queen!" she asked impatiently, squirming in her saddle.

"I'm getting to that, mistress," he answered indulgently. "You have to learn to have patience, too, it seems."

Scowling, she refused to look at him, staring down at her fingers, while he continued his story.

"The Roman soldiers came, taking pieces of Britain by sword and shield, eating up the land until they were at the very steps of *our* mountains, coming down through the passes like a devouring plague on our people, destroying fields, enslaving women, *selling* our beloved children into bondage, forcing us to *kneel!*"

Instinctively Gerald clasped the hilt of his sword as the story swept him back in time, a savage pride flowing through his veins, for he was of the glorious Iceni, the first people to settle this land.

"Yet," he continued, his voice ringing across the valley like steel, "for all their furious attempts at conquest, they gained a bit of sod here, a tree there, brook and meadow, but they couldn't defeat *us!* For we, peasant and aristocracy alike, are the heirs of the earth and the worshipers of the moon, a blending of the old and taming of the new. The land, our dear mother, protected her children well, swallowing the Romans in steep chasms, hiding the Iceni in shrouded caves or secret glens."

"Like the stone garden at Aberystwyth?" she offered, thinking of the secret hidden place with the curiously mounted stones and circular rings.

"Aye," he offered sagely, "just like Aberystwyth. But the Romans, out of swollen pride for all the battles they'd won, could not accept defeat at the hands of pagans and peasants. So they tricked Prastigus, King of the Iceni, into believing that they had given up, wanting only to negotiate peace, but in reality what they had in mind was a trap—a cowardly ambush from which neither he nor his men would ever escape."

Gerald's eyes burned as if with a fever, as though his ancestors' blood cried out the betrayal anew in his veins. He could see in his mind the Welsh king as he trustingly laid down his sword and entered the valley while the traitorous Romans closed in behind, cutting off his escape. Indeed, he could almost *feel* the confusion, the *hatred*. Looking up, he knew that the same lemon-yellow sun that shone down on him this day had lit the valley for his brothers centuries before and had witnessed their betrayal.

"There was no hope," he said softly. "None at all. All the men were slain or wounded, their red blood turning the floor of the valley crimson and staining the water settling in the bogs and boles a deep scarlet."

"What's happened to Queen Boudicca?" Charlotte asked breathlessly, knowing the next part of the story would be the best.

"She came," he said quietly, knowing that the ancient queen's motives went far beyond mere patriotism. "Boudicca had been the king's wife for eighteen years, and when she learned of the treachery, she rallied her people to follow her and her daughters into battle. Druid, she was—brave as any man, schooled in the arts of Star and Leaf and Sign. Before leaving her bourne, she retired to a sacred grove and prayed to the warrior goddess Adraste: 'If not victory,' she begged, 'then grant me but one last kiss.' And with her raven staff thrust out defiantly before her," Gerald told her, holding his sword out in the late afternoon light until the steel caught and reflected the sun's glow like fire, "the brave queen climbed into her fleet wooden cart and led her women and children, the old and sick, into a battle they could not possibly hope to win."

A quietness descended on the valley as they continued their ride. Gerald was so engrossed in the story that a crack seemed to develop between the past and present, a void in the fabric of time. In his mind he could see the beautiful Queen Boudicca, long since gone and turned to dust, leading her people courageously into a battle already lost.

"The Romans," continued Gerald soberly as his little mistress stared avidly into his face, "fought with precision, like a machine, mowing down all who opposed them. They were as cruel as their blood-reeking spears, showing no mercy. It was slash-and-burn warfare. The young and old, male and female, child, feeble old man, it didn't matter, all fell beneath their dripping blades. Yet these soldiers saw with their hardened, veteran eyes a beautiful woman in their midst with billowing clouds of jet-black hair shot through at the temples with lightning streaks of white, shouting orders, giving encouragement—in the very thick of it! Her eyes were alight and filled with blue fire! And she fought against them! Fought! Even when there was no chance of winning. Knowing the next spear would take her life as surely as the sun would rise in the morning! Ah!" He sighed in wonder. "Boudicca of the Iceni! More like the goddess Aeronwen of war that day than a woman! Boudicca struck again and again at the Romans with almost supernatural fury!

"They say the winds blew cold from the north, bitter winds howling like banshees, and the campfires the Romans set, their flames turned blue and no man could draw near them. Their fires gave no warmth but had turned to ice!"

Charlotte's eyes grew round with wonder. The thought of a warrior woman—a leader of her people—made her courageous little heart beat furiously. *She* would be a warrior someday, too, she vowed—and a *queen*, thinking how perfectly wonderful going into battle would be.

They stopped beside the River Mynach, near the town of Aberystwyth, beneath the cascading falls which tumbled over 300 feet into the valley below, to water their horses.

"Queen Boudicca fought for her people, the Iceni, for our freedom. She fought as our queen, but also as a woman passionately searching for her husband. She was a devoted wife, and it was told that when news came that her husband had fallen in battle, she refused to step down or seek safety by escaping to the coast. She could not be consoled, and feeling as though her life meant nothing without him to stand beside, she strapped her athamé to her leg, took her short sword and arrows, and led a fatal charge against the invaders from which there was no way back and no hope of victory."

He told her this part softly, watching the flicker of doubt register in her mind, clouding her eyes. "Aye, mistress. I'm telling you the truth. As hard as it may be for you to believe, she fought not just for the love of battle, but for a *man*, for Boudicca knew that she had been *born* to be with him, that she *belonged* to him and him to her since before the beginning of time."

"Why?" Charlotte asked curiously, too young to understand the mysteries of the cosmos or the devotion that true love brings to the lucky few who are fortunate enough to find each other.

"Because," he told her sweetly, "*it was meant to be!* When Boudicca found her husband on the field, he was badly torn and broken, nearer to the gates of death than life." He whispered her name fervently, a misting in his coal-colored eyes.

"How broken-hearted she must have been as she knelt beside him! They say that she cradled his head against her breast and cried softly until his eyes opened for one last look at his beloved wife. The Romans, out of respect for her bravery in battle, allowed them this time together, yet their swords were drawn, and their archers' bows were trained on the queen's fair form. Her hair, dark and wild as midnight, rained down around her husband, while her fair-skinned body formed a shield over him as she held him close. She did her best to protect what she loved most in this world—the King of the Iceni—her husband.

"The Romans intended to take the queen as a slave. Her beauty was legend. The general, Suetonius, was already hungering to possess her fire and display his prize.

"But the gods were kind to Queen Boudicca. Her life warmed her husband's form, and it is told he stirred in her arms and opened his eyes, gazing at her. Then the king whispered, 'Forever, my love,' and his voice was sweet. The sound of his words became a great, wailing wind and mist rose from the ocean unlike any other seen in the land as the words he said to his beloved wife carried magically for miles, echoing through the valley. Then he died, the great King of the Iceni, content in his beloved wife's arms."

Charlotte gasped.

"What happened to the queen?"

"It is said that when the king died, they all sensed a great thing had happened—a sorrowful event. Even the battlefield, covered in gore and broken bodies, moaning prisoners and gloating victors, had become oddly still, except for the Roman general Suetonius. Rude and impatient for his prize, he reached out to take the grieving queen, as was his due, but before he could claim her, she drew her dagger from beneath her tunic and lunged at him. He retaliated as she knew he would, turning the athamé toward her. The blade plunged deeply into her heart.

"'You'll never have me,' she vowed. 'I will never be your slave!'

"Suetonius was furious as he watched her fall to the ground

next to her husband with her life ebbing slowly away. She turned toward her king and reached for him, kissing him gently on the mouth.

"'Forever, my love,' she said and smiled triumphantly as she followed her husband into his long, dark night."

Sighing, Gerald searched the horizon, his throat constricted and tight, feeling instinctively what the queen had felt, knowing that the bonds of love could stretch to eternity and then some, but never—never—loosen, even in the grim face of death.

"Later," he continued quietly, watching as the sun began to dip toward the ridge of purple mountains in the distance, its passing stirring up the first faint rushes of cool night wind, "after the Romans had taken their captives and left the bloody field, one of Boudicca's daughters stirred from beneath the sweat-soaked body of a fallen Roman. He, too, had tried to possess a princess—his reward, the cold steel of an unforgiving sword!" exclaimed Gerald proudly. "But the girl found refuge beneath him, lying as still as possible under the huge man's body, pretending death.

"When the sounds of tramping feet had cleared the ridge, fading in the distance to only the rumble of distant thunder, she pushed him aside and stood up. Her muscles were cramped and painful, but she felt lucky to be alive. Yet when she saw the horrible carnage around her, a great cry burst from her lips, echoing forlornly for miles. Not more than a few feet away from her lay the bodies of her mother and father, locked forever in an immortal embrace, while above her in the darkening sky, cawing loudly and circling the battlefield, flew Adraste's bird—the raven.

"'Please!' begged the girl. 'Do not let their love be for nothing!' And she fell to her knees in despair, sacrificing her tears, pouring out her pain, offering her prayers on the altar of their love.

"Wherever her mother's tears had fallen, shimmering diamonds formed, and wherever her mother's blood met and mingled with her father's, a large, dark-red ruby glowed with secret life.

"'Thank you,' said Boudicca's daughter, gathering the sacred gems, knowing that it was Adraste's tribute to a love that would last through eternity."

Gerald smiled and stretched, heaving a great sigh as he gazed down at the little princess. The tired lines already forming around his dark eyes deepened as he watched the mist rise like a breath from the cooling earth, reaching with ghostly, ivory-colored fingers over the sharp, snow-capped Cambrian mountains as twilight flowed across the land, painting the valley in smoky, plum-colored shades and shadowy midnight hues.

So tired, he thought. So many regrets. There didn't seem to be much to look forward to except his little mistress's future. Some day she would be the one to unite the kingdom as it had been so long ago. It was her destiny and part of the seemingly invisible thread that wove the stories of history together, directing her future, stitch by invisible stitch, until her life became part of the colorful tapestry of time. Her life was written in the stars.

"The diamonds, little one," Gerald said, "have since then adorned the crown of our queen, and the ruby was embedded deeply into the hilt of a sword. It is with these symbols that the people of Wales recognize their true rulers. And these symbols, Princess Charlotte, belong by birth and blood to you!"

"To me?" she whispered.

The memory faded.

"To me," she said. She was in Lord Montgomery's garden, a prisoner of the present time, about to lose her birthright—her very identity—to Norman invaders.

Bishop came to stand beside her, and she knelt down, hugging his big shaggy head.

"Oh, Bishop! I must find a way to secure the Crown and Sword and return them to Aberystwyth and into Lon's safekeeping! I just have to."

The big dog, not understanding his mistress's words, only the desperate sound in her voice, licked her face with delicate, light strokes, trying very hard to console her.

"My good friend," she said, hugging him tight. She refused to let the tears which had formed in her eyes fall. Tears were precious things, and for all that she had been through and was worth, she still felt betrayed by those who should have loved her most. But she would not allow herself to fall into the trap of self-pity.

"If I would lick your face, would you care about me and perhaps hug me as well?"

Charlotte turned to see Lord Garret standing in the garden, gazing softly at her.

"Would you," he said, "at least, care about me, too?"

Chapter 20

Garret felt an alien fear solder his arms to his sides and his feet to the ground. A lump rose to his throat as Charlotte looked at him, loathing and pain in her clear sapphire eyes. He wished he could take his remark back, grab it from her mind and stuff it back into his mouth, swallow it… start over. He only wanted to talk to her, but every time he did, nothing came out but crass remarks and silly nonsense.

Awkward silence filled the space between them in the shadowed seclusion of the moonlit, mist-covered garden, and an intangible something else—a subtle electricity, an acute *awareness* of the other that was awkward and nearly painful.

"Let me go, Garret," Charlotte whispered brokenly. The words, spoken too softly, with the haunted, lonely look clouding her eyes, filled him with a tearing pain. "You have everything of mine now. Everything. And I have nothing. I *am* nothing."

The swirling fog rose lethargically from the damp, peat-green ground like curious, eavesdropping ghosts, enveloping her legs, making her seem transitory—a fading image Garret was afraid would vanish from his sight as all his other dreams had.

"You're my *wife,*" he said with feeling, advancing a step closer, needing the reassurance of her touch to chase away his doubts that she was an illusion. The desire to comfort her grew stronger by the second.

"You don't understand!" she cried. "That isn't what I *wanted!*"

She stood and stepped forward with her hand placed imploringly next to her heart.

For a moment he forgot to breathe, his heart skipping several beats. He would rather have taken a beating than hear those words from her. *He wanted her; she didn't want him.* It was his worst nightmare come to life, cutting fresh wounds into his soul. His expression remained stoic and didn't reveal the pain he felt, but it seemed as though a great part of him had begun to die. He could feel it as keenly as if someone had cut him and he was bleeding to death right in front of her eyes—and she couldn't see that it was *she* who held the knife.

"It wasn't my choice!" she tried to explain. "Men have ruled the world for so long now that you can't imagine a woman to be anything other than a wife or a mother or a wench. And I am none of these things!"

"Then what *are* you?" he asked harshly. Her rebellious nature fought against the very order of things, fought against the accepted tenets on which his life and all those of his time were built.

"I am a person," she told him softly, wearily, feeling as though she had said that sentence at least a thousand times before, with little, if any, results. "A *real, thinking person.*"

There was a beseeching light shining strongly from her eyes, and her lower lip trembled with emotion. "I have thoughts—dreams—of my own. I *feel*… as you do! I *love* as you do! I *hate* as you do! I am different than you," she admitted, watching as one of his black eyebrows shot up cynically. "But I am as *good* as you!" Seeing the confusion in Garret's eyes, she fell back on the use of a parable, wanting only that he at least try to understand. "If a thin man cannot heft a two-hundred-pound load, do his friends say that he is inferior? No," she supplied the answer, shaking her head vigorously, wanting desperately for him to understand the turmoil raging inside of her. "Those friends look for his other skills. Perhaps he is gifted at writing or reading or figures. Perhaps he can heal or sing. But in everything, though he is different, they still consider him *equal.* Because I do not grow a beard or stand when I pee—does that make me so much less than you?"

"The Scriptures say quite clearly what the natural order is," he told her patiently. "They explain your place and mine. Your obligations and duties, as well as those of every man."

"Who wrote the Bible?" she retorted angrily, assuming her "man-stance" with a fire glowing brightly in her eyes. "Moses, of course! A *man!* I believe in God as described by the Bible. I truly do! My faith in God the Father is strong. I just wonder at the interpretation."

"Divinely inspired, I might add!" Garret retaliated angrily, his square jaw jutting forward defiantly while a lock of his unruly black hair fell once again over his forehead.

"Stew strawberries in a kettle and sift them through cheesecloth," she responded furiously, "and you will get a clear, sweet jelly. But run the same mixture through netting, and you will get a coarse jam!"

"Are we talking about cooking here or the Word of God?" he asked sarcastically, rolling his eyes in a childish exhibition of superiority.

"God's Word, of course!" she replied hotly. "Are you so set in your ways that you cannot understand an analogy when you hear one? I have faith in Him! I pray to Him and believe He hears my prayers! I believe God the Father answers my prayers, too! That I matter to Him."

"To hell with your comparisons, woman!" he shouted, his features darkening like a thundercloud on a hot summer day. "Are you trying to tell me that if God had spoken to a *woman*—instead of His first created being, *Man*—the Bible might have been written *differently*?"

"Yes," she answered firmly, watching the horrified expression on her husband's face grow darker by the second. "By the way," she added haughtily, flipping her veil behind her back. "How do you know He doesn't speak to women? If women were ever allowed to learn to read or write, they might just put down what God tells *them!* I know God is good. I know that He loves all His children. Women would love to read the Word of God if they only could learn to read and write. We would all be so much better for this."

"Humph!" he snorted, folding his brawny arms across his chest. "Women who can read and write! What an oddity. Perhaps they would start their own circus: fat ladies, magicians, and—God help us—*thinking women!* Lord knows those creatures wouldn't fit in anywhere else except a circus—and no *sane* man would consent to harbor one in his own house, let alone *marry* one, I might add!"

"Oh?" she asked quietly, a dangerous light shining from her eyes. "Since you are a man—and so obviously learned—*you,* of course, know that even in the New Testament, Christ, our Lord, *never* speaks of the submission of women to men, only the submission of *all* to God's will. It is only the Apostle Paul and other *males* who speak of a woman's place, teaching submission and instilling guilt in the female of the species—*not Jesus!*

"I love the Scriptures, Garret. I see God as goodness, mercy and kindness, even allowing women to listen to His sermons and to hear His words."

"And how do you know these things?" he snorted, flinging back a wayward curl with an impatient toss of his hand.

"Because," she said angrily, "I can read!"

She expected the admission to bring laughter, or perhaps even a whipping, or a horrified exclamation. Hadn't he said that women who could read belonged in a carnival?

Perhaps she had been going about this annulment business all wrong. Maybe if she had told him at the start that she was literate, he would have sent her packing. Or perhaps his father would never have consented to the match in the first place. No, she thought suddenly with a shudder, Lord Charles would probably have had her burned at the stake. An educated female was probably considered an apostasy, an *unnatural thing*. Women simply did not read, nor did they write, the consensus being that what they harbored between their ears was only a place meant for growing hair and frivolity; a woman's mind held nothing but vanity and wickedness. They were silly, quarrelsome, nagging creatures so wayward that they were easily seduced into evil by a conniving, two-legged snake in the mythical land of Eden nearly six thousand years ago.

Garret looked as though the wind had been knocked completely out of his sails. A woman who could read! He remembered the note Armando had given him—a note he'd thought Charlotte had dictated to the monk, not written! *What next?* he wondered, thoroughly shaken.

"Is that *all* you can do?" he asked icily, coming nearer, remembering the accuracy with which she threw the dagger in the library and her cunning trick in the courtyard.

"No," she told him calmly. "I can write as well." She neglected to tell him, for fear that he would have a heart attack, that she was fluent in both Latin and French, could add and subtract faster in her mind than most scholars on paper, and had a fine understanding of the Greek philosophers. But in all honesty, she would also have to admit that she couldn't sew—not even a stitch—and she was a perfect horror in the kitchen.

"Humph!" he snorted, blinking rapidly as he felt a surprising surge of pride. *She* could read and write!

"Amazing!" he murmured. "Who taught you this?" he asked curiously, having heard so little of her past that he didn't know if her grandmother had granted her a tutor or sent her away to one of the new, revolutionary schools for women or to a nunnery. Women did learn things there. No, he thought to himself wisely. With her temper, she would never have stayed in a convent long enough to learn a single prayer, let alone how to read and write.

"No one," she admitted, a trace of pride coloring her words as she held her head a little higher. "I moved an empty barrel beside the schoolmaster's window and stole a stylus and an inkhorn. Every day I would pretend to take a nap and hide in my barrel. He, Master Talmidge," she hurried to explain, "would read the Psalms and the Greek epics to the thanes… and I learned," she told him sharply, defying him to criticize her. "I learned all that he could teach *them*, practicing at night beneath an oil lamp, hiding my stylus during the day behind a loose stone near the hearth. I loved the Psalms. I loved the way King David sang to God with his words. I had never heard anything quite so beautiful."

"Did your grandmother know?" he asked curiously, sitting down on the garden's solitary stone bench and watching as the fireflies darted around the garden, looking for all the world like glowing faerie-lights bobbing crazily in the mist.

"No," she said with a tired sigh. "But Gerald did."

"Your father?" he asked with a frown.

"No," she admitted, coloring slightly. "He is the Captain of the Guard—a very brave man, who taught me to fight and took care of me since…" And then she paused, coloring even more deeply, as a cool breeze teased at her veil of pale blue silk, a nearly tangible sorrow in her azure-hued gaze that seemed utterly fathomless.

"Tell me something, Charlotte," he asked kindly, watching the moonlight shimmer in the pools of her eyes, reflecting almost silver at times. "Were you always so sad?"

She started in surprise. He was the first person, outside of Gerald, to ever see through her facade, her fierce mask of bravado. *Like a banty rooster, she walks!* Gerald had always said with pride. *See how she pokes her head so belligerently forward and squares her little shoulders as though she's looking for a fight.* Fighting or laughing like a clown; that was her. Making jokes to fill the emptiness in her heart. And *he* had seen the sadness in her, and he knew that it had been there long before he was around. He recognized her sorrow because it was the same feeling that he had carried inside himself all his life. A fighter, too; a warrior to the bitter, bitter end, waiting and wanting only for someone to hold him and let him know that he was loved.

"Sit beside me," he told her softly, patting the bench beside him with one large, calloused hand. "Please…" A ghost of a smile turned his lips upward, a hint of irony in his words.

She hesitated, searching for the challenge in his dark eyes that must surely be there. A challenge—or a trick; that's what his invitation really held. But instead of the cold fire of distant starlight that could burn and torture a soul, his eyes held a rare, warm glow, like candlelight welcoming the weary traveler home.

Cautiously, she sat down, every muscle tense, expecting a headlock any minute, or a cuff to her ear, her flesh tingling as it brushed against his arm and her heart quickening its beat, ready to fight or run. But no attack came. Nothing moved. But his scent, borne on the soft southerly breeze, came to her, filling her with his presence. He smelled like cinnamon and cloves, with a hint of pine soap. Clean and masculine; dark and mysterious as the night. Sexy…

"Oh!" she murmured in surprise as her stomach did a neat little flip. She gripped the bench with both of her hands. Her insides were becoming more like acrobats every day, twisting and tying themselves into unpredictable knots, flipping and somersaulting whenever he was around. Almost shyly she looked up, expecting to see triumph in his gaze. She stared in amazement when she only saw compassion.

"Was growing up at the Vale really so terrible?" he asked, taking a very accurate stab in the dark, wanting to know her, if she'd only just let him in. The look she threw in his direction would have made any ordinary human cringe. Such pain and hatred!

"What would *you* know of how I grew up!" she snapped, sitting up ramrod straight. "You with your fine family!" She flung these words at him, jealousy clouding her heart simply because he had been fortunate enough to be born in the right place at the right time—or so she thought. "A mother and a father, brothers!" she ranted, clenching her jaw tight. "I never knew my mother! Not even what she looked like! Can you understand that?" she asked furiously, kicking at a tuft of dew-lined grass. "My grandmother had all my mother's likenesses destroyed! Every one of them! I used to stare at my reflection for hours in the bronze mirror in our great hall until my head ached and my eyes burned, wondering *who* I looked like. I would watch the servants walk past, or stare like an idiot whenever the nobles came to visit—searching, always searching for a sameness in them, wondering *who* I was, pretending to be this one's daughter because his hair was light, or that one's daughter because his eyes were blue. And as for my *real* father—I'm quite sure he was a very brave fellow indeed!" she told him bitterly, swallowing hard as bile rose to scorch her throat. "Although he was never brave enough to introduce himself to *me!*"

Garret knew that she was illegitimate but hearing her admit it made him furious—not at her, in her innocence, but at a man who would not take responsibility for his actions. Flushing slightly, he turned his head away to stare into the distance, thinking of the shame she must have had to endure, the torment of not knowing *who* she was, feeling a deep sense of pity for his little wife as he listened to her story.

"But Gerald," she added, in defense of her first friend and teacher, blocking his betrayal of her from her mind as easily as closing a door to a room she didn't want to enter, "he taught me! He helped me!" She told him this almost fiercely, looking frankly into his face. "He told me about the Legend and the Sword of Wales and about how I was destined to be a queen because of it! *He told me who I was!* Don't you see? He told me *who I am*—and now you've taken even that, and I am left with nothing!"

Garret didn't know anything about the Legend, only that his father had developed a fanatical obsession with the Sword of Wales. Even Alaric of York seemed inordinately interested in it.

"Charlotte," he said passionately, taking her by the shoulders, "I want you to listen to me. I had *nothing* to do with the taking of your sword or your heritage. I wouldn't do that to you!

"King Henry decreed that your property was to be distributed according to his wishes, and that the Vale would come under his rule. Henry II is a strong ruler. He has most of the island already. Even parts of France have fallen under his control. Now he wants Wales as well. He wants it all, and one way or the other, with Empress Matilda behind him, he will have it! At least," he reasoned with her, "with the Sword and Crown in *our* possession," he added, careful to use the term "our" to show her how he felt about his things and hers, "*you* will still maintain the right to rule Wales."

"With you by my side, no doubt!" she spat.

Shrugging, he dropped his hands to his sides, watching as she fought to control her tears, brushing her hand impatiently across her face.

"Always sad. Always on the verge of tears or fighting mad. Yet you never cry. Why is that?" he asked compassionately, having watched her control her sorrow at least twice now.

"Because!" she told him furiously through gritted teeth, beginning to feel her nose start to run and pinching it hard to stop it. "I just don't cry!" She didn't bother to tell him how often the tears had come in her life, filling her eyes with their salty wetness, and something inside of her, made of steel and stone, would instantly spring to life and clamp down on those weak, nasty things and drive them back inside. There must be a lake of them in her by now, a dam brimming full of unshed tears. But her life had no place for self-pity, and so that pool of sadness lay still and silent, becoming fuller as the years went by.

"You think," he told her, biting on his lower lip and studying a distant, wet-blackened yew, "that my life was so *perfect?*" He laughed. It was a hard, biting sound, devoid of humor, brittle and cold as ice. "Well," he picked her up as easily as if she were a child and set her down firmly on his broad lap, "it wasn't."

"Let go of me!" she cried.

"I won't harm you, Charlotte," he told her gently, holding her hands tenderly as she struggled. "Listen," he pleaded earnestly, cupping her chin in one hand and forcing her to look at him. "Please," he offered, granting her twice the gift of a word he very seldom, if *ever*, used. "I want to tell you a story. *My story.*"

A somber light was burning in his midnight-blue eyes, and she became still, unwilling to admit to herself that she wanted to hear what he had to say.

"Do you think that if you have a set of parents, your life is automatically wonderful? It's not. When I was young, I learned how to earn my father's attention and respect. It was easy. If I could run faster, fight harder, be stronger than everyone else, then he would notice me. I had to be the best or I was nothing. There was no gain for a runner-up or second place."

Garret remembered the day the tide turned in their relationship from indifference to interest. He could still see his father standing in the courtyard with his fierce, hawk-blue eyes glowing when he looked at his son.

Garret was taught to fight. Every day, bare-knuckled, he went to the courtyard where the older knights jeered that he'd come for his daily thrashing, which had become a local sporting event.

The matches were uneven; the weight and height of his opponents were out of proportion to his age and size. But Garret did not complain. He went and he stood his ground, lifting his arms and taking on the challenge.

"Life is not fair," said an older, seasoned knight. "At war with another, they won't count or let you sit it out or care that they are bigger than you. That is why you must be better than them, because it is your life that hangs in the balance, Lord Garret. Your life. Now fight!"

And he did. He became a machine. Beyond pain and thought. Technique, violence and anger directed with each blow. When the event was over, four older boys lay nursing a variety of wounds, and Garret turned to look belligerently at his father, sucking the blood from his wounded knuckles, expecting the older man to walk off as usual with only another reminder of his next session.

Instead, his father remained silent and nodded slowly. A gleam lit the older man's eyes, accentuating their sharpness, making them look like glistening, marbled glass. A slight tremor drove the corners of his mouth upward in a mirthless parody of a smile. Pride colored his features. His chest swelled. Charles strutted in the courtyard like a peacock. He had obtained his goal: Garret was a champion! And Garret? What was his reward for these brutal lessons? Why, that was simple: His father was finally proud of him!

So that's the key, Garret thought shrewdly that hot August day. Be the best at everything, then my father will be proud of me. Otherwise, I'm nothing to him.

"So that's what I did," he mused coolly, remembering the incident as clearly as if it had happened yesterday. "I became the best I could at everything he instructed me to do, always waiting, wanting to hear him say just once that he was proud of me. But he never did.

"I realized as I got older that my father could never say the words that I wanted to hear. Somehow that was a weakness that would wreck the iron-fisted rule he had over his sons. Over me. Yet he tried to show us in other ways."

For a moment, Garret was silent, remembering the velvet warmth of the cape and his father's hushed voice telling him that he loved him. "Possibly my father believes that to admit to someone that you love them is weakness.

"There is no place in a man for that, is there?"

Garret looked at Charlotte tenderly. A sad smile lit his features. His hands let loose of her arms, and he wrapped his arms protectively around her.

"So I learned early on to never expect affection from my father. It was beyond him. I expected anger, indifference, and disappointment if I should ever lose at anything, but never affection. I stood like a soldier in his presence and that is what I became. A knight of the realm coming home from war to cheers and a firm handshake, salted with a "Well done, my son," and somehow, Charlotte, that was enough.

"Red in tooth and claw, that is the world I live in—I fight for those who cannot. It is what I was trained to do. I am the King's man—a knight and proud to be so.

"But my mother," he went on cynically, sighing and shaking his head.

Charlotte watched in amazement as the dark god of war holding her blushed.

He lifted his head to look upward and his dark hair cascaded down his neck. He smiled recklessly, a flash of white teeth, and his blue eyes glowed warm in the light of the moon. "How do I describe her? A saint? Too good and beautiful for this world? Perhaps."

"She is very kind, isn't she?" said Charlotte. "Your mother Grace."

"My mother is a good woman," Garret said with finality, defending her at once.

For an instant Charlotte had the eerie sensation that he was trying to convince himself of that fact and not her.

"But you see, she never wanted to marry my father. He saw her when she was thirteen at the tournaments in Ashby. Her beauty was legend, yet she was modest and humble and hid amongst the nuns. The story goes that he couldn't live without her, begging her father for her hand, bribing him with nearly half of his fortune.

"And it was arranged. My mother was taken literally by force from the convent and into this house. It was the dead of winter. November. This house was made ready for their lady; every room shone and every hearth was lit. Her composure, they said, was amazing. Greeting everyone politely, she was escorted to her rooms. A year later, I was born in the dead of winter. My brothers followed later."

"What happened between them, your mother and father? They seem so distant. He spends all his time acquiring property and treasure, and she is up before dawn, with her rosary in the chapel. I heard her singing one morning, sweet as a nightingale singing the Lord's Prayer. She is so gentle with such incredible faith."

Garret smiled. He loved his mother very much.

"Yes," Garret said. "They have gone their separate ways and yet she abides by her marriage vows as any good woman would."

"Is that a barb sent in my direction?" Charlotte asked.

"More like a dagger," laughed Garret.

Charlotte smiled and blushed and felt like boxing his ears.

She left us one day," he said. "Not physically, but emotionally. Her days started in the chapel and ended there. She gave up her elegant four-poster and traded it for a nun's cottage, caring for the villagers bodily and for their souls as she began to pray unceasingly.

"Her kindness never abated. Her politeness toward her husband was ever present, yet she was distant. And her boisterous sons would tumble through the door, lifting her with hugs and kisses, and she would laugh, calling us her greatest joy. Her love for us was ever present, even to challenging Father when his sternness became too repressive. So little, she would stand between us and I kept thinking a strong wind would make her tumble, but Father would recant and his temper would subside. 'Go pray for me, Grace,' he'd shout, shake his head and be on his way."

Garret laughed. "I'm sure she did. For all of us."

"She loves you," Charlotte said. She had seen the way Grace looked at him: the tenderness in her eyes and the way she would hold herself as if she were holding her child against her.

"I know," said Garret. "That is one constant in my chaos I never doubted. My mother has always loved me."

Charlotte looked down, quietly envying such a strong love.

"Perhaps that is where you've learned to love, Garret. From your mother."

Garret smiled. "Maybe."

"I want my sons to love me as you do your mother," Charlotte said. Her decision was made.

"Our sons?" Garret said. One dark eyebrow arched above his eyes.

Charlotte was utterly quiet. Crickets filled the void, and the croaking of bullfrogs accentuated the music of the surf pounding like thunder against the coast. The clearing was now totally filled with ivory-colored mist, and the moon had hidden itself behind a gauzy bit of floating haze, becoming an obscurely shy, silvery light. The world seemed to have vanished, and all that existed were the two of them.

"Our sons," Charlotte said.

Garret nodded and gently pressed his lips against her mouth.

Above them in an ancient yew, a nightingale began to sing while the mist rose like the wings of a swan, covering their bodies in a garden of clouds.

Chapter 21

The first light of dawn was streaking the gray sky, but it didn't appear ashen and drab to Charlotte, it looked like silver, the color that lines all black clouds and eventually brings joy.

She was trapped, and, perversely, she didn't want to be free. Even though Garret had a huge four-poster bed and plenty of room, he was sleeping peacefully nearly on the edge, lying halfway across her. *He must weigh eighteen stones!* she thought sleepily. Yet for some inexplicable reason, she didn't mind the feeling of his weight one bit.

Garret's right arm was curled possessively around her middle, and every time she moved, even an inch, he would draw her back underneath him with a jealous growl, throwing one leg over her. She couldn't breathe very well, she mused as she studied the cracks in the ceiling, and she had a horrible cramp in her side. Yet, she thought with a dreamy half-smile, closing her eyes in contentment, she had never been happier in her life.

The door to the bedroom opened slowly. Charlotte peered over Garret's bulging biceps and watched as her little maid tiptoed quietly to her side.

"What is it?" she whispered softly, immediately eliciting an endearing snore from her sleeping husband and another possessive tug of his arm, until only the top of her head and two startlingly blue eyes were visible.

"Your grandmother," replied Sparrow as quietly as she could.

Her brown eyes were wide, and she couldn't help but flush slightly at the sight of the couple in their marriage bed.

"My *what!*" said Charlotte.

Muttering a Celtic oath only the gods could hear, Lady Charlotte tossed her husband's arm away, waking him with a startled oath.

"Your grandmother Isabel is *here*, Lady Charlotte," Sparrow replied nervously, looking at her sleepy-eyed lord, his broad chest exposed to the waist.

"My grandmother Isabel is here at Pembroke!?"

The anger in her voice caused Sparrow to take a cautious step backward.

"Yes, m'lady," Sparrow stuttered. "In the solar along with a big brute of a soldier, too! Got a wicked scar runs halfway down his face! He looks like an old knotted tree, he does, and as *mean* as a cornered bull! And those black eyes of his! Lord, but he gave me a shiver! I've never seen such eyes! So dark and piercing! He looks like a brigand! Or a *murderer!* Like he could slit a body's throat while he's sipping tea and not think nothing of it!"

"Gerald, Captain of the Guard," snapped Charlotte. "Enough of your insults. He has been with the family for years and is a good man."

She hurriedly pulled on her dressing gown.

"Here at Pembroke?" she said incredulously. She ignored the soft Moroccan leather slippers by her bed. Dumbfounded, she tied her sash with one vicious, wrenching tug. "What trick is that devious *woman* planning this time!" she muttered furiously as she headed for the door.

"Charlotte?" Garret called softly from their bed.

The princess paused long enough to stare at her magnificent husband, his dark head resting on his strong hand, his eyes still half-closed and heavy-lidded with sleep, looking like a sated panther curling beneath the linens.

A new emotion replaced the ambivalent feelings of the past: possessiveness. He made her feel selfish, wanting only his touch and determined that no other should ever take her place beside him in bed.

"Do you need me?" he asked calmly, one black eyebrow arching. "I'm always ready for a fight."

"No doubt," she said. "I'll always need you, Garret. But not for this! This is my home and that woman has no place in it!" Angrily, she slammed the door on her way out of the room.

* * *

"I wonder if she will see me?" murmured the Baroness de Clare softly as she stared out the window.

"I have no doubt of that, Isabel," answered Gerald familiarly, wrapping his arms around her waist to reassure her. "I just don't know what *weapon* she will choose."

"Humph!" snorted Isabel, with a wry smile. "How true."

She hugged the stout arms surrounding her, resting the back of her head against his chest familiarly. *So this is peace*, she thought with a sad, wise smile as she listened to the steady, rhythmic beating of her lover's heart. *This is what I was really searching for all my life.*

The door to the solar was thrust back with unrestrained fury, and a barefoot woman with silver hair and gleaming eyes bore down on the pair with murder blazing in her liquid gaze—coming up short when she saw her grandmother and Gerald in their intimate embrace.

"So!" she raged in disbelief, stalking around the pair, her hands welded to her hips. "*This* is what you betrayed me for, Gerald?" she snapped, tapping her foot angrily on the floor. Her jaw was clenched so tightly that her face had drained completely of color, making her eyes dance like livid blue flames in her pale face. "Is this what *she* promised you for becoming a traitor to me? A chance to romp in her bed?"

"It isn't what you think," replied Gerald quietly as they broke apart. His face blushed crimson-red, making him appear like a precocious schoolboy caught kissing behind the gate, while his gaze sought the floor, trying desperately to escape the accusations in his young mistress's blazing eyes.

"No?" Charlotte asked acidly, marveling at what a fool she had been all these years. Fool enough to believe that Gerald had truly loved her, thinking of him like the father she'd never had. But her grandmother, it seemed, had won again, manipulating *him* as she did everyone else, with frightening ease.

"No!" said her grandmother forcefully, breaking through her thoughts and coming forward to stand flat-footed and coolly in front of her glowering granddaughter. "No, Charlotte," she repeated in her powerful voice, a voice that seemed to reverberate and echo off the walls in the brightly-lit solar. "It isn't at all what you think!"

She was dressed in deep maroon. Her hair was still lustrous and full, and her eyes still glowed with a deep inner strength that seemed to defy the years. Silence filled the space as the two women eyed each other.

Gerald had the distinct impression of two cats squaring off, hackles raised, claws unsheathed, expecting one of them to leap any minute and the fur to begin to fly. Suddenly, to his surprise, Isabel smiled.

"You know," she told Charlotte with a rare grin, cocking her head to one side, "you really *are* more like me than you think."

"Don't insult me in *my* house!" retorted Charlotte icily, with a shudder. The image her grandmother had planted in her mind just then was not pleasant. "What are you doing here?" she snapped rudely, thumping the older woman on the chest.

Gerald shuddered, wondering how Charlotte expected to ever get away with *that* insult, pounding on Isabel like she was a melon, for God's sake! *A melon with claws,* he thought with a twisted grin. *Let's not ever forget her claws!* Isabel's eyebrows shot up in surprise as she studied her granddaughter. Then her gaze narrowed menacingly, and she swayed slightly, like a cobra, ready to strike. Gerald expected Charlotte's digits to wither on her hand, turn black and fall off, as he thought he heard the older woman hiss.

"Or, more precisely, you old witch, what is it that you want from me this time?" Charlotte asked.

"Don't insult my religion!" snapped her grandmother.

"Don't insult me!" replied her granddaughter.

"You're a Christian," said Isabel. "Just as the King of England requires, baptized at birth as are the knights who guard the island and all her people. I ensured your survival and the sovereignty of Wales by complying with the King's request."

Charlotte felt a coldness envelop her. She stared at her grandmother.

"I am of the old religion. A Celt," said Isabel, "as were our ancestors, but I am a Christian, too. Don't forget that the advisor to the King was Ambrosius, a very wise wizard indeed!

"But times are changing. You've had the best Christian education that I could give you so that you would be accepted. The world is changing, Charlotte. The old ways are fading. I must decrease so you will increase. You will inherit the relics, and it will be up to you to guard them and keep your people safe. This I know you will do. But I warn you, granddaughter, don't thump me again!"

Charlotte studied her grandmother quietly.

"You never leave the Vale, Grandmother. Like some ancient griffin, you guard the relics, as does Gerald. You never change. Like some phoenix, you disappear and reappear, ageless—no lines on your face, little silver in your hair. Is there an eternal spring you drink from, Grandmother? What pulled you in this direction, so far from your duty? You're the guardian of the relics. I know this, but why are you here?"

Isabel looked at her granddaughter and sighed.

"Magic, Charlotte. Magic will always be with you in one form or another. Wizardry is inherited. You must learn to use your powers for the greater good of others."

Princess Charlotte nodded her head quietly.

"Will you?"

"Yes," she said.

"Then it is so. As you say, so shall it be," said Isabel. "Magic will always be there if you so desire, Charlotte. To aid and assist you, to preserve your people, and for the good of Wales. Those powers will acquiesce to your will, as you know, and must only be used for the greater good of all.

"I've come to see you for a reason."

"What is it?"

"*You* are the only one that I can trust to get the Sword and Crown back, Charlotte! Brat or not!"

A low, bitter laugh erupted from Charlotte. "Still the same, I see," she murmured, the words dripping off her tongue.

Gerald detected a note of disappointment in them.

"I must get the Sword and Crown back," she repeated as she tapped out the syllables on her lips, coming to her own conclusion about Isabel's motives without any help. Experience was her guide—and all that she needed where this woman was concerned. "So that *you* may *keep* them—correct?" she asked sweetly, rocking gently on her heels.

"No," replied her grandmother, interpreting her reaction accurately. "Not for me, Charlotte! For Wales!"

"Since when have you become so *patriotic*, Grandmother?"

"I have always loved Wales, Charlotte. Always," she stated flatly, no hint of artifice in her voice. "Wales is everything to me! Surely you must know this by now!"

"You must forgive me, Grandmother," Charlotte goaded meanly, not believing a single word she said, "if I doubt you. You see, *Grandmother*, I've never known of your patriotism—only your greed!"

Charlotte watched in satisfaction as her grandmother's eyes flared brightly, going from black to translucent brown in a second. She mentally congratulated herself, knowing she had hit a nerve. The tables had turned; the tide had gone out. For some reason she couldn't quite fathom, Charlotte felt the power she now held over her grandmother—and relished it.

Slowly, confidently, she began to circle the older woman, who stood very still—*too still*, Gerald thought, holding his arms in the middle of the solar.

"The *truth* is a painful thing, is it not, Grandmother?" she prodded, poking at her with words. Trying very hard to hurt her; knowing it would take years to equal the pain she had felt growing up. "Your schemes have turned to dust," she mocked, cocking her head sideways and looking Isabel straight in her boiling eyes. "Everything you've planned is being destroyed. Everything you've acquired is being taken from you. How does it *feel*, Grandmother?" she asked wickedly, twisting the knife a little deeper, "What do you have to left to lose?"

Isabel's face contorted with rage.

"Truth?" Isabel spat harshly, rounding on her granddaughter and giving her a violent shove which caused Charlotte to stumble clumsily backward, issuing a muffled curse as she caught herself and sprang angrily to her feet like a cat, fists ready, murder in her searing blue eyes.

Gerald groaned, wondering who to grab first.

"I'll give you truth, Charlotte," hissed Isabel, her square jaw jutting out, her sturdy shoulders thrust defiantly forward, her dark eyes seething—just asking for it, Charlotte concluded darkly. "The truth is, the Sword and Crown belong to *you*, by birth—but they also belong to another, even more so!"

"*You*, Grandmother?" Charlotte hissed, hearing the triumphant edge in Isabel's words and wondering how much penance she'd have to do for brawling with her grandmother in the solar. She clenched her hands so tightly that her nails dug red furrows into her palms.

"No!" Isabel exclaimed exultantly. Both women had unconsciously adopted an exaggerated version of the "man-stance" as the distance between the two narrowed. Both spitting mad. Both ready to fight. Perhaps even curious to see who could best the other.

Even Gerald had his doubts about the outcome. What Charlotte had in her favor—youth and strength—Isabel made up for in cunning. Too bad he couldn't take bets on this one, he thought ironically. The odds wouldn't be that great. Pretty even on both sides. But it would be a good match. Close. Very, very close.

"Well?" Charlotte urged angrily, her eyes flaring brightly, cheeks blossoming with the adrenaline pumping through her. "*Who do they belong to?*"

"Your half-brother!" Isabel stated sharply, standing up as tall as possible, looking as imposing as she could, ready to cast her poison-tipped spear directly into her granddaughter's proud heart. "*Lon ap Llewelyn!*"

Charlotte went white and gasped, nearly fainting. The spear had met its mark, the poison began to flow through her veins as the words registered slowly in her mind.

For a moment, the expression of pain on Charlotte's face made Isabel forget her rage, her desire to hurt and best her granddaughter. Mentally she damned herself for her stupid temper. *Not this way!* she pleaded, biting the inside of her cheeks to keep from saying the words out loud. *It wasn't supposed to be this way, Charlotte! We were supposed to talk, to come to an understanding. Perhaps even part as friends, family once again… Not this way!*

"What are you saying?" Charlotte whispered hoarsely.

Gerald moved nearer, watching anxiously as his fiery little mistress regained her composure, scratching and clawing her way out of her shock, inch by painful inch.

"Why, why, why do you make me so angry!" moaned Isabel with her hands to her head, as though warding off a vicious headache. In that moment she knew Charlotte's will was as strong as her own. Charlotte's temper as great. They were just too, too much alike!

"Charlotte," she began again softly, trying hard to make her understand, the words slipping lifelessly from between her lips, "Lon is your *brother,*" she admitted, her mouth drying up and feeling as though it were full of sawdust. "He's your *half-brother.*"

"How can that be?" Charlotte whispered, images of the past flooding her mind. Her friend Lon. Her confidant. Her most trusted advisor. The man she had vowed to marry only a month before. *He was her brother?*

"How…" she asked, stunned and sick inside. "Why didn't you tell me?" she stammered, nearly shouting as she turned her back to the dark-haired matron and concerned-looking guard. "Why didn't… *one* of you… tell *me?*"

"I couldn't," Isabel replied, the fight leaving her in a sigh. "You see, many years ago, before you were born, I fell love with someone—someone I had no right to."

There was a long, empty silence. A moment when no one seemed to breathe or utter a sound.

"I fell in love with your father," she admitted sadly.

"My *father?*" Charlotte whispered, her world reeling.

"Yes," answered Isabel, and Gerald noticed the guilty blush staining her cheeks. It was as if all the black birds of sin had come and roosted right on her doorstep, staring up at her, knowing of her shame and listening to her belated confession with knowing, greedy ears. "Bren ap Llewelyn," she began almost dreamily, feeling a tearing pain at even the mention of her lost love's name. "Bren was Lon's father… and," she admitted, licking her lips but unable to work up enough moisture to do any good, "he was also *your* father."

"I don't believe you!" Charlotte cried, unable to accept, even after all these years, that Isabel could be this cruel. "Even if," she began again hesitantly, struggling to form the questions her mind was firing at her with blinding, demanding speed as she wondered for the millionth time in her life what her grandmother's motives were *this* time. "Even if it was true… that he is—*was*—my father," she added carefully, stumbling over the unfamiliar words, "what," she turned to face the silent woman standing before her, "what in all that's holy did it have to do with *you?*"

Isabel studied her granddaughter's face for a very long time.

"It had nothing, and everything, to do with me," she answered cryptically, hiding for as long as she could behind words. "You see," she began half-heartedly, pushing the curtain aside in the confessional of her mind as she mechanically began to profess her sins, kneeling before her granddaughter in both her heart and soul. "After Bren's first wife died—Lon's mother," she added, wanting to keep the family threads as straight as she could, "I petitioned the House of Llewelyn to contract a marriage between your mother Charlotte and the recently widowed Bren Llewelyn. I had one of my schemes going, as you put it so effectively.

"Everything was planned," she whispered, staring at a tapestry on the wall depicting a Viking attack, complete with bloody axes and dripping blades. "You see," she told her quietly, chopping away at her own facade until nothing remained but the *real* Isabel before Charlotte, who didn't recognize the contrite woman as her grandmother, "before you were born, the Llewelyn family held the Sword and Crown in their possession, as was only right. The relics have belonged to the Llewelyn family since the Roman invasion, since the very beginning of the Legend. The Llewelyn family are direct descendants of Queen Boudicca, as you are." She spoke quietly, spearing Charlotte with her dark eyes. "Part of the contract I negotiated with Lon's grandmother entailed the physical possession of the Sword and Crown, with the right to keep them at the Vale regardless of the outcome of the marriage. In other words, those ancient relics of Wales were to be brought to the Vale as part of the betrothal agreement. The de Clare wealth and prestige were pledged against the holiest relics of our land."

"So," Charlotte said, piecing together all the bits of her grandmother's story in her mind, "my mother and Bren ap Llewelyn were *supposed* to be married, and yet they weren't." She frowned. "And still you say I'm *his* daughter?"

"Yes," replied Isabel, and Charlotte watched as her grandmother appeared to age ten years within the space of a few minutes. The skin on her face seemed to sag like worn-out cloth. "He came to the Vale," she said softly, remembering that day and how handsome he was. How golden and fair, and how she ached to simply brush her hand against him. "He came, as was arranged, bringing the Sword and Crown. For all intents and purposes, my plan was working out just the way I'd wanted."

Gerald moved nearer to Isabel, placing a gentle, reassuring hand on her shoulder, which she covered with one of her own.

"Bren did come," she admitted softly. "The Sword and Crown were deposited in our vaults. Everything was arranged—except for one minor thing."

Charlotte watched in amazement as a tear slid down her grandmother's wrinkled cheek, sliding over the bumps and undulating through the crevices without losing its shape.

"You see," she told her granddaughter sadly, now crying outright, large, glittering tears dripping from her eyes, splattering on her cheeks, unrestrained by hand or will, "I fell in *love* with your father, and I..." she gave a heart-breaking sigh, "I tried everything in my power to entice him to marry *me*... instead of your mother."

One sin, she thought dejectedly, her hand clutching convulsively for Gerald, who was never too far away. "But it was too late—far too late! He and your mother were very much in love, you see. And together they had started a family. *You*, Charlotte. Your mother was pregnant with you, and Bren was your father. I didn't know this. I swear I did not know this!

"One day, I ran to find him. As greedy as I was for money and power, I hungered *more* for him. Can you understand this, Charlotte?"

For a moment Charlotte thought that she could. After last night, she could see how a person could give up everything they had to be with the one they loved.

"I was going to give him everything I had. Everything! Broker my own marriage and buy what I wanted using my fortune and everything I had. If Bren ap Llewelyn would only just love me," she said. "If he'd only just love *me*. But when I found him, near to bursting with my news, *they* were together. Your mother and Bren.

"I don't know how it happened, Charlotte. All I remember is the pain inside of my heart. My anger. I shoved him!"

Sin number two, she thought miserably.

"I shoved him, Charlotte, in my anger. I shoved your father, Bren ap Llewelyn. We were standing on the castle marches, and when I shoved him, he fell from the castle's marches to the ground below the castle's keep."

"You *killed* my father?" Charlotte whispered in horror.

"Yes. It was an accident. I loved him" came the broken reply.

Isabel tried to touch her. Charlotte backed away from her in horror.

"All of my life, you've treated me horribly. You're telling me that you killed my father. And you have the audacity to come here to my home and ask me for a favor?

"You're a murderer."

"It was an accident, Charlotte. I would have died a thousand times to save Bren's life!"

Suddenly a terrible thought occurred to Charlotte.

"Did you kill my mother as well?" she asked quietly, afraid she already knew the answer.

"No," Isabel said.

Sin number three.

"She died in childbirth."

Isabel remembered the frigid tower room with no heat and the strong, fierce winter wind blowing through the arrow slits.

"*Get out of my house, Grandmother!*"

"Wait," Isabel pleaded. "I need to tell you something!"

"There is *more?*"

"The Sword and Crown," said Isabel. "They are to be transported to Pembroke *tonight*. They will be in the Montgomerys' coffers by nightfall and possibly King Henry's within a week! You must find a way to return them to the Vale. The relics are sacred, Charlotte. They belong to Wales!"

"My *husband,*" Charlotte replied icily, "told me that he would talk to his father this morning. I *trust* him to do that."

"Charlotte," whispered Isabel, shaking her head from side to side, handing her a vial of purple fluid topped with a wooden stopper. "Take this… and listen!" Some of the old power had returned to Isabel's eyes, and her voice rose. "The Sword and Crown belong to Lon and you. *I don't want them! In fact, I never want to see them again. Find a way to give them to your brother Lon! He is the rightful heir to the throne!*"

"I don't believe you, Grandmother," replied Charlotte, refusing the vial of liquid. "You don't want the relics that you guarded all of your life?"

"No. And I don't want the Vale, either," she told her granddaughter firmly. She moved back to stand beside her towering guard Gerald, clasping his hand in both of hers, drawing strength from his quiet presence as she always had. "Gerald and I are preparing to leave, to go back to the village where we were born, farther north along the coast. It is there, with him and my people, that I wish to end my days in peace.

"But the Sword and Crown are sacred to Wales and the Welsh. They do not belong to the Normans or the Saxons. If you cannot do this for me, and well I understand why you wouldn't, do it for Wales and your people.

"We would fight to keep them, but that would only bring bloodshed and war upon our people. Yet if the artifacts simply *disappeared*," she said with a shrug of her shoulders, "then who could say who is to blame?"

Charlotte nodded, watching the two skeptically. She remembered being led to the treasure chamber as a child and Isabel pretending disinterest but watching keenly as Gerald asked her to lift a glittering sword. It was heavy, but she had held it aloft and the old guard had smiled. Unknown to her, so had Isabel. It was the fabled Sword of Wales that she held in her small hands. She had been tested and, without knowing it, passed.

Exhaling, Charlotte understood why her grandmother had taken such a great risk in coming to Pembroke. The relics belonged to Lon ap Llewelyn, and it was up to her to ensure that they were returned to him.

"Take this," said Isabel, giving her the jar of purple fluid. "Two drops in your husband's wine and he will sleep. Five drops, and he will wake no more."

"As I did?" Charlotte replied sarcastically. Her grandmother, past the point of artifice, nodded tiredly.

"The Sword and the Crown are in an ebony box," she continued. "The box is inlaid with lapis lazuli and rubies in the shape of a flaming dragon—the Llewelyn crest. Find the box, hide it, and send it to your brother Lon any way you can—for *he* is the rightful ruler of Wales and this land's true king!"

Nodding, Charlotte took the sleeping potion from her grandmother, feeling a sudden lump in her throat as she studied the woman whose face seemed to shine with relief.

"Who do I look like?" asked Charlotte as she studied the tall, dark-haired woman before her.

Immediately, Isabel understood. Her eyes, always so stony and hard, softened.

"Your face," she began quietly, cupping Charlotte's face in her gnarled hands, "is exactly like your mother's and your grandfather de Clare's. Your fine hands and elegant neck are like…" For a second she hesitated, picking up one of her granddaughter's hands as though it were the rarest of gems. "Your hands—your build—are like your father's." With a sad smile, she dropped her old wrinkled hands to her side as though trying to hide them in the folds of her dress, and Charlotte noted how they trembled. "And your will and temper," she added hoarsely, her voice choking with emotion, "your fire and your determination are gifts…"

She hesitated then, her dark eyes locking with her granddaughter's light ones while a proud blush colored her olive cheeks. "They are the very best part of a very… *very* foolish old woman."

The next moment, Isabel clasped Charlotte to her breast, holding her tightly, marveling at the beauty and strength in her granddaughter, feeling as though she had contributed, at least in part, to her will and courage, shedding her tears unashamedly on her granddaughter's sturdy shoulders.

In another moment they were gone, and Charlotte was left alone in the brightly-lit solar.

"I can't be like her," she said to herself.

In her mind she could see her grandmother in a whirling collage, beginning with her earliest recollections and ending with the image of the aging matriarch, broken and sobbing in her arms.

But the one memory that was stronger than all the rest was of a woman who made her own way, decided her own fate, and took responsibility for her choices.

"Yes," she murmured slowly, seeing fully the enigmatic woman she had been unable to know for so many years. The strength, the stubbornness, the will—hers and her grandmother's—the relentless drive was the same. *She was like her!* Yet, in her, the drive had not been twisted by guilt.

"Armando!" Charlotte shouted to the empty solar, rushing for the door, a plan forming in her mind. She must steal the Sword and Crown tonight, before it was placed in the sealed vault. It was the only hope she had of giving them to Lon ap Llewelyn, the rightful heir and the legitimate ruler of Wales. "Armando!" she called again fiercely, flinging open the heavy wooden door.

"Hurry!" she ordered a waiting guard, grabbing him frantically by the tunic. "I need my priest!"

"Yes, my lady," he answered politely, stumbling backward from the intense look in his mistress's eyes. "Right away!"

* * *

Lon ap Llewelyn stood alone on the narrow wooden marches of Aberystwyth, staring angrily at the choppy gray waters of Cardigan Bay. The northeasterly wind drove his silver hair away from his face, and his eyes glittered angrily in the wan afternoon light.

"Your lordship," interrupted a young page, "the House of Brecon has answered your call."

"Well," encouraged Lon softly, "how did they say?"

"They will join you, my lord," he answered proudly.

All Welsh houses had been told the news of a daughter of theirs forced into marriage with a Norman family and of the planned displacement of the ancient relics into the hands of Britain's king. All had heard, and of those who had replied, not one house had turned its back on Lon's call to arms. From the northernmost part of Wales, Anglesey, Llandudno, Denbigh, along the Cambrian Mountains, to the far reaches of the interior, the Houses had put aside their petty differences and found a common ground: Princess Charlotte. They were united in their desire to bring their little princess back to Wales, along with the Sword and Crown of Wales.

Together, the Welsh became a most formidable army, numbering well over a thousand able-bodied men.

Nodding silently, Lon turned his eyes back to the turbulent, foam-flecked gray waters crashing against the coast.

"Tomorrow morning, we will meet at Tregaron. A day's march from there, and we will be at the gates of Pembroke," he vowed harshly, slamming down his fist on the ancient stone, causing a weak piece to fall into the swirling waters below. "And if as much as a hair upon Charlotte's head has been touched—I swear by all that's holy—I will *kill* Montgomery with my bare hands!"

Chapter 22

Alaric wandered through the stalls in Pembroke's massive courtyard, his alert eyes taking in every detail, from the gatekeepers' position to the men-at-arms posted at various intervals along the stone wall.

Stopping near a wagon laden with fresh-baked bread, he tore a piece from a still-warm loaf and watched as two young squires fenced in the courtyard.

"Not very good," muttered a guttural voice near him. He recoiled slightly as he recognized the sound. Looking sideways, he swallowed his bread and viewed the man who had spoken. He was cloaked in a purple hood, head down and arms folded across his chest. But there was no mistaking the green glitter of his barely concealed eyes.

"What are you doing here, you fool?" Alaric muttered, his eyes flashing dangerously as he pretended to study the fencing thanes.

"*You said,*" answered Harold Halfdanson with a wicked grin, "that a *man* was to be sent to market on this day—to receive orders. I'm a *man,*" he said bitingly, "even with this withered stump. Tell me, *Lord Alaric of York*… what's your orders?"

If Alaric hadn't been worrying about drawing attention to himself, he would have buried his dagger into the idiot's throat. Halfdanson could ruin years of planning and careful work by simply being here now.

"I said," replied Alaric through clenched teeth, smiling charmingly as a pretty young girl passed in front of the pair while Harold only glared lecherously, "someone who wouldn't be *recognized.* For God's sake, you fool! They want to hang you!"

"Yeah, that's right. But they won't. Not before I get my hands on Montgomery!" he vowed. "Now, what's your bleeding orders?" He bellowed so loudly that turned toward the sound of his voice in curiosity.

"Take six men," answered Alaric, walking away from the wagon with the crippled Viking in tow. "Come to the garden door, the little one on the north side. Come tomorrow night. Knock three times. Nell will let you in."

"Got it," he muttered.

"The rest of your men," added Alaric, bowing elegantly to a matronly woman and her young son, eliciting a curtsy and a smile, "have them waiting behind the hedgerows until the main gate is dropped. By then we should have both Charles and Garret under control—the rest will be easy. By morning we will flag the ships waiting offshore, and the invasion will start."

"Aye," muttered Halfdanson, rubbing the end of his withered stump, his green eyes gleaming savagely. "You'll have Charles and Pembroke. And me… why, I'll take hold of his son and teach him a lesson he won't forget!" He smiled wolfishly, and Alaric saw the glitter of madness in the light of his predatory eyes. Halfdanson was worried about settling score with *one* man. *He,* Alaric of York, was contemplating the beginnings of a new nation with himself as its king!

"Go," he told him flatly, not bothering to keep the contempt out of his voice as he turned his back on the lumbering giant. "Get out of here, before they figure out who you are." He added, "Or I tell them" under his breath. But Halfdanson didn't hear him as he made his way out through the gate, hidden behind a mule. His mind was on revenge.

"First his arm," he murmured quietly, as he passed the gate-keeper without any problem. "First his arm. Then I'll hang him—slowly, though…" he whispered. "With a loose rope, placing the knots to the side—so's his neck won't break… and he'll swing! Oh, yes! He'll swing for a long, long time!"

Chapter 23

Armando entered the solar, watching warily as his blonde-haired mistress paced relentless up and down in front of the windows. His brown eyes bounced back and forth like a rubber ball, following her movements.

"There you are!" she snapped, turning on him with a flourish of silk.

Armando saw the agitation in her glittering eyes and wondered what was on her mind this time.

"Yes, my lady," he answered elegantly, covering up his wariness with a theatrical bow and a broad sweet of his pudgy arm.

"Cut out that nonsense!" she muttered, hating to see anyone, even Armando, bowing and scraping before her. "Armando, didn't you tell me once that you were an actor?"

"Why, yes, my lady!" he admitted proudly, puffing out his chest. "Quite a good one. As a matter of fact," he boasted dreamily, "perhaps even the best there ever was!" Extending his arm high in the air with a soulful, heart-wrenching, almost pathetic expression plastered all over his versatile face, he began to recite as sorrowfully as he could: "Oh, there is a distant isle," he fluttered his eyelashes a great deal, "around which seahorses glisten…"

"Yes, yes," she muttered, cutting him off. "Very good, Armando. "But what I want to know is, do you have any costumes?"

"Why, yes, my lady," he answered with an indifferent shrug. "Quite good ones,, I might add."

"Good!" she answered brightly, rubbing her hands together. "I need you to bring me the costume of a man!"

"What?!" he asked incredulously, stumbling backward and falling on his rump as though she'd slapped him.

"A costume of a man," she repeated in irritation, her foot tapping rapidly on the rug-covered floor and her dressing gown nearly opening in agitation. "Also, I'll need your help tonight."

"What help is that, my lady?" he asked fearfully, swallowing hard and keeping his eyes averted out of respect for Garret, not liking at all where this conversation was heading.

"I'm going to steal something," she told him fiercely, grabbing him by the cowl, her eyes glittering dangerously.

"Steal, yes, my lady. Does your husband know what you're planning to do?" he asked cautiously, fluttering his fingers together. He received a painful thump to the side of his bald head. "Ow!" he blurted out, rubbing his head in surprised shock.

"Of course not, you fool!" she said. "Do you think a man like Garret Montgomery is going to let me go traipsing around, all over this country, masquerading as a man and stealing, for God's sake?"

"No, my lady," Armando said. "I am quite sure he wouldn't!"

"It is something I have to do, Armando. A last resort to preserve the relics of my people's past. There is no other way." She knew that even if Garret spoke to his father, and she had no doubt in her mind that he would, a man like Charles Montgomery would never go against an order from his king. No, she reasoned firmly; if she wanted to save the Sword and Crown of Wales and return them to their rightful owner, Lon ap Llewelyn, she must do it alone.

"What, may I inquire, are you planning to steal?" asked Armando.

"The Sword and Crown of Wales," Charlotte said calmly. She settled back into a chair and draped her arms arrogantly along the arms.

Armando gasped aloud and held his hand to his mouth. He was shocked!

"You're going to steal from your husband?" he said in horror.

"It's done all the time!" she told him casually, sitting indifferently on her throne. "A penny here, not spent on bread," she murmured, dropping imaginary coppers into one hand as she remembered what the maids and scullery girls had always talked and laughed about in the kitchens. "A coin there, not spent on linen. Into a woman's private coffer it goes. Plink! Plink! Besides," she told him haughtily, springing to her feet, "I'm taking the Sword and Crown to the rightful ruler of Wales, and it has nothing whatsoever to do with my husband!"

"No," Armando agreed breathlessly, already planning to run to Garret with this information as soon as possible. "I can see why it wouldn't have a thing to do with him," he lied, breaking out in a sweat over what the woman was planning on doing to his hero.

Believing that Armando was on her side, she sat down once again, curling her toes into the plush woolen rug sprawling on the floor.

"This," she told him, holding up the vial of purple fluid that her grandmother Isabel had given her so that the light reflected through the glass, "goes in his wine. Just a few drops, mind you, and he'll sleep like a lamb. Then you and I will go for a stroll, to the baths. Have horses ready, Armando, and we'll intercept the cargo at Milford."

She smiled, and her smile sent a shiver down Armando's back. She was planning not only to steal from her husband, but also to lie and to cheat. And now, she was planning to drug him as well! Oh, what evil, villainous creatures these women were! A virtuous man didn't have a chance against them!

It was then that the door opened a fraction of an inch. A very flushed Sparrow poked her round face in.

"Oh, there you are, Father Armando!" she gushed in relief, opening the door more fully as Charlotte hid the flask behind her. "Begging your pardon, your ladyship, but I've need of Father Armando, now, if you don't mind, that is!"

"Are you sick, Sparrow?" Charlotte asked, frowning. The girl didn't seem capable of standing still.

"Oh, no!" she assured her brightly, still fidgeting about. "It's just that Father Armando told me this morning that if the fires of Hell in my privates get to burning out of control again, to come get him right away!" Turning more fully toward the man who appeared to be shrinking by the second, she grasped his hand and looked imploringly into his eyes. "And those fires, Father Armando, those devilish fires, are fair to consuming me!" she admitted woefully, grabbing the embarrassed-looking man by the other hand and pulling him toward the door. "Oh, they really, truly are!" Blushing, she gave him a serious tug.

"What?" said Charlotte suspiciously, rising to her feet. "'Fires of Hell'? Just what is going on here, 'Father' Armando?" she asked harshly, reminding Armando of his mother: *Armando, what are you doing back there? Armando? Ar-man-do! Let that little girl go! Armando!*

"Nothing, Mother! Er, uhm, mistress!" he told her sincerely, making a hurried sign of the cross in the air as the maid tried unsuccessfully to pull him out the door. Strong little wench! he thought fearfully, dragging his sandal-footed feet against the floor with all his might, and scraping the devil out of his big toe, while wondering just what his fast-talking forked tongue had gotten him into this time.

"Oh, Father!" Sparrow pleaded, letting one hand loose to fan herself. "You must drive the devil back through the gates! I'm fair to burning up, I am!"

"Drive the devil?" Charlotte repeated, her eyes narrowing as she looked at the sweating, heaving young woman and the overgrown man she was trying to drag through the door. "Just what is it you've been telling that girl, Armando?" she demanded, affecting her man-stance as she thought protectively of her naïve little maid.

"Nothing but good things!" said Sparrow in defense of her priest as she gained a few inches by grabbing onto his girdle and hauling on it with both of her hands. "Only things like… like when a woman's fire burns out of control, there's a secret ceremony, whereby… umph!" She grunted, pulling hard, as Armando gained a few inches by falling to his knees and trying to scramble away, doggy fashion.

"Whereby…" Sparrow began again, never letting loose of the man on the floor as she grabbed the doorpost with one hand, hooked her foot around the other side, gaining a remarkable amount of leverage, and continued to pull the crawling man backward to his doom.

Chapter 24

Armando walked stiff-legged and silently down the echoing stairwell. He was so exhausted that all he wanted to do was find a nice dry corner and curl up and sleep. The little wench with the brown eyes was draining him dry, and he didn't know how much longer his aging form could take such abuse. But now, he sighed wearily, he mustn't think about his own dwindling life-force. He must find Garret and tell him what his conniving little wife was planning… *again.*

Yawning, he entered the door of the library, relieved to see his lord writing at the long table near the opened window.

Armando paused, gazing with unabashed adoration at his hero. He had never seen a more regal human being in his long, eventful life, nor on any of his countless journeys. Even in a moment of ease, with his head bowed and his legs stretched out before him, there was a bearing—a *majesty*—about the man that caused his eyes to widen and his heart to swell with pride. *Kings*, he thought proudly, *are not crowned but created.* Garret de Montgomery was a king with the heart of a lion and the romantic soul of a poet.

"Your lordship?" he queried respectfully, closing the door softly behind him.

"Yes?" answered Garret, looking up in surprise to see his spy resting against the wall with his eyes closed and a yawn splitting his face almost in half. Armando looked ashen and totally exhausted.

"What is it, Armando?" he questioned, his crooked, wolfish

grin sparkling icy white in the muted afternoon light. "Well?" he prompted gently as he stretched his rugged arms high above his head and yawned. "Are you ill?"

His movements were curiously fluid, giving him a subtle grace as if each gesture he made were part of a divinely artless dance. A light, playful breeze whispered through the opened window, rustling pages on his desk and teasing the midnight-blue lights in his hair into a tousled mane of midnight fire.

"I've… must, ahhh…"

"Well?" prompted Garret, a look of patient interest flooding his face.

"It seems…" stated Armando conversationally, thinking that his lord was going to get a big laugh out of this new escapade of Lady Charlotte's. Any other man would have had her flogged and her hair cut off, but not Lord Garret. He didn't see things as other men did. He was different. He was *special.* He was *naive…*

"It seems that your lady bride has come up with another brilliant plan."

"Oh?" Garret said curiously. He frowned as he remembered last night and the closeness they had shared. For the first time in his life, it had seemed as though he had found someone with whom he could share even his soul. No thoughts or feelings had been taboo. No memory too horrible to relate. And the result of their closeness had been a feeling of satisfied peace, as though together they had sailed into a tranquil harbor where not even the evil winds that had blown steadily against them all their lives could touch them. Last night he had walked through the gates of Paradise with an angel on his arm, and now his darling had hatched another "plan" that threatened his heaven and his peace of mind.

"What is it this time?" he asked cautiously.

Armando walked over to the table and rested both of his hands on it. If Lord Garret thought the bathhouse caper hilarious, he was sure to burst a gut when he heard her new scheme.

"Your wife is going to dress up like a *man!* Can you believe it?" he asked, shaking his head in wonder as a double yawn cracked his face in two and he appeared to lose his nose somewhere in between his eyes. Grunting, he hefted his ample rump up, plopping down unceremoniously on top of the polished writing desk.

"A man?" Garret prodded, his eyes darkening subtly. "Why would Lady Charlotte wish to dress as a *man?*"

"To steal from you," he answered gleefully. He slapped his fleshy thighs and laughed. "She's going to put some sleeping potion in your wine, knock you out, dress up like a man, and steal the Sword and Crown of Wales."

He spoke casually, as though he were talking about the weather instead of a heinous, underhanded scheme. Pausing for a breath, he issued an exaggerated snort as he tugged on the corners of his mustache, wishing for a mug of muddy brown ale, while Charlotte's whole plan had been revealed in a single breath.

"Imagine!" he chuckled. "Lady Charlotte as a *man!*" He kept on cackling, expecting Garret to join him any minute, but silence was the only companion Armando's laughter had.

Garret's chair quietly moved back. Armando paid little attention to the movement. He just kept on talking, filling his lord in on all the gruesome details of Charlotte's impending deception.

"She wants me to *pretend* to take her to the *baths*—again! Huh! What a joke! I'm supposed to have horses ready, and then we—her and *me*, mind you—we are supposed to pose as a couple of brigands and steal the crown jewels of Wales! Can you imagine?" he said for a second time. "*Her* dressed as a man!" Armando pushed out his chest in an imitation of breasts and kept on laughing, not noticing that his lord no longer sat at the table nor sensitive enough to feel the change in the atmosphere of the room, which seemed to have heated up by several degrees.

"Dress like a man… for God's sake! What will that lady think of next?" he wondered, shaking his face and looking at the empty chair. "And then," he continued, swiveling around to see where his lord had wandered, expecting to see the giant of a man laughing hysterically, "when I asked her if she thought it was *right* to steal from her husband, she answered just as bold as brass. 'Oh,'" he began, mimicking his lady by tossing imaginary hair behind his shoulder and speaking in a forceful falsetto while his eyelashes batted energetically up and down, "she said, *'It's done all the time—a coin here, a coin there, not spent on linen.'*" He suddenly became aware that Garret didn't appear to see the humor in his story.

"Your lordship?" inquired Armando softly as he watched his master standing silently before the glowing embers in the fireplace. "Your lord—" he began, losing his smile as he watched Garret throw a thin, leather-bound book on top of the glowing wood chips.

"Where is my *wife*," he asked, choking out the words through gritted teeth, "to get the clothes that she will need to dress as a man?" He asked this quietly, the words grating harshly against his throat. He felt as though he had swallowed shards of glass, each word ripping at his throat as he stared bitterly at the book he had thrown into the fire and watched as the binding began to smolder.

"From me, my lord," Armando answered soberly, recognizing the wounded, agonized expression on his young lord's face as he stood up. "I have many costumes from my acting days," he added lamely with a shrug.

"Then," replied Garret softly, watching as a blue-tipped flame blossomed on the edge of the book, "bring *me* a costume as well."

"*You*, my lord?" whispered Armando hesitantly, watching as a muscle in Garret's jaw worked silently back and forth while the blue and orange flames caused his face to fill with shadows, and ghosts to peer out from behind haunted, searing blue eyes.

"Yes, *me*, Armando," he repeated darkly, his eyes narrowing into savage slits. "If my lady bride wishes to play dress-up, far be it from me to stop her."

Suddenly Garret turned, sweeping the chess pieces to the floor and toppling the table on which they stood, and as though his rage at being betrayed was more than he could bear, he lifted a chair and sent it crashing into the wall.

Armando jumped and edged away. The look in Garret's eyes would have scared the Reaper himself, and he (he admitted wisely) had never been known for his courage, so he sidled toward the door.

"If *she,*" hissed Garret furiously, the muscles corded and straining in his neck with fury, while his breath came in short, enraged gasps, "wishes to be a *man*—then I will *treat* her as one!"

"Yes, my lord," murmured Armando obediently as he reached for the handle of the door. "Of course." They were both crazy, he concluded. Hot-headed, stubborn, and completely uncontrollable, and he was caught right in the middle of them!

"Have my costume ready, Armando," Garret whispered. There was a dangerously cold edge to his voice as he turned to stare back at the cheerfully burning book. "Tell her that your *men* will meet her at Milford and help her *steal* those cursed relics."

He spat the words out, feeling as though a handful of gems and an old piece of steel meant more to his bride than he did.

"Yes, my lord!" gulped Armando, saluting and curtsying and saluting again as he banged clumsily into the wall. "Right away, my lord!" he agreed as he tried to undo the door, managing to push it open just wide enough for him to exit. "Immediately, my lord!" he confirmed for the third time as he shot through the narrow slit just as fast as his cumbersome girth would allow.

"So," Garret murmured softly into the empty silence of the room. "This is how it is!" He mocked himself and his stupidity. The cold edge of irony chilled his words until they became an unintelligible hiss as he clenched a small, solid-brass figurine in his broad hand. "Last night meant nothing to her!"

His mouth was dry and his pulse beat too fast, making him feel dizzy and light-headed. The nerves tingled in his hand with the force of his restrained will.

"It was all an act," he said harshly. The words, though thought often enough, carried a singularly deadly force when spoken aloud, as though they had somehow become living daggers, ripping his heart to pieces. His hand began to squeeze the noble seated warrior he held in his palm.

He had been a fool to think that she loved him. A fool.

Perhaps even a bigger one than his father had been all these years, he thought sardonically, never having imagined that possible. But she had been his *dream,* he rationalized, trying to garner some measure of pride out of what he had been so willing to believe. His destiny.

"Fool!" he whispered with a snort, hating himself at that moment. Hating the weakness in him—the weakness in him for a mere *woman.* Yet she was the vision that he had longed for all his life, and finally seeing her, *being with her* had driven him past the point of reason and control. For the first time in his life he felt totally powerless. It was like being caught in the very center of a wild current in a fast-flowing river. No matter how hard he struggled to keep his head above water, the pull was too strong and kept dragging him under, suffocating him with its power, threatening to consume him in its relentless tow. And he had reveled in it, drowning in her eyes and touch, surrendering to the force of beauty, even though he knew it might well cost him his life.

"Fool!" he bitterly whispered again, continuing to crush the seated horseman in his hand. Worse than giving up his control—worse even than knowing he would have followed her to the ends of the earth if she had only nodded her head and crooked her little finger—was the realization that the greatest moment of his life meant nothing to her. Nothing at all.

How could it? he reasoned. How could *he* mean anything to her if she was planning to steal the accursed relics, drug him, lie. Oh, he had been such a fool! Such a child! And the knowledge left a bitter taste in his mouth like the acrid bite of rotten wine, disguised and made palatable by too much honey.

For a moment, he even began to believe that she had faked her arousal—had played him like the commonest of whores. But then he remembered how she had acted in the bathhouse when she thought he was Robert of Gloucester. There had been no difference, he thought with disgust. The reaction had been the same. She had abandoned herself *both* times. The knowledge that the *man* didn't matter sickened him.

Love was blind—and deaf—and stupid. Love was the Devil's greatest lie, a joke, a trap into which he had fallen so willingly.

Well, this time he would pay her back for her deceit! This time she would learn not to practice her womanly tricks against him! This time she would pay for her guile!

With a muttered oath, he threw the figurine on the floor and stalked out of the room, leaving a destroyed knight to hobble and roll within inches of a fallen queen.

Chapter 25

The costume didn't fit. The brown trews were baggy, and where the crotch should have met snugly between her legs, half a yard of material sagged in an untidy-looking sack.

"I'd better fill this up," Charlotte muttered, tucking her hair into the striped bandanna and pulling the farmer's cap down low over her ears. "It's nearly dark."

She was amazed at her good fortune tonight. Although she hadn't seen Garret for most of the day, he had suddenly come up behind her in the garden, scaring her half out of her wits.

"Garret!" she had exclaimed in surprise. "You startled me!"

"Startled *you?*" he repeated sardonically, his dark brows shooting up cynically. "I thought nothing scared you." There was no warmth in his eyes, and when she wound her arms around his neck, he simply stood there, looking down at her as though she were a stranger, tolerating her touch.

"No," she admitted with a shaky laugh, momentarily confused by his coolness. "I mean *startled*—not scared."

"Oh," he murmured, unlocking her arms from behind his neck and pushing them gently but firmly away. "My mother used to tell me when I was a youngster that a guilty conscience usually leads to that kind of nervous behavior."

"Ha!" She tried to laugh, taking a faltering step backward. "Ha… hah!" she repeated, trying to sound nonchalant, but the sound was so phony that she cringed and gave up the attempt.

"Do *you* have a guilty conscience, my dear?" he asked innocently, pretending to tease her as the dark spears of his eyes bored holes straight through her heart.

"Of course not!" she snapped, her guilt making her defensive. For just a second, she wondered if he knew. But that wasn't possible, she reasoned. The only other one to know was Armando, and he would never betray her—the cost would be too great. No, she concluded, Garret couldn't *possibly* know. "My conscience is clear as a bell," she lied, crossing her fingers behind her back and trying hard to cross her toes.

"Good," Garret murmured, his eyes dancing darkly as he continued to stare at her with the unrelenting, probing light of his gaze. "I wouldn't want the Devil to come up and pinch you on the rump for being a *bad* girl."

"Don't be silly!" she muttered irritably, feeling so guilty she was ready to tell him everything and beg him to forgive her. But she couldn't do that. The Sword and Crown meant more than her personal feelings. So very much more.

"My conscience," she lied again, "is in fine shape!" With a haughty flounce as though she were indignant that he would ever doubt her veracity, she turned to leave. "It's time for supper," she added shakily, feeling the vial of poison beneath her robe as it bounced coldly against her leg. "Are you… Ow!" she shouted, stopping in her tracks to grab her behind. "What was *that* for?" she asked angrily, telling herself not to get mad. Tonight was too important.

"Just testing," goaded Garret, holding up the offending fingers for her to see. "Better me than Old Nick… aye?" he asked, working the fingers back and forth as though they were eager to pinch again, and then he grinned so evilly that she shuddered.

"Frankly," she retorted as she began to walk toward the hall with a slight limp, rubbing her injured fanny, "I really don't see much difference!"

Then he laughed, low and wicked. The sound caused her to swallow, chasing her into the dining hall, where she sat down and started to eat, not even sure what it was that she was putting into her mouth.

But then at supper, her plans had gone well. He drank his drugged wine like a good little boy, drank it quickly, giving her the most evil, enigmatic looks she had ever received. For the hundredth time that evening she wondered if this could possibly be the same man she had slept with the night before, who had proclaimed his undying love.

But he slept. His head drifted forward remarkably fast, and he stretched out on the bench—snoring to wake the dead—in no time. *Funny*, she thought uneasily as she adjusted the tunic across her shoulders, she couldn't remember him snoring like *that* last night. Oh well, she mused, stuffing hose down her pants until her crotch swelled like a ripening melon, perhaps he was just embarrassed at having revealed his feelings for her last night. It would pass, she concluded as she looked down, examining her artificial bulge carefully.

"Too small," she decided, adding several more stockings.

She didn't want Armando and his band of thieves to think she was anything less than a *real* man.

Turning, she tried to view herself in profile, comparing *her* bulge to her husband's—and *hers* won! Hah! she thought smugly, doing a little dance and watching it jiggle. Why, it was possibly the biggest, most awe-inspiring rod she had ever seen. It stuck out nearly four inches and filled the entire area between her slender legs. "Let them just say I'm not a *man* now!" she murmured happily as she slipped her cloak over her costume and pulled her hood up over her hat. She went out the door, accompanied by an eager, tail-wagging Bishop and her waiting, dubious "priest."

In the shadows of the landing Garret watched. He was dressed in his own costume, with a patch over one eye and a light brown beard and mustache glued to his face. He had one goosedown-filled pouch strapped to his back and one anchored to his middle, making him look both pot-bellied and hunch-backed.

Smiling evilly, with one blackened tooth exposed, he looked positively wicked and every bit the part of the bloodthirsty brigand he felt.

Torin opened the door, followed closely by a bad-smelling, dirty-looking Cole.

"Ready?" Garret asked Torin, and both men exchanged a knowing look as they walked grimly down the stairs, followed closely by a bewildered Cole.

Theirs was a sacred mission, a divine duty, and, Garret thought vehemently, his lips thinning in anger, a real pleasure. For tonight was the night when the order of the universe was restored, and the "woe" was put back in "woe-man" for good.

Chapter 26

"Armando," Charlotte asked quietly as she adjusted her migrating "jewels" once again, "do you think a wife ought to keep secrets from her husband?"

Turning his face so she wouldn't see his traitorous grin, he replied as prudently as he could. "Secrets," he advised, the wise man in him peering out from behind the eyes of a jolly, cunning clown, "are meant to be shared with *friends*, m'lady."

He offered this advice as softly as he could, neglecting to tell her he believed that in this world, at least, men and women could never truly be friends because, sooner or later, biology would interfere. They were alien nations, co-existing however uneasily from time to time, getting along for but one purpose: sex. They needed each other, *lusted* after one another, but they were *different.* It was that difference that made complete *trust* impossible. Hence how could they ever be truly friends? They couldn't. At least, *he* had never been able to accomplish that feat. Sniffing, he remembered the time he'd tried to tell his third wife about the habits of his first wife—just as if they were friends. *What?* she had demanded, rounding on him as though he had just committed the worst sin of his life. *You've had other women besides me!* He was thirty-four at the time and had been having them ever since the ripe old age of nine, so *Yes,* he had told her with a comradely smile and a shrug of his still-firm shoulders, just as if they were friends, *dozens of 'urn!* And that was the end of marriage number three. Oh, well, he mused, she *was* beginning to act a great deal like number one and number two, innocently unaware that his Casanova antics could transform mild-mannered women into shrewish, screaming harpies.

"Then," Charlotte mused, breaking into his reverie, trying to interpret his advice as best she could, "a wife—if she and her husband are friends, that is—shouldn't keep *any* secrets from her husband?"

"No," counseled the wily thief, "none. Other than the fact that a woman belches regularly, farts fire occasionally, and probably swears ten times better than her mate. Other than *those* indelicate items, no, I *don't* think a woman ought to keep secrets from her husband!"

"Fat lot *you* know!" Charlotte retorted guiltily as she shoved a piece of stocking that was traveling down her leg back where it belonged. "But I suppose," she said in defense of her transgressions, "that it's perfectly acceptable for a *man* to keep secrets from his *wife!*"

"Of course," answered Armando quickly with a shrug, eliciting a strangled oath from Charlotte and a well-deserved clout over the head. "Ow!" he shouted, rubbing his head. "I'm only trying to *help*, m'lady," he answered innocently, though secretly gloating.

"Your kind of help I can do without!" she snapped, muttering to herself. "I can't believe I just asked the Duke of Debauchery for advice on how a married couple ought to behave!"

Armando grinned as he guided her horse, which was sullenly following his lead.

"Does it always take this long to reach Milford?" she asked irritably.

"We are using the back trails," he lied, having gone in a giant circle now for more than an hour, praying she wouldn't notice the now-familiar scenery. "My friends will meet us shortly."

"Good," she muttered, wanting nothing more than to ride back to Pembroke and slip into bed, wistfully hoping that Garret would come and lie down beside her—but not now! Later, after she had returned, feeling a sudden surge of adrenaline as she prayed that he wouldn't wake too early!

* * *

"There!" whispered Torin.

Garret watched as Armando's mule came plodding into sight, followed by his lady's high-stepping palfrey.

If he hadn't been so mad, he would have laughed at her appearance. She looked like the most effeminate male he had ever seen, and when he noticed the huge bulge between her legs, bouncing on the center of the saddle, he nearly choked.

"Let's go," he murmured evenly, kicking the old horse beneath him gently and breaking into a trot as he heard his men giggle. He knew exactly what it was they were laughing at as he listened to Cole's adolescent chatter, mumbling to Torin how he wished he were "packing stones as big as hers!"

* * *

"By the way," Charlotte said loudly, thinking of a new thing to scold Armando about, "what is going on between you and Sparrow?"

Armando wanted to tell his mistress that the little maid was killing him with her sexual demands, *kiss me here, hold me there, touch this, do that.* It was beginning to feel like *work!* But he held back from telling his lady this as she might misunderstand and think he was taking advantage of an innocent. *Sparrow!* he thought, mentally choking. *Innocent! Why, she had shown him things he had only dreamt about… telling him she had heard about it from the stable hands. Heard it? Most likely performed* in *the very center of it!* But he could never tell his lady that. She would never believe him.

Sighing, he replied as evenly as he could: "Nothing, Lady Charlotte." He sniffed indignantly, finding it hard to swallow. "She simply asks for my guidance."

"Huh! Guidance from the King of Sin, the Prince of Lechery, the Duke of Lies!"

"Well," he began to admit, liking the high-sounding titles she had cast his way, unmindful that they were meant only to insult. But his reply was cut short as a group of men tore through the brush, a huge, villainous, evil-looking brigand in the center.

"Oh!" exclaimed Charlotte in surprise, lowering her voice an octave. "Oh, Armando. They are here." This was hard on her vocal cords, but it couldn't be helped.

"So it would seem," he said gaily, walking his mule toward the grim-looking leader with the leather patch covering one eye.

"John of Milford," he greeted the slouched, bowed giant and was hailed back with a wave of a brawny arm and a grunt. "He's a mute," Armando explained to Charlotte over his shoulder, and she nodded, careful to keep her head down and her pelvis thrust forward.

"Have you seen the wagons yet?" Armando inquired loudly as he sidled up against his master's horse. "Well met, my lord," he murmured under his breath. "All's ready."

Garret nodded, careful to keep the brim of his hat down as he made a few gestures in the air and pointed down a twisting path.

"John said the wagons are coming—over there."

Charlotte nodded, watching suspiciously as her dog—the most fiercely loyal canine in the entire world—wiggled his way to the grim-faced pirate, his tail shaking so much she thought it might come off.

"It seems," she said slowly, keeping her voice as low as possible as she studied the man with narrowed eyes from beneath the shadowed brim of her cap, "that he *likes* you."

For a moment, the pirate lifted his face, and Charlotte felt a sudden stab as a glittering eye—as blue as Garret's, except this one was framed in brown and gray—speared her.

The pirate began to gesture slowly, finally ending by locking his gaze on hers and running his finger slowly across his neck as though he were cutting his throat, then ending his pantomime by holding his two hands together in front of her and twisting them savagely in opposite directions, popping his knuckles in the process—the same fatal move one makes when strangling a chicken—and then he smiled diabolically, showing blackened gaps where teeth should have been.

"What?" Charlotte whispered uneasily, rubbing her throat as she wiggled a little, because now she was sitting on at least half of the hose she had stuffed in her pants. "What did he *say?*"

"Oh," replied Armando, yawning to conceal his smile. "He simply said that *all* dogs like him—something to do with the fact that he never bathes, and… and he rubs goose fat on his thighs to keep them from chafing in the warm weather."

"Ohhh…" she murmured, nodding her head, as Garret turned his head and rolled his eye. Perfectly logical. Bishop thought he was supper.

"Well," Armando offered, "shall we be off? The contraband is waiting." He rubbed his greedy hands together out of habit.

"Yes," agreed Charlotte, her horse fidgeting and ready to run, already planning on finding the Sword and Crown and hiding them from these rascally-looking thieves. She could pick them up tomorrow night and take them to Aberystwyth. There was just something about the ringleader of this crew that bothered her, something that she didn't trust. "Let's ride!" she said loudly, ignoring her fears and trying to roar like a man but only managing a strangled purr as all horses turned and followed the large, smelly brigand in the lead.

* * *

"When are they s'posed to get here?" grumbled a guard who had sat in the clearing now for well over three hours.

"I don't know—but I wish they'd hurry. I'm getting hungry."

About that time, they heard the familiar sound of breaking branches and the thunder of approaching horses.

"Make it good, boys!" shouted the oldest man-at-arms. "But watch out for the lady! She thinks this is for real!"

"Ayes" were muttered as men regained their seats and began to plod slowly forward, walking into the ambush as they had been instructed.

* * *

"Hist!" shushed Armando, cupping his hand to his ear.

Instinctively, all the men in their ragged group fanned out, melting into the surrounding forest with remarkable ease, which was slightly alarming, considering their beefy size and cumbersome horses.

"Charley!" snapped Armando, motioning for Charlotte to follow.

She stared down the trail the wagon was to arrive on with something like exhilaration on her face. It was her first *real* fight!

"Get over here!" Armando ordered, irritated by her "amateurish" behavior.

She dutifully pulled her reins toward her stomach, and her horse began to back into the cover of the midnight forest, just making the dense brush when the first wagon clattered into the clearing.

A few tense seconds passed as the first guard appeared, seated proudly on a barrel-chested warhorse. The guard seemed totally at ease, slouched low in his saddle and whistling a meaningless tune.

"Oh no!" Charlotte whispered excitedly. The sight of an "enemy" was just too much for her warrior heart to bear, and with a wild "Aye! Yah!" and the crash of underbrush breaking, she bounded after the first shocked man-at-arms with her sword drawn and flashing in the muted half-light, ready to cleave the scoundrel in two.

"Christ!" muttered Garret, springing after the bloodthirsty vixen with the bulging crotch. "She's serious!"

"What gave you that clue, Montgomery?" shouted Torin in agreement, following his friend and charging forward as Garret's horse rammed his lady's excited mare from the side, sending the horse spinning and her nearly flying. "Was it when she picked up a sword or tried to pin the man to the ground with her knife!"

"You fool!" she screamed, forgetting to keep her voice low, and she pulled up so hard on the reins her horse screamed and tried to break away. "I almost had him!" With a wave of her sword and an oath, she was off again, intent on the head of the unfortunate guard who had wound his way around the loaded wagon and was heading for the dense covering of the forest with Charlotte hot on his trail.

"Blast the savage wench!" Garret cursed, urging his horse forward and heading straight for the loaded wagon. "Come on, old boy!" he prodded. The bedraggled warhorse, who had one good fight left in him, felt the urgency in his master's words as he gathered his powerful body into one hurtling mass of muscle and bolted over the wagon, cutting Charlotte off a few feet from her prey.

"Get out of my way!" she screamed in frustration, cursing the clumsy pirate as Garret sprang from his horse and threw his guard violently to the ground. The man looked bewildered and terrified.

"Play dead, fool, or my wife will have you for supper!"

"Your *wife?*"

Garret nodded grimly.

"Poor devil," muttered the guard sympathetically. Obediently he shut his eyes as Garret plunged his sword downward, piercing the shoulder of his tunic in mock battle.

"He was mine!" shouted Charlotte, keeping her voice low, her words full of fury, as she jumped from her horse.

Garret ignored her, pretending not to hear her as he pulled his sword out of the ground—careful to keep the clean blade out of her sight—and wiped it on the dirty rag of his cloak.

"I said," she repeated, affecting her "man-stance," her foot tapping angrily on the mossy, leaf-covered ground, "*he was mine!*"

Garret turned the guard over, laying him face down on the ground, and continued to ignore her.

"I said," she stated forcefully, the anger boiling up uncontrollably in her, "HE WAS MINE!" And then she shoved him—*hard.*

"Oh, God!" whispered Torin fearfully, and Cole squeaked as Garret teetered and hit the ground.

Armando sprang boldly into action, jumping between the pair and wondering the entire time why he was crazy enough to do it.

"Charley!" he shouted, gripping his mistress's slender shoulders and starting to sweat as he watched the towering giant right himself out of the corner of his eye and begin to stand. "John can't hear out of that ear!" interjected Armando, who placed himself between his headstrong young mistress and the huge man who began to brush the dust from his clothes, his single eye glued menacingly to the arrogant female standing beside Armando.

"He *saw* me!" she swore, looking at the clearing and seeing nothing left of the "enemy" but a few scattered "corpses."

"He can't see none too good either!" quipped Armando, hoping his lies could keep up with her questions, as Garret stood up and began to walk past the pair as if he didn't see them, murder glinting in his solitary blue eye, managing to drive his shoulder against "Charley" with unrestrained force and knocking the little witch off her feet.

"Blast it! You're so clumsy!" she muttered hotly. "Watch where you're walking!"

The pirate kept on going as she rose painfully to her feet, apparently not aware that he had nearly knocked the stuffing out of her.

"I can't believe what a rude oaf he can be!" she stormed, throwing a tantrum, flinging her sword down and pounding the ground with her feet. She had lost her first chance at honor in battle all because of a deaf, dumb, and half-blind, stinking son-of-a-pirate who was as clumsy as a cow.

Standing sullenly in the middle of the clearing, she frowned as movement out of the corner of her eye caught her attention. Turning slightly, she watched as two of Milford's cronies climbed aboard the seat of the laden wagon, preparing to leave.

"The Sword!" she whispered. Consoling herself with the fact that there would be other fights in her life, she walked discreetly to the rear of the wagon. Swallowing, she looked for the old pirate, John of Milford, who appeared to be deep in a one-sided conversation with Armando. "Good," she murmured as she lifted the edge of the leather tarp and glanced down, feeling reasonably safe.

Her grandmother had told her she would put the chest near the rear so it would be easier for her to find. And there it was, a shining black ebony box with just the tail and the wing of a bejeweled dragon showing like scarlet fire in the muted light.

Licking her lips, she started to tug on the box, inching it backward, hiding it behind her as she pulled. Careful, she thought to herself, watching the men in the clearing with apprehension as she felt the hasp, which was directly in the middle. Then she lifted it, amazed by the weight of the thing, nearly grunting and walking backward with her booty in her hands.

"...To bring her to Milford?" questioned Armando, who took a respectful step backward. Those clothes really did smell, but he had wanted Garret's costume to be *authentic.*

"Yes," Garret replied, keeping his hunched back to Charlotte while he spoke. "Tell her John of Milford wishes to *reward* her for her bravery."

"Of course." Armando shrugged, wondering what his lord had up his sleeve this time. "Well now," Armando murmured in surprise, his attention caught by the diminutive little "male" inching backward with a concentrated groan on her face. "What's she up to now?" he wondered out loud.

Garret turned with a muffled oath, knowing of only one female in the world who could get into as much trouble as she could—and so incredibly fast.

Charlotte had backed toward a huge rock, and Garret spied the ends of the ebony box jutting out on both sides of her. Armando started to move forward, but a strong arm restrained him as Garret watched cynically while his little wife continued to dig her own grave with each faltering step.

Looking around, Charlotte was satisfied that no one saw her as she slipped the box behind the rock, dropping it gratefully to the ground. She began to cover it up with leaves and moss as best she could.

"There," she muttered, standing up and backing up a step, satisfied with her camouflage, when she felt a huge, round *thing* poking her in the back.

Gulping, her heart nearly stopping, she knew it was the pirate, John of Milford. She knew it because she could *smell* him. So she did the only sensible thing she could: she pretended to adjust her trews as though she had just been watering the vegetation.

"Had to whiz," she muttered gruffly, hoping she sounded manly enough as she walked past him, praying he would follow.

"Whiz away," said Garret evilly. He would have laughed, but he didn't. He did, however, match her step for step, always behind her like a great menacing shadow as she swaggered out of the forest, hitching up her pants.

"Charley!" Armando called jovially, slapping her hard on the back. "John here and his boys want to *reward* you for your bravery!"

"Oh," she inquired in her simulated bass voice, stretching to seem casual and sticking her crotch out to remind the others she was as much of a *real* man as they were.

"Yes!" Armando beamed impishly, calling on all his acting abilities to keep from laughing out loud as he said, as casually as he could, "They wish to take you wenching!"

She nearly fainted, feeling John of Milford's iron grip landing squarely on her shoulder with a thud.

"Wenching?" she squeaked, trying desperately to swallow.

"You do like girls, don't you?" said the pirate, John of Milford. He appeared to appraise her, looking her up and down with a skeptical gleam in his eye.

"Yes, of course, over for tea…"

"Hush, you fool!" said Armando. "Play along! They're a bad lot, and if you refuse…" He gave a shrug and a shudder, his eyes searching the darkened heavens imploringly. "I fear neither you nor or I will see the morrow."

"Dead?" she said.

"Dead," he confirmed.

Frowning, she turned to face the motley crew waiting and watching expectantly behind her. She stared into the glowering eye of the piggish pirate. Time to signal retreat, she reasoned glumly as she lifted her sword high in the air in a salute.

"Wenching we will go!" she shouted with as much enthusiasm as she could muster, her voice trailing away to a whisper as she told herself she would find some way to get out of this before her cover was destroyed—or worse.

A roar of approval went up from Garret's men while he only grinned his black toothless smile at her, then turned his horse and headed for the inn at Milford.

Suddenly, with a sadistic twist of thought, he imagined an army of pawns in ragged, stinking clothes cutting off a disabled white queen dressed in baggy, bulgy-crotched trews. He wondered just how far she would go!

Lord Garret Montgomery snickered wickedly.

Chapter 27

"Inns are inns, and wenches—God love them all—are wenches!" chanted Torin, happy for any excuse to go wenching. "And beer always tastes better the more you drink!"

And tonight, Torin thought with a mischievous grin and a wink at a smirking Cole, promised to be exciting! Both men knew what the set lines and dark expression on Garret's face meant: He was out for revenge and determined to get it any way he could before the night was through.

"What am I supposed to do?" whispered Charlotte, walking her horse beside Armando's mule, flanked on both sides and in the back by Garret's grinning men.

"Ah!" Armando waved merrily, thinking how good a chilled beer was going to taste sliding down his throat. "Just play along. Most likely they'll get so drunk, and the wenches will be so worn out—you have nothing to worry about."

"There is hope, then," said Charlotte. She gulped as the inn seemed to materialize out of the ground. Her mind was still on the artifacts lying low and covered behind the safety of an old rock. So little time!

Up ahead was a mean little cottage, gray-stoned and low to the ground, with a barn attached and pens for pigs, chicken and cattle affixed to the structure at various leaning angles. It looked like any unkempt farm except for the words "Bed and Board," which were burned into a flat piece of wood propped beside the door.

"Coming?" asked Torin sweetly as he jauntily passed her horse, and she started, only able to nod as his grin broadened, and he laughed all the way through the front door. The rest of the men slid eagerly from their horses and followed.

The interior of the inn was barely more than a hovel, with a few rough plank benches and crude tables for seating. The only light was provided by the peat burning in the scooped-out hollow that represented the inn's fireplace.

The tavern was a popular place, sporting music and men, beautiful women of all ages, lounging and laughing the night away. A mug of ale was shoved into Charlotte's hands and she followed her fellows to a table where many lounged, blending into the walls, resting and talking, playing dice and cards after a long day's ride.

Garret couldn't stop from smiling when he looked at her. "Foolish girl," he said beneath his breath. Yet he knew the legend of the Sword and Crown and why it meant so much to her, so part of him understood. Yet he wouldn't forget for a second what she had tried to do.

"What'll you have?" inquired a woman with a grin.

Garret smiled. He was thinking of a blue-eyed blonde who shared his last name, but instead ordered ale, put his foot on the bar, and looked over his shoulder at the skinny waif masquerading as a man.

Waiting.

Charlotte peered around the room. She watched as the men engaged themselves wholeheartedly in drinking the dark thick ale and flirting with the women. If she just appeared nonchalant, if she just acted as though nothing out of the ordinary was going on and made her way to the door, she could slip out unnoticed and claim the relics.

"What?" she said, startled, as she half-turned on the narrow bench to gaze into the sinister face of John of Milford and the sorrowful face of her friend, Armando the Letch. "What do you want?"

Armando was standing directly in front of the smelly pirate, looking at Charlotte with the sympathy of a relative who has just found out that their loved one is about to be hanged. "It seems," he started to say, acting as if he were frightened out of his britches, "it seems our friend John has a *present* for you, Charley."

"A present?" she asked suspiciously, her eyes narrowing as she saw the wicked gleam in the towering gangster's solitary blue eye.

"Yes," answered Armando, twisting his hands in front of him as though he were under great stress, even managing a glistening bead of sweat or two to complete the picture of nervous prostration. "John wishes to *reward* you for your bravery, Charley, by giving you this short sword."

The quiet in the room was deafening. Armando had gone off to one side of the room where a circle of women surrounded him and an occasional giggle was heard, while Charlotte, feeling quite pleased with herself and her new short sword, sauntered over to the ale barrel, conscious of all the eyes on her.

Garret grinned and took a long pull on his ale.

He decided it was time to end the charade. So saying, he turned toward her and started to walk toward what he considered to be nothing but a thin, spindly-legged, conniving, deceitful, meddlesome, wicked… nearly reaching her before the door burst open.

"King's men!" shouted Torin, who knew there wasn't any way on the face of this earth that they would believe a ragtag bunch of cutthroats like them were decent, respectable, chivalrous men of honor only out on a lark.

Half a dozen suited knights entered the room, ducking beneath the low lintel.

"Fight!" Charlotte cried in delight, seeing only the Norman enemy before her as she scrambled up on top of a table, grabbed the rope holding the oil lamp and kicked a surprised man-at-arms squarely in his jaw.

"What the deuce is wrong with her?!" shouted Garret.

Torin shrugged. "She's a lively piece of work, isn't she?"

"Lively? Is that what you call it? Just wait till I get you home, you bloodthirsty witch!" Garret said beneath his breath.

"Brigands!" shouted one young guard, drawing his sword and heading straight for an enemy he thought he could handle: the deformed little male with the bulging crotch who'd just kicked a very good friend of his in the face.

"Oh no, you don't!" muttered Garret, picking up a table and hurtling it across the room as he sprang to the right, rolling and coming to his feet, out of the way of a vicious, swiping blow. All his protective male instincts surged forward as he made his way to the other side of the room, intending to defend his little bride.

"Oh ho!" shouted Charlotte jubilantly as the eager-eyed lad bore down on her with his sword flashing and confidence in his young eyes.

"Here, lad!" shouted Maddy, the owner of the pub. Charlotte looked up just in time to catch the sword tossed in her direction.

"Give 'urn what for! Rowdy little fellow," she said appreciatively. Chuckling with glee, she wound her way through the fighting men with ease, Armando on his knees behind her, hiding his head beneath her skirts. As long as he stayed down low, he decided, he had a reasonably good chance of not getting hit, having to fight or dying.

"Thanks, Maddy!" Charlotte cried, sidestepping the first downward strike of the steel-covered guard. "Humph!" she snorted, watching in disgust as the youth tried desperately to pull his sword out of the table, where the blade had stuck. "You should've stayed at home and helped your mama!" she jeered, hefting her own sword and raising it high above her head, preparing to separate the boy's smile from his body—permanently.

"Bloodthirsty witch!" muttered Garret as he fought his way to her side, grabbing the back of her pants and the top of her tunic. He lifted her off the table.

"Hey!" she shouted in outraged frustration. "John of Milford! Let me go! You're not going to cheat me again!" she vowed, swinging wildly with her sword and nicking him on the cheek.

"You just cut me!" shouted Garret.

"Two for two!" shouted Charlotte, aiming high as Garret ducked.

Torin, who was fighting beside Cole near the front door, turned the chap he'd been exchanging blows with around and kicked him in the rump, sending him crashing to the floor.

"Let's ride!" Torin shouted, waving his arm and flinging open the door. Fighting was great fun, but he preferred to fight an *enemy*, not a friend.

The rest of the men, in perfect agreement, headed for the door. No one wanted the King's men after them; it was rather like a house divided, and they'd have a very hard time explaining themselves before being hung for treason!

Armando was the first man through the door; the coins he had scooped up in a brave attempt to "save them" jingling merrily in his pockets. About half a second later, Garret tossed a furiously thrashing Charlotte through the opening like a sack of old clothes.

"No!" she screamed, sailing through the air. "John of Milford!" she bellowed, landing with a bone-crushing thud in the muck beneath the horses' hooves. "You!" she began, spitting mud and debris. "PIG!"

"Get up!" urged Armando nervously, not willing to touch the dirty figure sprawling on the ground. "Do you want them to put you in *prison?*" He shuddered.

"No!" she spat, pushing up, her eyes throwing daggers as she recognized the huge form coming toward her with her horse in tow.

"I'm going to *kill* him!" she vowed, scrambling to her feet.

"Not now!" shouted Armando. "The guards…"

With those words, a host of angry knights poured from the tavern's door.

"Where there are a few guards," he said knowledgeably, mounting his mule in a great hurry, "there is usually a garrison not far away!"

Knowing that what Armando said was true, she jerked the reins from the drenched pirate, pointing her finger in his face.

"I'm not through with *you* yet!" she threatened, leaping up into her saddle with easy grace. Suddenly she stiffened as she became aware of his glance on her. There was something in the cold, dangerous glitter of his solitary eye that said *he* felt the same.

"Stop looking at me that way, John of Milford!"

Garret stopped and stared, and Charlotte felt an icy shudder course up and down her spine. There was something about his gaze, something familiar and altogether frightening when one black brow arched unexpectedly above one blazing blue eye.

"Scatter!" shouted Torin, breaking the spell.

And the men were off! Riding hard in different directions with the King's guard not far behind. Two riders veered sharply to the south, dodging trees and brush with the help of frequent flashes of lightning. One was a curiously effeminate-looking male in the lead on a high-spirited, nervous palfrey, and the other was a massive, wicked-looking pirate with blackened teeth and a hulking, crooked form, following the other as quickly as he could, both fleeing into the arms of a wild spring storm.

Chapter 28

Brilliant shards of lightning lashed the rainswept countryside, exploding in shades of blinding white and silvery gray. The night-time world of Wales was on fire with bursts of spectral, gleaming rays that illuminated the landscape into an eerie parody of day.

"Run!" urged Charlotte, her face pressed hard against the saturated silky fur of her horse's neck. The velvet farmer's cap that she had worn so proudly all night had fallen to the ground long before. Her hair, once pinned and bound in the striped bandanna, had sneaked loose of its confines to lie soggily in wild strands against her face and neck.

Behind her, the ground rocked with its own thunder. John of Milford rode hard in her wake while, behind him, three of the King's men did their best to catch up.

"Hurry!" she whispered, looking back just as a jagged bolt of lightning ripped through the sky, destroying the smooth, black fabric of night. They were gaining on John, she thought grimly—and on her.

The ground beneath the mare's narrow feet oozed with mud, sucking at the horses' legs and making traveling slow and hazardous. The palfrey was a skittish animal who kept tossing her mane and rolling her eyes wildly with each new crash of lightning or accompanying rumble of thunder. It was all Charlotte could do to hold her. To make matters worse, she didn't know the countryside—neither the shortcuts nor the hazards. But that would have done her little good anyway, she realized. In this darkness, there was only one way to travel, and that was by trusting in the superior senses of your horse.

The reins were slack in her hands, and her body followed each movement, loose and supple, parroting each of the horse's maneuvers as though they were her own.

"Run, girl," she urged quietly, feeling the stinging brush of a branch graze her cheek, scratching red webs into pale skin while the wet mane clenched tightly in her hands began to slip through her fingers. Then it happened! Sparks exploded in the heavens, splinters of a great burst of lightning fanned out like miniature stars moments before the parent bolt struck, seeming to curl down from the purple-hued sky like a huge, forked serpent's tongue, its branches veining out slowly, striking an oak and exploding in a blaze of orange-tipped fire only a few feet from them.

"Whoa!" Charlotte cried, pulling back hard on the reins as the horse reared up, her eyes rolling white with fear. "Whoa, girl!" she urged desperately, her fingers slipping on the reins as she tried to wind them around her hands. "Steady!" she cried, feeling the reins slice scarlet grooves in her fingers as she struggled to hold on. But trying to control the mare was useless. The storm had maddened her, and the ground was as slick as ice from the never-ending rain. She began to skid clumsily on her back feet, throwing Charlotte brutally to the rain-soaked ground.

"Blast it!" she screamed as she hit the muddy trail with a breath-stealing thud, remembering to roll quickly to one side and out of the crazed horse's way. Scrambling quickly to her feet, she tried to catch the mare before she ran off. "Whoa!" she cried again, waving her hands and trying to get in front of the mare, but it was too late. The horse was so frightened by the shrieking storm and blazing fire she refused to listen to any of Charlotte's taming words.

"Whoa," she cried again, knowing her commands were useless.

With a strangled curse, she jumped to one side, watching as the excited horse plunged headlong into the nearest thicket and out of sight—leaving her stranded.

"Anything else?" she whispered in disgust, reaching for her sword, which was stuck nearly to the hilt in the oozing mud, and jerking it out as the thundering hooves of her pursuers came closer, threatening to beat her into the ground with their force.

Looking up as the first rider approached, she automatically tensed, not knowing whether to be relieved or dismayed as she saw John of Milford reach for her with a determined scowl on his face.

Without breaking stride, he bent over and grabbed her around the waist, swinging her easily into the saddle ahead of him, then continued to ride.

There was no time for thanks; there was no time for anything. His horse was old but used to the games of war, crashing fiercely through the undergrowth with heart-stopping speed.

Breathing hard, she wound her hands into the stallion's mane, feeling the solid weight of John behind her and the security of his brawny arm surrounding her middle. He was hard as stone despite his misleading potbelly; and for an old man, she thought absently, his heartbeat remarkably clear and easy.

Not foolish enough to question her rescue, she looked ahead, just in time to see a large deadfall in the middle of the trail, blocking their path.

"Oh, my God!" she whispered incredulously as she felt his arm tighten protectively around her. "You're not—" she began to say, her eyes growing wide. "You're not going to try and jump *that!*" she cried, her voice rising excitedly and competing with the shrieking wind—and winning. Yet she already knew that jumping the deadfall was exactly what the old pirate intended to do as she felt his body stiffen behind her, tensing, preparing for the leap.

"It's too high!" she argued desperately, seeing visions of herself skewered on jagged branches, helpless and pinned.

But he paid no attention to her protests as he began to stretch out—his head beside hers, his chest covering her back—forcing her to lie down against the aging warhorse's bowed neck.

"Oh, sweet Jesus!" she shrieked, this time in real fear.

That was a perfectly *huge* deadfall, and this was a very *old* horse.

"You're *crazy!*" she started to say, feeling the stallion's muscles contract, feeling the sudden, dizzying surge of adrenaline coursing through her veins as the animal's body lifted into the air and lunged forward in one powerful motion. "John of Milford!" she screamed as she felt his hand tighten to an almost bone-crushing pressure around her middle. Either he was afraid she would fall off, or he was protecting her. The latter just seemed too hard to believe.

"You're insane!" she bellowed as the horse's forelegs cleared the top of the deadfall barely a moment before they hit the ground on the other side. Its back legs followed, nearly jarring her out of her seat in spite of the protective arm encircling her waist. She cried aloud in pain, as John's head thudded against her own with a loud crack. For one dizzying minute it felt as though the impact had split her skull wide open. It took a moment for her to realize that she wasn't dead.

Then the simple running beat of one horse, slowing now to a well-deserved walk. The singular rush of wind and rain against her face. The cold prickle of chilled flesh, and the warm, intimate feel of a powerful hand, sliding slowly upward, pulling her close.

"What…" she stammered in confusion, unable to make any sense at all out of what he was doing. He had just nearly killed them both barely half a minute before, and now he was acting… acting as though he were *excited* by the whole thing.

Grabbing his fingers to halt their intimate progress, she turned in the saddle. His arm, which had prevented her from falling to her death during the jump, now prevented her from leaping from the still horse.

"What are you doing?" she began, flushed and angry. "You're making a mistake!"

But then the lightning bit through the fabric of the midnight sky to reveal the man behind her. The brown and gray-striped mustache had fallen from his face along with his beard, and the wide-winged hat had flown from his head during the jump, while the scraggly, dun-colored brow was peeled away with the pirate's free hand, and the leather patch was removed to reveal a pair of scalding blue eyes.

"You!" she whispered in horror, recognizing Garret Montgomery, her *husband*, who had caught her red-handed in the middle of the biggest plot she had ever hatched and nearly gotten himself killed.

"No way out of this one," she muttered gloomily, shaking her head in disgust. "If it wasn't for bad luck, Garret Montgomery," she whispered, blushing furiously, "I'd have no luck at all!"

A subtle tightening of his arm made her suddenly wish that she was back at the Vale, climbing down the wall and battling with her grandmother again. She would rather face ten Isabels or an entire squadron of the King's men any day than those searing blue eyes which seemed to see right through her with agonizing ease. Yet even worse than the knowledge that it had been him all along tonight and not the smelly brigand, John of Milford, was the acutely painful awareness that he had outsmarted her, something her pride simply could not stand. *He had outwitted, outflanked, and outmaneuvered her every step of the way!* That thought nettled her like nothing else could, turning her cheeks a most embarrassed red.

Quietly Garret surveyed the small woman trapped in his arms, who was busy studying her fingers and turning various shades of crimson, finally settling on shameful scarlet, a color that suited her well. He waited patiently, anticipating an apology. Perhaps he even wanted to hear her beg for his forgiveness. He expected at least contrition, but what he got instead of submissive guilt was a sudden, sharp, stinging slap across the face.

"You tricked me!" she choked in fury. His eyebrows shot up in surprise.

Knowing of no other way out of her dilemma, she immediately took the offensive, preparing to confound and confuse her adversary, turn the tables, or even pout and throw a tantrum if necessary, but she would never admit that she was in the wrong!

"*I* tricked *you?*" he replied coldly, favoring her with a scalding, withering stare.

"Yes!" she replied indignantly. "You tricked me!" She pushed his hand away and leapt to the ground, thankful that she had hidden the Sword and Crown and praying he didn't know what she had *really* been doing behind that rock.

Laughter, a cruel, bitter sound that filled the clearing and caused her to shiver, rang out in the rain. Lifting one long leg over the tired horse's head, he jumped lightly to the ground beside her.

Any other human being would have had the good sense to be scared, and any "normal" human being would have looked into those furiously burning eyes and *run.* But first of all, she wasn't any other human being; and second, being "normal" was a matter of opinion. Last of all, and probably mattering the most, having good sense wasn't an attribute she could readily boast of. She just stood there, a dripping, wet mess, glaring back at him with her hands on her hips and her crotch bulging ridiculously in the brilliant, flashing bands of color that tore through the midnight sky.

"You lie," he began in a calm, even voice that couldn't hide the rage that boiled in him as he stared down at her. "You steal. You try and drug me. And then," he added, pushing the wet strands of hair away from his face before he grabbed her shoulders roughly, giving her a frustrated shake. "You dress like a man and ride off into the night, waving your sword like an idiot at anything that moves!"

An arrogant shrug of her little shoulders and an impatient toss of her hair were the only explanation he received.

"Do you have any idea what could have happened to you?" he growled furiously, licking the droplets of rain from his lower lip. "You could've been *killed!*"

Calmly, she looked up at him, too blind to see the worry and pain in his glittering eyes.

"What do you care?" she asked haughtily, and she held her breath, waiting for his reply, wondering why it should matter so much what he said.

There was a long pause, a moment when neither one spoke. The only sounds surrounding them were the rain beating down and the rushing *whoosh* of the scattering, frantic winds.

"I care," he said. He momentarily forgot his anger as he looked at her rain-soaked features and her sparkling sky-blue eyes. *I care so much that it hurts!* he nearly cried aloud, wanting to shake some sense into her belligerent little body. *Even in the rain*, he thought in wonder as he mentally cursed himself, aroused at the sight of her, still feeling his anger while bitterly acknowledging his need. *Even now…*

"You are the most conniving, underhanded, scheming…" he began, intent on giving her a serious tongue-lashing, if nothing else, until the bored *I've been through this a million times before* expression in her eyes halted his scolding and made him furious. With an agonized curse and a muffled groan, he grabbed her, pulling her to him so hard that she gasped, and he kissed her.

But his touch was not tender as it had been last night. It was hard and demanding and so very cruel in the way he tried to dominate her through her senses.

"You will submit to my authority," he told her furiously. "You're my wife and I won't have you jeopardize your safety by these dangerous escapades you are so intent on initiating!

"You could have been killed, Charlotte!"

The thought of her dying was more than he could stand.

Groaning, he pulled her close, nearly crushing her in his haste. But it was a bitter embrace, as cold and lonely as the wind moaning forlornly through the trees. It was a touch that told of desire, but one that had lost the sweet romantic gentleness of only a few hours before. And she knew, in that final, painful moment, that Garret Montgomery, if he was pushed too far, could be as cruel as he could be tender, as unforgiving as he could be sweet.

For him, she had been a bridge, a road that united his heart and his mind. Within her had been the power to lift him up and grant him the dream he had been searching for all his life. Passion was the key that melted the glacier ice surrounding his heart. She was his *passion.* But now he felt cut off, as though with her betrayal she had forever destroyed the way to his heart and the warmth that could have saved him from the cold existence he had witnessed in his father's life. He had been denied his chance at happiness. And yet he wanted her… wanted her badly.

"Stop it!" she cried, pushing against him. "Don't punish me, Garret, for something you don't understand! The Sword and Crown are more important to me than anything you could possibly understand!" She looked at him and he saw a beautiful woman before him, a maiden as fragile and white as the moonlight trying desperately to peer through the clouds above.

Garret did not let go.

"What," he said suspiciously "do the Sword and Crown have to do with what you've done tonight?"

She couldn't tell him. The Sword and Crown lay in a rough place, hidden from eyes without understanding. Only she knew where they were and why they were so vitally important. More important than her life.

"My penance will be my silence," she whispered, penance for having nearly failed. The relics were safe for now.

"You're hurting me, Garret. You promised that you wouldn't hurt me!"

"Hurting you?" he retorted sarcastically. He stripped the bandanna from her hair and flung it to the ground. "I haven't hurt you half as much as you've hurt me!"

"How?" she asked, her full lips trembling and her eyes wide with surprise. "How have I hurt you?"

It was the genuine bewilderment in her voice and expression that caused him to pause and gaze quietly into her eyes.

"You really don't know, do you?" he said softly, touching her lower lip with the tip of his finger before he reached down and ripped the servant's tunic from her shoulders in one savage gesture, eliciting a strangled gasp as she tried to cover herself with her hands. With little effort he wrapped his cloak about her. "My wife will never wear rags," he warned. "And if," he whispered dangerously, tangling his free hand into the strands of her wet hair, "I cannot have your trust and affection, I swear by God and all that's holy, I *will* have your favors, wife!"

"Stop it, Garret!" she cried, beating her hands against his chest. Instead of allowing herself the luxury of tears, she retaliated the only way she knew how. She slapped him as hard as she could.

With restraint born of a gentleman, Garret reached upward and touched his cheek. Quiet. Utter stillness filled the clearing, excepting only the pitter-patter of rain falling straight down, his icy silence telling her that this time she had gone too far.

She took a cautious step backward, hiding the offending palm behind her and wondering if begging for mercy would have any effect.

Slowly he turned to face her, his cheek blooming red with the print of her hand. A brilliant flash of lightning illuminated the clearing, making him look suspiciously devilish.

"How dare you!" he said, his voice booming and reverberating through the clearing, loud enough to compete with the storm's weakening thunder and winning easily.

Shocked, she stepped backward, then slipped and fell backward into the wet mud, smacking her cheek on a fallen log.

"Gentlemen," she cried fiercely, rubbing her stinging cheek and glaring up at him, the tears threatening to fall once again, "do not treat ladies in that manner!"

"I see no 'lady,'" he replied coldly. "I see only *you!*" he added, spitting the blackened tooth caps from his mouth. "A spoiled *brat!*"

"I am too a lady!" she shouted, wondering for a moment why she was arguing about something she never had any desire to be in the first place. "I'm as much of a lady as anyone!" She tried to push herself up in the slippery wet mud but failed to find a secure foothold.

"Only when it's convenient," he replied, beginning to come to her with his intentions very clear. "What you are," he informed her clearly, "is a spoiled, self-centered brat, a liar, and a scheming, conniving *witch.* Let us not forget," he added harshly, pointing his finger heavenward as he remembered the library and her hot and cold behavior, "a *tease!*"

"I am not!" she replied, but her rebuttal lacked depth because she was not sure what being a "tease" meant in the first place. In that moment, when she was contemplating the meaning of that word and wondering why it seemed to bother him so much, he sprang.

"Oh!" she cried in surprise as she tried to roll out of his way, looking like a chocolate-covered elf in her boyish clothes and mud-covered form. But she didn't roll fast enough, and she didn't jump far enough, and she didn't move quickly enough.

"Not that easy!" he muttered through gritted teeth as he scrambled through the mud after her. The sound of his voice was like the rumbling growl of a lion ready to attack as he grabbed her foot and pulled her backward.

"You'd better let me go!" she threatened, doing her best to kick him where she thought it would do the most good. Unable to reach, her blows fell only on the hardened steel of his chest and arms.

"Or what?" he retorted with a contemptuous snort as he twisted her foot around and threw her to the ground, pinning her easily under his weight.

"Or I'll… I'll…" She tried to think, digging a rut in the mud with her heel that quickly filled with water as she tried to twist her way free. "I'll…" she grunted, trying to get an elbow between them and still unable to think of a single threat ominous enough to make him leave her alone.

When she found she couldn't move, not even an inch, she tried a more subtle approach. "Just let me go!" she asked with a frustrated sigh when it became obvious that fighting him would do her no good.

"Never!" he promised.

"I thought…" she whispered, her lips trembling and her eyes glistening wetly as she remembered last night and the tenderness they shared. He had been so incredibly sweet, and his words—those precious, precious words he had uttered—had given her the first sweet dreams she had ever known in her life. "I thought you said that you *loved* me…"

It was those three words that brought him up short.

"What is this?" he growled in annoyance. "Another trick?" Those words made him close his eyes tightly against the memory of last night—his *special* night. "Blast you!" he cursed, furious at her for making him remember those miserable little words, which stabbed painfully at his heart and his conscience, making him sigh, making him weak, effectively chaining his anger as she had chained his heart the moment they had met.

A second later he stood up and hauled her to her feet. His desire to ravish and punish her had been diluted into simply the urge to put her in her proper place.

"A man," he began, as he pulled her resisting form toward the waiting horse, "will say a great many things." He told her this calmly as he began to tie her hands with the leather thong that had been holding his hair in place.

"What?" she whispered in disbelief, forgetting to struggle as he reached down inside her trews and pulled out the yards of saturated hose. "You *lied* about *loving me?*" she asked in a small, timid voice, unable to believe that Garret would lie to her at all, about anything!

"A man will lie through his teeth," Garret replied callously as he picked her up and tossed her over the horse's neck, bending down just long enough to tie her hands and feet together under the stallion's belly. "For a chance at a good roll in the hay. Even," he added cruelly, "for a pathetic tumble."

"Oh!" she cried indignantly. "A *pathetic tumble?* Is that what last night was to you?" she asked shrilly as he walked around to stand next to her face, answering her indignation by stuffing a wad of hose in her open mouth.

"Yes," he told her wickedly. "As a matter of fact, I think I would've had more fun by myself." He gave a shrug and a yawn as she tried to spit the soggy stockings out of her mouth.

"You wicked man!" she mumbled furiously, not sure if she wanted to kill him more because he had outsmarted her or because he thought that last night's tryst in the garden hadn't been worth the effort. She struggled furiously, telling him off as best she could in her circumstances, and he laughed, poking the hose back in with the tip of his middle finger.

"Not as good as the real thing, aye?" he teased with a mirthless grin, turning up the corners of his sensual mouth. "There is no reward in this world for *bad girls* such as you," he said devilishly. "Old stockings may be all you ever get!"

Her blue eyes were livid.

"Yes, *dearest,*" he answered sarcastically, batting his eyelashes at her as she had done only a few moments before. "I *love* you too!" he mocked, laughing as he sprang into the saddle behind her, pointedly ignoring the remainder of her muffled cries of wrath and obvious discomfort. "It's time to go home, *Lady* Charlotte," he told her loudly, turning the rested horse in the direction of Pembroke. "And it's also time you learned who wears the pants in this family!" he added dryly, swatting her as hard as he could on her provocatively soaked fanny as the rain continued to pour, and the thunder continued to pound, accompanying him all the way back to the manor.

Chapter 29

Tregaron was a natural fortress, protected on the north, east, and south by the formidable Cambrian Mountains, while on the western slopes, high walls of stone had been erected.

Seated on a sturdy gray charger high on a plateau above the village, Lon surveyed the assembled Welsh nobility with renewed pride.

The House of Brecon, with its lusty, dark-skinned lords, shadowed the side of the hill, proudly waving their armorial colors, as did all the other noble houses of Wales until the valley beneath him seemed alive with rippling, multihued silk banners waving in the late afternoon breeze like shimmering jewels cast randomly at his feet.

Over a thousand able-bodied men had responded to his call to arms, prepared to march to Pembroke and retake their relics and their future queen.

Suddenly, from the northernmost edge of his makeshift camp, a new banner popped into view. Deep purple silk was proudly unfurled and held beside a raven staff of ancient oak. The emblems were carried with dignity and thrust defiantly forward by a woman who glared haughtily at the assembled peoples as though daring them to defy her presence amongst them.

As she approached, Lon could see she was an older woman with jet-black hair boldly streaked with lightning white and eyes of volcanic fire that only hinted at the immense power of her magnificent will.

Accompanying her were twenty sturdy men-at-arms. Riding behind her was a singularly cruel and dangerous-looking Captain of the Guard, with a wicked scar that ran the entire length of his rugged face.

"So," murmured Lon in satisfaction, bowing low as she approached him, "Baroness Isabel!"

In the late afternoon sun, Charlotte paced silently back and forth in the study, wondering what to do.

Last night Garret had trussed her up like a goose, brought her home, and thrown her down on the bed, not speaking a single word to her all night—and not untying her either, she remembered darkly.

But worse than his silence had been the feeling of bitter loneliness that had crept over her when he refused to lie down beside her. He had sat on the window seat for the remainder of the night, gazing at the ebbing storm, looking utterly lost and as miserable as she felt.

Only after Sparrow had brought breakfast, exclaiming a startled "Oh!" when she saw her mistress's less-than-comfortable condition, did Garret allow the ropes to be loosened, instructing his guard not to "let this traitorous child out of your sight!" Then he left, shutting the door between them without even a nod or goodbye.

She still refused to accept the possibility that perhaps she had deserved her less-than-courteous treatment or that she was responsible for hurting him as deeply as it seemed.

Yet, despite her personal troubles, the more immediate problem still had to be righted. The Sword and Crown must be transported back to Lon. And now, with all that had been revealed to her last night—that traitorous Armando!—she knew that she could trust only herself to carry out such an important task.

A small gust of wind blew through the damper in the chimney, making something brown and white flutter in the black ashes. Frowning, she reached forward and lifted it out. It was the remnants of a small, leather-bound book all but destroyed by the flames. Blowing on the cover to scatter the ash, she opened it, seeing a strong, simple script etched on the page. Holding it toward the light, she read:

Rose of marble chiseled deep,
Music in material form,
Beauty in light, forever to keep,
Silently born.

And below the lovely verse a single, slashing, firm "G," and the explanation: "The rose is not forever, but the memory is."

"Garret," she whispered in wonder, trying to pry apart more of the tortured pages, seeing fragments of verse here, a word there; and on the last page a poem, all but obliterated by the heat. It began:

I was a warrior of stone,
Until the maid with hair of silver
And eyes of liquid blue,
Touched my heart
And broke my chains
Of loneliness
With her sweet love so true.

No more could be read. The flames had destroyed the pages.

"Garret," she said, and she held the remnants of her husband's book of poems close to her heart. It hurt to breathe. Tonight, she knew, she would have to find another way to slip out, and tonight, to Garret, her actions would seem like the ultimate, most unforgivable betrayal.

"God," she whispered, sinking into the chair beside the ornately decorated chess pieces, absently fingering the flowing robes of the white queen as she stared into space. "What shall I do?" she moaned, suddenly wishing with all her heart that the burden of her destiny could be shoved away or forgotten.

Angry and not fully understanding why—she threw the piece against the wall, not caring where it bounced. "Garret," she murmured, knowing she would have to lie again, scheme again, hurt him again, but not knowing if she had the heart and the courage to do that once more. "I'm sorry," she whispered, running her finger over the smooth hair of the lustrous black knight, apologizing now for what she was about to do. "So sorry," she repeated, seeing his face in her mind as clearly as if he stood in front of her. In absolute misery, she closed her eyes and laid her head against her arms, waiting for tonight…

Chapter 30

A day's ride through the rugged hills had brought no rewards, and the night promised to be equally as barren.

"Take another garrison of men tomorrow morning, Torin," ordered Garret tiredly, "and scour the seaside of Milford. He's got to be around here somewhere!" He raked back his unruly hair as he unstrapped the dusty sword-belt from around his narrow waist and let it clatter to the floor.

"Perhaps he's gone back home… or over to the Frankish side of the Channel," offered Torin lamely. He was tired of looking for the solitary red-haired, one-handed pirate with the mad green eyes. There had been no reports of sightings, no raids, nothing. Yet Garret refused to give up.

"He's here!" replied Garret firmly, sinking gratefully into a chair beside the study's massive fireplace. "I can *feel* him." Narrowing his eyes, he stared into the flickering flames, a tingling awareness of danger licking at the back of his mind like a renegade spark of fire about to ignite. He wasn't sure if his premonition was due more to lack of sleep and fuzzy thinking, or if his sense of impending danger was accurate.

Torin, who could never feel anything outside of his basic desires and his various bodily functions, knew only what his five senses could tell him. And what they told him was that Harold Halfdanson had vanished off the face of the earth, or at least this little piece of it. It was time to move on to other things. There were tournaments to be fought… and women; disputes to be settled… and women; ale to be drunk… and women…

He was preparing to argue his perfectly valid point about more important things than a one-handed Viking when a small figure with a loose cape of flowing silver hair walked demurely into the room, followed close at her heels by two wary, armed guards.

With a sudden intake of breath, as though someone had just hefted a hundred-pound stone at his midriff, Garret stared. Charlotte wore nothing but a light dressing gown so transparent that even in the study's dim light, her silhouette was completely visible.

Any other woman would have hidden her face in shame at such an outrageous display, but then, he mused, no other woman of her time would have had the brass necessary to walk around thus attired. Yet, remarked Garret grudgingly to himself, her head was not bowed in submission, nor did her cheeks flame in shame. Arrogant pride showed in the square set of her shoulders and the haughty tilt of her nose. Despite his still-smoldering anger, and thoroughly sure that she was scheming once again and her garment was simply the bait she was using *this* time, his heartbeat ten times faster at the shadows displayed so clearly beneath her robe.

Ignoring the gaping Torin and seemingly unaware of the embarrassed, furtive glances of the guards, she approached her husband and stood quietly in front of his chair, barely half a foot from his knee. He wondered if she knew that every color of the rainbow shimmered in her hair when the firelight played across it. Or how the golden light caused her ivory skin to glow like a dusky, pale rose.

"Well!" he snapped, breaking free from his thoughts as the twin demons of lust and desire burned fiercely in his eyes. "What do you want?" he asked roughly, refusing to look at her as he wondered just what she had up her sleeve this time.

"I wish to speak to you," she said quietly.

As she moved nearer, he heard the rustle of silk and smelled the heady aromas of rose and lavender with *her* scent beneath it all, attracting him like no earthly flower ever could.

"So," he replied, with an indifferent shrug and slight wave of his hand, still staring into the flames. "Speak."

"Privately," she answered firmly, moving nearer, enveloping him in her cloud of silk and scent, causing the heat to build in him till the ruddy rush of fire coursing through his veins made him burn. For a moment he wondered which would sear him worse: jumping into the hearth, where the fire snapped and blazed orange, or standing near her, where the fire began white-hot inside of himself, consuming him in a blinding rush of desire until he became a helpless moth and she temptation's hottest fire.

Frowning, he watched as a splinter of wood ignited, flared brightly, and then was gone, all in a puff of gray smoke. He was tired, dirty, and not just a little bit depressed. His mental powers were at low tide, and he was not in any mood for games. Thinking of a hundred reasons why he didn't want to be alone with her—and only *one* powerfully strong reason why he did—he replied as cruelly as possible, "Go to bed, woman. I've no patience with your childish games tonight!"

Torin's dusty eyebrows shot up, and one old guard, who'd been married for over twenty-five years, coughed in his hand, sure of what was coming.

"What I have to say to you," she began evenly, apparently not affected by his remark or his tone, "is important."

Garret then looked long and hard at her, yet she neither flinched nor looked away but remained standing coolly in front of him, holding his gaze confidently. His resolve to send her from the room vanished, just like the puff of gray smoke he had seen scurrying up the flue only a moment before.

"Leave," he commanded the others softly, turning his head to gaze into the flames again as the guards withdrew quietly from the room.

"Garret?" called Torin quietly.

Garret turned to look at his friend, whose face was puckered in a worried frown.

"It's all right, Torin," he answered, with an exhausted grin. "I think I'll be *safe.*"

Torin nodded, fixing Charlotte with a scathing look before leaving the room, shutting the door behind him with a very loud bang.

"Well?" Garret asked testily, refusing to look at her in her gauzy, translucent silks but wanting to so much that his mouth watered.

"I want to apologize," she told him simply and clearly, most of her secretly wishing to do so, most of her hating herself for what she was about to do.

"Oh?" he asked in surprise, sitting forward and cupping his chin in his hands as he rested his elbows on his knees. There was a look of anticipation, perhaps even pleasure, on his face, and there was no way she could miss the soft fires of hope lighting his blue eyes.

"Yes," she told him quietly, surprising herself by the sincerity in her voice, unable to meet his gaze. "I'm sorry that I hurt you."

"When did you hurt me?" he asked innocently. Having revealed himself once before, he would be damned if he'd ever do it again. At least not until he trusted her. With the way he felt, that wouldn't occur for several lifetimes.

"Last night…" she started, before losing her composure and beginning to stammer. Her speech had been carefully prepared, each point rehearsed, each maneuver outlined. And he had destroyed her strategy with one remark.

"You didn't hurt me," he told her calmly, yawning slightly and stretching his booted legs far out in front of him. "You see, Lady

Charlotte, in order for someone to hurt me, I must first think something of them."

His words caused her to gasp. His remark hurt ten times more than his slap, as he knew it would.

"You said," she reiterated slowly, picking through her words carefully and wondering why her heart was hammering so loudly and why she suddenly felt ill. "You said that I had hurt you and that… and that… you *loved* me…" she insisted, moving nearer and placing a hand uncertainly on his shoulder. She felt him flinch, and he stood up, laughing darkly as he turned his back to her.

"I thought I had explained that to you last night," he replied with a bitter sigh, still feeling her fingers, so warm against his burning flesh that he trembled slightly.

"I don't understand," she said quietly. "I won't. You said that I had hurt you. The only way that I could hurt you is if you love me!"

Turning, he glared at her with burning, reproachful eyes, thumping his massive chest with one powerful fist.

"I'm the lord of the manor!" he thundered. "Loving someone, anyone, is a weakness that I cannot afford! I won't give you or anyone the power to hurt me again! Do you understand? I gave up my humanity a long time ago, Charlotte. I became the lord of the manor, and this man you see before you is made of cold, hardened steel and unfeeling stone! I won't be played like a puppet for your purposes."

He came towards her. His sensuous masculinity and unearthly good looks gave him the appearance of a dark, sinister lord, like Pluto stepping from his chariot. But it was his eyes that arrested her attention: intelligent and sharp-edged, they cut her to the quick faster than a rapier and with more accuracy than an arrow. She remembered his poem of the stone warrior and she saw it embodied in the knight before her.

Sensing her appraisal, Garret smiled, and the flash of his white teeth made him appear feral in the firelight as he nodded.

"Yes. You see it, don't you? The knight and the warrior, the lord of the manor. I wield justice with my sword and am just as capable of tearing down as building up!

"I won't be addled by your charms, though they are legion. And understand this: I'm not a lapdog to be petted into submission or tamed like one of your horses. You've put not only yourself at risk, but this manor. And I'll do whatever is necessary to ensure the safety of my family, and you, Charlotte, willing or not, are my family, my beloved enemy and my wife.

"But be warned. I gave up my flesh, blood and tender heart years ago! So, you see, Charlotte, you and others like you cannot hurt me, not ever again, because I've no heart left to hurt!"

She saw bitterness and fire in his eyes as they roamed over her face and form. Instead of confusion and anger, pity filled her. Pity so sharp that her heart began to ache. So, she thought sadly, she *had* hurt him. Hurt him badly.

Something special had happened to her the other night in the garden of silvery clouds and pale moonlight, something sudden and sweet. That night when he had touched her, he had reached a part of her that she never even knew existed, and at that moment she was willing to believe that you could fall in love with someone you've only just met. That perhaps there *was* destiny and magic in the universe. Because that night it had touched her with its blessed light.

Swallowing, she turned and walked to the decanter of wine, the image of the box with the Sword and Crown lying on the moss-covered ground filling her mind while she knew her impending betrayal threatened to condemn her to a guilty existence for the rest of her life—a life that might well have to be lived without him.

Her resolve began to crumble until she saw Isabel's face in her mind and heard her words:

> *"...do not belong to Normans or Saxons. They belong only to the Welsh!"*

Only to the Welsh. A legacy that would probably cost her Garret. It seemed a high price to pay to fulfill her obligations. A very, very high price to pay indeed.

Careful not to be observed, with trembling hands she poured two goblets of wine and dripped two drops of the sleeping potion into one goblet. Licking her lips and taking a deep breath, she turned, offering him the wine that had been drugged.

"You don't give up, do you?" he snorted, looking at her with contempt, which hurt her far more than his anger ever could. "You really think I'm a fool, don't you?"

"Garret," she said, speaking as softly and as clearly as her hammering heart would allow, "I would have never hurt you—never lied to you—if I thought there was any other way. You must believe me!"

"There *was* another way!" he said angrily, reaching her in only a few long strides to stand glowering over her like some dark, malevolent god, his eyes dancing with building fury. "You could've trusted me," he answered bitterly, thumping his massive chest. "*Me!*"

"Possibly," she whispered, unable to look at him as she extended the wine toward him in the most casual gesture she could make. "But it would not have only been up to you," she reminded him. "Your father would have had the final say."

"I would have done my best," he argued, unable to dispute the fact that Charles would have the last word on the disposition of her property and those damnable relics. *Speaking of which...*

"By the way," he told her, looking suspiciously from her to the extended cup, "if you think you got away with anything the other night," her heart skipped a few beats in fear, "you didn't!"

Careful to look down, but not too obviously, she didn't try to lie this time. There was no point.

"You have them, then?" she asked, trying not to sound too anxious.

"No," he admitted, and her spirits soared. "But I know the rock that you've hidden them behind, and tomorrow you and I will go and retrieve *our* property."

Yes, Garret," she replied meekly, again offering him the drugged wine as she reached for the other goblet with her free hand.

"Now, let's see," he murmured, looking at her from beneath lowered lids, and she marveled at the remarkable length and thickness of his lashes, suddenly feeling a desire to hold him, to touch him. "Since I still have not found the potion that you tried to poison me with, there is a good chance that you've dumped some more into my wine. But which one is it?" he asked, the deep baritone of his voice booming loudly through the room. "Since you offer me this one," he tapped the goblet with his little finger, which bore a sapphire ring as deep as his eyes, "and you hold the other one away from me, and since I *know* that you've tried to trick me before... you are obviously trying to make me believe that *this* one is drugged so that I will want the other one. Except you knew I would think that, and so—this one," he concluded, grasping the goblet she offered, "is really the wine that *hasn't* been drugged!"

His logic was good, but in this instance, it was flawed. Smiling triumphantly, he downed the entire goblet, ending with a merciless "Aren't you going to drink yours?"

"Of course," she whispered, knowing the effects of the potion was almost immediate. Silently she began to sip her wine, feeling extremely depressed and wishing her plan hadn't worked so well.

"Garret?" she started to say, turning fully toward him and staring in horror as his eyes suddenly seemed to lose their focus. He began to sway lightly on his feet.

"Charlotte?" he whispered in surprise, unable to focus as the painful realization sank through the cottonlike haze enveloping his brain that she had tricked him again. With a sudden flash of anger also came an equally unbearable feeling of fear—the fear that something might happen to her, and now there was nothing he could do to prevent it. "How…" he began, the room starting to darken as he felt her arms steady him. "How could you do this… to me?"

"I'm sorry!" she whispered fervently, struggling under his weight as she lowered him to the floor. "I'll make it up to you, Garret! Even if it takes the rest of my life! I swear!"

For a full minute she gazed down at him, tracing the lines of his face with her finger, touching the lush lashes and the full, sensuous sweep of his mouth, memorizing every feature.

"Sleep well, darling," she whispered, kissing him softly before she went to the study's window and put on the clothes that she had hidden there earlier that day. And with one of the tricks she had learned at the Vale, she began her acrobatic climb to the ground, keeping as far back in the shadows as she could.

"Time," she murmured, looking up into the starlit heavens, "to fulfill my destiny."

Chapter 31

The night was clear. Above her in the velvet-black sky, accompanied by a glowing half-moon, the North Star, so solid and always stationary, winked its approval as she brushed aside the wet moss and leaves.

"There!" Charlotte whispered in relief as the first glittering wing of the dragon appeared beneath her hurried touch. The Sword and Crown were there, unharmed, where she had left them last night. "Now to return you to your rightful owner," she said firmly, and then, as she lifted the heavy box, she vowed that she would do her best to make amends for ever causing Garret Montgomery one single moment of pain.

Walking slowly, with a back-breaking effort, she lifted the box containing the Sword and Crown onto the wide rump of her mare and tied her precious cargo securely. Mounting up, she turned north, keeping Polaris glittering above her, always before her, like a twinkling beacon guiding her way.

She took the coast road because it was the shorter route. Now she could smell the tang of salt in its fresh perfume and hear the gentle hiss of rolling surf boiling and crashing on the breakers beside her.

"Well, Bishop," she said gaily, cantering lightly, her spirits lifting. "Our task is nearly complete."

He barked in reply, making Charlotte laugh until the guilty memory of her husband's still form lying on the study's floor reasserted itself forcefully in her mind. For reasons she couldn't understand, she had a sudden, powerfully urgent, thoroughly illogical desire to bolt straight back to Pembroke, straight back to him. *Danger*, a voice seemed to murmur in her mind, sounding remarkably like the hissing surf. *Danger*, it whispered, and the sound had become a sinister omen, making the hairs on the back of her neck stand up in response.

"Bishop…" she said softly, slowly, her nerves tingling as she picked her way carefully along the beach. "Either my sins are finally catching up with me and my conscience is beginning to bother me, or—" The sentence was never finished, wedging itself in her throat and forgotten in the next breath.

A figure lay before her on the deserted beach. A still, white figure, half in the water and half out, eerily reflecting the weak light of the moon by giving off a pearly phosphorescent glow.

"What?" she began in alarm, pulling her horse up short, her eyes narrowing as she studied the partially submerged form. "Bishop! It's a boy!" she exclaimed in concern as she jumped quickly from the back of her horse, running before her feet even hit the ground. "I wonder what happened," she murmured, suddenly startled into silence as she looked up and saw another body, not ten feet away from this one. "Sweet Jesus!" she whispered, catching her breath as she stood up and turned halfway around. There were more of them. Many more. Perhaps a dozen still, lifeless forms lying on the cold, wet beach, gleaming like white porcelain statues in the gloomy, muted light.

"The storm," she concluded softly, grasping for the only explanation that seemed possible as she turned slowly around, staring in shock at the horrors surrounding her. "There must've been a wreck," she reasoned with a shudder, her flesh beginning to prickle and pucker—gooseflesh, the old ones called it—and then she turned cold as she realized that all the victims were stripped completely of clothing.

Suddenly it felt as though she were walking through a graveyard instead of on a lonely, deserted stretch of shore. Even the pleasant hiss of the surf seemed to grow louder, beginning to sound like the whispered wailing of these poor lost souls in her ears.

With Bishop at her heels growling and her own sword unsheathed, she tentatively approached the first body. Carefully, she turned it over with the tip of her boot, jumping back as it rolled over, not knowing what to expect as it fell on its side.

A young, light-haired boy peered blankly up at her. His skin was bleached white and bloodless, not bloated and blue, as if he'd drowned. Peering closer, she noticed that around his neck, like a cruel, carnelian ribbon, was a gaping wound. The edges were white and ragged, completely washed clean of blood.

"What is going on here, Bishop?" she asked in surprise, her curiosity effectively snuffing out her fear as she walked cautiously to the next one: a young girl with long flaxen braids and wide, staring, ice-blue eyes. Her throat had been slit as well, and other than that awful, hellish gash, there were no obvious marks of violence on the bodies, except around the hands where leather thongs had bound them together, rubbing their wrists raw.

Swallowing and fighting the wave of nausea washing over her, she peered closely at the bindings, noticing a piece of wood with crude, sticklike drawings carved into it hanging from each one.

"Runes!" she exclaimed in horror, realizing that could only mean one thing. "Vikings!" she hissed, staring hard at the murdered girl.

These poor children were Viking children. They had been sacrificed in the storm, their throats slashed and their bodies cast over the side like so much baggage to appease their pagan gods. *But,* she thought darkly, staring out at the dark, churning waters, *close enough to shore for the tide to drag their bodies in—barely three kilometers from Pembroke!*

"Garret," she whispered, feeling sick to her stomach and shutting her eyes tight at the thought of what she'd done. He was helpless. Drugged and helpless, lying without protection of any kind on the study floor.

"Come on, Bishop!" she shouted, jumping onto the nervous palfrey's back. "We've got to go back!"

There was no thought in her mind for the Sword and Crown strapped to her mare's saddle, nor for her promise to her grandmother Isabel, nor even her consuming obligation to her people. The only thought that dominated her mind was Garret. She must reach him—warn him! There was nothing else that mattered at this moment except *him*. The thought that she had traded his safety for cold artifacts and a bit of legendary lore sickened her.

"Hah!" she shouted, kicking the horse savagely in the flank. "Hurry!" she urged, laying her spurs into the mare and taking off at a full gallop, back toward Pembroke... afraid that she was already too late!

Outside Pembroke's solitary garden gate, several men waited. One, with wild red hair and crazed sea-green eyes, tapped furtively on the unlocked door. A moment later, it opened.

"Hello, Nell!" whispered Halfdanson in delight, smiling wickedly as he walked into the deserted garden with but one thought on his twisted mind. "Where's Garret?"

Chapter 32

Charles dimly perceived his room, squinting dumbly at the woman who led him to his bed. He was lost, lost and forgotten, in a terrestrial world of senses, where colors vibrated to the cadence of words and time was nothing more than a forgotten dream.

Drugged. He had drunk wine and fallen to the floor, awakening in his chambers.

"More wine, love?" whispered Nell, laughing. "I warned you that rejecting me had a price, Lord Montgomery!"

This was going to be far easier than he thought, concluded Halfdanson from the shadowed corner of the room where he had hidden, and he nearly chuckled as he made his way over to elder lord. "Far easier…" he muttered, reaching with his one good hand for his scabbard.

Nell watched dispassionately as something shiny and silver arched over her head. Something that glinted and sparkled as it curved downward. Something sharp. Like the Reaper's tooth, she mused, shearing away all of Charles's *noble* illusions, forever…

"Good night, love," she whispered fondly, stroking his mane of steel-gray hair.

And the blade slammed home. He jumped once—only once—as though too tired to make a second effort. And then Charles Montgomery, the great, fierce lord and protector of Pembroke, lay still.

"The kiss of death." Halfdanson chuckled with a wink, wiping his blade on the silken sheets.

"I warned him not to spurn me," said Nell bitterly. "Hurry up! We've a need to hide his body, and he's quite heavy!"

Not far away, in the quiet, still recesses of Pembroke's chapel, Grace prayed fervently on her knees.

"Lord," she whispered, daring to look upward into the compassionate, forgiving eyes of Christ, "give me the strength to bear the burdens that you've laid upon my doorstep," she asked, unable to shake the image of Charles and Nell walking out into the garden from her mind. "Grant me peace and patience of spirit..." she murmured as a stray breeze caused the candles to flare brightly, illuminating the chapel in eerie, phosphorescent glowing light, making the painted saints decorating the stained glass appear alive and so unutterably sad.

"Rather you should ask your God to grant you courage, Lady Grace—courage to live your life instead of hiding behind a wall of mystical hypocrisy" came a sly, masculine voice from the shadowed recess of a darkened alcove.

Startled, Grace turned, helping herself to stand with one arm placed against the cold stone of the altar.

"Who?" she stammered, not needing to ask that question again as she recognized the voice in an instant.

Alaric of York stepped forward, appearing like a ghostly white after-image on her startled mind.

"It is only I, fair lady," he murmured silkily, coming toward her with his gleaming, darkly-hooded eyes. "Only I..." he soothed as he reached for the fragile, shaking woman, smiling slightly as he watched her eyes widen in fear and... *something else?*

"You've no need to *fear* me, good lady," he whispered huskily, his long fingers grazing her chin gently. She flinched. "I've only the best intentions…"

Gasping, she felt his hand slide around her waist, felt him tug her forward, moving her as easily as he would a child.

Mesmerized, she watched as the candlelight's glow reflected perfect, glowing orange flames in his dark eyes. She stared, transfixed by his gaze as he brought his head forward, angling it to one side, preparing to kiss her slightly opened lips.

"No…" she murmured in protest, the sound coming out as an inaudible squeak. "You mustn't," she begged, but there was no force in her words as he brought his lips down hard on hers… And she *shuddered*…

Chapter 33

Grace's wimple had fallen to the floor in the great hall. Her hands were still bloody scrapes from having fallen as she pushed away from Alaric. She could still hear his laughter chasing her along the corridor and feel his kiss like tainted wine upon her lips. And the tears, which had begun in fury, still fell, but now with the force of utter despair. She was wrong! So wrong! And she had been for so many years!

She had to find Charles. She had to tell him she was sorry, beg him to forgive her cold and cruel behavior all those lonely, long nights. Ask him if they might try again…

As she stood in front of her husband's bedroom door preparing to knock, an image that she had repressed for years reasserted itself. In her mind, she was once again at the Abbey of St. David with its thick, dark stone walls and windows cut only an arrow-slit deep—the abbey where she had taken her first vows as a novice. She was barely a day into her fourteenth year.

Snow had fallen all through the night, covering the entire countryside in whirling drifts of glittering white, making the high Cambrian Mountains appear like glistening ice castles against a violet sky. It was near the feast of Michaelmas, and a fierce, cold wind had blown through the chapel, making her shiver while Sister Margarite had shorn her locks and placed the coarse wool around her face. Smiling gravely, she had listened intently while she repeated her vows of fealty, devotion, and humility. It was a very sacred moment—until the hushed solemnity of the chapel was shattered by the sound of a door bursting open, and *he* entered, with her father straggling mutely behind.

"Stop this ceremony!" he yelled as loud as he could, and she gasped in horror. "Stop it, I say!" he commanded, stalking imperiously down the aisle, with an angry scowl setting fierce color in his cheeks and painting blue fire in his eyes. Comte Charles de Montgomery, Lord of Pembroke—young, impulsive, and arrogant enough for ten men. A man who had ordered the prioress of the abbey to stop what she was doing, as though she worked for *him* instead of God.

Pausing near Grace, he gallantly offered her his hand. She refused, looking in confusion from her father to this towering, dark-haired giant with the glinting blue eyes.

"Go with him, Grace," ordered her father quietly, refusing to look into his daughter's incredulous dark eyes. "He will be your husband now."

"But I am *married*," she insisted, taking a faltering step backward, as though Charles's presence dominated the area around him, making it impossible to get too close. "To the Church!"

"Not any longer, daughter," replied her timid father, the sire of her and nine others—a cleric and a potter.

He had been poor by any man's estimation until Charles had given him half of his family's wealth—half of everything he possessed—not just to satisfy his lust and then drop the girl as so many nobles had done before to so many others, but as part of a marriage proposal—along with a vow that Grace would be treated with the utmost respect.

"Go with him," her father repeated. He was trembling. "He will treat you well," he added in a hushed whisper, stepping back to make room for her new lord and master.

She wanted to scream! Fight! Yell! It wasn't fair! It just wasn't fair!

The abbey was the only place a woman had any measure of freedom in her stifling time. Outside of prostitution, only the Church offered the opportunity for a woman to have a voice in the choice of her destiny. And now, even that meager chance at independence was to be taken from her forever!

Looking away from her father, she turned to face the man who had "bought" her—and she watched in wonder as the towering Comte de Montgomery, in his black satin cape and thick gold chains, bent over, retrieving every single strand of her fallen ebony hair from the floor as though each piece were part of a precious treasure, and the treasure just happened to be *her*...

A light, embarrassed, boyish smile filled his face as he placed his hand out for her to take—and she took it *willingly*, forgetting, in the warmth and adoration of that smile, her vow to be celibate and her desire to be independent.

In the years that followed, Charles kept his word. He was devoted and tender indeed. But the very fact that she had been told to marry him—had been *ordered* to be his wife—caused a certain peculiar perversity to seize her mind, compelling her to punish him—not by sword or word but by indifference and passivity.

The harder he tried to show her his love, the more she resisted—until her behavior and his became nothing more than a polite habit. Soon they knew of no other way to treat each other except as strangers who occasionally shared the same bed.

"Charles..." she whimpered, pressing her hands against the rough oak door, thinking of his great mane of thick black hair spreading out lustrous and full on the white satin pillows and the singular fire of his passionate blue eyes that no one's could equal.

Crying bitterly, she remembered the Christmas he'd had a book of psalms copied in the most elaborate, elegant script she had ever seen… just for her. How beautiful it was! How unique!

That Christmas Day as he handed it to her—blushing furiously, she recalled—he had offered to teach her to read it.

"Read?" she'd repeated, as though she couldn't comprehend the word.

"Yes," he'd offered shyly. "I would like to teach you to read!"

Closing the book, she had set it aside as though it meant very little to her, even though her fingers had tingled, wanting nothing more than to browse through the brilliantly colored pages and trace the elegant script with her fingers. *Yes*, he had said with a shy, sweet smile. *I'll teach you to read…*

And she had replied that all a woman needed to know, her husband could teach her, and anything else was superfluous because no woman could understand more. *So no, thank you, husband. I do not care to learn to read. Please, take your precious, precious gift back.* And that was the end of that.

"How wicked I was!" she murmured aloud, leaning her head against the thick oak door as she remembered how unhappy he had looked that day. So many gifts he had offered, so many times he had tried, and she had rewarded his love and devotion with coldness and indifference.

"Charles!" she called, beating her fist against the door.

"Charles!" she begged, praying. *Don't let it be too late. Please, God, don't let it be too late!* "Please, open the door!"

In response to her furious pounding, the door swung wide, revealing a scantily-clad red-haired woman with pale hazel-green eyes.

"Well, if it isn't her ladyship!" Nell smiled, pushing the door open as far as she could. "Come in! Come in!" she offered, curtsying low. "It's so good of you to call!"

Grace nearly fainted. The bedroom was in a shambles.

The scarlet drapes that hung from the windows and bed were lying in a heap on the floor and the tapestries had been torn from the walls.

In the middle of the room, in his immense four-poster bed, barely covered, with his back to her and his hair falling in dark, salt-and-pepper waves across his shoulders, lay her husband, naked and still as though he were sleeping.

"Do come in, Lady Grace!" invited Nell with a wicked leer.

Grace stumbled backward, righting herself as a sob tore from her throat.

"Well, what is it, *Lady* Grace?" asked Nell curiously, her eyes narrowing into feral slits.

"Please," moaned Grace, as wave after wave of shock rolled over her. "I," she began with a stammer, a jealous rage building in her to the point that all she wanted to do was grab handfuls of that russet hair and pull and pull and *pull!* And gouge those sea-green eyes and rip that alabaster skin! The impact of those basic human emotions flowing through her rarefied soul was nearly as shattering as the experience of seeing her husband with another woman.

"Too late!" she whispered aloud, white with shock.

"Pardon, your ladyship?" inquired Nell politely, smiling her honeyed, wicked smile.

"Too late!" she repeated. It was too late to save their marriage.

Crying bitterly, Grace turned and ran down the shadowy, half-lit corridor, suddenly realizing that she had loved Charles all along.

"Did you see that?" Nell asked, pointing her finger and giggling madly at the frail woman running blindly down the corridor.

From behind the door, Harold Halfdanson and a short, coarse-haired Saxon emerged, laughing, as Alaric of York approached the trio from a darkened corner of the hallway, drying up their hysterics with a searing glance.

"All's ready?" asked Alaric sternly, glancing at the bed and the still figure of the lord of Pembroke.

"Of course." Nell shrugged, momentarily pleased by the look Alaric cast at her exposed breasts.

"Good," he replied, lightning flashing in the pools of his dark eyes in anticipation of his success this night. "You," he told the slouching Halfdanson, "take your men and open the gate. As soon as our men secure the castle, we'll light the fires on the beach at dawn."

"All I want right now," growled the deranged Viking with the missing hand, "is his son!" He pointed his one good hand at the figure of Charles slumped on the bed.

"You'll have him," replied Alaric with a tired wave of his hand. "As I promised."

Suddenly, from the bedroom, where Harold had purposely shoved and propped Charles up on his side, a feeble moan was heard. Like puppets tied to one string, all heads turned toward the sound.

"It looks," advised Alaric lightly as Charles shuddered and rolled onto his back, "as if you two didn't do your job properly."

"Humph!" snorted Halfdanson, his eyes glittering in embarrassment, already reaching for his dagger. "I'll finish him this time!"

"Wait," ordered Alaric, grabbing him by the wrist and stopping him. "I have a better idea," he said, looking at the trembling form lying so helplessly on the bed. "You two," he commanded arrogantly, jerking his head in their direction and indicating that the Saxon knight was to help him, "take Charles to the keep *before* you open the gate."

"You're good at ordering people around, aren't you!" roared Halfdanson angrily, jerking his hand away.

Alaric nearly slapped the idiot. He didn't even have enough sense to keep his voice down, he thought with disgust.

"But while me and Ned here are putting Charles in the keep," he continued belligerently, ignoring the sneer on Alaric's feral face, "what'll *you* be doing?"

All Halfdanson could think of was getting even with Garret, and anything that was delaying what he felt was an inevitable battle irritated him greatly.

"I," replied Alaric piously, looking furtively down the darkened corridor where Grace had fled, "feel a need to *pray!*" he told them evilly, exchanging a knowing smile with Nell.

"Give my regards to her ladyship," she said politely.

Then they both laughed as he turned and followed the path that Grace had taken, wondering if the pious little woman had had a healthy enough dose of reality yet.

Chapter 34

"Whoa!" whispered Charlotte, pulling up hard on her reins, half a kilometer from Pembroke. Staring fixedly at the castle marches, she could detect no sign of a struggle.

The watch fires were lit on the south side, and all appeared calm. But the image of the sacrificed Viking children—along with the guilty memory of her husband asleep on the study floor—was still so vivid in her mind that she shuddered.

Sliding deftly from the saddle, she tied her horse out of sight of the main road, making sure that the Sword and Crown were firmly secured as well.

"Come on, Bishop," she whispered.

The dog either sensed the danger ahead of them, or perhaps he could smell the coppery whiff of fear in her sweat. He began to growl.

"Come on," she commanded, slapping her thigh, and he fell in step beside her, ready to protect his mistress with his very life if nccessary.

Remembering everything Gerald had taught her, Charlotte crept around the wall of Pembroke, heading for the garden's open gate. Beside her, as if he sensed that something was wrong, Bishop whined deep in his throat.

"Hush!" she warned, drawing her sword with her right hand as her left hand went to the gate's latch. "You'll give us away!"

She shoved the gate open, springing through it as quickly as she could. When she hit the ground, her feet were already spread and balanced, and her knees were bent. *First position*, a fighting stance, which made it easy to protect herself from all sides. But silence and mist were the only enemies that greeted her. No Vikings, she sighed in relief, taking a deep, cooling breath. *But no guards, either*, her suspicious mind reminded her.

Cautiously she looked around. There were always guards patrolling the garden currently: a pair of them, walking along the wall at least ten times a night. Stranger still than even the missing guards was the fact that not one watch fire was lit on the north side. Something was wrong. She knew it. She could feel it in the pit of her stomach, like a cold, heavy rock, making her cramp and tense; making the tiny hairs on the back of her neck rise; making her heart pound and the sweat start to bead.

Bishop paid no attention to her warning to keep still as the hackles on the back of his neck rose in direct proportion to his growls. Crouching low, he approached a thick old yew.

"What is it?" she whispered tensely, following her shaggy friend. Her sword was drawn and ready. "Bishop?" she hissed as the big dog barked once and leapt.

"No!!" screamed a huge figure cloaked in a deep purple drape, who fell toward her from behind the tree. Charlotte nearly had a heart attack but prepared to lunge and spear the hulking form when the drape fell away, and Armando's moon-shaped face peered out at her, followed a second later by Sparrow's.

"Mistress!" breathed Armando gratefully, scrambling to stand up and tripping several times over Sparrow.

"What's happened, Armando?" Charlotte demanded, pushing the two back into the shadow of the tree.

"York!" Armando exclaimed excitedly. "Sparrow and I were… were *praying* in a secluded little corner of the hallway when I heard Alaric of York tell that infernal Nell to let the Vikings in through the garden gate! I tried to find Garret," he told her softly, noticing how pale she had become and feeling a genuine stab of remorse for not being able to locate him. "But before I could, the bloody heathens had taken over Pembroke! We just barely escaped ourselves!"

Charlotte muttered an oath, her eyes flashing dangerously, while Sparrow, for the first time in her life, was utterly quiet. All eyes turned fearfully in the direction of the manor, wondering what was happening inside.

Chapter 35

The fever which had afflicted Harold Halfdanson since the severing of his hand, burning and twisting its way through his mind, had cooked his brain into a jellied, maddened mess of gray tissue which could think no other thought than *REVENGE!* Straining under Charles Montgomery's massive weight, he and the Saxon had gratefully dumped the older, half-dead Montgomery on the dirt floor of the keep.

"This way," murmured Nell, who had accompanied them to show them the way to the gatehouse, and they had followed. Their way was virtually uninterrupted as all the soldiers' eyes were trained on the perimeter *outside* the walls and not on the relative safety of their own courtyard.

Within minutes they had subdued the gatekeeper—Halfdanson snapping his neck with a vicious tug and merry chuckle—and the gate was lowered.

Seconds later, the ground seemed to be alive with moving bushes and running, shouting soldiers, and the fight was on!

"C'mon!" Halfdanson grunted, grabbing Nell and heading back into the manor, weaving through the fighting men with ease. "I got some business to take care of!"

And he found his *business* sleeping peacefully on the study floor, covered by a velvet drape with a cushion beneath his noble head.

"Ha!" he laughed, lifting Garret's hand in disgust between two fingers. "This is not what I wanted," he snorted in disgust. "Either Montgomery is drunk… or drugged."

Nell only shrugged. Whatever he was seemed irrelevant to her.

"Help me!" ordered the red-haired giant, and Nell, with more common sense than conscience, bent to grab the young lord's feet as Halfdanson grabbed his shoulders, sliding his good hand and withered stump beneath him, lifting him up.

"We'll take him to meet his father," he told Nell with a grunt and a wink. "Then when Sleepyhead here wakes up, I'll have *my* own particular brand of fun!"

"The bastard's heavy!" huffed Nell, nearly stumbling and trying to keep up with Halfdanson's hurried step as the Viking made his way down to the dimly-lit room beneath the keep, with the wine of vengeance and the war song of the Valkyries filling his demented mind with bloody fire.

Alaric walked into Grace's room. He smiled when he saw the fragile, dark-haired woman with the ivory skin lying on her bed, crying her eyes out.

"So sad," he whispered under his breath, untying the laces that bound his shirt across his chest. "Perhaps I can cheer her up!" he added with an evil chuckle, and he went to her, looming over her bed like a dark cloud threatening to obscure her life forever.

"Grace," he whispered, turning her to him gently, letting her struggle as he knew she would. But her movements lacked power and purpose. Her resolve to be virtuous had vanished with the vision of her husband and that *woman* in his room.

"You see," he offered quietly, brushing back a tear-soaked strand of midnight hair, "it was just as I had said, wasn't it?"

Grace looked into his dark eyes, and she felt the rage build, growing stronger by the second. He *had* told her. He had chastised her to live her life—*take* what she wanted. But, oh! she thought bitterly, all she wanted was Charles, and it was far too late for that!

"Well," he prodded, letting his finger slide down her cheek, "did I not tell you the truth?"

"Yes," she murmured in a broken whisper, unable to meet his gaze. She felt so betrayed. So *wronged.* Yet she knew she was partly responsible for Charles's actions. If she hadn't been so *cold*, if she hadn't ignored him, denied him, toyed with him—glorying in her own sense of twisted power as she sensed her ability to hurt him. If only she hadn't treated him as though he didn't matter one whit to her. But it was too late now, and it seemed at this moment that her whole marriage had been nothing more than a singular act of vengeance—and Charles had been the victim.

Could she, she wondered, staring vacantly at the white face hovering above her, with tears clouding her eyes—could she be so narrow-minded and mean? In a second she knew she could, as she saw herself in her thoughts, reflected a thousand different ways, like an image caught in the facets of a diamond. Self-awareness had come to her with the cruel clarity of hindsight; she saw all her mistakes but was unable to do anything about them.

"Now, Grace," murmured Alaric, pushing her gently back onto the bed. "There are *ways,*" he began smoothly, kissing her forehead, stroking her cheek with his long, slender white hand. "Pleasant ways—to get even…" With a smile that promised her pleasure and revenge, he covered her lips with his own as she thought of Nell and Charles… thought of them *together*, letting her anger rise to conceal her guilt, acknowledging her desire to repay Charles's unfaithful act with one of her very own.

"That's better," crooned Alaric in delight as she pulled him to her. "Much better!" he murmured evilly, licking her salty tears, which seemed as sweet as honey to him.

The door into the great hall opened, letting a shaft of yellow light hit the dark, swirling ground outside. Charlotte crowded back as far against the ancient yew as she could and watched with her hand poised over the hilt of her sword. Two men entered the garden, one dressed in Saxon garb—green tunic and dark-brown hose—while the other, much taller and fairer, wore leggings of leather and a vest of the same material, studded with silver. Both men held swords that were dark and dripping to the hilt.

"Look over there!" shouted the taller man clad in leather.

The shorter Saxon began to walk along the garden wall with his sword drawn, occasionally stabbing at a bush or under a patch of lush ferns.

"Get back!" ordered Charlotte, and Bishop started to growl as Armando became an amazingly small shadow, holding the shaking Sparrow in front of him. "Hush, Bishop!" hissed Charlotte, clamping her hand around his muzzle and holding her breath, preparing to strike as the man came within several feet of their hiding place.

"Hey!" shouted the taller man, grinning as he peered into the kitchen. He pulled out a beautiful leg of roast lamb. "If you're hungry," he called, "get on over here!"

"Sure," muttered the Saxon. With one final thrust into a clump of lavender, he grunted in satisfaction and obeyed the other man's command. Charlotte breathed a sigh of relief, not realizing until now that she had grasped the sword's hilt so tightly that she had drawn blood with the tips of her fingernails.

"Listen to me, Armando," she said firmly, taking hold of the quaking man by the shoulders. "You and Sparrow must go to Aberystwyth! To my half-brother, Lon ap Llewelyn!"

Sparrow began to whimper, nestling against Armando's wide shoulder for protection.

"Listen to me!" Charlotte said, shaking the girl as a high, piercing scream ripped through the night. "Take Bishop," she repeated, the sound of that cry echoing dizzily in her mind. "Leave through the garden door. Do not follow the coast. Go first to Milford—to the inn—and ask Maddy to lend you a horse. If she will not do that, then steal one! But find Lon! Tell him what is happening here! Tell him the Vikings are preparing to invade Wales!"

Another scream filled the night, followed by still others, and Sparrow fainted against Armando.

"Go now!" she told them, giving them a shove as Armando gently shook the swooning girl. Charlotte's heart was beating so fast she was afraid she would be the next one who crumpled on the ground.

"My… m'lady," stammered Armando, propping Sparrow up by the arms. "Aren't you coming?"

"No," she said quietly, staring at the castle with burning eyes. "I have to find Garret first."

"But, my lady," whispered Armando, shaking his head in sympathy. "Perhaps…" And he hesitated, coloring slightly as he saw the pained, watchful expression grow on his mistress's young face. "Perhaps it is too late…"

"Don't say that!" she said furiously, her eyes glittering.

The fear that had gripped her insides, twisting them into knots, became almost unbearable. "He is all right!" she said with conviction, ignoring the *what if!* voice in her mind that threatened to shatter her confidence and her hope. "I know he is!"

"Lady Charlotte," said the wise old thief with the shining, wonderfully warm brown eyes, "how can you possibly know this?"

Swallowing, she looked at the darkened study window, just visible from where she stood.

"Because," she said, her heart in her eyes, "if anything happened to him—I would know it. I would *feel* it, in here," she whispered, touching her heart.

"Yes, my lady," murmured Armando gently, placing his large

hand on her trembling shoulder. Without his support propping her up, Sparrow slid to the ground with a moan, her eyes rolling up once again in her face.

"Go!" Charlotte ordered furiously, as the crashing, crying, and screaming filling the manor became the most hellish din she had ever heard. "Or it will be too late for everyone!"

"Yes, m'lady," replied Armando quietly as he half-lifted, half-shoved Sparrow before him. But Bishop refused to go, whining loudly.

"Go, boy!" she hissed, looking furtively over her shoulder as the sound of running came closer. "Get out of here!" she cried, bending down to pick up a rock and throw it at him, striking him squarely on the shoulder. "Go!" she repeated angrily.

Bishop, not understanding her words, only understanding the stinging reprimand of the stone, thought that his mistress was mad at him. So, with his long, shaggy tail tucked between his legs and his heart in his soulful amber eyes, he followed Armando and Sparrow out of the garden's door, glancing back longingly at his mistress every few steps.

"God be with you," whispered Charlotte as she turned and walked a few paces, diving behind a bush just seconds before another bunch of shouting, sword-waving men entered the garden.

"Kill every Norman!" bellowed the short, dark-haired Saxon who had accompanied Halfdanson to the kitchen. "Don't let one of those men live!" he cried, spittle flying and the bloodlust blazing in his eyes, along with the sweet fire of revenge.

"God *help* me," she choked, swallowing hard, shrinking down into the foliage and trying to become as small as she could. "God help us all!"

Chapter 36

The small rectangular room at the base of the keep held several small cells, shackles, and even an iron maiden with cobwebs adorning her tragic face and deadly interior, and discarded weapons of torture—relics of another owner—that delighted both Nell and the misbegotten son of perdition, Harold Halfdanson.

Grinning, Harold dropped Garret to the ground, ignoring the grunt of pain.

"Look at this!" he marveled in glee, lifting the rusty shackles and playing with the iron pincers used for rending and tearing tender flesh.

"Well?" asked Nell eagerly, getting into the spirit of the place with remarkable ease. "What shall we do to him?"

"Nothing yet," answered Halfdanson begrudgingly, wishing Garret Montgomery would wake up so he could have a little fun. "What good is it to torture someone if they're not awake enough for you to enjoy their misery?"

"True. True," admitted Nell, adjusting a stray lock of hair as she peeked into the cell where Charles lay, pale and gleaming white, but still breathing. "Tough old bird, isn't he?" she mused out loud. "How long do you think he would have lasted in *this?*" she asked speculatively, trailing her finger tentatively over the dusty iron maiden.

Halfdanson's eyebrows shot up at that remark, and then he shrugged.

"I don't know," he admitted, adding, "But it might have been fun to find out!"

They both looked at each other in silence, and then they laughed, the sound dying in their throats as Alaric walked through the door, shoving a bedraggled Grace before him.

"Well, well," he said, giving her a vicious push that sent her crashing down the stairs to lie on the floor, inches from her sleeping son. "What've we here?"

"A family reunion?" offered Nell with an innocent grin, and then she laughed at her clever remark.

"Is he dead?" asked Alaric indifferently, and Grace moaned, moving toward the still form of her son, placing her fragile arm across his broad back as though she had the power to protect him from these devils.

"No," admitted Halfdanson, unable to keep the disappointment out of his voice as he crossed his hands over his chest and watched the progress of Garret's mother with all the interest of someone who has spied a bug and wants nothing better than to place a foot over it and end its miserable existence. "Drugged, I think," he replied, still thinking about exterminating insects before adding, with his green eyes all aglitter, "What should we do with him?"

"Have you found his wife?" asked Alaric as with narrowed eyes he watched Grace try to rouse her son.

"No," admitted Halfdanson with a frown. "My men have practically torn this place apart." He rubbed the end of his stump, which still throbbed. Sometimes, at night, he had the sensation that his hand was still attached, and he would run to find a light, disappointed when the glow illuminated his arm and no hand was there. Nothing but a ragged stump, and then he would think of Garret…

"We must find her," mused Alaric, absently tugging on his

chin. "I have searched the coffers of the manor for the Sword and Crown and have found nothing for my efforts but a few archaic relics from the Holy Land."

Suddenly, as though seized by another perfectly *evil* idea, he grinned broadly, which pulled the skin so tight across his high-boned face that he resembled a skull with gleaming, malignant eyes.

"Take *Lady* Grace," he said quietly, peering at Garret through narrowed eyes. "Put her with her husband. Then help me prop our sleepy friend up. I think it's time he joined the party, don't you?" he asked with a wicked chuckle.

Harold grinned as he walked down the steps, grabbing the sobbing woman by her delicate wrist and hauling her violently to her feet.

"Grace?" called Alaric in his loveliest, most cultured voice as Harold jerked her around to face him. "Madam?" he inquired a little more sternly when she refused to answer. The mistress of Pembroke looked up, her eyes filled with guilt and suffering—a sight that pleased him to no end. "Thank you," he told her with a gallant bow, "for entertaining me this afternoon!"

"It was not my choice," she said. Her courage stunned him.

"Nevertheless," he said, "I had a good time."

Blushing furiously, terrified and humiliated, she was unable to hold her head up again as Halfdanson pulled her toward the cell where Charles lay, throwing her in and locking the door with a cruel chuckle.

"Now," said Alaric, "there appears to be a good stout brace over there." He gestured elegantly with his long, heavily-ringed fingers. "A coil of stout rope is only a few feet from it. It seems as if Providence is supplying all our needs!" he added with a dry snicker, and the unholy trinity laughed until their sides ached, already feeling as though they'd won.

"Well, go on, Harold." Alaric chuckled, wiping his hand across his eyes. "Help him up!"

"Sure," growled Halfdanson as he walked over to the still form. "I'll help him… all the way to Hell."

He bent over, locking his arms under Garret's shoulders. Grunting, he lifted him up, holding him steady as Alaric wound the rope around Garret's middle and each one of his arms. They had positioned him against a huge oak brace that ran between two supporting pillars. His arms were stretched along both sides until the sinews bulged and the veins looked like swollen rods running between his slack wrists and bent head.

"There," congratulated Alaric as he tied Garret's wrists to the brace, pulling the rope so tight that the blood was nearly cut off from his hands. "That should hold him!" he said loudly, smiling in satisfaction as the future lord of Pembroke stood before him with his head bowed, an unconscious captive—and, as far as Alaric was concerned, a dead man.

"Well?" urged Halfdanson with a snort. "How you going to wake him up?"

"With water, of course, you oaf!" snapped Alaric, picking up a bucket filled with stagnant, thick water and stinking moss from the side of the wall. "Wake up, Montgomery!" he shouted, dumping the pail over him.

Garret snorted, shaking his head as the lukewarm liquid slid over his face, wondering for a moment if he were dreaming. But no, this couldn't be a dream. In dreams there was no pain… And he pulled instinctively against the ropes, trying to break free.

"That's a good boy!" offered Harold jubilantly, running hand across Garret's massive chest before he grabbed him by the hair and shouted in his ear, "Wake up, Montgomery! Judgment Day has come!"

Slowly, Garret opened his eyes, trying very hard to focus. The images surrounding him seemed blurred and fuzzy, as though he were looking up through muddied water. He was only dimly aware of an aching pain in his arms and back which seemed to grow more intense with each passing second.

Seeing the blue eyes flicker open, Alaric could contain himself no longer, brushing aside the Viking as if he were a small child.

"Where," he asked, pulling Garret's head back as far as he could, a single, burning question in his mind, "are the Sword and Crown of Wales?"

"The Sword?" Garret murmured clumsily, his tongue barely able to move as he tried to focus.

Suddenly, in his fogged mind he saw the firelight dancing in the study's hearth. Saw it… and remembered his wife standing before it in her filmy nightdress. Wanting her. Wanting her and drinking the wine she had offered. *The wine*, he recalled, licking his dry lips but unable to work up enough moisture to do any good. The wine was so bitter. *Poison*, he thought angrily, but he couldn't believe it at the time—didn't want to believe it. She was planning to trick him again. Yet the wine had left him feeling strange. So dizzy, and then there was nothing; nothing until now…

"I said," repeated Alaric cruelly, slapping him brutally across the face several times in quick, stinging succession until the blood flowed from his nose and the corner of his mouth, "*where is the Sword?*"

Garret only shook his head weakly, able to see quite vividly in his mind his wife, dressed as the brigand Charley with the ridiculously bulging crotch, hiding an elaborate chest behind the rock a few miles from Milford. The image caused him to smile, which only made Alaric furious.

"Do tell us what is so *humorous!*" he hissed, pulling his head back and glaring hatefully into the deep blue eyes that still hadn't regained their normal clarity.

"Go to Hell!" Garret growled, and Halfdanson, like an obedient dog, instinctively knowing its master's wishes, delivered a vicious kick to his groin, eliciting a strangled groan. For one dizzy moment, Garret thought he was going to vomit, and he hoped Alaric would move just a little closer.

"Watch your manners," whispered Alaric, a scant few inches from Garret's face, "or I'll let my friend there teach you some." Halfdanson grinned, popping the knuckles of his hand and grunting with satisfaction. "Now," began Alaric calmly again, remembering the gossip he had been hearing about a silver-haired woman who could wield a sword better than most men. A woman who believed the Sword and Crown were *hers.* "Where is your *wife?*" he asked, pushing his face to within a fraction of an inch of Garret's.

"Go to Hell," he whispered again in reply, enunciating the words perfectly this time as his tongue became more cooperative a second before he closed his eyes.

With a strangled oath, Alaric drove his knee upward, and Garret nearly passed out from the pain.

"I *said,*" he repeated fiercely, pronouncing his words just as carefully as Garret had, "you *filthy, stupid Norman!* Where is that Welsh witch?"

Garret only shook his head weakly, refusing to tell him where he suspected she had gone. *The Sword,* he thought darkly. *She's gone to get her Sword!*

"You amaze me!" shouted Alaric, punching him as hard as he could in the stomach and making Garret bend over as far as the ropes would allow, coughing and trying to catch his breath. "*She betrayed you!* You are a stupid idiot! And I suspect that she is also the one who drugged you as well! Hmmm?" he asked, but Garret refused to answer, making Alaric snort in disgust. "It is because of *her* that you are *here!* And yet, noble fool that you are, you protect her!"

Garret only looked at him, keeping his gaze as firm and steady as he could. He would never tell Alaric where she was, because despite what she had done, he still loved her, and he would protect her with his dying breath.

A sly, wicked smile replaced Alaric's maddened gaze. "Perhaps," he said softly, "since we are dealing with such a family of martyrs, we should treat them as such."

"What do you mean?" mumbled Harold, whose personal ideas of torture had very little to do with a couple of kicks and a few girlish slaps. Alaric's revenge was as exciting as a bowl of milk toast and just as fulfilling, he mused gloomily, toying with the metal pincers once again.

"They're such *Christians*—don't you see? They sacrifice themselves so readily for one another. Perhaps we should make an example of Garret—honor him, if you will."

"I don't want to honor him!" answered Harold angrily. "I want his bloody head on a platter."

"Oh," replied Alaric lightly, with a wave of his hand, "that is another story altogether. We shall show our regard for his selfless devotion by… *crucifying him!*"

At the mention of that word, a shocked expression settled over both Nell's mobile features and Harold's crazed ones.

Crucify? Alaric could see the question in both of their eyes, and the hatred burning in Garret's.

"Yes," he whispered, moving toward a bench where various tools of torture had been left to rust and corrode, letting his hand linger on the metal as if by touching them, he could witness all the crimes that their cold forms had ever participated in. "Crucify—as the Romans did, I might add."

Quietly he picked up two rusted spikes, each the width of a woman's little finger and the length of one hand-span.

"These," he related, holding the rusted nails outward in all reverence, "should do nicely, don't you think?"

Halfdanson, whose face had suddenly blossomed into a leering grin, muttered, "Yeah!" nodding his head and finally feeling as though he were going to get some satisfaction out of this tea party.

Turning, Alaric took the thin, wickedly sharp stakes and walked toward his prisoner, chuckling.

Chapter 37

Outside in the shadowed garden, Charlotte made her way stealthily toward the separate building that housed the kitchen fires. In there, underneath the cellar ladder beside the massive hearth, Sparrow had told her that a small passageway had been cut through rock, which served as the wine cellar and a favorite place for an afternoon tryst. And hopefully, she thought with a silent prayer, an inconspicuous way to enter the great hall.

Cries of pain filled the night, and fires burned out of control along the narrow marches. *This, then, is war*, Charlotte thought, horrified, and she cringed with each new frightening sound. This was not like her games, nor like her dreams. This was a nightmare that had somehow trickled over into reality. The evil genie had fled the bottle, and there was no one who could stuff him back in.

"Courage!" she whispered, shaking so hard that she had to clamp her teeth together to keep them from chattering. Swallowing and trying desperately to still the wild hammering of her heart, she flattened herself out as much as she could against the cool stone walls of the outbuilding. All was dark inside. But sounds came to her ears: the soft sounds of crying and the ringing sound of metal being struck again and again. The air was heavy with the smell of smoke from fires gone wild and the wails of despair, as if those who wept cried not for help or salvation—believing there wasn't any—but for release from this dark, consuming dream. Such was the evil face of war and such was the beginning of the white queen's wisdom.

Taking a deep, calming breath, with her sword drawn, she flung the kitchen's broad door open, making it thud loudly against the far wall, and sprang inside. All was still. Silent. The room was empty, her way was clear.

"Garret," Charlotte whispered, her mind becoming numb with the thoughts reeling through them. *What if she was too late?* No, she must not think about that! Garret was alive. He had to be, she prayed as she started to make her way down the narrow cellar steps, plunging into utter darkness with only the cold, wet wall to guide her.

In the cell where she had been thrown, Grace had found her husband, nearer to death than life. She realized with a sickening shudder that the castle walls had been breached and her husband stabbed while she lay in the arms of the devil outside the door, enjoying his kisses.

"Charles," she whispered, lifting his head from the floor to lay it upon her breast. "Forgive me," she pleaded, letting her tears fall unimpeded on his ghastly pale face.

"There," he croaked, barely able to make out the form above him and marveling at the fact that he couldn't feel anything, as if he were somehow divorced from his senses. "There isn't anything to forgive…" he whispered, wishing that he could touch her face, feel the weight of her hair in his hand, kiss her… *one last time.* A sadness, the fruit of the seeds of the love he had sown so many years ago, filled him, along with a bitterness born of the knowledge that he had cast his lot on the side of the Devil and lost.

"Charles," she whispered, cradling him in her arms as her hair fell like a dark wing to envelop him. "I do *love* you," she confessed sadly, feeling her heart tear in half as she admitted this, and seeing, as only one can see when looking back along the road they've traveled, all the days wasted, all the times of joy missed… Charles had been *her* gift from God—not a burden or a pestilence, but a gift, a rare and precious thing. *Too late*, a sad, wise voice whispered inside her head. Grace wept, while her soul, a rare and fragile thing, began to bleed.

Her words had reached him, seeming to vibrate across a great, dark abyss.

"Another time," he whispered, his hand reaching unsteadily for her face. "Another time… we'll be together… again…" he promised. The walls of darkness surrounding him began to grind open, wide enough to reveal the glory behind, and then he was gone…

Above him, Grace cried, knowing that what she had held in her hands for years had fled. She was left all alone, with an ache in her heart that time would not heal.

Chapter 38

"Stretch his arms out!" ordered Alaric, lifting a thick iron mallet from the bench where it had lain shrouded in forgotten webs. "And stretch his palms out flat."

Garret tried to struggle, but the ropes held fast. He could only glare at the man who approached him with a sinister, gloating grin on his cunning face, swinging a mallet in anticipation.

"Let's see," muttered Alaric thoughtfully as he positioned the first spike above Garret's open palm. "Here, do you think? Or," he asked a gloating Halfdanson, moving the spike a little to the right, "here?"

"Looks good to me," he grunted, holding the mallet in his one good hand, aching to give it a try.

"Well," encouraged Alaric, seeing the eagerness in his eyes. "Give it a go."

Smiling, Harold Halfdanson aimed the rusted mallet at the spike, and with a strangled oath from Garret, he brought it down with all the force he had.

"Ahhhh!" screamed Garret as the tip was driven through the layers of skin, past the muscle and gristle, right into the wood behind the hand. *Pain!* Such pain! Such misery, concentrated in the very center of his palm as the shock of the blow seemed to send him upward, spiraling high above his head, as though he could feel the throbbing heat of his tortured flesh only in an abstract way.

"You oaf!" snapped Alaric, grabbing the mallet from Harold's hand. "Not so hard! You see?"

Grabbing a handful of Garret's hair, he jerked his head upward. "He nearly passed out. You tap," he told him delicately, "just a little at a time. Like so," he replied, ready to demonstrate as he brought the mallet up. "Hold his fingers, Nell," he muttered impatiently, and the sullen woman, who had stood so silently for the last few minutes, frowned.

"You're not going to miss, are you?" she asked skeptically.

"Only," replied Alaric with a dark little grin, "if you don't get over here this very minute."

"Humph!" she snorted, pulling Garret's fingers back and keeping hers as far out of the way as possible.

"Like this," Alaric instructed, striking sharp and fast, but with only enough pressure to drive the tip halfway through the other palm.

"CHARR-LOTTE!" wailed Garret, and Alaric stared at him in amazement.

"You call her name as if she were your god!" he sneered. "She *betrayed* you, Montgomery! Used you—and yet you call out for her as though she is your salvation! You," he spat, pulling his face back sharply, "are more of a fool than I thought!"

Pulling Garret's curled, bloodied fingers back, he was ready to deal the next blow. "Tell me where the little Judas is, Garret," he crooned gently. "I'll make it easy on you. One swipe with my blade, and it will be done. No more pain. No more anything."

Through all of Garret's torture, he could only gaze at Alaric of York with loathing in his eyes and defiance. Yes, he had called on her as though she were his god, but it was not with the idea of salvation in mind, only the pain of regret—and the knowledge that, even now, he loved her, and he always would.

"You're a fool!" hissed Alaric, slamming the mallet down again and tearing a scream from Garret's throat.

Another scream accompanied the first one. But this one was a little weaker, a little higher, but no less filled with pain. That scream came from his mother, who looked helplessly from her cell to the tortured form of her son nailed on the beam.

In the great hall, a drunken revel was taking place. Wine casks were split open and flowing, and women lay scattered and broken—the spoils of war—around the room.

She had made her way quietly past the door, nearing the study when, suddenly, a cry rang out that froze her to the spot. *CHARR-LOTTE!!!* she heard, and she knew the voice that called her name so desperately.

"Garret!" she whispered in horror, wondering what had been done to him to make him sound so hopeless, so lost. "I'm coming!" she vowed, diving beneath the cover of a tapestry as a group of men, carrying thrashing, crying women like sacks of potatoes across their shoulders, entered the hall. "I'm coming!"

Chapter 39

Alaric stared shrewdly at the half-crumpled form of the man he hated above all others. *So incredibly noble*, he thought with disgust.

"Garret," he called quietly. "You haven't gone to sleep on us again, have you?" he asked cruelly, taking a dagger from his belt. "Those ropes seem awfully tight," he muttered, cutting through the bands that held Garret's wrists and upper arms to the beam. With a grunt, he pulled the restraining ropes away, and Garret moaned as all his body's weight now rested solely on his hands for support, which were bloody, mangled, throbbing messes, bolted to a piece of aged wood.

"Better?" whispered Alaric, tugging sharply back on his middle fingers and letting them slap back against the wood as Garret moaned.

"Stop it!" cried Grace, who had fallen to her knees, praying beside her husband. "For God's sake, please, Alaric—stop it!"

"Ahh!" hissed Alaric, turning toward the bowed figure kneeling behind the door. "The mouse speaks!"

Nell smiled and bent to kiss Garret, laughing wickedly when he turned his mouth away in disgust.

"Harold," ordered Alaric, "bring *Lady* Montgomery here. I think it is high time for her son to know just what kind of woman she *really* is!"

Grinning, Halfdanson did as he was told, bringing the broken, tiny woman to stand before her son.

"Garret," Alaric said in a soft, conversational voice, as if they were preparing to sit down to tea and discuss the weather. "Behold, I bring you your mother!" he mocked, introducing her with an elaborate bow and a sweeping gesture of his arm.

Slowly Garret looked up. Grace could not bear to look at him. He seemed so tragic and lost, simply because she knew of his incredible power and determination. His betrayal and bondage seemed blasphemous.

With the clarity of someone who has just awakened from a dream, she saw the last twenty years of her life as nothing but a span of nonexistence, like a dream-walk through the corridors of life, refusing to face it, preferring to live in the fantasies of her devotion and the pettiness of her make-believe world.

But Garret was not make-believe. He was flesh and blood. Hers. And her husband's and he suffered so! She could see it in his eyes. Did he know that his father lay dead within the other room? Did he know what a fake she was? How she had pranced and prayed through all of their lives as though she was above them, so superior? Ah, but she was none of these things! She was the worst kind of liar, because not only did she deceive and betray her family, but she lied to herself so frequently that she had begun to believe all of her phony claims.

"I'm sorry," she whispered, with desperation lacing her words as his eyes, so like her husband's, gazed on her for the longest time before closing. "I'm sorry!" she repeated, this time out loud, and Garret raised his face to look at her. "Garret!" she cried, starting to run to him when Alaric grabbed her, holding her tightly against him.

"Well, Grace," he chastised, bringing his dagger out and holding it to her ribs, eliciting a growl from the bound prisoner on the beam. "Go on now," he encouraged, holding the blade beneath her breast. "Tell your son exactly what I did to you this afternoon and what happened to his father."

At the mention of his father the old power flickered to life in Garret's eyes. "My father," he growled, the pain in his hands traveling up his arms and sending lightning bolts of agony through his body. But that was good. The pain brought him awake, made him aware. "What of my father?"

"Why," answered Alaric brightly, "he's dead, of course."

Garret gasped, starting to move against the stakes.

"You killed my father!" he shouted menacingly, straining against the spikes. The blood, which had ceased to flow, becoming a mere trickle, began to pour afresh from the gaping wounds.

"No," answered Alaric honestly. "Harold did."

Garret threw him a look that should have dropped him in his tracks, but he only smiled in satisfaction.

Nell became curiously silent, backing toward the cellar door as she watched Garret work his hands back and forth, pushing against the iron that held him in place, ignoring the pain.

"All your mother did was sleep with me. True, it wasn't her idea, but mine," Alaric said, then laughed. "While your poor father bled to death, of course. Shall I tell you what I did to her?"

Garret's eyes flashed and his mother dropped her gaze, moaning like a sick child.

"Now you listen to me, Norman." The pleasant voice and the artificial smile were replaced by a look of pure hatred. "Either you tell me where that witch you married is, and where the Sword and Crown are, or your mother dies!"

Garret's face contorted with rage. His mother was mistreated by Alaric while Nell tried to seduce his father, and Harold killed his father when Nell's plan failed.

Garret knew this whole scheme had been planned from the start! But there was one small flaw in Alaric's plan: Charlotte!

The Sword, which he seemed to covet with an obsession matching Garret's father's, and his wife eluded his grasp.

"Tell me!" hissed Alaric, seeing the anger and the glow of something else in his dark blue eyes that he did not understand.

Triumph? Alaric thought in confusion. Surely not! But there it was, a hint of a smile grimly curling his lips upward and a look of satisfaction on his face, all because of a clever, devious little woman with hair of silver and eyes of palest blue.

"I see," murmured Alaric dangerously. "I don't like to be laughed at. Did I ever mention that? I don't. Not at all. The gloating in your eyes! I see it! I know why you revel in your misery. You're right, you know? Absolutely right.

"I do not have the Sword or the Crown and, yes, I want them badly. But tell me, friend, how badly do you want to see your mother die?"

There, amidst the ruins of a hundred tortured souls, with the wind moaning through the chinks in the stone walls stained brown with blood, was the question he dreaded. In spite of everything, Garret loved his mother and did not want to see her die. She was the gentlest, kindest soul he had ever known. She loved her family and her faith in God held them together through many a long night.

Smiling, Alaric noticed the hesitancy in the pain-filled eyes. He was too noble, too fine, to let his mother be murdered for the sake of a sword and a woman he barely knew. He would tell.

"No, my son," Grace murmured softly, giving him the gentlest, most intimate smile he had ever seen. "I will not be the cause of yet another innocent death." With those words her hands, which had been folded into a twisting knot at her side, she turned to push against Alaric, to free herself from his grasp. The hilt of the dagger he held plunged deeply into her stomach.

"Mother! My god, my mother," wailed Garret, straining now

against the ropes. "I'm going to kill you, York!" he promised as his mother's frail body, swathed in bloody white, slid to the floor. "Mother!" Garret whispered, horrified and heartbroken.

Rage, unlike any he had ever felt, filled his body. Staring at Alaric, he pulled on the spikes, watching helplessly as she reached one trembling hand upward, toward her son.

"I love you, Garret," she breathed, wishing she had said those words years ago, wishing she had held his ebony curls to her breast and kissed away all his tears. "I have always loved you. Remember me." She sighed as the light left her eyes forever.

There was a moment of quiet. A time that seemed to stretch all the way to eternity and back as the full realization of what Grace had done and *said* registered on Garret's shocked mind.

"I'll kill you!" Garret swore slowly, looking up from his mother's limp form to Alaric's startled face. He jerked as forcefully as he could on the spikes that bound his hands to the beam. "I'll kill you for what you've done to my family. I swear to *God*," he vowed as his right hand broke free of the spike. "I'll kill you!"

Alaric's eyes opened wide in shock as the huge man before him bared his teeth and growled, jerking his other hand free with a strangled cry of pain.

With eyes wide and unbelieving, Alaric began to back away. Nell had made her way to the door long before Garret had broken loose from his bonds.

"Let me kill him!" screamed Halfdanson as Alaric retreated from the straining man, running up the few stairs to the door.

"No!" shouted Alaric, putting his hands on Halfdanson's chest to stop him as Garret stumbled to his feet. "He may be able to pull thin nails from his palms like a cheap magician, but he will never be able to dig his way out of here!"

Slowly, a deliciously cruel smile lit Halfdanson's mad features. Starvation seemed an excellent way for a man like Montgomery to die. It was a coward's death—a death that would find no reward in Valhalla, no redemption. A fitting end cruel enough to satisfy his need for revenge.

"It isn't as though we've left him with nothing to eat!" snickered Alaric, nearing the door, as Garret took a few weak steps, dropping down beside his mother.

Laughing darkly, the two men backed out of the door, slamming it shut just as Garret regained his footing and headed for them with murder in his eyes.

"Lock it!" shouted Nell excitedly, not wanting that brute to get a chance to get near her.

Alaric did, dropping the key to the floor just outside the door, within Garret's range of vision.

"Let me out!" he shouted, rattling the door with his bloody hands. "God damn your souls! Let me out!"

"Not on *my* life," whispered Alaric, staring triumphantly into the glittering blue eyes. "Goodbye, Montgomery," he added jovially, followed by a salute. "I'll give your regards to your wife when I see her!"

Laughing, the three walked off, leaving Garret to stand alone, locked in a cell with the bodies of his parents to remind him of his failure, and a new fear to battle with: the fear of what would happen when Alaric found his wife.

Chapter 40

Rounding a corner at the base of the stairs that led to the lower room of the keep, Charlotte ran headlong into a half-drunk soldier with a stolen leg of lamb dripping from his hand. "Huh?" he grunted as he turned the twisting corner and saw the miniature warrior, her hair tied back with a leather thong and her tunic covered with blood.

"Well." He smiled. "It looks as though I've found something more interesting to chew on than a leg of lamb!" he gloated, drawing his sword and dropping his supper on the stairs.

"In a manner of speaking," she answered coldly, raising her sword, "so have I. But you seem more like a pig than a lamb!" She caught his forward blow and countered with a quick upward slash that caught the soldier near his eye.

"You'll find out!" he shouted, holding one hand to his bleeding face as he rounded on her, losing confidence seeing the easy way she stood. "I thought I would have a little fun with you!" He grunted, swinging boldly, trying to catch her off guard. "But now," he said, his arm reverberating as she met his blow and countered with a deep slashing right, "I see I'll just have to *kill* you."

"If you can!" she retorted, retreating two steps up the landing, not liking the unfair advantage he had gained from his height.

"I can," he replied, parrying deftly to the right, the clash of the sword reverberating off hers, then feinting to the left and drawing sparks. "And," he added, shoving her back against the wall and knocking the sword from her hand, "I will."

As he moved closer, preparing to pin her arrogant little heart to the wall with something other than a sword, a sudden, sharp stab of pain shot through him, growing stronger and radiating outward. With a surprised "Huh?" he looked down and saw the blade of a curiously ornate silver dagger buried to the hilt in his stomach.

"I don't think so," she replied calmly, yanking her dagger out and sending the soldier plummeting down the stairs with a vicious kick, beginning to tremble as she realized what she had done. She had just killed a man. *Enemy*, her mind rationalized, seeing him lying crumbled on the landing like a broken toy soldier. *Enemy*, she repeated, swallowing the bile that rose in her throat, knowing she would see his face in her dreams for the rest of her life.

Picking up her sword, she continued to make her way to the secluded room at the bottom of the keep, hugging the walls and preparing to fight again at any moment.

Ahead, in the narrow corridor, light streamed from the window of the dungeon's solitary door. Holding her breath, she approached the room, peeking inside. What she saw in there filled her first with gladness, then despair. Seated on the floor was her husband, and cradled in his arms like a baby was the fragile body of his tiny mother.

"Garret," she whispered, but he was so wrapped up in grief that he didn't hear her.

Running feet and voices overhead caused her to look around, desperately searching for a key, a bar, anything with which she could free her husband. And then she saw it. A single iron key cast carelessly onto the floor. Its position indicated that it was in full view of whoever was unlucky enough to inhabit the shadowy recesses of this dismal, seldom-used chamber.

Picking it up, she inserted it gently into the lock, turning it until she heard the squealing grind. The door swung open at her touch. With one furtive glance over her shoulder, she ran into the room, straight to the silent, rocking figure.

"Garret," she whispered, touching him timidly on the shoulder. So much blood on the poor woman's dress, she thought sadly, and then she saw her husband's hands, and the horror of what had been done to him filled her with a boundless pity, a desire to comfort him, and a *need* for revenge. "Garret!" she whispered again.

The beautiful face that filled all her waking thoughts, haunted her dreams, drove her to risk her life in coming back to find him, looked at her through a veil of tears.

"We have to go, Garret," she whispered softly, seeing the water beading on his lashes and knowing it wasn't bathwater or dew but tears of grief and pain and betrayal. How she longed to wipe away those tears and beg him to forgive her.

"I thought…" he murmured softly, the pain ebbing and flowing in his eyes like a living tide of torment. Yet in their depths she saw a glimmer of joy as he gazed at her, and her heart leapt. "I thought you had forsaken me," he whispered brokenly.

She shook her head slowly, knowing that she could never leave him, never hurt him again—because she loved him.

"Never," she promised. "I'll never leave you," she vowed, and he closed his eyes with a sigh as the voices upstairs came closer.

"Garret," she told him kindly, "we can do nothing for her now. We must go. The Vikings are preparing to land at first light. There is no one to defend this land or our people."

He heard her words, but the pain in him went beyond the words, echoing back over the years, as though the price everyone had paid in admitting that they loved him was death. The words always came too late. Much too late…

"I should have killed that mangy dog when I had my chance," he said fiercely, the power returning and flowing strongly in him once again, steeling into his gaze. "I should have killed him," he repeated, taking full responsibility for this as he did for everything else.

Standing up, he lifted his mother gently as if she weighed less than the air around her.

Charlotte watched as he took her into a narrow cell. Following him, she gasped when she saw Charles lying so still on the cell's cold floor.

Both dead, she thought in horror. *Both of them!*

With infinite tenderness, Garret placed his mother beside her husband. And then, as if remembering something, he smiled—a sad, lost smile—and took his cloak of blue velvet and laid it gently over the pair. A moment of silence followed, and when Garret again turned to look at her, she saw the stony mask of a warrior instead of the tragic poet. The fire of revenge was blazing in his eyes, and he looked once again like the god of war.

"Which way is clear?" he asked.

"None," she replied. "I came through the wine cellar, from the kitchen. The garden gate is open."

"Let me have your sword," he told her.

With his tortured hand wrapped around the hilt, he entered the hall. He would find Alaric of York and kill him, and Harold as well. He would find them and make them pay for what they had done. But first he must save his people.

Silently, the two wound their way up the stairs and out into the darkened courtyard, becoming two shadows in the late hours of the night.

The horses had been let loose to run because there was no one now to take care of them, and in the middle of the village green, Arion grazed. As quietly as he could, Garret whistled. The warhorse, used to his master's call, pricked his ears forward and ran to do his bidding with a furious snort. Concealing themselves beside him, they walked until they were clear of the manor's wall.

"Whoa, Arion," murmured Garret. Grabbing a handful of his glossy black mane, he swung up onto his back, then reached down with one arm to pull Charlotte up in front of him. Clucking softly, with nothing to hang onto but the horse's mane, they were off, bounding across the midnight-darkened moors of Wales—a threatened queen and her gallant black-haired knight, struggling valiantly to save their land.

Chapter 41

The white cloth was wound carefully around his hands, each tug causing him to grimace in pain.

They had reached Milford, riding hard. There they'd found refuge, as had several of Pembroke's weary inhabitants.

"Maddy!" Charlotte had shouted, forgetting the woman wouldn't know her. "Please, we need some bandages and water!"

The woman had obeyed, instantly recognizing the young lord of the manor, then frowning at his diminutive consort. *She does look rather familiar*, the woman thought with a curious glance. *Reminds me of someone*, she mused as she handed her the bowl of water, the confused look still lighting her fleshy features.

"It's *me*, Maddy," Charlotte hastened to explain. "*Charley.*"

"Charley?" she said in disbelief, narrowing her eyes and studying the woman who was busily cleaning her husband's wounds. "Say, you do look kind of like him…" she admitted, scratching her hair. "What's going on, anyway?" she asked, staring at the roomful of refugees she had inherited.

"Vikings," Garret said softly. "Vikings are preparing to land on our coast."

"Oh, dear God!" she whispered, having lived through an earlier invasion of the bloodthirsty bastards only fifteen years before. They were utterly without mercy—cold killing machines. She shuddered at the thought of what they'd do.

"What's all the ruckus?" came a familiar voice from Maddy's

private room, and several of Garret's men came into the main room, with a yawning, rough-looking Torin scratching his head in the lead and a wide-eyed Cole behind.

"Jesus!" he breathed, looking at his friend's bloody, weeping hands. "What'd you do to him?" he bellowed, pushing Charlotte.

"Yeah!" shouted Cole, talking to his new sister-in-law for the first time and standing between her and his injured brother, blocking her way.

"Stop it," Garret said tiredly, restraining Torin's arm. "The only thing she's done… is save my life."

Blinking rapidly several times, Torin looked at Charlotte, who boldly held his gaze, while Cole flushed and turned an embarrassed scarlet.

"If you please, Torin, Cole," she answered with dignity, forgetting about Torin's shove and Cole's rude behavior. "My *husband* needs my help."

"Of course," Torin stammered, moving back and pushing his crop of unruly sandy hair away from his now wide-awake eyes.

"The Vikings," Garret repeated. "They're in league with Alaric of York. They've taken over Pembroke, killed Mother and Father, butchered perhaps a hundred of our people."

"Oh, God!" whispered Torin, damning himself for picking this night to go wenching.

"I should have been there!" shouted Cole, feeling guilt flowing in him, fresh and hot. Feeling tears and pain. His mother and father gone, murdered—and he had been here, learning how to be as big a carousing knight as Torin.

"Why?" said Garret flatly. "So that now you two would be lying dead and bleeding in the courtyard? There were too many of the bastards, Cole," he told his brother gently, seeing the pain in his young eyes. "Over a hundred by my count. We have to get help—call the other houses to arms—but in the meantime," he added, not looking Charlotte in the eye, "I must try and find a way to stop them from landing any more of those devils on our soil."

"That is certain suicide!" Charlotte cried hotly, eliciting a strangled "Ow!" as she pulled too hard on the winding cloth.

"Suicide or not," he stated firmly, "these people are under Montgomery protection, and until there is not one of us standing, we will honor our vow!"

"Then I will go with you," she told him softly, remembering how the dagger had felt in her hand, the moment of resistance when it met the enemy's flesh—and then the thought sickened her. "I'm a Montgomery now!" she told him weakly, her heart in her eyes, and something else: tears. Tears had escaped the lake of misery in her heart, flooding her eyes.

"Let me go with you," she begged. "Let me fight by your side."

Smiling gently, he looked at her with such tenderness she was sure her heart was melting under the warmth of that gaze.

"If I must commit suicide," he whispered, "don't let me take your death to my grave as well."

"But…" she argued, bowing her head to conceal her expression, and Garret felt something warm touch his hand, washing the wound.

"Tears?" he asked quietly. "You're wasting your tears on me? A smelly brigand and a pig?"

There was a gentle bantering note in his voice, and when she looked up, with her eyes glistening and her pert little nose bright pink, he reached over, brushing the tears from her cheek.

"I," she began, gazing into the enigmatic, endless depths of his eyes. "I love you!" she whispered, saying the words he had longed to hear all his life. "I love you, Garret Montgomery!" she told him in front of everyone, the wonder in her voice and eyes making him laugh with joy.

Standing up, he wrapped his arms around her. "And I, my

fierce little *Montgomery* bride," he replied, kissing her gently on the forehead, "have *always* loved you!"

The misery had come to an end, at least for a moment. All her life she had forced herself to believe she was above all need, all want. But the truth was that what she had required—needed—all her lonely life, was to be loved by someone as passionately as she could love, and now she was! Oh, how she was!

"Don't leave me… ever!" she begged, furiously wishing she could turn the hands on the clock back—all the way back to their first night, wishing for more *time* to be with him, because she had the sudden, strong conviction that should he pass out of her sight, she would never see his beautiful face again.

Gently brushing the hair away from her face, he lifted her in his arms.

"Your hands," she argued weakly, recognizing the spark of dark fire that ignited his eyes, turning their black centers into bright blue flames.

"It would take more than little holes in my hands to keep me from loving you," he whispered passionately, striding swiftly across the inn and entering Maddy's little back room, kicking the door shut behind them.

"I want to give you something," he told her as he laid her down on the soft, warm rushes, kneeling beside her.

"You," she began, licking her lips and unable to meet his gaze, "you already have…"

"How is that?" he asked as he pulled his shirt over his head, pausing for a moment to look at her, the puzzlement clear in his magic eyes.

"You gave me… *you*…" she answered in a whisper, glancing up shyly and holding her breath as she watched his confusion turn into a brilliant smile.

"But what I want to give you, little one," he replied huskily, stripping off the legs of his trews and lying down beside her, drawing her near, "is *me*... a part of me that will be with you even... if I cannot. I want you to have my children, Charlotte," he whispered hesitantly, feeling a deep emotional need to give her a child—a part of himself—that would continue on.

"Just hold me, Garret," she murmured, drawing his arm around her and nestling into the protective shelter of his embrace. Yes, she would gladly have his sons—and his daughters. She would receive his seed and bear his fruit with pride and dignity. With that decision she felt an emotional bond grow between them, building in her like a warm, glowing spark. "Hold me, Garret and don't ever let me go."

"Never," he whispered, sealing his vow with a kiss as he entered her, slowly and gently, filling her and igniting the dormant ember that she had carried in her for a lifetime into a radiant blaze, burning brighter and brighter, until her soul seemed to flow outward, uniting with his. And the spark became a light, and the light a glowing universe, and in the center of the glowing universe, a brilliant new sun was formed.

Chapter 42

The balance between night and day began to tip, and the hush that precedes the eerie whiteness of dawn settled on the valleys and hills, chilling Armando to the marrow of his bones with its cooling, settling mists.

"How much farther?" whispered Sparrow, her arms wound so tightly around Armando's middle that he could barely breathe.

"A long way..." he murmured, fearing the sound of his voice would wake something in this preternatural light. "A very long way." They were nearly to Tregaron, their mule plodding slowly and carefully along the twisted, mountainous paths.

Too far, he thought in despair. *Too far to Aberystwyth. Too far to go for help.* A sudden, inexplicable sorrow filled him, making a solitary tear fall from his eye. It was a full minute before he realized that the emotion he was feeling was grief, a deep sense of anguish, as he realized that behind him lay only destruction and quite possibly the loss of the two best friends he had ever had.

Sighing, he tapped the side of his mule's head, urging him on, lost in his own misery, when a brilliant yellow light suddenly winked into existence before his eyes. And then another, and another after that.

The valley beneath the ridge he had just cleared was alight with fires—campfires—and a sudden, terrifying fear seized him.

"Vikings!" he muttered, and he felt Sparrow stiffen against him as he kicked the flanks of his mule and tried to get the lumbering beast to turn around, not sure where to go but certain he wasn't going *down there.*

"Hurry, Armando!" she cried, and then she screamed as the underbrush around them exploded and horsemen tore through, surrounding them and cutting off any chance they had of escape.

"Please!" shouted Armando, clasping his hands in prayer.

"We meant no harm," he begged as Bishop growled menacingly, his hackles up.

From within the circle ringing him, a solitary rider rode forward. He was cruel-looking with a wicked, slashing scar traveling the entire length of his face, and his eyes burned dark and cold.

Suddenly, Bishop let out a playful yip and bounded forward, leaping eagerly at the tall man in the saddle.

"Bishop!" murmured Gerald in surprise, surveying the pair he accompanied with narrowed eyes. "Where," he asked, fixing Armando with a fierce stare, "is your mistress?"

Chapter 43

She was aware of the emptiness *inside* of her before she was aware that he was gone.

"Garret!" she cried, sitting up on the rough pallet of rushes, her heart beating madly. He was nowhere in sight, and his clothes were gone along with her sword. Dressing hurriedly, she scrambled for the door shouting, "Maddy! Maddy!"

She threw open the door, nearly stumbling over the woman she called, who was propped up against the wall near her door.

"Maddy?" she asked, a question in her eyes.

"Gone, dear," she whispered, her arms wrapped beneath her solid breasts, hugging herself. "All of them. They've taken every bloody weapon in the inn, and Lord Garret said that as soon as you awaken, we're to leave—follow you and Cole to the Vale. He told us," she repeated with a sigh, closing her eyes, "that you'd take care of us."

"They've gone to stop the Vikings!" Charlotte cried, shaking her head at the utter insanity of it all, suddenly feeling very cold inside. "Listen to me, Maddy," she said firmly. "You take your women and the villagers and go through the mountain passes to Aberystwyth. Cole will lead you," she told her confidently, motioning to the sleeping boy on the other side of the hearth. "Tell Lon ap Llewelyn that he is to give you refuge, and tell him what is happening here!"

It was virtually the same message she had given Armando, but her faith in him was flawed. She couldn't be sure if he had done as she asked or was halfway to Salisbury by now.

"Look, Charley," Maddy told her sharply, struggling to stand up, not liking the desperate light shining from Charlotte's young eyes. "He left you here with no sword or weapon so you *wouldn't* get any foolish ideas in that thick skull of yours! He left you with us, Lady Charlotte—so that you might *live!*"

Part of her—the steel and stone core which had been built upon rocks of pain and loneliness—was crumbling. It was as if the tears, once let loose, had washed away the mortar that held that bitter tower together. Those tears and those words that she had uttered last night to the man with the eyes of a magician had been a baptism and a rebirth. *Life* had flowed through her veins because she loved and was loved in return. Without him, the world that would be left for her would seem as lifeless and cold as the one she had escaped from in his arms.

"You don't understand," Charlotte said slowly, quietly, resting her eyes on the gentle figure before her. "Without *him*," she whispered, "there is no life. Without him, there is nothing." She smiled, a small, wise smile, the smile of someone who had aged a hundred years in the space of a single night.

"You've no weapon," argued Maddy weakly, seeing the determination burning like an unquenchable fire in her eyes.

"Oh, yes, I do!" she replied with a sly smile, remembering the ebony box still strapped to her horse's rump and the Sword resting securely in its bed of red velvet. "A most remarkable weapon."

"Girl..." pleaded Maddy sadly, with a worried shake of her head.

"Don't worry, Maddy!" she told her jovially, feigning a confidence she didn't feel. "We'll be back," she assured her, giving her a hug and a peck on the cheek. "We'll *both* be back!" she vowed, heading for the door and going through it as the first hint of whiteness washed the night from the horizon.

Chapter 44

Twelve men against a legion.

Dawn was in Garret's eyes, pale and silver, and anger, bright red, filled his mind. He lay flat against a ridge of chalky limestone with Torin to his left and five of his best men to his right. Their horses had been hobbled and now waited in a line of brush behind them.

Along the coast of Carmarthen Bay, Alaric's men were hauling limbs and pieces of driftwood, lighting signal fires all up and down the beach. In the distance, barely visible behind the ever-present, low-lying clouds, a score of Viking dragon ships waited—waited for the signal fires that would welcome them to their new home.

"We'll have to stop them here," Garret said quietly, his eyes narrowing as he focused on the arrogant figure of Alaric of York, shouting orders, and his lapdog, the mad Halfdanson, riding back and forth, whipping the men into a victorious frenzy.

"Stop *them?*" snorted Torin. "In case you've forgotten," he reminded Garret lamely, "there are only *twelve* of us and there are at least eighty of *them!*"

"Pretty fair odds, wouldn't you say?" Garret answered calmly, grinning his devilish grin and making Torin smile despite his fear.

"I suppose," Torin agreed, staring into the sparkling eyes of his best friend. "I suppose we should let our men go. That might even it up a bit more!"

Garret smiled, happy to see the cocky Irishman back again.

"Help will come," he told him earnestly, hoping Armando had gotten safely away to alert the other families. "Until it does," he grinned and shrugged his massive shoulders, "we'll give those sons of perdition more trouble than they know what to do with!"

"Sure!" agreed Torin, nodding with as much enthusiasm as he could muster as he scrambled up to follow in Garret's footsteps, noticing the small trail of blood on the ground.

Garret's hands still bled. Every time he held the reins or moved so much as a finger, the wounds were reopened, and the blood would flow.

Torin could not imagine the pain his friend was suffering, but whatever he bore, he bore in silence. *That Garret Montgomery*, thought Torin, with admiration shining from his eyes, *is brave!* Suddenly, against all reason and logic, Torin felt sorry for those men on the beach.

"We could lie like dogs beneath the rocks in caves and alongside the roads and let them pass us by to wreak havoc where they will. Or we can stand and fight, knowing we've done our best for the people.

"The reward of a coward's life is a thousand deaths. If we've but one life to give, let it be for our people," said Garret, once they were on horseback.

Torin nodded.

Both knights lifted their swords and held them aloft. Fire gleamed along the edges of their blades and in the wellsprings of their noble eyes.

"To the last breath!" they shouted. "For our people!"

A pale ridge of pink lit the horizon, and the fog began to lift. Morning had dawned, and the day of reckoning had arrived.

Carefully laying the ebony box on the ground, Charlotte opened it. Still inside, safe and unused for centuries, lay the fabled Sword of Wales. Beneath its impressively sharp blade, in a little nest cut into the very grain of the wood, the Crown gleamed with the secret lives of hundreds of diamonds.

The Queen's tears, she thought sadly, finally understanding the Legend in all its bittersweet glory. With a lump in her throat, she lifted the blade, and Maddy, who had followed her outside along with most of the girls, gasped.

The jewel—the red, glittering eye, the very soul of Wales—seemed to search out the illusive rays of dawn and draw them into its crimson heart.

"I'll be!" whispered Maddy, crossing herself reverently as Charlotte swung the blade, creating a high, arcing figure eight that seemed to shimmer with rainbow fire. It whirred menacingly as it sliced through the air, the sound of its passing like a high-pitched wail.

"It's the Sword, isn't it?" asked Maddy in a breathless whisper. "It's singing, isn't it!"

"Yes," said Charlotte. "It is the Sword of the Welsh. Our blood has forged this blade a thousand years ago!"

For a moment, time stopped. Charlotte lifted the mythical sword and let the rays of sunlight travel the length of the blade. The fire of the rubies ignited crimson and the diamonds shimmered.

With all of her skill, Charlotte held the blade aloft and called out to her ancestors to ride the winds and aid their people. A spectral light gleamed above them, and Charlotte turned toward the old woman, suddenly feeling very calm, as though in that moment she had stopped struggling against her fate and accepted it.

Princess Charlotte felt the Sword's power flow through her until she felt as though she were lifted several inches from the ground, though still touching the earth.

"Maddy," she added, closing the lid of the box and carrying it across the small space that separated them, "when you leave, take this. It's the Crown of Wales."

Maddy's hands flew up in the air as though she were afraid of getting too near it.

"I'll be dead if I touch it!" she cried. "I'm not worthy!"

"The Lord bestows courage on those who need it. This is for our people. This is for Wales!

"Take the Crown to Aberystwyth and give it to Lon. Tell him," she added thoughtfully, her frown turning into a radiant smile, "tell him that his *sister* sends her love."

"Charlotte!" cried Maddy. There was real sorrow in her voice. "You must come as well, before it's too late."

"No, Maddy," she replied with a determined little smile and a stubborn shake of her head. "The day I met Garret Montgomery was the day I found my destiny. I can no more run from that," she realized with an accepting shrug, "than I could from his love."

Solemnly Maddy took the box. Charlotte had no doubt in her mind that it would find its way to its rightful place in those good and capable hands.

"Goodbye, Maddy!" she said softly, springing up lightly into her saddle. And then, as if a sudden, sweet thought occurred to her, she looked out onto the deepening rosy glow of the horizon and cried aloud for all to hear: "If not victory," she prayed, "then grant me one… last… kiss!"

Seconds later she was gone, turning her horse in the direction of Carmarthen Bay.

"Through the front door?" Torin asked politely, with a bow. "Or couldn't I perhaps persuade you to sneak around back?"

"Through the front door, of course," replied Garret with a roguish grin. "Unless you happen to be a fish!" he added, looking out across the sea. The two men then looked at each other fondly, and what Torin saw before him was a man of unmistakable charismatic power. He would have been a king no matter where he had been born.

With a deep in-drawn breath and the eyes of all his men trained on him, Garret raised his sword high above his head and shouted, "Engage!" Then he pounded down the hill, leading the charge and grinning like the Devil himself, with a dozen brave men close at his heels.

"It is about to happen!" murmured Alaric passionately as he stared proudly out to sea. Fires all along the beach were being lit, inviting the invaders once more into the land. *But not invaders*, he thought arrogantly. An *army—my* army!

"Do you see them, Nell?" he asked excitedly, studying the plunging black ships hovering just a few miles from shore. "There," he told her, pointing, and she yawned.

"Yes," she replied with a bored sigh. "It's all very grand."

She had something more important on her mind than the war games of men: survival. Now that her part was through in Alaric's elaborate scheme, where did that leave her? Frowning, she turned to look at him, staring for a moment at the odd, nearly ecstatic look on his narrow-featured face.

"*Lord* Alaric," she began, careful to coat her voice with enough syrup to make it palatable to the egotistical maniac seated like some great king on his little gray horse. "Now that my part is finished," she said, trying to smile as seductively as she could when he finally turned his attention to her, "what is to—"

Her question was never finished for, suddenly, Alaric's deadly pale face went three shades lighter, and his eyes bulged in disbelief.

"Oh my God!" he whispered, staring with the most horrified

expression on his face at the northwestern ridge of chalk hills that ran the length of the beach.

"What is it?" she asked with a frown, turning to look where he did.

Coming down the north slope of the ridge on a large black stallion, with his sword drawn and his eyes blazing, was Alaric's nemesis, followed by a dozen fierce-looking men-at-arms.

"Garret Montgomery," he whispered incredulously, his hands automatically tightening on the reins while his eyes darted nervously back and forth like a trapped animal's, searching the hundred or so men around him for *one* man in particular.

"Halfdanson," he choked, barely able to get the word out. "Harold Halfdanson!" he bellowed, bolting across the sand toward the red-headed pirate with Nell close at his heels. "Look!" he shouted, pulling up sharply and pointing. "Look who's come to settle the score!"

Scowling and thinking the wild-eyed man insane, Halfdanson dropped the load of firewood he had been hauling to the beach and looked where Alaric pointed.

"By Thor!" he hissed, feeling the bloodlust rise in him and his body grow rigid. Breathing hard, he reached for the double-edged ax he had cast on the ground.

"MONT-GOM-ER-YY!" he bellowed, raising the ax high over his head. "IT IS TIME!"

Chapter 45

"MONTGOMERY, YOU BASTARD!" shouted Halfdanson as he whipped his murderous lust into a frenzy, whirling his long-handled ax in the air, moving it faster and faster in killing arcs until the blade was little more than a blur, screaming: "IT'S TIME TO DIE! MONTGOMERY! DO YOU HEAR?" he bellowed. "TIME TO *DIE!*"

Garret's hands were racked with pain, but he tried not to dwell on it. Pain was no stranger to him, so when the hilt of the sword pressed too hard into his palm, sending needle-like flames up his arm, he pushed the feeling away, concentrating on only one thing—the mad Viking with one hand.

"I'll take him," offered Torin, who would be giving away well over a hundred pounds in the fight, all to a man who had twice the experience and ten times the cunning he possessed. But he offered to do this willingly, knowing Garret's wounds were more painful than he let on.

"No!" growled Garret, so close to the shouting lunatic with the red hair and whirling ax that he could see the color of his eyes. "He's *mine!*"

With a kick and a wild shout, he closed the gap between them.

"HALFDANSON!" he roared, ramming the Viking's charging horse with his own and jarring both riders nearly out of their seats. "IT'S TIME I SENT YOU BACK TO HELL WHERE YOU BELONG!"

"Only," shouted the other man, recovering his balance with remarkable ease, "if I don't kill you first!" He brought his horse around and rammed Garret's with as much speed as he could, making Arion scream in rage, as the wicked-looking ax vaulted forward, whistling through the air.

Grunting, Garret countered his attack, feeling a numbing shock that nearly sent him spinning into darkness as his sword connected with the ax flying toward him.

"You'll have to do better than that!" he laughed, recovering from the blow and slashing upward with his right hand, countering with a defensive thrust that nearly sent Halfdanson to the ground.

"My ax," shouted the Viking, beginning to breathe hard and struggling to keep the reins wound around his withered stump as the two stallions began to bite and kick each other, "is called *Blood Drinker!* And she," he shouted proudly, pretending to bring her upward, but feinting slightly to the left as he tried to find an opening, "is thirsty!"

Garret countered, his muscles bulging and sheened in sweat, as he kicked Halfdanson's horse in the head, causing him to buck and send the Viking crashing to the ground.

"Then she had better be prepared to taste yours!" he roared.

Laughing, the Viking stood up, thumping his chest with his withered stump. "No weapons!" he shouted, challenging his opponent. "Only our hands! Man to man!"

"Man to man it is, then!" Garret agreed, sliding deftly from his horse, thinking about his father and the brutal knife wound he had seen in his back. "Just like my father and you!" he sneered, and Harold only laughed.

"He wasn't worth a fair fight, Montgomery!" Halfdanson said, scratching his beard and watching in delight as the fire built in Garret's eyes to a blazing inferno. "All he ever was is a drunkard and a whoremonger… I just put him out of his misery," he added cruelly, and from a half-crouch position where it seemed that he was laying his weapon down, he sprang upward, the blade of his ax coming down directly above Garret's shoulder.

"Scum!" Garret shouted, trying to move out of the way.

But he was not quick enough this time. The tip of the ax grazed his shoulder, giving him fresh pain to deal with and more blood while the mad laughter bubbling out of Halfdanson's cursed throat galled him to the marrow of his bones.

"Do you hear the Valkyries singing, Montgomery?" The Viking laughed, preparing to lunge once more. "They're coming for you, boy!" He chuckled as he raised his ax. "Coming to take you home!" he sang, swinging the ax and aiming for Garret's unprotected neck.

Farther back, behind the warring men, Alaric had lit the rest of the signal fires. Out on the ships, the pale blue eyes of the Norwegians saw the flames. Their oars picked up speed, beating in perfect time, heading for the beach.

Charlotte followed the tracks in the powdery dust of the trail. Her heart was beating so fast that it was hard to draw even a single full breath as she crested the ridge, staring in horror at the scene before her.

"So this is war," she whispered, suddenly weak at the sight of all the blood and the deafening clang of steel reverberating on steel for miles. Garret's men were badly outnumbered. Scanning the beach with anxious, worried eyes, for a moment she didn't see him. "There!" she murmured, her heart in her throat. He was a little farther down the beach than his men, and he wasn't fighting from the back of his horse, but on the ground, grappling with a huge, red-haired Viking.

"I'm coming," she whispered quietly, feeling the familiar surge of adrenaline and pushing back the thought that she was about to ride to her death. "Hah!" she cried, kicking her mare in the sides, and then she shouted, loud and sweet, her war cry undulating across the valley for miles as she raced down the hill into the very thick of the battle.

"Montgomery!" panted Halfdanson, shoving against him with all his weight. "Do you see the Choosers of the Slain, the maidens in shining armor, coming to take you?" he asked with a throaty chuckle, barely able to talk as he tried to reach Garret's throat with his one good hand, keeping his crippled arm between them like a wedge.

"Yes!" Garret replied with a grunt, struggling to keep the hand from reaching its destination. "They must… uhm!" He grunted in pain as fingers tore into the wound on his hand. "They must be coming for you!" he shouted, kicking the Viking's feet out from under him.

"Ooomph!" Halfdanson groaned, the wind leaving him for one very frightening second as he hit the ground, and he thought he heard the maidens singing—right next to his ear. His eyes went wild with fear and he turned, scrambling for the ax that he had dropped during their struggle. But Garret was quicker, snatching it from the ground and lifting it over his head in one fluid motion. Halfdanson could only stare.

All too vividly Garret saw his own body reacting to its instincts and the experience of many, many fights as it brought the ax down, curving it at an angle and laying all his weight into the blow, burying it to the hilt in the stunned Halfdanson's chest.

There was a moment of awful silence while both men looked into each other's eyes.

Halfdanson grunted, touching the ax, and he seemed almost surprised. Then he smiled as the Valkyries he had waited so very long for welcomed him into Valhalla, a hero at last, and the life that had burned so fierce and green in his eyes winked out forever.

With barely enough time to recover, Garret saw a flash in the periphery of his vision. In that same instant, he jerked the ax free and rolled to the ground, heaving the ax straight up as he lay on his back, catching a Saxon between his legs. Blood spurted, drenching him as he jumped to his feet, feeling the first wave of fatigue wash over him as he watched the man grimace in pain and fall to the ground. But there was no time for rest now. There was no time for anything except the *fight.* That was all there was.

He began to run, looking for his horse and seeing him only a few feet away. But his gaze caught something else besides Arion's glossy black mane: a long tail of bobbing silver hair crowning a small woman surrounded on both sides by sword-wielding Saxons.

"Charlotte!" he cried in disbelief and fear as he ran toward his horse, springing upward from the back, pushing off with one hand on the horse's rump, and landing firmly in the saddle. "Yah!" he shouted, spurring the horse on and sending him screaming and biting, hurtling through the fighting soldiers, toward the woman he had held in his arms all last night.

Too many! her mind screamed as she continued to work her blade up and down, slashing sideways, thrusting, feinting, weaving. But there were too many, and she didn't know how long she could hang on. A ragged gash oozed blood from her back, and her head was on fire where a savage blow from a Saxon's shield had landed. *Garret!* she thought desperately, unable to believe she would make it out of this battle alive. She felt suddenly vulnerable and weak, and she needed him and his strength beside her now more than ever.

"Haughty bitch!" roared a Saxon to her left, meaning to send her to her death with a fierce downward strike of his blade. Her sword hand had just finished its own downward strike, and she knew with the same clarity that someone in an accident knows that they are dying that she would never be able to raise the sword in time to deflect the blow. But she tried, gallantly she tried, putting all her power—concentrating it—into the blow, watching as if in slow motion, her death arcing downward in a cold, silver spiral… And then she did something completely cowardly and utterly feminine: She covered her eyes with her hand and waited…

Suddenly a startled scream escaped the man, and he fell forward, clattering loudly to the ground at her feet. Knowing she wasn't dead and wondering why, Charlotte peeked out from between her fingers, seeing the Saxon who had meant to kill her dead himself with a double-headed ax protruding from his back. And thundering to her rescue on the back of a ferocious black stallion, with an angry scowl on his face, was her husband.

"Garret!" she cried gratefully as his horse rammed another unsuspecting soldier intent on Charlotte's head and sent him to the ground where Arion proceeded to stomp him into the dirt with outraged snorts and sharp hooves.

"Why," asked Garret, grabbing her and shaking her furiously by the shoulders, "are you here?!"

"To be with you," she stammered, staring into his angry eyes, drinking in their beautiful, deep-blue depths as though his gaze was the rarest, most addicting wine. "To be with you," she whispered again, suddenly wanting to cry and realizing how much her back hurt and how incredibly tired she was, wanting nothing more than to go home and curl up in bed with him.

"AND I'M NOT A COWARD, EITHER!" she shouted, and Garret knew that if she were standing at this minute, her legs would be spread, and her hands would be soldered squarely onto her hips.

"That's it," he murmured with satisfaction, dodging a blow and countering with one equally as savage. "Keep fighting, my little queen…" he whispered desperately. For every Saxon he felled, ten more seemed to take their place. "Keep fighting…"

Along a ridge, well away from the fight, Alaric gloated.

Smiling, he watched as the *valiant* band of Norman filth was being mercilessly destroyed. Out in the bay he could just make out the first dragon's-head prow of a Viking ship.

"Splendid!" he whispered, congratulating himself on how well his plans were going.

"Lord Alaric," whined Nell peevishly, intending to tell him that she was hungry and tired and to ask his leave.

But a haughty gaze pinned her to her seat, and he said with an arrogant sneer, "*King* Alaric, if you please, Nell. Or *Your Highness* will do." And then he snickered, unable to wait for the day when all the Normans were lying face down in the dirt.

Now only six of Garret's men were left, and a very small woman with as much courage and fire as any man. They barely had time to think as the Saxons bore down on them from all sides.

Yet even during all this turmoil, Garret couldn't help but be proud of Charlotte. *Was there ever*, he wondered, the adoration shining from his eyes as he watched her fight a man twice her size and win, *a woman such as her?* Her speed with the blade was remarkable; her reflexes fast and immediate. But watching her, with her tunic spattered in blood, he noticed, too, the unmistakable imprint the horror of battle was leaving in her eyes. She had aged. No more valiant games or noble thoughts of war. War was only one thing: the will to survive, and not some battle fought on a chessboard.

"How much longer," shouted Torin, bleeding now from several places on his body, "can we last?"

"I don't know!" Garret growled, keeping an eye on the lady fighting between them with the curiously beautiful sword that flashed fire in the light with each blow. "Not much…"

And then he heard her shout.

"Look!" she cried jubilantly, stabbing her blade toward the northern ridge and nearly forgetting to defend herself.

Norman and Saxon alike looked to where she pointed.

For a moment, Garret couldn't believe what he was seeing. The ridge was one brilliantly covered, *moving* mass of bodies.

"Soldiers!" he breathed gratefully as he struggled with two young Saxons, dispatching them easily with Torin's help.

"Yes!" Charlotte cried, her eyes growing wide with wonder as she noticed who led the charge. "Grandmother!" she breathed, unable to believe her eyes.

Ahead of all the horses and flanked on the right by Lon and on the left by Armando Bustamante, in full armor was her grandmother Isabel, proudly waving her purple banner and leading the charge with a blood-curdling cry at breakneck speed.

A lump rose in Charlotte's throat as she watched the proud woman, defiantly holding the oak-hewn raven's staff before her while her hair flowed around her face and figure like a black-winged cape. Behind her (as always), near her (as always) rode Gerald, the Captain of the Guard, with his sword flashing and his cruel-looking face set in a perpetual scowl.

A cry of joy went up from the rest of Garret's men, who took heart at the sight of the thousand-man army approaching, and they fell to fighting with renewed hope.

Saxons, one and all, saw nothing joyful about the approaching army. All they saw was their death bearing down on them with fresh horses and men, and an old Welsh witch leading the charge.

"Let's get out of here!" shouted one, and then soon they all took up the cry of "Retreat! Retreat!" With one mind, they turned their horses around, fleeing from the battle as fast as they could.

Alaric watched from his perch on the hill in disbelieving horror as his army turned tail and ran. "Stop!" he shouted, trying to head his men off. But they ignored him, not willing to die for his pride.

"You traitors!" he screamed as the last of his soldiers vanished in the distance.

Suddenly, in the silence of their wake, he realized that, with them gone, he had no protection.

"Nell," he started to say, preparing to tell her to run, but when he turned around, she had wisely beat her own retreat, outdistancing him by a quarter of a mile, safely on her way to her next escapade.

"Traitor!" he screamed as he slapped his horse's rump and attempted to follow her, wanting to get as far away from Garret Montgomery as he could. "I'll kill you!" he bellowed, knowing how weak his threats must sound. "When I catch you, Nell Gwynn, I'll kill you!" he vowed, running away as fast as he could.

"There," whispered Charlotte, pointing to the east, at the far edge of the retreating men. Garret swung around, just in time to see Alaric make the first ridge.

Without a moment's hesitation, Garret's horse broke into a run, bearing down on Alaric of York while vengeance raged through Garret's mind.

Charlotte followed him, watching as, along the rocky coast, Garret veered off sharply east, knowing that Alaric's present course would take him right out onto a little lip, surrounded on three sides by water. There would be no escape for him this time!

As Garret had predicted, Alaric made for the cover of the inlet and skidded to a halt, staring in horror at the water surrounding him on all three sides. Turning wildly, he prepared to backtrack, suddenly pulling up short and staring ahead of him.

At the opening of the lip, preventing his escape, was Garret Montgomery. There could be no mistaking his intentions as he began to walk his horse forward, destruction on his mind.

Behind him, Charlotte skidded to a halt just in time to watch the two men fight. She didn't pray for Garret's safety, trusting in the strength of the arms that had held her last night and the courage of his noble heart.

"Get him, Garret," she whispered, nodding her head as Torin approached from the other side, suddenly feeling very glad that she was *not* in Alaric of York's boots.

Laughing, Alaric threw aside his shield. Holding up his sword, he motioned arrogantly to Garret.

"Well, *boy*," he shouted haughtily, pretending not to be scared. "Come get me!"

His baiting did not affect the gait of Garret's horse nor the expression on his handsome face. When he looked at Alaric, he saw the murderer of his mother and his father. That vision of his mother, Alaric thrusting a knife into her stomach, made him furious. He had never wanted to do more than fight the good fight. Win honorably. Play fair. But right now, with the blood pounding in his veins so hard it made him dizzy, he wanted nothing better than to rip the man to pieces with his bare hands, to make him suffer as he was sure his parents had.

"Today," boasted Alaric, sweating profusely now and wishing he could wipe his hand, which was clammy and slid too easily off the hilt of his sword, "is a good day to die, boy!"

"I agree," murmured Garret. "A good day for *you* to die!" With a strangled cry of rage, he swung his borrowed sword, which thudded heavily against Alaric's.

"Clumsy!" muttered Alaric, trying to disturb his concentration. "Did I tell you about your mother?" he asked evilly with a wink.

Garret swung too soon, feeling a stinging counterattack as Alaric's blade pierced his side.

"Garret!" Charlotte cried, beginning to ride to him, intent on helping him if she could.

"Hurt, didn't it?" asked the cunning Saxon, feinting upward

and parrying away to the right, knocking Garret's blade from his hand. "Tsk!" he chortled. "You seem to be defenseless."

Looking upward from beneath his dark lashes and seeing the triumphant smile on Alaric's face, Garret did a most unexpected thing. Weaponless, he jumped from his horse, knocking the hand that held the blade to one side and sending the two of them tumbling to the ground.

"Garret!" Charlotte cried, and he looked up, just in time to see a flash of red spin through the air and hear a *whirr* like the sound of beating wings.

Catching the mythical Sword of Wales in his hand, Garret looked deep into the frightened eyes of the man beneath him.

"This," he said quietly, standing up and slicing down between Alaric's legs, "is for my mother!"

Alaric howled in pain.

"And this," he said, slamming the blade of the sword through Alaric's black heart, pinning him to the ground with all his might, "is for my father!"

With a surprised grunt and a slow release of breath, Alaric of York breathed his last.

"Garret!" Charlotte cried, flinging herself from her horse and landing squarely against his chest.

"Yes, Charley?" he whispered with a grin, gathering her to him and winding his arms protectively around her as the sound of a thousand stamping feet came closer.

"I," she started to say, looking *way up* into his gorgeous face, "I *love* you!"

"Yes," he admitted. "I know."

And then her features darkened subtly, and a frown pulled her black eyebrows together over her nose as she pushed away from him. Squaring her shoulders and affecting her "man-stance," she stared at him fiercely.

"I am not a coward!"

"I know. But you *are* a liar," he added, laughing as he ducked her blow. "And a conniving little Welsh witch. And let us not forget..." He started to run away from her. "A *tease*..."

"Ahh," she said, pulling absently on her chin and tapping her booted foot as he pranced back and forth a few steps from her, wiggling his eyebrows and flexing his rounded pectorals. "Fox and Hen," she mused in delight. "And I'm the Fox and you're..."

He pounced on her, silencing her with a kiss.

"A rooster," he said warningly. "*You're* the hen..." he reminded her sternly. "Now, shall we *play?*" he asked, and they both giggled like a couple of children, lying in the middle of the beach.

Above them the sky began to darken with the first shadow of night and the full moon rode the crest of waves, sailing into the harbor.

Garret was silent.

"I'd die for you, my lady," he said seriously.

"I know," she said. "But my wish is that you will live for me and with me. That your promise to be my husband, though it was spoken by another on your behalf, will be your pledge to me this night and forever." She turned toward him and reached upward, surrendering herself as she surrounded his neck with her arms and drew him to her. Her body was weary from war, yet her heart was filled with love.

"I neither want a surrogate in my bed nor in my arms. I want you, Garret. No other man will ever posses my body or soul as you do."

She was gentle in his arms, soft and more beautiful than he had ever imagined. The moonlight shined her hair to platinum and lit her skin with a magic that radiated from within.

He kissed her. Then whispered, "I take thee, Charlotte de Clare, to be my lawfully wedded wife, to have and to hold, in times of plenty and times of hardship, in times of health and times of sickness, from this day forth, keeping myself only unto thee, forever more."

Charlotte's eyes glowed softly, so filled with love and happiness that Garret laughed gently and pulled her against him.

"I love you, Charlotte," he said quietly. "You're my lady and my wife."

"It's only fitting that two warriors should wed on the battlefield," said Charlotte ironically.

"Then for a third time," promised Garret. "In the chapel at Pembroke so that others may know and celebrate our love for one another, and our vows be witnessed by God and the parish."

Suddenly, from the north a fierce wind began to blow across the land. There was a banshee wail in the wind and a hint of ice and mist.

Charlotte heard in her mind her grandmother's voice: *Magic will always be a part of your life, granddaughter. It will arise when least expected and most needed.*

The north winds surged across the terrain with a ferocity that startled the men. In the harbor, the limp sails of the invading ships began to fill with wind, pushing the marauding ships away from the island's well-defended shore!

Charlotte watched as her enemies began to fade in the distance, escorted by the relentless arctic winds. The Sword of Wales was thrust deep into the earth; the rubies glittering like fire in the moonlight.

"Wales is the land of my father," said Charlotte with pride as she gazed at her husband. It was a victory. The Welsh had won and routed the Vikings from their land.

"Wales is for the Welsh!" she said.

"Is there room in Wales for a Norman knight?" Garret asked sweetly.

"Yes, for you, my love," said Charlotte.

Garret smiled in satisfaction. He was bleeding in several places; his arms ached from lifting and hefting the sword. He was a knight, a warrior who had given his all to keep his princess safe and defend her land.

Together they watched as the Viking ships' oars struck the sea in rhythmic beats, turning away from Pembroke's well-defended harbor!

"Forever Wales!" shouted Garret, lifting the Sword proudly.

He knew the men would follow him into battle without question. He had earned their loyalty and trust.

"Forever free!" said Princess Charlotte.

The soldiers began to cheer! They knew the Vikings would never be back.

The Welsh were free at last.

Life at Pembroke resumed its slow and easy rhythm within a few weeks after the attack. There were casualties and grief, but it was summer, and the gardens were ripening with the promise of a good harvest and full days ahead.

The Sword and the Crown had been given into Lon's keeping, as the rightful ruler of Wales. Charlotte remembered, as she stared up at the ceiling in her bedroom, the happy smile on his face when he had walked up to her, embracing her and calling her "Sister."

"Do you," she started to say, wanting to ask her sleeping husband what he thought. "Do you think Grandmother and Gerald will be all right?" She had tried to convince them to stay at the Vale, but Isabel had refused, taking only a handful of clothes and the barest possessions, admonishing Charlotte to come visit her from time to time.

"Yes," he murmured sleepily. "I think that woman would be all right no matter where she was."

Suddenly the door to their room burst open, and a very frightened Armando ran through it, jumping squarely onto the middle of their bed.

"Save me, master!" he begged, kneeling in the center of the bed with his hands clasped.

"From what?" asked Garret sharply, pulling the sheet up to cover his wife's exposed breasts.

"From," began Armando, stammering in fear as he pointed a trembling finger at the door. "From her!"

At the mention of "her," Sparrow came running into the room, flapping her apron and hyperventilating, looking just like a chubby little bird preparing to take off.

"There you are, Father!" she cried in relief.

Armando scooted up to the headboard, right between Garret and Charlotte, becoming as small as possible and tugging on Charlotte, which didn't hide him and only got him a well-deserved clout on the head from Garret.

"Oh, come along now!" she said irritably, tapping her foot and flapping her apron. "You are a *priest*," she reminded him. "And you have a *sacred* duty to perform… an obligation to one of your flock!"

"No!" he yelled, unable to take any more "exorcisms" today and quite possibly for the rest of his life. "No, I don't!" he repeated, standing up on the middle of the bed. "I don't have any sacred duty to you or anyone else! And you're not my 'flock,'" he added as he ripped the worn habit from his body, his spittle flying. "I'm not even sure if I like you, Sparrow!" he admitted, ripping the girdle from his waist and tossing it on the floor. "See!" he shouted, his eyes bulging and his face livid with color. "I'm not a priest, Sparrow! I'm just an ordinary man!"

"Not to mention a liar," added Charlotte with a yawn, receiving an indignant snort from Armando.

"So you see, Sparrow," he explained more calmly, convinced now that she would leave him alone, "I can't exorcise you! I'm just a regular man and not an ordained priest!" With that he hopped off the bed and stood in front of her with his arms out, looking very relieved.

"You're not a priest?" she questioned, looking his striped pants up and down.

"No," he admitted, shaking his head, with a grin blooming on his face. "I'm just a lecherous thief, Sparrow. Ask Lady Charlotte." He motioned toward his mistress hopefully.

Charlotte nodded in reply to the questioning look from her little maid.

"Well," Sparrow sighed, coming closer, "if you aren't a priest," she began, sorting through his confession and suddenly starting to smile, "then you and I can get *married!*"

"Oh, no, we can't!" argued Armando, backing up.

"Oh, yes!" she replied. "Why, it'll be perfectly lovely! We can live with my folks, have lots and lots of babies—and, incidentally, did I tell you I was pregnant? You can exorcise me on a regular basis! Why, every day! Twice a day! It'll be perfectly *lovely!*"

"Help!" he squeaked, leaping over the bed and running out the door as fast as he could, followed by a determined maid with a devilish fire burning in her night and day, shouting, "It'll be lovely, Armando! Perfectly lovely!"

"Garret?" Charlotte asked slowly when they had stopped laughing, and she began to tickle his ear. "Do you think a woman ought to keep secrets from her husband?"

Garret snorted. There was a motive behind her question, he knew, as there was a motive for everything she did. Keeping his eyes shut, he grinned, tightening his grip around her waist.

"What sort of secrets?" he asked softly.

"Oh," she replied, struggling to find the right words. "If a person *did* something," and he chuckled, turning more fully toward her so that his hand could continue caressing her.

"You mean," he goaded gently, "if *you* did something, right?"

"Well, yes," she admitted, not sure why that should matter so much as she began to squirm uncomfortably under his gaze. "But I did it because I thought it was the right thing at the time—only now I deeply regret it. Since I'm sure you don't feel it's right to keep secrets, I'm having a very hard time dealing with my guilt."

Frowning, he opened his blue eyes more fully, staring down at her with a cynical expression lighting his eyes.

"You know," he said, "I'm going to have to get you another maid. You're even beginning to sound like Sparrow."

"Stop it!" She groaned. "I'm trying to tell you something—something I'm very sorry for."

"What is it?" he asked with a knowing grin.

"Well," she began, swallowing hard and beginning to twist the bedsheet into a knot, "do you remember when I slept with Robert on our wedding night because I was desperate for a way to break the agreement?" The last part of her question came out more like a muffled squeak.

"You mean about the pre-arranged marriage?" he asked. "The agreement where neither one of us had a choice?" Garret pretended to look hurt.

Charlotte sighed. He was the most handsome man she had ever seen and found it nearly impossible to resist him.

"Yes. I just wanted to tell you that I wish with all of my heart that it could have been with you," neglecting to mention that her memory of Robert of Gloucester and the bathhouse wasn't entirely unpleasant.

"Well," he murmured, bending over to nuzzle her neck. "You

wish it had been me?" he repeated, smiling against the side of her throat as she wrapped her arms about his shoulders. He nipped her gently. "You've lied to me, poisoned me, imprisoned me and tried to kill me more than once."

"Yes," she admitted guiltily. "But that's before I knew you. Before I fell in love with you."

Garret nodded.

"I've been to confession several times over all of it. Father didn't have enough time for all my sins in one session, so I kept going back," admitted Charlotte.

"No doubt," said Garret, laughing.

"But our wedding night, Garret, I wish it had been you with me!"

"The wedding night," Garret said softly. "Oh, yes, I remember it well. Did you say something like 'Robert of Gloucester, let's get this unfortunate business out of the way?'"

"What?" she cried, sitting bolt upright in bed and making him bite his tongue as the realization began to dawn on her that Robert was *not* Robert, but the one and only *Garret Montgomery!* "That was *you?"* she asked, nearly shouting. She was not sure whether to be happy or mad. He had outsmarted her every step of the way.

"Yes," he told her firmly, pushing her shoulders back down on the bed. "Life is a game of chess. You can castle your queen, rout my bishop, but in the end, the king always wins."

He pulled the sheet across them.

"Checkmate," he said. "That was me, on our wedding night, not Robert of Gloucester." It still made him angry. "The man who lies beside you in bed will always be me, Charlotte!" he vowed, settling next to her with a happy sigh. "I am your husband, the lord of the manor, and you are my lady, and I demand that you kiss me."

"Do you love me, Garret?"

"Yes. Now kiss me."

"Gladly," she said. She heard the irritation in his voice, so she bent until their mouths nearly touched.

Suddenly another thought occurred to her. "But where," she asked with a confused light glowing in her azure eyes, "is Robert of Gloucester?"

It was then that a surprised light spread over Garret's handsome face and he started to laugh, rolling over on his back and bringing her with him.

"I forgot to let the fool out of the cellar!" he admitted, and the two of them laughed until the tears rolled down their cheeks.

In the cloistered chapel at Pembroke there was a simple stone of granite which had been placed there nearly 700 years ago. Embedded deep within the rock was the Sword of Wales. Four times a year, at the solstices and the equinoxes, sunlight and moonlight would stream into the chapel, striking the magical sword.

Quietly, unobserved by anyone, the celestial clock of heaven moved. A gentle wind lifted the tapestries adorning the walls of the tower that depicted the life of King Arthur and his Court at Camelot.

Moonlight fell through the window at precisely the right time, as it did every year, striking the legendary sword, and the darkened room filled with light. The windows had been set in place by a master builder who designed the tower with its high turrets to sport twelve windows.

Throughout the year, the full moon was captured each month in an artfully designed window that allowed light to spill through, illuminating the features of a noble knight of the realm. In the center of the Great Tower was the Winchester table where a knight's name was inscribed before each seat: Sir Lancelot, Sir Gawain, Sir Geraint, Sir Percival, Sir Bors the Younger, Sir Lamorak, Sir Kay, Sir Gareth, Sir Bedivere, Sir Gaheris, Sir Galahad, and Sir Tristan.

There was a vacant seat at the table: a seat made ready for the knight of the Grail. The single door to the tower opened and Gerald, Captain of the Guard, respectfully approached the table. With purpose, solemn grace and speed, he walked to the empty seat and worked diligently and with expertise, scribing the name of the Grail knight into the weathered wood with an ancient silver athamé.

"Sir Garret Montgomery," he said firmly. "Take your place amongst the noble knights."

In answer to Gerald's declaration, the wind rose steadily outside, and the sound of chain mail and the thundering beat of horses' hooves and the clash of swords could be heard in the distance. The tower filled with the sound of masculine voices and ancient, cavalier whispering. Satisfied his work was done, Gerald, Captain of the Guard, respectfully left the room and closed tight the tower's solitary door, sealing it shut. The wind abated as the iron key turned in the lock, and peace once again settled over the land of the Welsh and all was right with the world.

Beneath a pale moon,

Under a starlit sky,

Nightingales sing songs of love,

For dreamers like you

And I.

Don't miss the romantic adventures of

Victoria Morrow

Jenny's Dream

Beneath a Pale Moon

Angel in My Arms

The Eagle and the Dove, Montlake

The Theft of the Magi

Victoria Morrow

Born October 3, 1957, Victoria Morrow is a mother with a wonderful son, Dan, who is married to a lovely girl, Heather, and she has two grandchildren, Jacob and Drew. A graduate of Patricia Stevens Business College and the University of Nebraska at Kearney, Victoria earned a degree in business and a Bachelor of Science in Psychology, and currently works in healthcare while finishing her education degree in Social Science. Victoria enjoys writing, music, medicine, art and spending time with her family.

Made in the USA
Columbia, SC
21 February 2021